MONSTER IN DISGUISE

VERONICA LANCET

MONSTER IN DISGUISE

VERONICA LANCET

PREFACE

Dear Reader,

Before proceeding further, please be aware that this book deals with *extremely* sensitive themes. My advice would be to read only if you have **no** triggers at all, as this is a very dark book.

This was previously published as Morally Blasphemous but it has since been re-edited and re-worked.

Trigger Warnings

attempted rape
blood and gore
child abuse
death
derogatory terms
domestic abuse
extreme graphic violence
forced animal abuse
graphic sexual situations
incestuous situations
kidnapping
miscarriage
murder
self-harm
suicide
descriptive rape
uncomfortable religious situations
extreme depictions of torture

Marcello

Silence hangs heavy in the air, broken only by the soft rustle of leaves and the distant hum of cicadas. I've been sitting at Tino's grave for what feels like an eternity, my heart aching with grief. Ten long years...ten years since I last saw my brother. And now he's gone, buried beneath the earth that I can't seem to stop staring at.

In this lifetime, I've carried many regrets with me. And now, here at this graveside, I find myself adding another one to the list. With one last lingering look, I stand up and brush off my knees before turning to leave.

But as I make my way through the cemetery, a familiar figure catches my eye. Vlad, hands tucked into his pockets, stands waiting for me with a grim expression on his face.

"Vlad," I acknowledge him with a slight nod, knowing that his presence here can only mean one thing—bad news.

I had thought that with Jimenez dead, it would all be over. But as Vlad approaches and begins to speak, I realize that everything is just beginning.

"Capo Lastra."

A sly smirk spreads across Vlad's face, and I can feel the corners of my lips twitch in annoyance. "What is it?" I ask, trying to keep my voice steady.

"You need to take your position back, my friend. War is coming," he says with a hint of amusement in his tone. I scoff at his choice of words, the memory of bloodshed and betrayal still fresh in my mind.

"Not interested ten years ago, not interested now," I reply sharply, brushing past him.

"What about your sisters?" he asks, and I stop in my tracks, turning to face him with a cold glare.

"What about them?" I have two sisters, Assisi and Venezia. Both young... far too young to know about the cruelty of the world. My stomach twists at the thought of them being caught up in the violence that looms on the horizon.

"They'll be fair game for anyone looking for legitimacy. Still not your business?" Vlad taunts, knowing exactly how to hit a nerve.

"They'll manage," I lie through gritted teeth, knowing deep down that there is no way they will ever be able to handle what's coming.

There was a reason I left that life behind a decade ago. A dark secret that still haunts me to this day and prevents me from sleeping at night.

"You know they won't. Venezia is what... fifteen?" Vlad casually remarks as if it's no big deal, but I can feel the anger boiling within me. She'd been just a small child when I walked away without looking back. But as much as I want to ignore it, he's right. They will be easy targets if I don't intervene.

As hard as I try to cling to my old identity as Marcel Lester and pretend that everything is still normal, that Tino is still alive and well... I can't deny the grim reality staring me in the face. War is coming, and I can't keep running from it forever.

Reluctantly, I give in to his demands. "I'll make the move into the house soon."

"I knew you'd come around." Vlad's face lights up with satisfaction. "The Gallaghers have already made their first play. It's time for you to make yours."

"I know. I'll pay a visit to Enzo and make amends now that we have the truth about Romina's death."

"That's not what I meant." Vlad's eyes bore into mine. "You need to solidify an alliance. Through marriage."

"Venezia is too young, and Assisi is on her way to becoming a nun," I interject quickly.

"I wasn't talking about them," Vlad says pointedly.

"I cannot marry. You know better than anyone why that is," I emphasize, my voice laced with bitterness. My past has stained me, making it impossible for me to even consider marriage. The thought of being intimate with a woman fills me with revulsion.

"But you must," Vlad insists firmly. "It's the only way to secure your position."

"There's only one woman I would ever entertain marrying. And she is no longer here." With a heavy heart, I lift my gaze to the sky, picturing her face in my mind once more.

"Exactly. She's gone. Which means you must marry whoever Enzo proposes. You need to realize that times are changing." Vlad's being more forceful than I've ever seen him.

"I won't shirk my responsibility... if only for my sisters."

"It can be a marriage in name only," he suggests, his tone serious and calculating.

I grunt. A marriage in name only is the only type of marriage I am capable of.

"If that is all," I say curtly, already beginning to turn away.

"No," Vlad interjects, placing a file in my hands. Suspicious, I raise an eyebrow at him.

"What is this?" I ask warily, wondering what other plans Vlad has up his sleeve.

"Your first assignment as capo," he states plainly. With a sense of dread building inside me, I reluctantly open the file.

Inside are numerous FBI reports documenting a string of brutal serial killings. My stomach churns as I flip through the pages, taking in the gruesome details.

"How long have you known?" I demand, my voice trembling with fear and anger.

"Long enough," Vlad replies nonchalantly, shrugging his shoulders. He then points to the last page with a sense of finality.

5th May, Philadelphia

I stare at the horrific details before me, my stomach churning in disgust. The photos show a family of four, their limbs gruesomely sewn together in a twisted display of death. Two children, once innocent and full of life, now reduced to mere body parts. I can feel the bile rising in my throat.

"This is last month," I say, my voice trembling with horror.

Vlad nods grimly, his lips pursed in deep thought. "You're right. But if it's not Chimera, then who is it?"

I take a deep breath, trying to steady myself. This can't be happening. Not again.

Our sins always catch up with us. And mine have been chasing me for an awfully long time.

MARCELLO

AGE FIVE

"I can keep it, can't I?" I look up at Mother's disinterested expression, silently begging her to say yes. With Mother, you never know what you're going to get.

Sometimes I think she's in a good mood, but just asking for a hug might set her off. Last time it wasn't pretty. I'd bruised my knee and wanted some comfort... I don't know why. Sometimes I just want some human contact. She'd said yes, initially, but a second later she'd shoved me off her and thrown me to the floor, saying it's a sin for a son to touch his mother.

She is unpredictable like that. But I've learned to keep myself out of her presence, mostly because I don't want to be berated for sinning all the time. I don't even understand exactly what sin is, but Mother says I do it. And considering her reaction, it must be *really* bad.

Maybe I *do* sin... but why can't she teach me how not to do it anymore? If not her, then I don't know who else. My brother is twenty... I think that's a lot. But he doesn't like to talk to me. He usually just nods at me and leaves.

And my father... I'm simply happy when he doesn't notice me. Honestly, I've wanted to learn how *not* to sin for a long time. My mother says that if I don't stop now, I'll sin even more when I grow up.

I don't want to sin when I grow up. I want to be normal... And maybe if I don't sin, then Mother will like me too.

"Sure." She takes one look at the puppy in my arms and shrugs. We'd just returned from a parent-teacher meeting at my kindergarten when I saw a tiny ball of fur outside my school. I'd nestled it in my jacket and given it something to eat. All this time I'd been waiting with worry, thinking she'd say no. But she agreed. I can't help but beam at the thought, hugging the little furred body closer to my chest.

I think the puppy likes me. And now, since Mother says I can keep it, I won't be alone anymore. I'll have a friend.

I've always wanted a friend. Other kids at kindergarten have friends, but they never talk to me. They told me their parents warned them not to become too friendly with me because my father is an evil man. I know my father is bad, but I'm not. I'd tried to tell them that. I do sin sometimes, but I try to be a good boy. At least not to anger Mother. But they ignored me.

Mother rolls her eyes at me and leads me towards our car, where the driver is waiting for us.

The drive home doesn't take too long, but Mother keeps clutching her cross necklace in her hand and whispering something. I try not to think about that since she's scary when she's whispering things.

When we get to the house, I hurry out of the car, taking the puppy with me. I don't want to wait around in case Mother changes her mind, or worse, she has one of her fits. I immediately dash to my room and close the door.

Our house is enormous. I sometimes get lost in it, but I try not to wander too much. Father's already told me off for going where I'm not supposed to. My room is on the third floor, but I'm the only one living there and it's a little scary.

My brother, Tino, used to live here too. Now, he rarely comes home. But he always brings me a chocolate bar when he comes. I like that... even though he doesn't speak to me, at least he remembers I exist.

I tried once to go downstairs, but some areas are forbidden, especially the basement. I'm really curious though. I've been curious ever since I heard some maids talk about it. They're not allowed there either. I once tried to go to the basement, but my father's men stopped me.

Father has a lot of men obeying his orders, and they are always around the house. He told me there are monsters in the basement and that they could hurt me. I don't know why, but I don't believe that. If there are monsters there, then why are they allowed to go? Do the monsters not harm them too? Or maybe the monsters prefer kids... I don't know, but I don't think I want to risk it.

And it's not only the basement. I'm not allowed on the first floor either. That's where Father and Mother live. Mother told me she never wants to catch me there, or I'd regret it. She said nothing about monsters, though.

But it would be weird if they lived with monsters, wouldn't it? How could they survive that? Unless they're monsters, too. But I know they aren't. Because if they were monsters, I'd be a monster too. And I'm not... At least I don't think so. I know my mother says I sin a lot, but I don't think I'm that different from other kids. I just don't have any friends.

I unbutton my jacket and carefully take out the puppy to place it on the floor. He looks at me with wide eyes, and I can't help but smile at him. He gives a small yapping sound and then runs around the room, inspecting every corner. His body is so small, his fur a warm shade of brown. As I watch him energetically running around my chair, I think of a name.

He should have a name.

He barks a few times at me, and I assume he wants attention. I scoop him up again and nuzzle him with my cheek. That's when I catch a sniff of something bad. I don't know what this smell is, but the puppy reeks of it. Probably because he's been living on the streets.

"Let's get you cleaned!" I tell him. He shakes his head and nuzzles his nose against my foot, as if he understands me. Maybe he does.

"You'll feel better clean. I always do." I open the bathroom door, and since I can't reach the sink, I drop the puppy in the bathtub. I take off my own clothes, folding them aside so they don't get wet before joining him inside.

Setting the water temperature to warm, I scrub the puppy clean, lathering a good amount of shampoo on the fur, and rinsing it well. The puppy doesn't seem too happy, and he tries to jump out of the tub a couple of times. I frown at him and try to tell him in a stern tone that he can't do that.

Somehow, he stops being that restless, and that earns a smile from me. I think I got myself a friendly puppy.

Back to the name... I keep thinking about it as I clean him, and only one thing comes to mind. He will be my first friend... my first *amico*. That's why his name should be Amico.

Satisfied, I take a towel and try to dry him before doing the same for myself. Amico runs out of the room before I'm finished, though.

I try to hurry as much as I can, and when I catch up with him, I take him in my arms.

"From now on, your name is Amico."

I don't think Father would approve of him.

I'm not worried that Mother will tell him though, since she probably forgot about it already. In the days after I adopt Amico, I see Mother only a few times around the house, but she doesn't take notice of me. It's okay though. It's usually like that. And since she takes most of her meals in her room, there's really no reason for us to meet.

The maids like Amico too, and they sometimes sneak food for him. One of them even got him dog treats. I feel bad, since I can't afford to buy Amico actual dog food, and he usually gets my left-overs. But he hasn't complained yet.

———

IT'S BEEN three days now that I've had Amico, and I don't know how I managed before. It's so different having someone to talk to, even if Amico can't talk back. And he's so playful... he's always in the mood to run around.

"Signorino Marcello," Amelia, a maid, calls me over from the hallway. She's one of the few ones who asks me how I'm doing. I know it's her job, but it feels nice.

"Melia." I go to her and look up, curious why she'd want to talk to me. Amico is nestling in my arms, and he makes a small noise. She looks at the puppy with an almost sad expression.

"The Signor is home. Be careful," she says in a hushed tone, before heading for the stairs and going back to work.

I sigh deeply, already uncomfortable at the thought. I'd imagined Father would be gone for much longer. He rarely comes home.

I go back to my room to drop Amico off, hoping Father would quickly return to his business as usual. I don't know what will happen if he finds out I brought a dog home. He has strict rules...

I open the door and stoop low to put Amico down. He's barely out of my hands when he dashes back into the hallway and down the stairs.

"No..." My eyes go wide with horror, and I run after him. I see him hopping down a few stairs, and I do the same, trying to catch up. But he's smaller and faster than me. He rushes down to the second story, and I'm horrified.

No... it's the first floor. I run even faster after him, needing to catch him before... before...

Amico yelps in pain. I stop, my eyes traveling up, taking in Father's form as he's holding Amico by the nape in a distasteful manner. He scoffs at him before finally zoning in on me.

I try to mask my feelings, having learned that Father despises weakness above all. His mouth curls up in half a twisted smile, smirking at me.

"This yours, boy?" he asks me in his usual leisurely way. I can only nod.

"Words, boy, words." His tone is clipped this time, and I'm almost afraid I angered him.

"Yes, sir. It's mine," I answer. He chuckles for a second before his features go blank. He turns his back to me and goes towards the end of the corridor, Amico still in his hold.

I'm not supposed to be on this floor...

"Sir?" I muster the courage to ask, hesitantly taking a step forward.

"Follow me." His voice booms in the empty hall, and I steel myself. I continue to walk after him, trying to control my trembling limbs so he doesn't realize how scared I am. Amico is all that matters now.

Father goes deeper into the wing, and it's an area I've never seen before. He finally stops in front of a door, and opens it carelessly, stepping in. I do the same.

It's a dark room, only lit by the million candles surrounding the walls. There is a wall full of crosses. In front of it is a table housing a case of some sort. Mother is on the floor kneeling, her front bent towards the table, a black scarf covering her face. She's whispering something.

I don't like it when she's whispering.

"Liliana." The moment Mother hears Father's voice, she scurries back, hitting the table.

"Giovanni... What are you doing here?" She valiantly tries to put on a smile, but she's just as afraid as I am.

Father lifts the hand holding Amico and shakes him in her face.

"Want to tell me what this is?"

"I..." She starts but frowns, her eyes moving from Father before settling on me. Her face is set in a deep scowl as she addresses me. "Didn't I tell you no?"

"But..." She said yes... she did.

"So you disobeyed your mother?" Father immediately takes over, looking at me.

"No..." I whisper, keeping my gaze down, not knowing how to reply. What is even the correct answer? If I say Mother let me keep it, I'll get her in trouble. But if I say I disobeyed... What will happen to me?

"Speak!" Father commands.

"I... I wanted a friend," I admit, hoping this answer would be a good one.

It's not.

"You wanted a friend?" Father's voice takes a sinister tone as he laughs at me. I keep my head down. I can still see from the corner of my eye Amico struggling within Father's hold. He must be hurting.

"Amico..." I look up as Father suddenly flings the puppy to my feet. *Amico!* I immediately scramble, lifting Amico in my arms and trying to comfort him to the best of my ability.

"He wanted a friend... He even named him *Amico*..." Father shakes his head, looking towards Mother this time. Her face is blank as she stares at the puppy.

"Wrong answer, boy." Father takes a step towards me, his hand going straight to my shirt's neckline. He wrenches me closer so that his face is right in front of mine.

"There are only two answers. Either your mother told you no, and you disobeyed. Or your mother told you yes, and she's lying. Which one is it?" Mother has a look of horror on her face as she hears Father speak, and I think she fears what awaits her if I choose the second option. So I don't. I choose the first.

"I disobeyed," I whisper.

"Good. We are getting somewhere. You disobeyed because you wanted a friend." He doesn't let go of my shirt, and his serious gaze settles on me. "You need to be punished, boy."

I nod, because what else can I do? I knew what I was getting into... I knew and yet, I risked it.

He moves suddenly and I flinch, closing my eyes. I expected him to hit me.

He doesn't.

I slowly open one eye to see Father regard me pensively.

"I have just the punishment for you, boy. One that will remind you to never disobey again."

He casually saunters to the table behind my mother, picking up a cross... or what looks like a cross, because one end is sharp. Father tests the sharpness of the blade, and I'm shaking with fear. Is he going to cut me?

I instinctively curl into a ball, hugging my knees and holding Amico to my chest.

"So, boy. You have a choice. You either take your punishment, or I must believe your mother lied. And if she lied..." His gaze strays to her, and she's petrified.

I slowly loosen up.

"I'll take my punishment, sir," I say slowly and wait for my punishment.

"Not that easy. Your punishment will be to get rid of that pest you're carrying." He motions towards Amico, and my eyes widen in understanding.

"No..." I whisper, and I try to crawl away from him.

"No?" he asks, amused. "Fine." He shrugs, gets up, and turns to my mother. Even though she is terrified, she doesn't move from her spot. She calmly turns her back towards my father and unfastens her gown so it falls to her midriff.

I don't even see Father move around to grab a piece of rope. My gaze is stuck on Mother's back. Even in the poor lighting of the room, I can see that her skin is mangled, barely any inch of skin unblemished. She's already resigned to this.

Just as Father is about to hit her bare back, I yell.

"I'll do it." My voice is trembling. I don't know what made me choose to spare Mother, when I know she would have *never* done the same for me. But I did. My eyes go to Amico, who is looking at me with his big puppy eyes. I can feel the tears in my eyes as I realize what I've chosen.

Father comes next to me again, and puts the knife in my hand, wrapping my fingers around it.

"For a quick death, you always go for the jugular," he mentions.

I keep staring at Amico, trying to talk myself into this. I know I'm hesitating when I'd said I'd do it, but I don't know if I can.

"Liliana, don't dress yet," Father says with a hint of warning in his voice.

My hand is shaking uncontrollably as I bring the knife to Amico's throat. Father covers my hand with his own.

"Do it!" he commands, his grip tightening to a painful degree. He guides my hand and with one swipe of the knife, blood gushes out of Amico's throat, flowing down my hand and covering my clothes.

I can't move. I just stand there, watching Amico struggle for a second, before dying—by my hands.

Father chuckles at this.

"Maybe I can still make something of you," he adds before leaving and closing the door behind him.

I'm cradling Amico's dead body in my arms, finally letting the tears flow. In my head, I keep asking for forgiveness, knowing there is no one to grant it.

I must have stayed like that for a while, rocking back and forth with Amico's body, silently begging him to forgive me, when Mother suddenly pushes me to the ground.

I fall on my back and my attention finally snaps to her. She has a crazed look as she's holding a bottle in one hand and a cross in the other.

"Cleanse... must cleanse the sin," she keeps repeating as she sprays me with the water and hits me with the cross. I take a defensive stance, and she mostly hits my arms and legs.

I don't know when she stops doing it, or how I end up in the backyard, covered in blood and bruises and trying to give Amico a proper burial.

But there is one thing I learned that day.

I am a monster.

I am a sinner.

And there is no redemption.

Marcello

As I stand in front of the imposing Lastra mansion, memories flood back to me with a force that takes my breath away. The grandeur and opulence of the building only serve to amplify my feelings of discomfort and unease.

This was a place I never thought I would have to return to—not after finally escaping this life for good. But as always, fate has a way of pulling us back into the places we thought we had left behind.

It's been a week since my brother's sudden death, and I still can't fully process it. Despite our lack of closeness, his passing has hit me harder than expected. He may have caused me pain and suffering in the past, but in the end, he did me the greatest favor by helping me escape this world. And for that, he earned my loyalty and respect.

It's a strange feeling to mourn someone who was both a source of torment and salvation.

But now, I am faced with the consequences of my actions. My best friend is in the hospital, and I only have myself to blame for it.

Guilt gnaws at me as I think about him lying on a hospital bed, fighting for his life. His wife, Bianca, has forbidden me from visiting him—and rightly so. I deserve her wrath, and his absence only serves as a constant reminder of what I have done.

I take off my coat, already sweating under the weight of guilt and anxiety, and nod at two bodyguards before approaching the doorbell. An older woman answers the door and gives me a quizzical look—of course she wouldn't recognize me. It's been too many years, too many lies and secrets built up between us all.

"I am Marcello," I introduce myself, watching the woman's face light up with a smile.

"Signor! Venezia will be overjoyed to hear that you have finally arrived."

"Finally?" I question, curiosity piqued.

"Yes, Signor Valentino had informed us of your impending return. It is such a shame he passed away. May he rest in peace." The woman makes the sign of the cross with her hands as she speaks.

"Please, come inside," she gestures for me to enter the grand hall. As I step inside, I am hit with a wave of familiar scents and sights. Memories flood my mind, unbidden. The screams... The pain...

"What is your name?" I ask the woman, trying to push away the unwelcome thoughts.

"Amelia, signor," she replies politely.

"Amelia..." Her name triggers a memory within me. "That Amelia?"

"Si, signor. Your brother rehired me after you had left," she confirms, and I feel a small sense of relief wash over me.

A soft voice, laced with uncertainty and longing, drifts down from the top of the grand staircase. As I lift my head to meet the gaze of the speaker, my heart tightens in recognition.

It's a young woman, her delicate frame clad in a flowing blue dress that brushes lightly against the stairs as she descends. Her mahogany curls cascade down her shoulders in perfect ringlets, framing a heart-shaped face with strong cheekbones and slanted hazel eyes.

She looks just like her mother.

"You must be Venezia." I manage to relax my features into a pleasant smile, not wanting to frighten the girl away with my own troubled expression. She nods shyly before taking a few hesitant steps toward me and Amelia, who hovers protectively at my side.

"Signorina." Amelia greets her with warmth and affection, clearly showing a close relationship between them.

"You've grown so much," I remark, trying to find common ground with this girl who once seemed like a mere child to me. "Last time I saw you, you were only about this tall." With a gentle gesture of my hand, I indicate that she had only reached my thigh when we last met...when she was just five years old.

"One does that in ten years," she says, but immediately lowers her gaze as she realizes her tone.

"Signorina!" Amelia's outraged voice chides.

"I know I've been gone a long while. But now I'm here. And I'll do my duty for this family."

"Really?" Venezia snaps at me, her eyes narrowing. "Like you did with my sister? Tell me, will you send me away too?"

"Signorina Venezia, your brother meant well," Amelia tries to interject, but Venezia does not stop.

"He meant well when he called her a *Devil's child* and gave her away to a convent?" Her voice is full of malice as she emphasizes Devil's child. I have to briefly close my eyes at her accusation. How does she even know? Venezia's tirade continues, and I know I have to do something about it.

"Enough!" My booming voice reverberates through the room, causing both women to shrink back in surprise. Their eyes widen as they stare at me, caught off guard by my sudden outburst.

"Last time I checked, you were under my guardianship, Venezia. And now that I am the head of this family, you will do well to respect my authority."

Venezia's face pales as she realizes the weight of my words. She opens her mouth to protest, but I continue speaking before she can.

"You're right. I did send your sister away. And it would be quite easy for me to do the same to you," I say with a calm demeanor, although inside I am seething with anger and frustration.

I watch as Venezia's features contort with fear and rage. "How much easier everything would be if I didn't have to worry about you," I muse aloud, almost taunting her.

Panicked, Venezia stumbles over her words in an attempt to defend herself.

"But...you can't do that!" she exclaims, taking a step closer to me.

"Oh, but I can," I reply coolly, enjoying the control I hold over her.

"It's up to you, really," I state matter-of-factly. "You can either behave and we can all get along, or..." I trail off suggestively.

Venezia looks at me with defiance in her eyes for a brief moment before finally admitting defeat.

"Yes," she mutters grudgingly.

"Yes what, Venezia?" I prompt sternly.

"Yes, sir," she adds meekly before turning and running up the grand staircase in a huff.

Turning to Amelia, who has been watching our interaction silently, I expect to see fear or submission in her eyes like Venezia's. But instead, there is only disappointment as she looks at me.

"I thought you were different, Sir," she says, her tone laced with disappointment and disapproval before turning and following Venezia up the stairs.

Left alone in the grand hall, I let out a heavy sigh. Was this truly who I had become? A tyrant who used fear to control those around him?

No... I had thought I was different too...

Until I wasn't.

THE HOUSE IS STILL as I remember it... And that's the problem.

I enter the guest room on the ground floor, my small luggage in tow. It's a modest space, but it will have to do for now. I've never been one to accumulate many possessions.

It's become a habit since the day I ran away from home. As I unpack my few belongings—some shirts and pants, and a small bag of toiletries—I can't help but feel a familiar urge to flee.

But I push it down, reminding myself of why I'm here. This isn't just for me anymore. It's for my sisters. Tino's death has left a dangerous power vacuum, and my sisters could easily become pawns in any potential takeover. Especially with Venezia being so young and Assisi still a novice in the convent, their safety is my top priority.

And then there's Vlad's proposal... the thought alone sends shivers down my spine. But for now, I must focus on securing my sisters' future above all else.

Despite my dread, there are tasks that must be completed. As much as I despise the role thrust upon me, I cannot deny its necessity for the resources it provides. To jumpstart the succession plans, I have met with Tino's lawyers and accountants.

They have provided me with a plethora of documents to sift through and analyze. Along with these materials, I have been given a comprehensive list of all the people who were previously under Tino's command.

Being the Capo doesn't just entail taking charge of the business side of our famiglia. It also means gaining the respect and loyalty of those within our ranks. My profession as a lawyer has prepared me for the legal aspects of running a business, though my focus has mainly been on criminal law.

However, my experience with the corporate side should prove useful in this new role. Yet, it is not my knowledge that concerns me most. It is the weight of earning the trust and acceptance of my new family members that weighs heavily on my mind.

Tino, may he rest in peace, had taken care of everything before his untimely passing. He knew his end was near and meticulously planned for every possible outcome. His succession order has enough loopholes to ensure that I am the most viable option to take over as capo. But that does not mean there won't be opposition from within.

A formal meeting must be held within the famiglia where I will officially introduce myself as their new leader and hope they accept me as such. Though Tino saw to it that all preparations were made, there is no guarantee that everyone will welcome me with open arms.

As I pore over the intricate list of names involved with the infamous famiglia, my eyes immediately land on my uncle Nicolo's name, listed as the Consigliere. He may not have been the ruthless monster that my father was, but he was far from being an angel. I couldn't let my guard down around him.

Lost in thought, I am abruptly pulled back to reality by a sharp knock at the door. With a hesitant creak, it opens slowly and Amelia peeks her head inside. She hesitates for a moment before making eye contact with me, silently asking for permission to enter. I give a small nod and she enters, her hands nervously fidgeting in front of her.

"Signor," she starts, keeping her gaze downcast. "I wanted to apologize for Signorina Venezia's behavior earlier. She is young and headstrong, and has never had proper guidance before."

I can already see the judgment in her eyes, no doubt assuming that I am just like my father. As much as I want to prove her wrong, I know that there are always ears listening in this house. I must maintain a strong facade, even if it means being seen as a cruel and self-serving man. Though my motives may not be entirely selfish, they certainly aren't pure either.

"Yes, go on," I say sternly.

"I... please forgive her impertinence towards your absence. She did not mean it with malice."

"I understand that she may have her own opinions about my absence. However, that does not excuse her tone and lack of manners. Who has been responsible for her education?"

"That's the thing, Signor... no one," Amelia replies somberly.

A deep frown creases my brow, my confusion growing with each word from Amelia's mouth.

"What do you mean, no one?" I ask, my tone sharp with disbelief.

Amelia fidgets nervously, as if she's trying to reveal a secret but can't decide if she should. "Signor Valentino was never the same after Signora Romina died," she finally admits, her voice hushed with sadness. "He closed himself off, and left Signorina Venezia on her own."

"That was eight years ago," I interject, my mind reeling at this new information. "You mean to tell me that no one has taken care of her since then?"

Amelia looks away, her disapproval of Venezia's treatment evident in her expression.

"Yes, that is correct," she confirms reluctantly. "I've tried to take her under my wing, teach her some things... but Signor Valentino did not like her getting too close with the staff. There was only so much I could do."

My brows furrow as I try to process this revelation. So Venezia has been essentially alone all this time? No wonder she acted out and sought attention in any way she could get it. And it explains why she was so upset by my absence; in her eyes, I had abandoned her just like everyone else.

I purse my lips in thought, feeling a pang of sympathy for the young girl who never had someone to guide her and show her how to behave properly.

"Thank you for your information. I will see that she receives a proper education from now on."

Amelia looks as if she's about to add something, but then she just nods and exits the room.

As I unpack my bags, my mind swirls with concerns. Venezia going to school on her own feels too risky, and I can't shake off the anxiety. Perhaps I can arrange for her to be homeschooled. But there is the matter of finding the right person for the job...

I decide to take a drive, hoping the change of scenery will help calm my nerves. But just a few miles away from home, my phone starts ringing. Instinct tells me to ignore it, but when I see the caller ID displaying Vlad's name, I pull over and answer.

"Vlad," I say, trying to mask my curiosity.

"Marcello," he replies in a serious tone. "I thought you should know about a sudden development."

My heart sinks as I wait for him to continue.

"All entry routes through NJ have been shut down."

"All of them?"

"Including mine." The anger seeping through his words is palpable. This news does not bode well. I hope no one is near him.

"I assume ours are affected as well then." My family has a long-standing partnership with the Russian mafia based in Brighton Beach. My father was close friends with their former Pakhan. And our businesses mainly involve drugs—the same trade the Russians are known for.

"Yes." Vlad's answer is clipped.

"The Irish?"

"Unconfirmed. Maybe." That is unusual. Vlad is in the loop

about everything. Either he truly does not know, or he doesn't want *me* to know.

"If not them, then who?" I inquire.

"Cartels. Jimenez's death created a power vacuum. There are too many factions fighting for power. It's hard to pinpoint which one did this." He takes a deep breath before continuing. "But I will find out. And *you* will help."

"*I* will help?" I ask, almost amused. But I already know what he's going to say.

"This will be the perfect opportunity for you to prove yourself to the famiglia. Clear the way for the merchandise, win their favor. Simple."

"So simple," I repeat mockingly. Vlad chuckles.

"Come on, it will be like old times," he adds with a little too much enthusiasm. That much is true. I'd run away while Vlad had succumbed.

"It was worth a try." He pauses and changes the subject. "How's the famiglia treating you so far?"

"I have yet to meet most of them. But there was no homecoming party."

"Did you expect one?"

"No," I add drily. Sobering, I ask something that's been nagging at me for a while, "How safe is Sacre Coeur?"

"Safe enough. For now. Are you thinking of taking your sister home?"

"If that's what she wants... but I highly doubt it."

"Don't worry about that. She's not the only *principessa* hiding there."

I grunt and hang up. I have a visit scheduled with Assisi tomorrow to inform her of Tino's death. Although I doubt she'll want anything to do with me.

I sigh. I don't think I can ever make amends for everyone I've hurt.

———

SACRE COEUR IS UP NORTH, half an hour off Albany, in a remote area.

I maneuver my car off the road and scan the area for a parking spot. This place is not meant to accommodate casual visitors, so there are no designated parking spots in sight. After ensuring that my car won't get towed, I exit the vehicle and make my way towards the main gate.

The first thing that strikes me about Sacre Coeur is its sheer size. It looms over me like a fortress, its Gothic architecture radiating an unwelcoming aura. The similarities to the Met Cloisters are uncanny, except this structure is magnified in both scale and foreboding presence. A towering two-meter concrete wall surrounds the convent, separating it from the outside world.

Every inch of the perimeter is covered with CCTV cameras, and guards are stationed at every entry point. If I didn't know better, I'd mistake this for a maximum-security prison. Even barbed wire lines the top of the walls, adding an extra layer of protection. Vlad had mentioned that security was tight here, but now I understand why. What could have prompted such high levels of precaution? Surely a group of nuns wouldn't be trying to escape...

As I approach the main entrance, the guards demand to see my ID and cross-check it against their list of approved individuals. Once satisfied with my identity, they instruct me to remove my shoes and pass through a metal detector.

It's all a bit excessive for a religious institution. I can't imagine what would happen if there were any physical pat-downs involved—things could go south quickly. Thankfully, the inspection ends there and I am allowed to proceed inside.

As I enter the convent, I am met with an imposing presence. An older woman, dressed in the traditional black and white robes of a Mother Superior, stands before me with a stern expression.

Her mouth is pinched tightly at the corners, etching a scowl onto her face. I bow my head respectfully.

"Mother Superior," I greet her.

She acknowledges me with a nod before speaking again. "Mr. Lastra. I understand you are here to see Sister Assisi."

"Yes, that is correct," I confirm, but she continues talking as if I didn't answer.

"Sister Assisi is a kind and charitable soul. She will be taking her vows next year, on a path of light. I hope your visit will not disrupt that."

"I assure you, Mother Superior, my visit is only to convey some news. It will not interfere with Sister Assisi's ceremony."

"Very well," she responds, eyeing me suspiciously.

Together, we pass through a narrow passage lined with low pointed arches until we reach an open clearing. Lush green spaces surround us, and nuns clad in their signature attire wander about, deeply engrossed in conversation.

In the center of the clearing stands a square stone outline filled with rows of meticulously tended flowers. And at its heart, a replica statue of Michelangelo's Pietà gleams in bronze. I am taken aback by the peacefulness of this place, almost in awe as Mother Superior motions for me to take a seat on the stone outline.

"I will fetch Sister Assisi for you now. Please wait here," she instructs before departing with purposeful strides.

In the distance, a small figure catches my eye. She's dressed in a drab gray uniform dress, her hair neatly tucked under a white head-dress. But as she draws closer, her eyes captivate me. They are a brilliant, emerald green that seem to shimmer in the sun. For a moment, I am taken aback by their intensity and the striking resemblance they bear to another pair of green eyes from my past.

Lost in my memories, I barely have time to react before she stands directly in front of me, regarding me with curious eyes.

"Who are you?" Her voice is filled with childlike wonder, as if I am some sort of exotic creature.

"I'm Marcello." I offer her a half-smile, and she returns it with enthusiasm.

"I'm Claudia," she declares proudly. Just then, a sharp voice echoes through the courtyard, calling out her name.

"Oh no!" she whispers urgently, waving goodbye before rushing off towards the sound.

As I watch her disappear into the bustling crowd, I can't help but wonder if my sister Assisi was ever like that. Carefree and playful in the courtyard of our childhood home. And although parting ways with her was difficult, I can't help but feel that giving her away was better than the alternative.

As I sit on the stone bench, Mother Superior approaches me

with a young girl in tow. The girl's face bears a red mark above her right eyebrow, revealing her identity before she even speaks.

"Mr. Lastra, Sister Assisi. You have one hour," Mother Superior's stern voice echoes through the quiet courtyard as she departs.

Assisi and I gaze at each other, both of us unsure of what to say or do. Her eyes scan over my form, and I notice her jaw trembling with emotion.

"Marcello?" She finally manages to speak, but my throat constricts and no words come out.

"Assisi," I eventually reply, my own voice barely audible.

"It's really you." Her tone is filled with awe and disbelief. I can see the thoughts running through her mind as she takes hesitant steps towards me. My hand instinctively reaches up to create some space between us.

Her expression falls at the rejection, but she forces a sad smile onto her lips. I feel compelled to explain myself.

"It's not that I don't want to... I just can't," I mutter, unable to elaborate further. But Assisi seems to understand without any further explanation. She looks at me with understanding and gestures towards the stone bench I had been sitting on just moments ago.

Taking a seat next to me, Assisi leaves just enough space between us. Her face lights up with surprise and joy as she recognizes me.

"I didn't think I'd see you again," she exclaims, her voice bright and warm.

"And I didn't think you'd remember me."

"Of course I do. You're my brother." Her expression is full of forgiveness and love.

"I'm sorry," I add, feeling the weight of my past mistakes.

"Why are you here?"

"Valentino is dead." A gasp escapes Assisi's lips and her hand flies to cover her mouth.

"Dead?" she repeats in shock, her eyes wide.

"Yes... suicide." The word hangs heavy in the air, like a dark storm cloud.

"Suicide?" Assisi whispers, her tone laced with horror. For Catholics, it is perhaps the worst way to die.

"He was diagnosed with a degenerative disorder. He was already dying... slowly."

Tears well up in the corners of her eyes and she uses a piece of fabric from her headdress to gently wipe them away.

"I had no idea... He visited a few times but never mentioned it."

"I don't think he wanted to burden you."

"Maybe. How is Venezia?"

"She's... coping. She'll be okay. Maybe I'll even bring her to visit sometime." As soon as the words leave my mouth, Assisi's entire demeanor changes.

"Really? You would do that?" There is wonder and hope in her voice, and I can't help but nod.

"It would mean so much. Thank you!" She leans forward as if to hug me, but pulls back at the last second and instead gives me a bright smile.

Despite the mark on her face, Assisi radiates such warmth and beauty that any imperfection melts away in comparison.

For the first time, I think I made at least one right decision in sending her to Sacre Coeur.

We talk a little more, and I tell her about my career as a lawyer and how I've been away from the family. She tells me about her mother figure and best friend, and how she is really happy where she is.

The more I talk to her, the more I realize that she has no idea what our family does for a living. Mother Superior knows, going by the way she received me. But Assisi has no clue. And *that* makes me entirely too happy.

Mother Superior interrupts us, telling us that our time is over, and we say goodbye.

"I'll come again," I promise, but I can see in her eyes she doesn't believe me, even if she nods in agreement.

"God Bless you!" She comes over to me, still keeping some distance, and does the sign of the cross with her hands over my body.

"Thank you, Assisi."

"*Sister* Assisi has other duties," Mother Superior interjects, leading her away.

With one last glance, I leave.

CATALINA

"Claudia!" I call out, cupping my hands together to amplify my voice. The nuns may disapprove of such noise, but I don't care.

As usual, I have no clue where that mischievous little rascal has scurried off to. I just hope she doesn't cross paths with Mother Superior; that always seems to result in both Claudia and me being scolded for our behavior.

Of course, most of the blame falls on me because apparently, I didn't raise her well. I roll my eyes in disbelief at their judgmental attitude.

It's not like I haven't been through this before; I knew what I was getting into when I decided to have a child. But I made sacrifices for Claudia's well-being. That doesn't give these holier-than-thou nuns the right to criticize my parenting.

Over the years, there have been countless instances where other nuns would make snide comments about Claudia and me within earshot of her.

There had been that time when she'd asked me what *whore* meant because that's what other nuns refer to me as. How can you explain *that* to a child? I'd made something up, of course, but Claudia is unusually perceptive. She'd realized by herself that it was a negative word.

I go towards the cloisters' garth, thinking I'd find her there. She likes open spaces a lot. We have only one room, and I feel terrible when she gets cooped up inside, so I indulge her whenever I can.

Of course, I was right that she'd be in the garth.

I come to a stop and watch as she's running around, to the chagrin of the other nuns. I'm enjoying their discomfort too much to stop her now, but then she suddenly runs towards a foreign man. I frown. Who's that?

I go a little closer and see him smile down at her, his mouth forming some words that I can't understand.

That's it!

I shout out my daughter's name once again, my voice cutting through the air like a sharp knife. Finally, she responds to my call and scrambles back towards me, her feet kicking up dirt as she dashes.

"Mamma," she says in a sheepish tone when she reaches me, knowing that she might be in trouble. I can't help but smile at her bashfulness as I scold her, "To the room, little troublemaker, you've terrorized enough nuns for today!" She revels in the attention and readily agrees to retreat to our accommodations.

But as I turn to follow her, something catches my eye. Mother Superior and Sisi are walking towards an unknown male figure. My curiosity is piqued, and I can't resist lingering for a moment to see what is happening.

"Go on ahead, my dear. I'll join you shortly," I tell Claudia, urging her forward with a gentle push. She gives me a pout but eventually skips off happily towards our room.

Intrigued by the unknown figure and his connection to Sisi, I stealthily make my way towards an arch that allows for better visibility. Once my spot is chosen, I strain to make out the stranger.

And Lord, is he beautiful. Wait... can men be beautiful? I frown a little at that. I'd never thought about it, mostly because I'd never interacted with any males who weren't family. My brother, Enzo, could be considered beautiful, but he is too perfect. No, this stranger is beautiful in a different way.

If I were to cast him in a biblical play (technically I'm only allowed to read those), he'd be Lucifer. Bright, yet with hidden depths. His dark blonde hair is messy and falling down his forehead in unruly strands. His skin has an olive hue, and his features look as if they've been chiseled in stone.

Ahh... I release a dreamy sigh. I guess you can tell how deprived I've been of male eye candy. Enzo had sneaked me a phone with an internet connection, but Lord is it slow. Even now... in this day and age. The images are the worst to load. But considering the fact that I'm breaking the rules just by owning that phone... well, I'll just take what I can get.

For now.

But I do have my celebrity crushes, like Marlon Brando... (the young version, of course). And this man... well, he could give Marlon Brando a run for his money, if he doesn't become obese in old age.

As usual, I start thinking about something, and I lose the thread... My brain really must have gone into overload mode. I'm even feeling a little flushed, and as I fan myself, I imagine what it would be like to be kissed by such a man.

I sigh out loud.

Probably better than kissing Marlon Brando... and I have imagined that quite a bit. I mean, have you seen that clip where he bites his lip? I rest my case.

It must be because I've never been kissed. I've fantasized so much about it that every slightly attractive male becomes my next fixation. But this is the first time I see someone that appeals to me in a non-digital format.

Since that incident, years ago, I've given up hope that I will ever experience that type of feeling in the flesh. But no one can take my fantasies away.

Honestly, even if it happened in real life, who is to say I wouldn't react badly to it, given my trauma?

It's better to admire from a distance. And that man will be the protagonist of my dreams until I get a better internet connection.

I'm once again so lost in my thoughts I don't realize both Sisi and the stranger are now standing up, looking as if they are saying goodbye.

I wait around until both he and Mother Superior are gone before I dash to Sisi's side, ready to get more answers.

"Who was that?" Sisi's startled by my words, and I have to stifle a chuckle at her expression. She puts one hand up and one on her chest, indicating she's catching her breath.

"I told you not to sneak up on people." She shakes her head with a smile, and taking another big gulp of air, she proceeds to tell me all about the foreign male.

"He's my brother."

"Your brother? *That?*" I ask, my reaction a bit too telling. Sisi narrows her eyes at me.

"Yes. *That.*" She laughs. "He came over to give me some updates regarding the family. My other brother, Valentino, committed suicide."

"I'm so sorry," I add immediately, feeling a little silly over my previous gushing when Sisi received such bad news.

"Apparently he was already ill. It doesn't matter now, does it? It's all water under the bridge. I feel bad about it, but it's not like we ever had a close bond... He was essentially a stranger."

"I know what you mean." I take her elbow and we head towards our room. We'd managed, against all odds, to stay together in the same accommodation for years now.

"It's sad. But it is what it is. Marcello promised he'd visit again, and maybe even bring my sister with him," Sisi says, and I can see the longing on her face. She's always had a problem with her family abandoning her at the convent.

Over the years, I'd seen her overcome some of her issues, but that doesn't mean she's stopped hoping that at one point she'd be reunited with them. While she's now resigned to taking her vows soon, it doesn't mean it is what she wants. And I know that better than anyone. She's just making the best out of the hand she's been dealt.

"Marcello?" I ask. Is that his name?

"That's my brother."

"I've never heard you talk about Marcello before," I add tentatively. She's talked about her family in vague terms, and I know Valentino visited sometimes.

"He left the family years ago... it seems he's back now to get the affairs in order."

He left the family? That's interesting. It also paints him in a much more positive light. Sisi knows very little about our families, having been raised in the convent since birth. And I'd never had the heart to tell her they are criminals. I've also had enough interactions with men within the famiglia to know that we are both way better off without them.

My brother is the only exception I can think of. Ever since I was a child, he's protected and shielded me from our father's wrath. He'd even prepared a suitable match for me before the incident. After... he promised to get me out of Sacre Coeur when he inherits.

It's been ten long years now, but I still have not given up hope. I trust Enzo, and I know he will keep his promise. When my father is no longer a concern, Claudia will finally be able to enjoy the outside world. Just thinking about that makes me smile. It's the only thing that's been keeping me going all these years.

"And what did he do?" I probe. I'm a little too curious about the man, I admit.

"He was a lawyer. He put away criminals." Sisi smiles, pride reflected in her gaze. That's definitely a commendable profession. He's earning even more brownie points.

"He's very good looking," I add shamelessly, and I can feel my cheeks immediately redden.

"Lina!" Sisi exclaims in outraged amusement. "So that's why you were so curious." She teases, and I blush even more.

"It's not as if I see a handsome man every day," I argue, but she's having none of that.

"Maybe next time you can meet him, too."

"And do what? Swoon at his feet?" The mere thought of that is hilarious. A scene slowly paints itself in my mind. Me tripping unceremoniously and landing on Marcello's lap.

Meeting his eyes for the first time, and him realizing that we're meant to be. All of it ending, of course, with a kiss. I'm so lost in that scenario that it takes Sisi physically shaking me to get me back to reality.

"You were really gone this time," she chuckles.

"I'm sure he'd want nothing more than a semi-nun with a child," I mutter drily, the reality of it being rather depressing.

"Hey, don't sell yourself short! You are *not* a nun, and you are beautiful. And I mean really beautiful. Any man would be lucky to have you." She tries to comfort me, but I shrug it off. So what if I'm pretty? My circumstances are decidedly *not*.

"Never mind." I try to change the subject. I know dreaming is dreaming... but when it becomes hoping, then it has the potential to become harmful.

"Mamma! Aunt Sisi!" Claudia greets us when we get back to our room. "You were gone for so long!" She pouts in her usual fashion and I just shake my head.

"We have baking duty at four," I suddenly remember, my head snapping back to Sisi. Her eyes widen for a moment before checking the time.

"One more hour," she sighs in relief, and I follow suit. Mother Superior would never let us hear the end of it if we're late. The only saving grace is that I can take Claudia with me for all the duties, including cooking and baking. It's one of our most fun activities.

Tomorrow is Sunday, and we have a special banquet for a new priest that's coming to Sacre Coeur. Together with Sisi and a few other sisters, we have been assigned to baking duty to ensure that we have some cakes and pastries to greet the priest with.

———

"ADD A LITTLE MORE FLOUR," I say, squinting at the lumpy mixture Claudia is vigorously stirring. The aroma of freshly baked goods fills the air as we all work on our assigned tasks—chocolate chip cookies and corn cupcakes. Mother Superior herself had paid us a visit earlier, inspecting our recipes and giving her seal of approval for the new priest's welcoming reception.

"Do you know why everyone seems so eager for this new priest?" I inquire to Sisi, who is expertly frosting a row of golden cupcakes. The other sisters are also hard at work, but they are far enough away that we can speak freely.

"I have no idea. It's not like we're in dire need of a new one." Sisi mischievously dips her finger into the creamy frosting, but I quickly swat her hand away and give her a stern look.

"You don't want them to see," I whisper, trying to protect her from their judgmental stares.

Sisi's eyes dart around as I adjust my body to block her from the view of the other sisters.

She rolls her eyes at me but swipes her finger in the frosting again, this time bringing it to my mouth. I raise one eyebrow at her, but seeing that no one's watching, I quickly taste it, too.

The sweetness of the frosting mixes with the bitterness in my heart.

"Not bad," I nod, and Sisi gives me a rare genuine smile.

"See! You need to be naughty every once in a while." She winks at me, a glimmer of rebellion still alive in her spirit.

But Sacre Coeur is not a place for rebellion or fun. It's a place of God, or so they say. Yet, Sisi has tried everything she can think of to break out of the monotony and rules. Falling asleep during prayer, shouting expletives out loud, even switching ingredients during her cooking duty. If she could get away with a prank, she'd do it without hesitation.

But she's mostly grown out of it now. The harsh punishments and endless lectures from Mother Superior have worn her down. But I can't blame her for trying to rebel against this suffocating environment.

Funny how it's always my fault according to Mother Superior. As if being a pregnant teenager was something I intentionally caused. She loves to remind me that I wouldn't even be here if not for my family's influence.

"If even a place of God wouldn't take you, what does that say about you?" Her words still sting like fresh wounds, reminding me of all the times she'd insulted me.

But the real bullies here are not us. It's Mother Superior and her army of nuns and novitiates, who have turned their backs on us because of our "sinful" actions. As if we weren't still human beings deserving of love and forgiveness. But I've learned to ignore their hateful words and focus on protecting my daughter from their cruelty.

"We should have used salt instead of sugar," I say, my voice laced with a hint of bitterness. They are going to great lengths to impress this new priest, and I can't help but feel a little resentful. What is the point?

"Lina, showing some rebelliousness? Who would have thought?"

Sisi teases, her eyes sparkling mischievously. But then her expression changes, and she leans in closer.

"I'm not sure how true this is, but I overheard the other novitiates talking. Apparently, the new priest has some powerful connections. That's why Mother Superior is so obsessed with everything being perfect."

"Connections?" I furrow my brow in confusion.

Sisi glances around before leaning in even closer, her voice dropping to a whisper.

"The Italian mafia." She reveals, and a disbelieving laugh escapes me.

But as I lean back and catch her suspicious gaze, she questions, "Did you already know about this?"

"No, no, of course not. It's just that I can't believe that," I immediately say, not wanting to admit that I was laughing at the irony of the situation. But if the new priest *is* mafia... then I have to wonder which family he belongs to. I can't say I know a lot about our world either.

Most of the things I'd heard had been by eavesdropping. No one would tell me anything otherwise. I'm most familiar with the New York mafia and the five families. Agosti, my family, and then there's Lastra, Sisi's family. There are three others, Marchesi, Guerra and DeVille.

"That's what they were saying," she shrugs.

"I want some too!" I look down to see Claudia pointing at the frosting. She must have seen us earlier. I can't refuse her, so I make sure no one's watching before sneaking a spoonful of frosting to her.

"It's good," she smiles as she licks the spoon, and I can't help myself. I lean down and kiss the top of her head.

"Are you done with your batter, moppet?"

She nods, and I go over to check the texture. Seeing it's all right, I prepare it for the oven, breaking it up into smaller pieces. Claudia joins me while Sisi continues her own decorating task.

By the end of the day, we have enough batches of cookies and cupcakes for the entire nun population and the special guest. I am a little biased against the man already, if he is indeed mafia. My lips curl in distaste at the thought.

We finish cleaning the kitchen, and then we go back to our room. There are three beds inside now. Until a few years ago, there had been only two, as I'd slept with Claudia on one and Sisi on the other. But with my little troublemaker growing so fast, we'd had to request another bed. It hadn't been the smoothest process, and I'd had to get Enzo to intervene.

Speaking of Enzo... he hadn't visited in a couple of weeks. It's worrying since he sometimes visits weekly. I've been meaning to call him to make sure everything is ok. Maybe I should do that soon...

———

THE FOLLOWING day we all gather together for Sunday service. Familiar sermons echo through the church walls, filling the space with a sense of peace and devotion. But towards the end, Mother Superior's voice rings out above the rest.

"Sacre Coeur is honored to welcome Father Antonio Guerra, one of the brightest priests of his generation. He has been blessed to study under the greatest theological minds at the Vatican, and we are grateful that he accepts our invitation."

A young man, no older than thirty, steps forward from behind the altar. It's Father Guerra.

His appearance is nondescript, yet there's something about him that immediately sets me on edge. As he surveys the congregation, his gaze seems almost predatory—like a hunter searching for prey.

A cold shiver runs down my spine as his eyes lock onto our group, and for a moment, I think I see a sly smile tugging at the corners of his mouth before it disappears just as quickly. Maybe I'm imagining it...or maybe not. I always trust my instincts when it comes to people, and in Father Guerra's case, they're telling me to be wary.

Little do I know that my initial impression of him will prove to be true in ways I could never have imagined.

MARCELLO

AGE EIGHT

A noise jolts me awake. I take a moment to realize I'm not dreaming and that my eyes are wide open. It doesn't seem like it, though. Maybe because everything around me is enveloped in darkness.

Trapped in this tiny place, my legs are stiff from crouching. I once again attempt to test the strength of the lock with my hands. I push once... twice... it doesn't budge.

I don't know how long I've been here. I've slept a few times, but with no light, I can't even tell if it's day or night.

I take a deep breath, trying to calm myself. But memories of how this all started assault me.

It had been during Sunday lunch. For what seemed like the first time in forever, Father had demanded we eat together like a family. It had been a tense meal. We had all sat down in silence until Mother started with her crazy whispering.

Father's head had snapped in her direction, and with a snide smile, he'd watched Mother pour holy water on her food, all the while saying prayers.

The more I grew up, the more I realized there was something seriously wrong with Mother. And Father just took advantage of that.

"Liliana," he'd casually said, leaning back in his seat, still watching.

My mother hadn't reacted, so deep in her prayers she was that I don't think she even realized he'd spoken. Big mistake.

"Liliana!" This time, his voice held a threat to it, and it seemed to snap Mother from whatever trance she was in. But she didn't snap gracefully. No... she had to throw the holy water on Father.

"Demon... you're the devil," she'd whispered, and Father's sinister smile appeared once more.

"Devil, huh?" He'd mocked her one moment before his fist had shot out and connected with her cheek. I'd gasped as I watched Mother crumple to the floor, eyes wide, a hand going to the redness appearing on her face.

"Monster..." she'd continued. Father had sat up, tilted his head at her, and in a taunting voice asked,

"And what are you going to do about it?"

Mother's hands had gone to her cross, and she'd stuck it forward, as if hoping to repel the evil in Father. It just made him laugh.

"Your God isn't very generous today, is he?" He'd picked up the knife from his plate, slowly wiping it clean with a napkin. Upon seeing this, I'd realized I couldn't just sit and watch.

Mother was ill... she wasn't herself. But Father didn't care.

"No!" I'd burst out, putting my body in front of Mother's and hoping it would be a good shield.

Father had looked stunned for a moment before laughing once more.

"Boy, you want to defend her?" He'd raised one eyebrow at me, as if challenging me to admit it. "You want to defend this faithless whore?" He'd hissed at her before grabbing the front of my shirt and lifting me in the air.

"Fucking useless piece of shit." It had been very sudden. One moment I'd been hanging in the air, the next I'd been thrown across the room and into the wall. As my back had connected with the hard surface, I'd grimaced. The pain had been too much, and eventually I'd succumbed to it.

The next time I'd woken up, I'd been here. In a small, two-compartment chest of drawers. Or at least that's what I assume it is, since I'd tried to feel my way around it.

Father had shown up a little later.

"Let's see if you feel the same after spending some time in there." He'd chuckled and left me.

And now?

I don't even know what's worse... being deprived of light for so long, or sitting in my own piss and shit for hours upon hours. At first, the smell had made me gag.

Now... I think I've grown desensitized to it.

I try to stay awake for a while longer, but thirst and hunger overwhelm me. I close my eyes.

"Shit dude, it smells like shit in here."

"Fucking hell, you're right. But boss said to bring the brat down... Hold your nose."

There is some rattling, and I realize someone is opening the doors.

"Fuck... ew," a man says. As the doors open, my eyes struggle to get used to the light.

"Grab the brat and let's go," the other man orders dismissively. I am so weak... I don't have the power to struggle against his hold when he tugs me by my clothes.

They keep on making weird sounds and complaining about how disgusting I am, until they bring me to the first floor, to Mother's prayer room.

My eyes widely roam about, wondering what's about to happen. The man carrying me throws me on the floor and they both leave.

I bring my knees close to my chest and link my hands over them, slowly rocking myself. It's not over. I know, with everything in me, that it's not over. I'm here for a reason.

I don't know how much time passes, but suddenly the door to the room opens. Father comes inside, dragging Mother by her hair.

"There he is."

Her eyes are blank as she looks at me. She doesn't react. Father's fingers tighten in her scalp, and even then, her face doesn't betray the pain she must be feeling.

"Now, son. I'll teach you how to treat a faithless whore." He purses his lips for a second. "It just happens that she's your mother.

Are you going to interfere again?" He looks straight at me as he asks this.

I can't help but shake my head. Again... and again.

"Good... Good. Why don't we put that to the test?" He flings Mother to the floor and slowly rolls his sleeves up.

"First, you never want to stain your clothes." He explains with an evil smile as he grabs a large cross from Mother's altar.

"Blasphemy..." my mother finally utters as she stares at the cross in Father's hand.

He gives her a bored look, waving the cross around before hurling it onto her face with the flat side. Mother flinches in pain, and I can already see the blood falling down her face.

As if that's not enough, Father grabs her collar, and in one movement he rips the material from her body. Her scarred back is on full display, and he doesn't waste any time in aiming the cross onto her back time after time, until her cries become screams.

"See that, boy?" He turns to me, and I can only watch, stuck as I am in my useless body. I'm rocking even faster, and tears roll down my face as I watch the bloody scene in front of me.

"Liliana, dear." Father makes a tsk sound. "This is a lesson for your boy. Why don't you behave?" He grabs her by the neck and tosses her towards the altar. Mother stumbles and her hands catch onto the altar table for support.

"Yes. Just like that." Father hums in approval. He casually strolls over and, gripping her nape, forces her face down on the altar. Using one hand, Father lifts her skirt and stuffs it around her hips. Somehow I know I'm not supposed to see this.

Mother is... bare.

But I'm stuck. I rock even faster, my sobs caught in my throat.

Father unzips his pants, and he turns to me. His hand is gripped around his penis.

"Watch and learn, boy. This is how you treat a whore." There is so much venom in his voice...

He turns around and mounts Mother from behind. There's only a pained sound coming from Mother's mouth, but Father is quick to push her face down onto the altar.

He keeps moving over her, grunting every time.

I don't want to watch this.

I don't want to see this.

But I can't move.

I keep rocking.

At some point, I think I must have zoned out, because I hear Father say a few more unintelligible things before leaving.

I try to focus... Mother is breathing hard as she drags her body to the floor.

"You... it's all your fault." She keeps repeating, dragging her knees up and imitating my posture.

"Monster!" she says as she rocks herself, just as I was moments before.

"I'm sorry." The words are barely audible, but I say them anyway.

I *am* sorry... and yet I couldn't do anything to help her.

Weak.

I'm too weak.

Marcello

The elderly man in front of me takes a long drag from his cheroot, the smoke swirling around his head like a gray halo. I raise an eyebrow at him, intrigued by his boldness.

"You're not what I expected," he finally speaks, exhaling a cloud of smoke.

"And what exactly did you expect?" I ask, curious to hear his answer.

"A coward," he states matter-of-factly, a sly smile creeping onto his face, revealing yellowed teeth.

I can't help but feel a twinge of amusement at his response. "What makes you think I'm not one?"

"You're here," he gestures towards me with his cigar, "unarmed and without an army of bodyguards." He continues to grin at me.

"Should I have brought some?" I play along, taking on a more serious tone.

"Perhaps," he chuckles, taking another leisurely draw from his cheroot. He then motions for me to take a seat in front of him.

"Call me Francesco," he introduces himself with a polite nod. I oblige and take the chair across from him, wondering what kind of game this old man is playing.

Francesco had been my brother's underboss and trusted right hand. And he was among the only ones to join the ranks after father's death. I'd read the report. Valentino had helped Francesco and his family, bringing them from Italy to the States and promising a better future for his children.

Francesco had sworn fealty to my brother and had quickly climbed the ranks to become a most trusted asset. After a week at the Lastra house, I'd realized that things were more dire than I'd expected. The finances were a mess, and over the years someone had been siphoning money from almost all accounts. Valentino, in his quest for revenge, hadn't seemed to care that much to keep up with the business.

His sole focus had been Jimenez.

I'd immediately guessed that the problem lies with father's men. Aside from Francesco and the young soldiers, all the important men in the famiglia were among father's inner circle. Which is also why I'd come to meet Francesco. If I want to make a change within the famiglia, it has to start from the inside.

Francesco's sharp gaze meets mine as I slide the stack of papers across the table. The evidence of irregular activity is neatly compiled, every detail meticulously researched and documented.

"I think you know why I'm here," I say, my voice firm and steady. Francesco takes his time perusing the sheets, his brow furrowed in concentration.

"So?" he finally says after placing the papers back on the table.

"I thought you might have some insight," I reply calmly.

He scowls at me, clearly irritated by my assumption.

"And why did you think that?" he challenges.

"Because I've been told that you don't play well with others," I respond, not backing down. Francesco regards me silently for a moment before speaking again.

"And who told you that?" His tone is accusatory.

"I can't reveal my sources," I shrug, knowing that much of the information came from Vlad, a questionable ally. His relationship with Valentino had been closer than anyone realized, but Vlad's motives were never clear. He likes to manipulate and toy with people, giving them bits and pieces of information but never the whole truth.

But I'll take what I can get. My goal is simple: gain power within the famiglia, solve the ongoing shipment crisis, and eliminate any traitors or corrupt members. It sounds straightforward, but dealing with old-school mafia men is anything but easy.

These are hardened gangsters who have weathered decades of violence and betrayal from both enemies and law enforcement. I know that approaching this situation recklessly will only lead to disaster. That's why my first step is finding allies I can trust.

"Things are going to change," I state firmly. Francesco's lips curl into a snort of disbelief.

"Change?" he scoffs, taking a long drag from his cheroot. "You think your brother didn't try that?"

"Not enough," I reply calmly. "I won't pretend to know the full extent of how Tino ran things around here, since I wasn't privy to it at the time. But what I do know is what those reports are telling me. The business is on the brink of collapse, and factions have formed within the famiglia. Factions that would love nothing more than to see me fall from my position now," I pause, letting my words sink in.

Francesco grunts, studying me through narrowed eyes before exhaling a cloud of smoke.

"Valentino couldn't achieve what you're hinting at in ten years. What makes you think you can do it now?"

"My brother had distractions," I state firmly. "Romina's death weighed heavily on his shoulders and he was not fully focused on the famiglia. But I am." I lean forward, locking gazes with Francesco.

"And more importantly, I have something that Tino did not."

His eyebrows furrow in curiosity as he takes another drag from his cheroot.

"What's that?" he asks cautiously.

"Knowledge about the inner circle," I say cryptically. "And enough disdain for their kind that I will not fail. The question is... will you join me?"

"What makes you think I'm not *with* them?" His eyes study me closely, but my face gives nothing away. Father may have been a monster, but he trained me well.

"You're not." I push forward another document. He picks it up and frowns at the contents.

"This..." His voice is full of disbelief.

"Your son is free to do as he pleases now," I explain. Nicolo and his associates had been trying to get blackmail material on Francesco for a long time. He thought he'd finally succeeded when Francesco's teenage son had been caught by the police in a stabbing gone wrong.

"But how?"

"I'm a lawyer. I also worked with the D.A. Your son's case was fabricated. It was just a matter of untangling the web of evidence."

I can already tell I have him. I stand up to leave, but not before I hear him say,

"Grazie, capo."

I nod and take my leave.

One ally.

It's a start.

———

THE PREPARATIONS WERE in full swing for the highly anticipated meeting with the famiglia. I had spared no expense in planning an ostentatious banquet to mark the beginning of my leadership. As much as I despised being in this position, I knew that maintaining control and respect within the famiglia required certain actions.

In this world, respect was earned through fear. And for now, that was enough.

I admire the opulent hall before me, all previous worries wiped from my mind. Amelia's gasp as she enters echoes through the grand ballroom, her hand flying to her mouth in awe.

"Now, Amelia," I raise a finger to silence her. "Please escort our esteemed guests to the drawing room. Once the attendance list is complete, they may be led here."

Her face drains of color, but she nods slowly nonetheless.

Nearly an hour later, the doors to the ballroom swing open. Leaning casually against the wall, champagne flute in hand, I watch as each man comes in wearing their finest tuxedos.

The first group stops dead in their tracks at the sight before them, some swallowing nervously before cautiously moving forward. This pattern repeats until all have arrived and taken their place inside the grand hall.

The dimly lit room fills with the aroma of costly cigars and aged whiskey as I stand tall and proud, my glass raised in a toast.

"Good evening, gentlemen!" I declare, tipping my head to acknowledge their presence.

My uncle Nicolo steps forward, his eyes narrowing as he surveys the scene before him. "What's the meaning of this?" he demands.

With a smirk, I gesture towards the north-facing wall where my gift to the famiglia is on display. The men's gazes all follow my gesture, absorbing the gruesome carnage depicted on the wall. Rows of decapitated human heads are nailed to the wood, forming a T-shaped junction at the center. It's a chilling sight, one that I've meticulously planned and executed. Despite its horror, a sense of satisfaction washes over me.

Six heads adorn the wall, representing six men who have betrayed our famiglia. They thought they were above the code of omerta, but they were wrong. Traitors deserve no mercy in our world. As I look around at faces of my fellow made men, I know they understand what that T symbolizes—betrayal.

It has been difficult obtaining evidence against these six men, but I have succeeded. When they refuse to give up any further names under torture, there's no choice left but to end their lives. Some may view it as a pity that they don't break under pressure, but not me.

Now my job becomes even more challenging as I work to root out any other traitors among us. But now there can be no doubt that I'm not playing games.

"Please, everyone, take a seat."

There are three rows of tables in the room, all of them carefully prepared in advance. They also have name tags. This isn't only a show of strength; it's also a study. By seating them strategically, I can observe the interactions between different members. It should be fun.

There is some shuffling as the men search for their names on the chairs, but shortly everyone is seated.

"In front of you, you will find evidence of the crimes committed by the traitors. This is my gift to you all. As the new capo, I can promise that there will be no rotten apples. In fact, the lucky six are only the first in a long list of people who have been exploiting the resources of the famiglia for their own gain."

"So where are the rest, then? You don't know who they are, do you?" A portly man laughs at the end of the table. I give him a sharp look, followed by a smile.

"Oh, I do... I really do." And as I say this, I let my gaze roam around the room, sparing a glance at every individual. "But I'm just waiting."

"For what?" My uncle barks.

"For them to trip."

People are already uneasy. It helps that the room is filled with hidden cameras. Body language *will* be telling.

"But enough of the morbid talk," I continue. "Let us enjoy a peaceful dinner before talking business."

At my signal, select staff enter the ballroom with the first course and start serving the tables.

Small talk ensues. From my spot at the top of the table, I observe.

Some men keep glancing at the decapitated heads. Others try very hard not to. But then there are those that are completely unbothered by the bloody mess on the wall, and I know it's those I need to look out for.

Starting with my uncle Nicolo. Because of his position as Consigliere—a position that unfortunately he still holds—he is seated next to me.

"I must confess it was unexpected that you took the leadership," Nicolo starts. I tilt my head and, looking wholly unbothered, I answer.

"I would assume so, given that you *expected* the role to go to you." I smile. He does the same. Both our mouths are straining to portray the opposite of what we're feeling.

"It was a natural assumption... with you leaving the famiglia. Do you really think they will accept you? You've shown yourself unreliable before. Maybe you didn't precisely betray the famiglia, but you *left* it."

"And now I'm back."

He laughs.

"You think this little stunt of yours will get you anything? Sure, the cowards are going to recoil in fear, but is that what you want?"

"No... I want to do a clean-up. It's simple. In order for the famiglia to thrive, we need some rules."

"And you're the one to make them?"

"I'm here, aren't I?"

"Not for long."

Nicolo challenges me with his gaze, and I don't back down.

"Hmm... I wonder. Maybe we should keep this conversation for after dinner. I'm sure others will be interested in what I have to say..." I trail off, and I watch my uncle grimace.

He's right in one aspect: I don't really care for cowards. But usually, a coward is also a traitor by extension. The severed heads were just the appetizer; a small reminder that I too am a made man. After dinner, I must remind them that *that* is not all I am.

Nicolo switches his focus to the other people at his side, and our conversation is dropped. At least one thing's clear now. He *is* after power, and he thinks he is entitled to it.

The courses come and go, and the men become more relaxed. Maybe it's also because alcohol flows freely.

It's soon time to discuss business, and where better than in the basement? The men are reticent when they hear the destination, but already ruddy from alcohol, they bring their cigars and we move the party to the basement.

They probably expect yet another bloody crime scene, but I already cleaned that up when I had some people dispose of the headless bodies.

The basement is split into a few chambers, the biggest one almost the size of the ballroom. I'd arranged for it to be decorated for a loyalty ceremony. We need to make this thing official.

There are two guards standing at the end of the room, where I promptly take my place. Francesco is already there, and he gives me a nod of approval.

"Gentlemen, shall we begin?" I ask as I take a seat in front of them. I give Francesco a look, and he takes the floor.

"Before we discuss anything of importance, every one of you will be required to swear loyalty to Marcello Lastra as your new capo. I'm sure you were already expecting this." He looks around at the myriad of faces. Some men scoff, others seem rather interested, while others emanate pure malice.

Nicolo is the one who steps forward and, as expected, states his challenge.

"How can we trust a kid," he sneers. "Especially one that left the famiglia behind. He may be the direct heir, but how can we trust that he won't bail again?"

There's a lot of hushed tones discussing; some in agreement, some raising questions.

"Are you saying you are better fit, *uncle?*" I look him straight in his eyes and he tips his head back in arrogance.

"Why not?"

I smile. It's not as if I was not expecting this.

"Then it seems we are at an impasse. Tell me, *uncle*, are you officially challenging me?"

His eyes widen as he understands where I am going with this. He cannot back down, however, since he's already made a claim.

"I believe you are."

"I am," he immediately adds. I smirk.

"Francesco, tell me the rules again?"

"The challenged can choose the type of challenge," Francesco adds so that everyone in the room can hear. There are hums of approval, some of them may be too eager. If they want a spectacle... well, they will have one.

I rise to my feet, casually walking towards Nicolo.

"So what? Fists, swords, pistols?" Nicolo looks at me and smirks.

"Chess." I enjoy the look on his face when he hears that. His smile slowly falls, and he frowns. The other men around are baffled as well.

"Chess? You're joking."

"It's my right as the challenged to choose the challenge. Does it have to be a type of combat, or violent?" I turn to Francesco and ask.

"No. It can be anything," he replies.

Everyone is quiet.

I motion to Francesco, and he brings over a chessboard, placing it on a table in the corner of the room.

With my hand, I motion Nicolo to follow. He looks like he wants to argue with my suggestion, but he must realize by now that he's fallen into my trap. And there's no return.

"But what would chess say about the new capo?" He sputters in a last attempt to divert attention.

"Then tell me," I begin, crossing my arms in front of me, "why would a capo need any fighting skills when he has his soldiers? Better yet, wouldn't you say," I turn and address the rest of the men, "that a good capo should be smart enough to strategically weigh his moves... almost like on a chessboard."

Nicolo's face falls, and I can tell I've won the argument in the eyes of the other men as well.

We sit down in front of the chessboard, and after arranging the pieces, the game begins.

It doesn't take long for me to win. After I capture his Queen, it's only a matter of a couple of movements until his King is cornered. It's something I counted on when I thought about this encounter.

Nicolo might be smart and cunning, but he is the type of person who belittles any type of intellectual pursuits—including chess. I'd narrowed down on his weakness, and I'd just made sure he was the one to challenge me. I knew he'd expect some type of corporeal challenge, like sparring or shooting, both of which he excels at.

He's not much older than Valentino had been, his body fit and in shape. But he'd been overconfident. I'd just played on his hubris... and won.

"Checkmate."

Nicolo's nostrils flare at the pronouncement, and he's doing his best to keep his temper in check. I don't let my satisfaction show.

"Good game, uncle," I tell him, taking a step back to put some distance between us.

In an unprecedented gesture, Nicolo inclines his head and half-bows to me.

"Capo," he says through gritted teeth.

He knows he's lost, but at least he still has his dignity. For now, the plan is working. Although I'm not so naïve as to think this would stop Nicolo from further plotting to take over the famiglia.

One by one, the other members of the famiglia repeat the gesture, swearing fealty to me as the new Capo.

When the entire ceremony is done, I announce my next intentions. Knowing that Nicolo will just lay in wait, I need to quickly consolidate power. Being Capo is not enough.

"There are two things that I'd like to discuss, and which are on my agenda as the official Capo," I start. Francesco had gotten in touch with the staff, and more drinks had been served before my speech.

"Before Romina's death, the Lastra family enjoyed good relations with the Agostis. I intend to rectify that by marrying within the Agosti family. In fact, I will have a meeting with Enzo Agosti, the new Agosti Capo, in the following days."

There's a lot of cheering, and people seem in favor of this decision. I can see from the corner of my eye that some don't look too happy. The same ones that had looked suspicious during the dinner. Interesting...

"Aside from that, you must all be aware by now of some problems in New Jersey. Some of our shipments to New York have been stopped and seized at the NJ entry points."

Everyone nods. It's not news for them either—most of them being directly involved with the chain of supply.

"I'll be partnering up with Russian Bratva and the Agosti family to find whoever is responsible for this and make sure they pay for this offense. I want everyone on standby for future orders."

My speech is interrupted by a phone's beep sound. It's followed by more ringtones, including my own. Everyone in the room is now checking their phones.

"Yes," I answer at the same time as Nicolo picks up his phone.

"Irish attack in Newark," Vlad's grim tone greets me on the other line.

"And?"

"Stolen merchandise and casualties. Both our sides. It's a declaration."

I purse my lips.

"At least we know who's doing it now," I reply.

Vlad chuckles on the other line.

"They don't know what they've unleashed."

I smile at that.

"It's on," I add before hanging up.

The men are all sporting a worried look on their faces. Everyone's heard about the attack by now.

"And we are officially at war with the Irish. I want everyone to send me a report with what you do, how many men you have under you, and your precise schedules and locations."

"Yes!" Everyone agrees in unison.

"Good. Meeting over." Nicolo is watching me with an inscrutable look on his face.

"You'll be the end of this family, boy. Mark my words."

I freeze at his appellation, something that father used to call me. Trying to mask my features, I answer.

"Be careful about *your* end, uncle. It might come sooner than you think." I leave the threat hanging.

After everyone's left, Vlad texts me a meeting spot, and I join him to assess the casualties.

THE ATTACK HAD BEEN TOO WELL COORDINATED. Both Vlad and I came to that conclusion, given the timing and the location. Aside from the merchandise, we'd also ended up losing a few people.

"A mole," Vlad's grim voice echoes my thoughts, and I can't bring myself to disagree.

The situation is spiraling out of control at a rapid pace, forcing me to make a swift decision. I waste no time in scheduling a meeting with Enzo for the next day.

And now here I am, in his opulent foyer, waiting to be received in his study. The tension hangs thick in the air as I anxiously wait to meet him.

"Signor Agosti can see you now." A burly man glares down at me before leading me down a long hallway to Enzo's study.

Enzo's warm smile greets me as I enter the room. "Marcello," he says with genuine warmth. "It has been too long."

I fight the urge to roll my eyes at his superficial charm. The man is dangerous, and I can't afford to show any weakness. But for the sake of our business partnership, I put on a polite smile. "It is always a pleasure to see you, Enzo."

Or not long enough, I want to say.

But instead, I take a deep breath and prepare myself for what needs to be done.

"So many surprises lately, wouldn't you say?" Enzo's movements are sluggish, and it's obvious he is still not completely recovered. Just a week ago, he'd been in the ICU fighting for his life. He's resilient... I'll give him that.

"My condolences for your father."

"Good riddance." Enzo waves his hand dismissively. "Just like your own old man."

"Indeed." I purse my lips but don't comment.

"Do tell, Marcello. What is the purpose for this visit?" His smile is cunning, but he must be aware of the *purpose*.

"To bury the hatchet, so to speak."

"You know, just because your brother is dead, that doesn't mean our conflict ends."

"I'm sure you've heard how Jimenez died." I go straight to the point. That he received me this civilly tells me he is willing to have a proper discussion, regardless of the past.

"Some." He looks intrigued, so I continue.

"I was there. So was my brother. Valentino was the one who killed Jimenez—retribution for Romina's death." I stop to gauge his reaction.

"Go on," Enzo urges me.

"Jimenez used Romina's death to drive a rift between our families."

"And then he picked on us one at a time." Enzo interrupts. "I must admit, I'd been thinking about this for a while. You just confirmed my suspicions. When my father first got involved with the Irish, I advised him to keep our options open, but he was bent on pursuing that partnership. But, alas, I will not blame my father for this entirely, since I didn't exactly do much to stop it. I was blinded by the possibilities too."

"So you suspected them?"

"Suspect? Hmm... I wouldn't say suspect, in as much as I didn't trust their intentions. But I never thought they would work for Jimenez. And *that* was my mistake."

"I don't think anyone could have known. The Irish aren't known to work with the cartels."

"And that's why it was such a brilliant move. They played us on our expectations." Enzo taps his pen on the table. "The world is changing, but we aren't. Our families are too steeped in tradition."

"Maybe we can do something about it."

"Hmm... lofty aspirations for someone who *left*, Marcello."

"It might be doable," I continue.

Enzo shrugs. "Then you might as well get to why you came here."

I clear my throat, the tension in the room palpable as I speak. "I want an alliance. I want our families to get along as they did before."

Enzo's dark eyes flicker with interest as he stands up from his seat and heads towards his decanter. Pouring two drinks, he hands me a glass with a slight nod. "Are you saying what I think you're saying, Marcello?" His voice is smooth and controlled, but there is a hint of amusement in his tone.

I take a long sip from my drink before answering firmly, "Yes."

A small smile tugs at the corner of Enzo's lips as he raises an eyebrow at me. "I must inquire about the marriageable girls of age. I have to warn you, though. You won't have too many choices."

"As long as she's of age," I say, forcing myself to remain composed despite the unease that gnaws at my gut. The thought of marrying someone so young sends a shiver down my spine.

"Not picky," Enzo chuckles, swirling his drink in his glass. "I like that."

"You'd be in favor of a match?" I ask, feeling a glimmer of hope ignite within me at his words.

"It would be the solution for both our problems, wouldn't it?" Enzo takes a slow sip from his drink, his gaze locked on mine.

"Indeed," I agree, emptying my glass with one final gulp before standing up. "Let me know who you've chosen, and we'll set a date."

Enzo studies me for a moment longer before asking with genuine curiosity, "You really don't care?"

I pause for a moment, considering his question carefully before responding with conviction, "No, I do not." But deep down, I can't help but wonder if this arrangement is truly the best solution for both our families, or if it is simply a means to an end.

"What's there to care? It's my duty," I shrug.

CATALINA

"Enzo!" My voice goes up a notch. "I've been worried."

"*Piccola*, I am fine." He coughs. "Not that I was fine *before*."

"What do you mean?"

"We were attacked. Rocco's dead." My fingers tighten on the phone. He is?

A surge of happiness envelops me. My father is dead.

"What about you? Please tell me you're okay!"

"I'm out of the danger zone, don't worry. They discharged me from the hospital a couple of days ago."

"Good! That's good! But... does that mean?" I ask hesitantly.

"Not now, *piccola*... It's extremely dangerous. I barely made it out alive myself. We have enemies gunning for our territories. I can't expose you to that." He explains, and my face falls. "Soon. Just wait a little longer."

"Ok," I whisper.

"How is my favorite niece?"

"She's good. She can't wait to see you. When will you be visiting?"

"I'll try to be there by the end of the week. I'll see you then, *piccola*."

"Yes, thank you, Enzo. I am really glad you're fine."

"Don't worry about me, I am a hard man to kill." He chuckles, but I don't share the sentiment.

As soon as I end the call, I slip my phone into its secret hiding spot. Although inspections in this place are rare, I can never be too cautious. Mother Superior has always held a grudge against me, and I know better than to give her any reason to lash out. She would just take her anger out on Claudia, and I couldn't bear that.

Enzo's absence is weighing heavily on my mind... he's injured and couldn't make it here. I close my eyes and take a deep breath, trying to steady my nerves. This is just another reminder of why I despise my family's line of work.

There's always danger lurking around every corner. I don't want that for Claudia, but at the same time, I don't want her to grow up confined within these convent walls either. It's not an ideal situation, and it weighs heavily on my heart.

With a joyful squeal, Claudia flings open the door and leaps into my arms. Her golden curls bounce as she clings to me with all her might.

"Mamma!" She exclaims, burying her face in my shoulder.

"There, there, little troublemaker," I chuckle, but her excitement is contagious. "You'll make me lose my balance."

Giggling, she pulls back and thrusts her hand out towards me. In it sits a small chocolate bar, already half-melted from the warmth of her palm. I frown at the sight.

"Where did you get that?" I ask, knowing that only an outsider could bring such a treat inside our strict community.

Her face lights up even more as she proudly proclaims, "Father Guerra gave it to me! He said I was an obedient child."

I feel a twinge of surprise and guilt. In the days since Father Guerra's arrival, I had let my own biases and prejudices cloud my opinion of him. But he had proven to be nothing but kind and understanding towards our family. He hadn't let rumors or societal expectations influence how he treated us, and for that, I am grateful.

Especially now, as I watch him interact with Claudia and see just how much she craves a father figure in her life.

I give Claudia a stern look. "You can have it after dinner," I say firmly.

"But can't I have just one piece now?" She pleads, batting her long lashes at me.

"No," I respond with a smile, unable to resist her charm. "After you finish your dinner."

Reluctantly, she hands over the chocolate bar and I set it aside for later.

"Now, where is your Aunt Sisi?" I ask, wondering why Claudia was alone when she was supposed to be with Sisi.

"She got held up by Mother Superior," Claudia explains with a shrug. "She told me to go ahead."

I find it odd that Sisi was delayed, but I push the thought aside.

"Let's get you dressed."

The anticipation of Sunday dinner always fills the air with excitement and warmth. Claudia is allowed to dress up in one of her nicer outfits, although they are not what I would consider pretty. I open our closet and ask her to choose her outfit for this week's meal.

After careful consideration, she selects a dusty pink dress. I pull out one of her crisp white shirts from a drawer and hand it to her to put on first. Then, with gentle guidance, I help her slip into the dress.

"Can you do my hair too?"

She eagerly plops down in front of the small mirror on the desk as I comb through her light brown locks, tinged with sandy blonde highlights. She looks like a miniature version of me, except for her hair.

As I separate her hair strands and begin braiding them into a long plait, my thoughts drift to that fateful night... to Claudia's biological father. A shudder runs through me and I quickly try to push the memories away by focusing on Claudia's lively chatter about her school lessons.

"All done."

"Thank you, mamma." She wraps her arms around my waist and gives me a tight hug.

"There you are." Sisi's breathless voice interrupts us as she enters the room. Her disheveled appearance suggests she may have just run a marathon.

I furrow my brow as I eye her panting figure, throwing herself onto the bed with frustration. "What happened to you?" I ask, concerned.

"That... ugh... that blasted woman!" She punches the pillow beside her. "Sisi?"

"Mother Superior," she growls, her expression contorting with anger. "She told me I'm not doing my chores properly and that now I will be assigned double the load... to 'learn how to work properly,' she says." She shifts restlessly on the bed before jumping to her feet.

"I've never had a complaint before, but suddenly I'm doing everything wrong."

"Sisi..."

"You know what, never mind. I'll do what she says...but that means I won't have that much time to watch Claudia." Her voice softens as she mentions our daughter's name.

"I'm sure we can figure something out," I offer, trying to ease the tension.

"And I'm a big girl. I can look after myself," Claudia chimes in, causing both Sisi and me to smile at her independence.

"Let me get dressed and I'll come with you to dinner." She sighs and reaches for a clean outfit from her dresser.

We make our way to the large dining hall, trying to avoid the judgmental stares and malicious whispers of the other nuns. We find a table in the farthest corner and take our seats. Despite the uncomfortable atmosphere, the food turns out to be surprisingly delicious, and we all enjoy our meal together. When we finish, we gather our trays to return them for washing.

"Can I go eat the chocolate now?" Claudia tugs on my sleeve eagerly, her eyes sparkling with excitement. Seeing her hopeful face, I can't bring myself to refuse her request.

"Sure, you can go ahead."

"Yay!" she exclaims before darting off towards our room.

"You're spoiling her too much," Sisi says, playfully reprimanding me.

"It's the least I can do," I reply with a smile, knowing how much Claudia has been through in her young life.

"I wish my mother was like you," Sisi's wistful tone catches me off guard, reminding me of the time when she had asked me to be her mother all those years ago.

I give her hand a quick squeeze in comfort, silently conveying that she is loved and appreciated.

As we make our way back to the room, the convent is cloaked in silence. The usual bustle of nuns preparing for lights out has ceased, leaving only a serene stillness. I call out my daughter's name as I open the door to our room, but receive no answer. A ripple of unease courses through me as I step inside.

"Claudia? It's not funny," I repeat, my voice tinged with worry as I search every nook and cranny of the tiny room. Sisi joins me in the search, but there are only so many places one can hide in such a confined space.

"Where could she be?" Panic blooms within me as I frantically scan the room. My eyes land on the spot where I had left her chocolate, untouched.

"I don't think she came here."

Sisi's words echo my thoughts as we exchange worried looks.

"You take the west wing; I'll take the east. We'll find her."

Without hesitation, we split up and begin searching. I approach every nun I come across, asking if they have seen Claudia. Some scoff at me, making rude comments about my ability to care for my own child. But I push their hurtful words aside and continue my search.

Finally, someone offers some information.

"I think so. I'm not sure if it was Claudia."

Desperate for any lead, I plead with them to tell me more.

"She was heading towards the chapel."

"Thank you!" Gratitude pours from me as I take their hands in mine.

As I approach the chapel, all is quiet and still. The wooden doors are unassuming, but as I push them open, they give way with ease. Inside, the atmosphere is hushed and reverent, like a miniature gothic church. Though it is spacious enough to hold all the nuns within the convent, by other standards, it is not particularly large.

The interior is adorned with two rows of pews on each side leading towards the ornate altar, and on the right is the confessional booth. Stained glass windows depicting scenes from the Bible line the walls on either side of the chapel.

Moving further into the chapel, I pass down the central nave towards the altar.

The only source of light in the dimly lit church comes from a few flickering candles at the altar. As I approach, my eyes gradually adjust to see two figures standing near the front. One is an adult, and the other is a small child. As I draw closer, their features become clearer...and so do their actions.

My heart stops as I realize what I am witnessing—Father Guerra's hand is up Claudia's dress. Without hesitation, I lunge forward with one goal in mind: to rescue my little girl from this man's grasp.

In that moment, they must have sensed my presence because Father Guerra quickly removes his hand and attempts to compose himself. Claudia turns towards me, her expression betraying a mix of fear and shame. But before I can even process what has happened or confront them both about their twisted relationship, something inside me snaps and I let out a guttural scream of rage and disgust.

My voice is stone, cold and demanding as I command Claudia to go to the room. Her shoulders tremble ever so slightly, whether from the recent events or the steely tone in my voice, I cannot tell. "Now!" I reiterate sharply when she hesitates.

"Mamma..." Claudia's whisper barely reaches my ears before she runs out of the chapel.

"Catalina, please understand, this isn't what it looks like," Father Guerra jumps to his own defense. His hands are raised in a placating gesture.

"Fixing her dress? Or her underwear?" My feet carry me swiftly towards him, a sudden urge to do harm overtaking me. How dare he touch my nine-year-old daughter? The thought alone makes me want to break down and cry, but I can't allow this man to walk away without facing consequences.

"Catalina, surely we can come to an understanding," he persists.

"What kind of understanding? That you're a disgusting pedophile?" My voice rises with each word, thick with disgust and rage. "Mother Superior will hear about this. You'll get what you deserve, you waste of a human being." There is so much venom in my words, yet it still doesn't seem enough for what I feel towards him.

Father Guerra chuckles. He actually has the audacity to laugh.

"And who do you think will believe you? You, who slept around and got pregnant by who knows who? Your own family didn't even want you." My face falls at his cruel words. "Oh, did you think I didn't know? You actually thought I was being nice to you? Whores like you have no place in a house of God." His mention of God only fuels my anger further. Without thinking, my hand shoots out and connects with his cheek in a loud slap.

My voice catches in my throat, unable to form words as I stare at him in disbelief. His hand quickly moves to his cheek, rubbing it slowly as if trying to erase the red mark that is surely forming.

"Fucking whore!" he yells before his hand wraps around my neck, cutting off my air supply. I stumble backwards until I feel the hard edge of an altar table against my back. Panic sets in as I struggle for breath, his grip only tightening with each passing second.

"No one would even miss you if you're gone," he sneers, his voice dripping with malice and contempt. In that moment, I realize my mistake. I should have listened to my gut instinct. Instead, I allowed myself to be lured here by him... and now who knows what he did to Claudia. The thought ignites a fierce determination within me, and I begin searching behind me on the table, desperate for something to defend myself with.

Seconds tick by agonizingly slow, and I can feel myself fading...until finally, my hand closes around something cold and sharp. With all the strength I have left, I plunge the knife into his neck. He stares at me in shock as blood gushes from the wound, his grip on my throat loosening as he clutches at the blade protruding from his skin.

Gasping for air, my lungs burn and ache as I stumble away from him. The metallic scent of blood fills the air, mixed with the sickeningly sweet smell of death. Father Guerra's shaking hand reaches for the knife protruding from his neck, his eyes wide with shock and fear. In a burst of crimson, blood gushes out in spurts, flowing like a geyser out of the wound and onto the floor.

His breaths come in ragged gasps, his face turning pale as he falls to his knees and then collapses on the floor with a heavy thud.

As my heart races and adrenaline courses through my veins, I slowly begin to comprehend the gravity of my actions. I...I killed him. The realization hits me like a ton of bricks, and I start to freak out. My hands tremble uncontrollably as I stare at the lifeless body before me, struggling to process what just happened. The weight of taking a human life is almost suffocating.

But then I remember why I did it. He touched Claudia...He was going to kill me... A fierce rage rises within me, warring against the guilt and confusion that threaten to consume me. I can't decide if I should regret what I did or not. Part of me revels in the fact that a monster is dead; but there is also another part of me that can't believe I've taken a life with my own hands.

I try to rationalize it. It's not the end of the world, right? He was a wicked man who deserved to die. Yes...He was an evil man, and the world is better off without him.

But what about me? What will happen to me when they find out? They'll probably send me to prison...No! That's not an option. Panic sets in as I realize the consequences of my actions. I can't leave Claudia. I can't leave my daughter alone to face the world without me.

Think, Catalina, think!

My resolve renewed; I go into fixing mode. I can't allow this to separate me from my daughter. He won't win!

Think, Catalina!

It's a Sunday night... no one will know if I get rid of the body. Yes... I just have to get rid of the evidence and no one will know. I pick up the knife and, using a cloth from the altar, I wipe it clean and deposit it back in its original spot. But looking around the chapel, I realize I'm in a pickle. What do I do with the body? There's absolutely no way I can get rid of a body on my own...

Think, Catalina... Think!

With wide eyes, I frantically scan my surroundings for any sign of inspiration. My gaze finally lands upon the confessional booth, an idea forming in my mind. I grab Father Guerra's limp hands and begin to drag him towards the booth, struggling against his larger size and my own lack of strength.

Eventually, with great effort, I manage to maneuver his body inside the booth, stuffing him inside until I can close the door. But there is still a trail of blood on the floor, causing me to let out a shaky breath. I quickly attempt to clean up the blood as best as I can, though my resources are limited and the result is messy.

As the adrenaline starts to wear off, panic grips me. I can't just leave a dead man in a confessional booth. But I also can't risk dragging him out alone to dispose of his body. I'll need help from someone else, but who? And what will I do after disposing of the body?

Placing a trembling hand over my pounding heart, I desperately try to calm my racing thoughts. I steal a glance at the confessional, waiting for the guilt to consume me. Surprisingly, it doesn't come. The thought of that man touching Claudia fills me with anger rather than remorse. Shaking my head to clear it, I focus on figuring out my next steps.

But first, I need to get rid of this evidence. Glancing around, I spot an organ on the other side of the aisle covered with a red cloth. With determination, I make my way over and uncover a long piece of fabric that could potentially cover my bloody clothing.

Divesting myself of the stained dress, I drape the cloth over my body and tie a knot around my shoulder in a Grecian style. Then, with my already soiled dress, I wipe down the floor again, in the most obvious spots.

I'll do the rest later.

Closing my eyes for a second, I try to calm down again. I can do this... I can do this. With one last glance at the chapel, I make my way out and navigate through the halls, careful to avoid populated areas. The faint scent of incense lingers in the air, a constant reminder of where I am. When I reach the room, I turn the knob slowly and push open the door, revealing Sisi and Claudia on the bed. Sisi's head snaps towards me.

"Lina?"

"Can you come out for a second? And bring me a dress." Sisi furrows her brow in confusion but obeys without question.

I wait outside for what feels like an eternity before Sisi reappears with a dress in hand.

"What is going on?" Her eyes widen as she takes in my disheveled appearance. It must be obvious that something is wrong.

"Something bad happened. Like terrible."

"Lina... you're scaring me."

"Did Claudia tell you anything?" I ask, bracing myself for her answer.

"No... she only mentioned you were with Father Guerra." At the mention of his name, all of the emotions and memories come flooding back, and I break down.

"He was touching her..." I whisper, tears finally starting to stream down my face.

"What do you mean?" Sisi asks, concern etched onto her features.

"He was touching her under her clothes..."

"No!" she exclaims, horrified.

"Where is he? What happened?"

"I... I killed him."

"You're kidding."

"No... I really killed him. I didn't mean to but..."

I tell her every detail about what happened, including how I disposed of the body in the confessional booth.

After a prolonged silence, Sisi finally speaks.

"We need to do something about that." My heart sinks as I expect her to condemn me for being a murderer.

"You... I killed a man," I repeat, waiting for condemnation.

"Yes, and I would have killed him, too. That wastrel! Now, about the confessional booth," she adds pensively.

"That's why I came back. I can't do it alone. I know this is too much to ask but..."

"No buts!" Sisi shuts me up and continues. "Come on, dress, and we'll figure it out." She gives me a big hug and lets me change into something more decent.

"I need to talk to Claudia first," I say, and she nods, stepping back to allow me into the room.

"I'll be here. Let me know when to come in."

I leave Sisi outside and tentatively open the door to the room.

"Mamma!" Claudia exclaims and comes towards me. "I'm sorry," she mumbles and starts crying.

"No, baby, no. It's not your fault."

"But you were mad... you screamed at me. You never scream." She mumbles, her small hands rubbing at her eyes.

"Shh..." I slowly pat her hair and lead her towards the bed.

"Claudia, my love, please tell me... has Father Guerra touched you like that before?" I don't know how I manage to mask the tremor in my voice. Claudia raises her dewy green eyes to look at me.

"Once... he told me he'd give me a chocolate every day if I let him." My heart is breaking as she tells me this.

"Did he... did he do more than that?" I almost don't want to know, but I must.

Claudia shakes her head.

"Are you sure? You can tell mamma; I promise I will not get mad."

"No." She shakes her head even harder. I want to believe her... My daughter... my daughter almost went through the same thing I did all those years ago. I bring her to my chest and I tighten my arms around her. She's fine... She's okay. And he's dead... He can't hurt her anymore. That's what I tell myself as I rock her in my arms.

A while later, Claudia is deep asleep. Sisi takes me aside and tells me her idea.

"It might work. No one will know if we bury him in the cemetery."

"How are we going to carry him there, though?" I whisper back at her.

"Your luggage case?" she suggests. That might just work.

We empty the luggage of all its contents, and then we leave for the chapel.

"Sisi, are you sure you want to do this? It's my fault... I can just tell them what happened." I don't want to drag her into my mess... The situation is getting out of hand. And it *is* my fault.

"And who'd believe you? You already said he's from a prominent family. They probably have enough influence to make sure you get blamed for everything. Think about Claudia. What would happen to her without her mother?" She asks, and I freeze. That's exactly what I'd been thinking about. What would happen to my daughter? Turning myself in doesn't seem like a good possibility, especially given that Father Guerra was Mother Superior's favorite.

"What if Mother Superior was in on it too?" Sisi suddenly asks. I turn sharply.

"What do you mean?"

"She knows that when you are on duty, I take over watching Claudia. With me doing double the chores, Claudia would be left alone."

"And vulnerable. You're right. He's been plying her with sweets to gain her trust since the beginning. And no one would have turned an eye if she went somewhere with Father Guerra. He's a priest after all." I add, but this just makes me even sicker to my stomach.

Were they planning this? To defile my beautiful baby? I can barely control the rage I feel inside at the thought... but I know I can't regret killing him, even if it was in self-defense. He wanted to hurt my baby.

Inside the chapel, we head straight for the confessional booth. Sisi is quiet as I open the door. She looks at Father Guerra's bloody body with an almost inscrutable expression.

We open the suitcase and lay it on the ground. Then, the both of us grab onto Father Guerra and dump him in the suitcase.

"He's too big," she scrunches her nose.

"We just need to fold him a little." She tilts her head to the side as she considers this.

"How about we try a fetal position?" She circles the suitcase, her face sporting a big frown. She's probably imagining the different angles.

"Let's try."

We rotate his body, trying varying angles to fit him inside. Lucky for us, he's not a very tall male, probably only five inches taller than my own five-foot-three frame. After much trial and error, he's folded nicely in the suitcase.

I grab onto one zipper while Sisi holds onto the other, and we try to meet halfway. It takes a little sitting on top of it to make the suitcase close, but we manage.

"Damn." She wipes the sweat off her forehead with the back of her hand.

The convent has its own cemetery. Sacre Coeur has a history stretching back almost two hundred years, and this cemetery was inaugurated during the 1918 influenza outbreak. Since then, it's been used sparsely, when nuns pass away. The advantage is that the cemetery is located close to the chapel, so the body can be put to rest right after the religious services.

There are maybe two administrative buildings that we have to pass on the way to the cemetery. Sisi's idea to place the body in the luggage was brilliant. The luggage's wheels make it easy to carry it towards the cemetery. Once there, we look for a hidden parcel, where the presence of fresh earth would go unnoticed. We find just the place, right next to a willow tree. The shadow cast from the tree should mask the turned earth.

"Wait!" Sisi says and dashes towards one of the smaller sheds next to the cemetery. She only takes a few minutes before returning with two shovels.

"Now's the hard part." She sighs and thrusts the shovel into the ground before scooping up some earth and dumping it to the side. I take the other shovel and do the same.

It must be a couple of hours later when, almost drenched in sweat, we finish digging.

"Honestly, this wasn't that bad," Sisi comments, and my head snaps towards her. Is she serious? "I think I'd rather dig up graves than wash dishes. Do you think I can apply for the position?" She's extremely serious as she asks this, and I can't help but laugh.

"Sisi..." I start, but I can't stop laughing. "You really want to trade dishes for graves?"

"It's still work." She shrugs, but I can tell she's amused as well.

"Let's do this!" I bring forward the suitcase and together we throw it into the hole.

"I say it's deep enough."

"I think so," I agree.

We grab the shovels once more and cover the hole with earth. This doesn't take nearly as long, and we soon find ourselves back at the chapel, trying to wipe away all evidence of the crime.

CATALINA

Claudia hasn't mentioned Father Guerra since the incident. I'm relieved that she doesn't seem to be deeply affected, but it's clear she doesn't fully understand what happened.

I tried to explain that what he did was wrong and that she should never let anyone touch her like that. However, she seemed more concerned about me yelling at her.

I reassured her multiple times that it wasn't her fault and that even adults can misbehave, using Father Guerra as an example. Our talks may have had an impact because she no longer brings up the event.

Similarly, Sisi has also acted like our late-night escapade never occurred. She doesn't mention Father Guerra at all, and everything appears to be back to normal.

Or so we thought.

As it turns out, not everyone has forgotten about Father Guerra. A few days later, rumors start circulating that he abruptly left. Some nuns claim Mother Superior is distraught over his sudden absence. After hearing these whispers, I finally give in and ask Sisi:

"Do you think they'll try to find him?"

"Don't worry. There's no chance of them finding him, right? There's no trace of him," she answers in a hushed tone.

The burden of guilt continues to press heavily on my heart, regardless of how much I attempt to rationalize my deeds. The vision of Father Guerra with his hand up Claudia's skirt haunts me, and I can't shake the memory of his eyes just before he met his end. It's a secret I've yet to share with Sisi, but each night since that ill-fated evening, Father Guerra has invaded my nightmares.

Previously, it was only the monster with amber eyes who tormented me. But now... my dreams have shifted.

They always start with that enigmatic man, the one with piercing amber eyes. His features remain indistinct, but the overwhelming dread he stirs forces me to flee. Yet, he always catches up to me, pinning me from behind. In the past, my dreams ended when he lifted my skirt and forced himself upon me. But now... I resist.

I shove him off and defend myself. However, every time I lash out at him, he morphs into Father Guerra.

And I kill him.

I had hoped that reason would help me forget about that night. But it seems my subconscious is adamant about clinging to those memories.

Tonight proves no different as I find myself tossing and turning in bed, sleep eluding me. Glancing at the clock reveals it's nearing six in the morning; quietly slipping out of bed, I pour myself a glass of water.

"You're not okay," Sisi's voice surprises me as she props herself up in bed, observing my every move.

I respond by shaking my head.

"He deserved it, right?" She pats the spot next to her and I join her on the bed.

"In my mind... yes," comes my sad reply. "But guilt keeps gnawing at me."

"Just try to forget about it. Time will make it easier," Sisi offers her advice.

Just then, a blood-curdling scream shatters the silence. My frown deepens as I glance at Sisi, instantly recognizing the voice of another nun.

Sisi quickly springs out of bed, hastily donning her habit as we both dash towards the source of the screams.

"What are you doing?" I hiss.

"Aren't you curious?" She asks, her voice a mere whisper amidst the constant screams in the distance.

I glance over at Claudia, still sound asleep, and give in to Sisi's prodding. As we make our way out of the room and lock the door behind us, I can feel my heart pounding in anticipation and fear.

"It's coming from the grotto," Sisi points towards a direction and takes off running.

As we approach the grotto, I see a group of nuns gathered around, their faces etched with terror. Some are frantically crossing themselves, others kneeling and praying fervently. Sisi pushes her way through the crowd impatiently, pulling me along with her. But as she reaches the front, she suddenly freezes in shock.

"Mother of God... What..." Sisi stammers, her gaze transfixed on something ahead. I shift to the side slightly so I can see what has captured her attention. And then it hits me like a wave.

In the center of the grotto stands a replica of Michelangelo's Pietà sculpture. But instead of Christ cradled in Mary's arms, there lies Father Guerra's bloated and discolored body. His naked form is covered in brown bruises and purple blotches, his chest cavity exposed and his organs spilling out onto Mary's dress.

Flies buzz around him hungrily while maggots crawl over his skin, some even falling onto the ground below. The stench of decay fills the air, causing nuns to faint mid-prayer.

But that's not even the worst part.

As I approach the base of the statue, I notice a dark liquid staining the stone. A closer look reveals that it is blood, and upon further inspection, I see a message scrawled in the crimson substance—five words that send shivers down my spine.

I KNOW WHAT YOU DID

The words seem to jump off the stone, taunting me with their ominous weight. The air feels thick and suffocating as I read them over and over again. My hand shakes as I reach out to touch the words, feeling the cold stickiness of the blood beneath my fingertips.

"Blasphemy!" one nun yells, her voice breaking through the tense silence.

I turn to see Father Guerra's head hanging loosely at the neck, his once-human features distorted by putrefaction and the scavengers that have been at work. His flesh is thin and rotting, his spine fully exposed. Even in death, his head continues to move slightly up and down until finally, with a sickening thud, it falls to the ground. The nuns scatter away from it in fear.

My heart races as I take in this macabre scene. My feet feel unsteady beneath me, but before I can collapse, Sisi grabs onto my arm.

"Lina?"

"Who..." I whisper, unable to form a coherent thought. "I can't."

"We need to leave." Sisi's urgency breaks through my shock and she pulls me towards the back of the church. Just then, Mother Superior appears.

The moment she sees Father Guerra's remains, she crosses herself and drops to her knees, her eyes wide with horror.

"Let's go." Sisi urges me on, pulling me away from Mother Superior's gaze. We make our way back to our room as quickly and quietly as possible.

Claudia is still asleep in her bed when we enter. We try to keep our voices low so as not to wake her.

"Someone saw me... Oh Lord, someone knows." Panic begins to overtake me as I think about the implications. The image of Father Guerra's mutilated body, displayed for all to see, will haunt me forever. I can't unsee it...

"You don't know that."

"It was written there. You saw it too." I bring a hand to my forehead and close my eyes, willing the disturbing images away. "I need to do something... We can't stay here. It's too dangerous. What if whoever did this comes for us next? Or worse, Claudia?"

"Maybe it was just a prank," Sisi suggests, trying to calm me down.

"A prank?" I turn towards her, incredulous. "Did you see what they did to his body? They debased him in death... No, I can't stay here. I won't wait around and become their next victim." The fear and urgency in my voice are palpable as I make my decision. We have to leave. Now.

"I understand, but what can you do?"

Bringing my nails to my mouth, I bite them, the anxiety eating at my sanity. What can I do?

Think, Catalina, think!

"I need to call Enzo, tell him everything," I blurt out. I don't know if Enzo can do anything, but maybe he can at least protect my daughter.

I don't even wait for Sisi to reply. I go directly to my hidden spot and take out my phone, dialing Enzo. He picks up on the first try.

"Lina?" he asks, clearly surprised I'd call this early.

"Enzo... I need help. I screwed up," I start, my voice trembling as I try to explain what happened.

"Slow down, *piccola*. What happened?"

And so I tell him. Not in great detail, but I think he understands enough because he immediately tells me,

"I'll be there in a couple of hours. Don't move! Don't leave your room, understood?"

"Yes," I whisper, and I hang up.

"You're leaving?" Sisi asks.

"I don't know. Enzo told me to wait for him. I'm more than scared, Sisi... I'm terrified. What if something happens to Claudia? You saw that thing outside. No sane person would do that."

"No, you're right. You can't risk her safety, or yours."

"What about you, Sisi? You helped me!" I'd hate for anything to happen to her because of me.

"I'll be fine," she says dismissively, but I'm not convinced.

"At least call your brother. Let him know you might be in danger," I add.

"I don't think it's necessary. Chances are security will be tightened because of the incident. Don't worry about me, please." She takes my hands in hers. "Let's get you packed up. You need to get out of here."

I reluctantly agree, and we fill a few bags, mostly with clothes. I then gently wake Claudia up and explain to her we may need to leave. In her confused, sleepy state, she just agrees with me, not really asking questions.

True to his word, Enzo is here an hour later. He calls me to come down, as he is waiting in front of the building.

"Enzo!" I call out as I rush to hug him. He kisses the top of my head.

"It's going to be okay, *piccola*." He swoops Claudia up and swirls her around.

"Are you ready, moppet?"

"Yes!" Claudia exclaims. I don't know whether she understands that we are leaving the convent, given that she's never seen the outside world, but she's open to it.

"What about Mother Superior?"

"I had a few words with her. She was too distraught to argue with me."

"She was probably glad to see me gone," I add drily.

"I just told her I couldn't in good faith leave you here, at the scene of a crime." He grimaces at the word crime, and I look away. I hadn't told him everything, given my mental state at the time. But I will.

"Let's just get out of here," I say, and he nods.

We soon find ourselves in the back of Enzo's car and on our way to his house... my childhood house. Claudia, still a little sleepy, nods off. I am thankful for that, as I can discuss things with Enzo more freely.

"Guerra, you said?"

"Yes." And then, in a hushed tone, I give him a full account of what happened, from the moment I saw him touching Claudia, to Sisi and I burying him in the cemetery.

"And you have no idea who could have left that message?"

I shake my head vigorously.

"It was like a spectacle... of death. I feel like whoever did that was mocking me."

"It's not the best situation," Enzo grimly admits. "More so because he was a Guerra. We've never been on good terms with them."

"What do you think they'll do?"

"At best? Take revenge. At worst... take revenge," Enzo says cryptically, but I try not to think too much about it.

We get home and Enzo suggests I take my old room.

"I'll keep Claudia with me for now, since this is a foreign place for her."

"Go rest, *piccola*. If you need anything, just let me know. Allegra won't come home anytime soon, but Luca is here. I'll introduce you later. Maybe he and Claudia will get along."

"That sounds good," I nod.

Enzo takes Claudia in his arms and lays her down on my childhood bed.

"Everything is the same..." I remark as Enzo is about to leave.

"I told you I'd get you back, *piccola*. Maybe the circumstances aren't ideal right now, but this is your home."

"Thank you!" I kiss his cheek.

Closing the door, I take a deep breath and look around my old room. It still has my teenage clothes, and everything I'd not been able to take with me to Sacre Coeur. Shifting my gaze to a sleeping Claudia, I can't help but smile.

I don't care where I am, as long as she's with me—safe.

She's all that matters.

———

THE FOLLOWING DAY, Enzo asks to speak with me. From the tone of his voice, I can tell he doesn't have any good news to share. After we'd woken up, Claudia and I had headed to breakfast, where we'd also met Enzo's son Luca.

As expected, Claudia and Luca had become fast friends, especially when Luca had invited her to play with his toys. For a little girl who's only ever lived within the confines of a convent, this was a whole new adventure. I'd encouraged her to have some fun.

As I take a seat opposite Enzo, I can't help but fidget.

"Lina..." He starts and shakes his head. He's holding a letter in his hand, which he passes to me.

"What's this?" I ask. His mouth is set into a rigid line. With a trembling hand, I grab the letter and open it.

Skimming the contents, I feel my stomach drop.

"This... but how?" I ask.

"I don't know. I really have no idea how they found out. Whoever dumped Guerra's body into the grave must have told them about you."

"What now?"

The letter detailed the things the Guerras would do to me if they caught me. They stated that they knew I was the one who killed Father Guerra, and that I'd suffer in kind for the insult afforded to their family.

"It's not an optimal situation. They feel slighted because you are a woman."

"And a woman can't possibly kill a man, you mean?" I ask sarcastically. Enzo grimly nods.

"You need protection, Lina. Both you and Claudia need protection."

"We have you, right?"

Enzo shakes his head. "It won't be enough. You need someone who will protect you at all times; and someone that they can't cross. As much as it pains me to say... I'm stretched too thin. Between running the famiglia and our businesses, there's also an ongoing conflict with other organizations."

"We could just stay here. Hide here," I add, trying to convince him we can be safe here.

"And if they attack? Who is to say they won't attack when I'm called away to deal with something? It could happen."

"Then what can I do?" I'm trying very hard to hold back the tears. What Enzo is saying... does that mean that we'll never be safe? That we will have to always look over our shoulders? I can't have that for Claudia... even Sacre Coeur is better than that. But the convent is no longer safe now.

"Get married." Enzo drops the bomb on me. My mouth hangs open in shock. Marriage? But who... no one would have me.

"Marriage?"

"Yes. You could get married to a powerful enough man that would ensure both your safety and that of your daughter."

"But... Enzo, surely you know that no one will have me. I'm damaged goods." I drop my volume at the last words, ashamed of myself.

"Don't say that. Lina... never say that again. You are *not* damaged goods," he reprimands, and I turn my head, not wanting to see his reaction.

"Who will have me, Enzo?"

"Someone will. In fact, just a few days ago, he came over to see me regarding an alliance. He would never say no to you." Enzo says confidently, but I can't help but be skeptical. Surely once that man realizes who I am... and that I have a daughter, he will no doubt back down.

"Who is it?" I ask. Before Enzo even tells me his name, I make a vow to myself. Whoever it is, as long as he accepts me and my daughter, I will also accept him, and do my duty as a wife.

Enzo purses his lips. "Marcello Lastra."

My eyes widen and I gasp when I hear the name.

"Sisi's brother?" Enzo nods.

"If the situation wasn't this dire, I would have never given you to him. Trust me on this, Lina. But right now, I fear he might be our only chance."

The good-looking man...

"Do you have anything against him?" I ask, almost hesitantly. Appearance-wise, Marcello Lastra was handsome, maybe even too handsome.

"There's something off with him... I can't put my finger on it. He asked for your hand before, you know. I never approved of him, but father was ready to marry you off."

"What?" I'm shocked at that piece of information. "Marcello asked to marry me? When?"

"A little while before the incident," Enzo says, looking extremely uncomfortable bringing that up. "Of course, it never came to pass because of that. After, his father died and Marcello just disappeared."

"I didn't know that," I add slowly, trying to digest this. Marcello had wanted to marry me? A foreign feeling of warmth was developing in my stomach. Maybe... maybe not all is lost. Just thinking about that glimpse I'd had of him, and how much I'd liked him...

"I'll marry him," I say, maybe too fast. "For Claudia," I amend. And for me.

Enzo sighs. "I really didn't want it to come down to this. But... I'll call him. Have him come for a meeting."

———

A WHILE LATER, when Enzo informed me that Marcello would come for a meeting tomorrow, I barely kept a straight face. I nodded, thanked him, and ran to my room.

I have to admit to myself that I'm entirely too giddy at the prospect of meeting him in the flesh... talking to him. It will be like a scene from my dreams. He'll even kiss me...

My hand goes to my lips, and I sigh. I don't want to think about what comes after kissing. Not now, when I am so happy at the idea of marrying someone—a handsome someone.

But what if he doesn't like me? The thought suddenly makes me pause. What if... Yeah, he wanted to marry me, but that was over a decade ago. I was an untouched young woman back then. Now... I come with baggage; emotional and physical. I'll just have to be extremely honest from the outset. Let him know everything about me. Then, he can decide if he wants to marry me or not. Decision made; I already feel a little lighter.

I'm still worried that he will *not* want me, maybe because *I* want him so much. I know I am projecting as I don't know the guy. But my attraction to him had been so sudden and so surprising that it had left a mark on me. Then, I'd used all the information I had on him to create this ideal person who would sometimes visit me in my dreams.

I groan out loud, internally cringing at my behavior. I need to stop. Whatever happens, happens. I need to worry about my daughter, not about some man that I don't even know.

Claudia seems to like that we've left Sacre Coeur; she keeps on raving about all the things in the house she's never seen before—especially the technological stuff. When Luca had shown her his toys, she'd been in awe. I felt bad because I'd never been able to give her something like that. But there is still time, right?

The only thing that seems to be a problem is the fact that Claudia is missing Sisi something fierce. Then the thought occurs to me. What if I can convince her brother to get her out of there, too? She could live with us... if he accepts me, that is.

I don't think Sisi's ever wanted to be a nun; she certainly doesn't have an inclination for it. But she's never known anything else. Raised by nuns since birth, that's all she's ever known. I've noticed multiple times how she tries to convince herself that taking her vows is what she's meant to be doing, because deep down she doesn't dare hope that there can be anything else for her.

With everything that's happened in the last week, I hope I can put in a word for her. I just can't let her waste away at Sacre Coeur.

The next morning, I head early to the kitchen for a cup of tea. My nerves are killing me. I'd like to think that everyone in my position—with danger looming over our heads—would be this anxious. I settle on Valerian for my nerves. I'm at the kitchen table, enjoying the tea, when a woman saunters in, her makeup smudged all over her face, her clothes in disarray.

"And you are?" She stops in her tracks at the sight of me, her eyes narrowing. I'm about to answer, but she just goes ahead with her tirade.

"I can't believe this! He's now bringing his whores home." She plants herself in front of me and studies me from head to toe. Her lips curl in disgust. "It seems his type changed too." She tips my head with her finger.

"You got it wrong." I move out of her reach. "I'm Enzo's sister," I try to explain, although it's odd that she wouldn't recognize me. We'd met a few times in the past. "Catalina."

She frowns for a second before she laughs. "That's simply great! He's into incest now? I should have realized." She mumbles some more before stumbling out of the kitchen, throwing her shoes around on her way out.

Good Lord, how is that Enzo's wife? And where was she that she came home looking like that? When Enzo comes down a while later, I mention what happened, but he just shakes his head.

"Don't mind her. She's not well," he grimly adds.

"She thought I was..." I blush, and Enzo quickly picks up on that.

"I can imagine what she thought. Don't listen to her. If possible, ignore her. That's what I usually do." He shrugs, going to the counter and pouring himself a cup of coffee.

"She didn't recognize me," I muse more to myself.

"Doesn't surprise me." Enzo adds with a scoff before collecting himself. "She's not well... mentally."

"Oh." I drop the subject, realizing it's one that bothers Enzo. I'll just do my best to avoid Allegra in the future.

"Marcello will come by around noon." He brings his coffee to the table and joins me. "I'll talk to him first, then you two can meet." Enzo lays out the plan and I just nod, the anxiety I'd felt before returning full force.

"Lina," Enzo puts his hand on top of mine. "We'll get through this, I promise you. No one is going to harm you, or Claudia."

I nod. I hope so too.

———

IT's hours later that I keep pacing around my room, waiting for Enzo to be done with his meeting. The cook, Melissa, had offered to take both Claudia and Luca shopping. Since this is all new to Claudia, I'd agreed, especially when she'd assured me they would be accompanied by several bodyguards.

My palms are sweaty, and when a maid comes to let me know Enzo's called for me, I try to compose myself to the best of my abilities. I go down the stairs and see Enzo with a cigarette in his mouth. He nods his head towards his office.

"How did it go?" I whisper.

"He agreed, but only after he talks to you. He said he wants to get your express consent."

The moment I hear that, it's like a weight has been lifted off my chest.

"Really?" My hopeful tone must be too obvious, because Enzo grimaces.

"I don't like this," he reiterates. "But it's the only solution to our problems." He takes a deep drag of his cigarette. "Go on. Settle his mind, and we'll convene to discuss the details."

Leaving Enzo behind, I head towards his office. With a deep breath, I muster the courage and knock on the door before opening it.

Marcello is with his back towards the door, sitting leisurely on a chair.

My heart races as I tentatively greet him, my voice laced with nervousness. He slowly turns around, and his piercing gaze travels up and down my figure. Suddenly, I feel self-conscious in my simple blue Sunday dress that reaches my ankles. It cinches at the waist, giving me a slight hint of definition.

My palms feel clammy and I try to discreetly wipe them on the fabric of my dress.

Marcello rises from his chair and gestures for me to take a seat across from him. As I step forward, I extend my hand in greeting. But he only spares it a passing glance before fixing his intense gaze back on my face. Feeling foolish, I quickly retract my hand and smooth down my dress awkwardly again before taking a seat. Does he not like what he sees? Why isn't he saying anything?

"Catalina." He nods at me, finally breaking the tense silence as he settles into his chair.

"My brother must have informed you of the circumstances," I begin, trying to maintain a calm facade despite the butterflies fluttering in my stomach. Marcello looks just as handsome as when I last saw him...maybe even more so up close. His warm whiskey-colored eyes meet mine, and I realize that I hadn't noticed their depth before.

His gray suit gives off an air of sophistication and his groomed hair adds to his overall sleek appearance. Once again, I can't help but wonder what he sees when he looks at me. Should I have worn makeup? But having never really worn any before, I wouldn't know how to apply it anyway.

"He has," he replies, his voice sending shivers down my spine. There's a husky quality to his tone that makes me want to ask more questions just so he'd keep on talking.

He leans back in his seat, still observing me. I try awfully hard not to fidget under his scrutinizing gaze.

"Are you agreeable to this match?" His voice is smooth and confident, and I find myself nodding without hesitation.

"Yes." But a wave of guilt washes over me. He probably doesn't know... "But before we go any further, there's something I need to tell you. You can decide if you still want to marry me after." I steal a glance at him, but his expression remains nonchalant. He simply nods, and I take a deep breath.

"I'm not..." I pause, struggling to find the right words. "I'm not pure," I finally blurt out.

There's a flicker of surprise in his eyes, quickly replaced by indifference. "That doesn't matter to me."

"But that's not all. I have a daughter..."

"Enzo mentioned that," he interrupts. There's an intensity in his gaze that sends shivers down my spine. Gathering my courage, I continue.

"I won't be separated from her." He nods understandingly.

We sit in silence for a moment as he takes me in.

"How old is your daughter?"

"She's nine and a half," I reply, feeling the weight of his scrutiny. "She's very well-behaved; she won't cause you any trouble," I add hastily. Perhaps he assumed my daughter was an infant or toddler, and I can understand why he might hesitate.

His eye twitches for a split second before he turns away slightly. "What's her name?"

"Claudia."

"Good," he says with a hint of approval. "You and Claudia won't have to worry about anything."

"It's not... an issue?"

"No," he states firmly. "I have a younger sister at home. She and your daughter are close in age and could get along well." A sense of relief washes over me at his words. "However," he adds seriously, "I do have some ground rules. That's why I asked Enzo to arrange for us to speak beforehand."

I freeze. What does he mean? I wait for him to continue.

"This will be a marriage in name only. I will give you my name, and I will provide for you and Claudia. You will want for nothing. You will be given your own room in the house. How you spend your time is up to you. I will only impose on you if there is an event we are invited to, or if we are hosting one."

My heart plummets at his words, like a stone plummeting to the depths of a dark, frigid ocean. A marriage in name only? There's no way I can conceal my disappointment, yet I attempt to camouflage it behind a forced smile.

"That's fine with me," I respond, striving to appear unfazed by his pronouncement. But inside, my heart is splintering into countless fragments. Doesn't he like me? That's the only plausible explanation.

"And one last thing. Don't touch me." His words smack me as if they're physical blows, and I jerk my head around to stare at him in disbelief.

"What do you mean?" I question weakly.

"Just that. I don't like to be touched. Even something small, like a brush of a hand. Don't." His tone is firm and decisive, allowing no room for negotiation.

I'm too shell-shocked to reply, so I just numbly nod.

"It's better to lay out our expectations from the beginning," he states calmly. "That way, there will be no disappointment."

But his prior declaration has already left me spinning and grappling to process everything.

"That doesn't mean that you can see other men," he abruptly interjects, causing my head to jerk up in surprise.

"What about you then?" The question slips past my lips, and suddenly my mask of indifference drops.

"Me?" He arches an eyebrow at me, as if amused by my query.

"It will be a marriage in name only, as you've said," I persist, fighting to keep my voice steady. "But I'm not allowed to see anyone. Then what about you?"

He throws back his head and laughs; the sound reverberates throughout the room. It's a cruel laugh that twists my stomach with unease.

"You don't have to worry about that, Catalina." He leans forward, so he's closer to my face. "My affliction, so to speak, extends to everyone. I'll be true to my vows; of that you can rest assured." He takes a moment to breathe deeply, before adding, "If I could..."

He shakes his head, a bitter smile forming on his lips.

"If we're both in agreement?" Marcello asks, and I nod.

"Good. Let's get Enzo so we can talk about the formalities."

And so we do. The wedding will be a small affair, to be held in three days. And after that, both Claudia and I will move in with Marcello.

It all sounds lovely, but why do I have this nagging feeling of disappointment?

Marcello

A FEW HOURS BEFORE

My aversion to touch cannot be pinpointed to a single point in time, although there was one specific event that might have triggered it. Maybe it all started in childhood. There is a study that proved infants who have close physical contact with their mothers grow up to be better-adjusted individuals than those who lack a mother figure. I belong to the latter category.

It wasn't hard to find out what had happened at my birth—the staff always gossiped. My mother had taken one look at me and declared me a sinner. She'd said that an infinite number of baptisms could *not* cleanse my soul. Father had, of course, relished the thought that a son of his would be the devil incarnate. And so he'd done everything in his power to strip the humanity from me. My mother had either kept her distance or abused me for the sinner I was.

It all converged to a single event that proved to be my breaking point. And so, from then on, I'd developed a phobia of touch. Although my phobia applies to everyone, it is especially traumatic when the person in question is a woman. And so, for the past decade, I've avoided all interactions with the opposite sex.

Even at work, people assumed I was gay simply because I kept a respectful distance from all the ladies in the office. And now I have to get married... likely to an eighteen-year-old. The thought of it makes me ill.

That's not to say that there have been no accidental touches throughout the years; it's practically impossible to live completely isolated. But each one of those touches caused me physical pain and so much mental anguish that I needed time to recover. Aside from that, I want to believe that I adjusted well enough to live in society as a normal being—or as normal as I can ever be.

"Someone's here to see you, Signore." Amelia's voice startles me out of my thoughts. I remove my glasses and rub my temples, trying to relieve the tension there.

"Show them in."

In strolls Vlad, his cocky grin in place as he plops down on the chair across from me.

"Marcello." He greets me with a smirk, audibly chewing gum between words.

"What brings you here?" I ask, already knowing that Vlad wouldn't visit without a purpose. We had been trying to unravel the mystery behind the recent attack, but according to him, both Quinn and Matthew Gallagher had disappeared after Jimenez's death.

"Not much, same old stuff." He shrugs nonchalantly, his eyes darting towards the clock behind me.

"And what does that entail?" Getting information out of Vlad is like pulling teeth.

"You know," he adds innocently. "Ortega's cartel teaming up with an MC chapter, Quinn returning to town... nothing new."

"But you said there were no signs of Quinn."

"Did I? Well, there are now. My sources say he's gearing up for a big fight. They've even added more arenas in the Bronx."

"And you didn't think that was worth mentioning?"

"I'm not concerned about Quinn. He's like a machine, but not a very smart one. His father, however? Haven't seen him since the Agosti attack. Now if we could get some intel on him, that would be a real development." Vlad leans back in the chair, wearing a relaxed expression that conceals his true intentions. His acting skills are top-notch; it's hard to see beyond his facade.

"My people want revenge for our losses," I remind him.

"And you think I don't want the same?" Vlad asks, feigned offense coloring his tone.

"I don't know what you want. Actually, why did you come here?"

"Marcello, Marcello, must you always be so rude to your guests? No wonder people can't stand your grumpy attitude." Vlad shakes his head in mock disappointment.

"Cut to the chase, Vlad."

"Hmm..." He studies me for a second. "You've made the correct choice to assume your role as capo... and so you will reap the benefits."

Furrowing my brow in confusion, I ask, "What are you talking about?"

"The thing you've desired most... it's almost within your grasp," Vlad says cryptically before rising from his seat and striding towards the library. The way he moves is fluid and confident, like a predator on the hunt. "There was a recent death."

"Chimera?" I interject, finally understanding why he has come to me personally.

"Yes. Saratoga Springs."

"What? That's..." My words trail off as the weight of the situation hits me.

"It's getting closer and closer, faster than before. If this were a normal serial killer, I'd say their cooling-off period is decreasing. But we both know this person is not ordinary."

"What are the police saying?"

"No prints, no evidence to speak of. The locations are chosen so chaotically that they can't establish a pattern."

"So nothing." Vlad nods in agreement.

"But we have something they don't. Motive."

"You've mentioned before that you believe this killer is after me. But I cannot fathom who it may be."

"Think, Marcello. There must be someone."

"There were countless individuals, Vlad." I shake my head, feeling overwhelmed and helpless. Trying to remember would only lead to more pain and frustration.

"This Chimera, whoever they may be, knows every detail of the real Chimera's methods. Unfortunately, I cannot assist you if you do not help yourself." Vlad sighs and tosses a file onto my desk.

"Perhaps something in there will trigger your memory."

With a mocking salute, Vlad exits the room with purpose.

I stare at the file in front of me, almost not daring to open it. When I finally do, however, it's to see my biggest nightmare staring me in the face.

There are pictures of the crime scene in Saratoga Springs. Chimera always left behind a signature, to show that the boogie man was in town. The original Chimera would assemble the teeth of its victim in the form of the letter C.

This Chimera seems to have deviated from that, ever so slightly. Although he'd stuck faithfully to script until now, it seems this copycat is trying to leave his own mark in a way. There is still the letter C, but this time it is assembled in a big, showy way using the ribs of the deceased.

The victim, a man it seems, is cut in half. His torso is set on a table in the middle of the room—the centerpiece. The chest cavity is empty of its organs. Instead...

I can't help but avert my eyes.

A dead baby is curled up in a fetal position within the man's chest cavity, where his other organs would have been. Simulating an in-womb death, the baby is strangulated by the man's intestines —probably used instead of an umbilical cord.

I can't look anymore. I throw the papers on my desk and close my eyes for a second, trying to think of something else.

But as much as I want to, I can't.

Because ultimately it is my fault these people are dead; my fault that this copycat has something to prove.

It's always my fault.

———

THINGS HAVE BEEN CALMER in the famiglia as of late. Francesco has been monitoring the activity and has been giving me daily reports. Nicolo seems to have swallowed his pride for now, but I wouldn't put it past him to be plotting something. It's just as well that the alliance with the Agosti is almost completed. Just a moment ago I'd received a call from Enzo that he had something to discuss with me and that he has a candidate in mind for me. We scheduled the meeting for after noon.

In the meantime, I have to review the files for the governesses that Amelia had vetted for an interview. After the disaster with the first governess who'd gone as far as to call Venezia mentally impaired for her lack of formal education, I'd decided to vet each candidate myself. There are ten in total that seem to have the qualifications. Of course, on paper even the last one had looked spectacular, but her attitude towards Venezia had been abysmal. I cross-reference their availability with my schedule and decide to see them starting next week. By then, I should be done with most of the urgent things within the famiglia.

Once I've allotted a time for each candidate, I give the list back to Amelia.

"You won't stay for lunch?" she asks when she sees me heading for the door.

"I have a meeting. Tell Venezia I'll see her at dinner." Amelia grunts, but it's obvious she's none too pleased with that. I can't exactly blame her, since I have not been entirely too present in the house ever since I'd moved in. My interactions with Venezia had been limited. Amelia had been adamant to remind me every single time how neglected the girl had been and how much she needs some attention.

Her suggestions haven't fallen on deaf ears, but right now time is of the essence for me too. I have to solidify my position in the famiglia, and that requires meetings upon meetings. When I get some time by myself, I have to review business plans and strategies. It doesn't exactly leave too much time to spend with Venezia.

I'd promised myself I'd deal with that, though.

I get in my car and start the ignition. Enzo's house is not too far off. I look at my watch and see I can take my time.

I can't help but think back to my friend, Adrian. I'd tried to get some updates from Vlad, since I know he still talks to Bianca, but so far he hasn't been too forthcoming.

Whenever I ask, he just tells me he has not woken up yet. Even when he recovers, I don't know what I can say to him. I take full accountability for my part in betraying his trust, and I don't see how he'd ever be able to forgive me for something like that. But I still want to explain my side of the story; be honest for the first time in my life with someone.

I shake myself from my musings and park my car, having already reached my destination. Inside, a maid takes me to Enzo's office.

Enzo's presence is grim as I greet him with a nod. He offers me a drink, but I decline. Pouring one for himself, he brings it to his desk and lights a cigarette before taking a drag.

"The situation has changed, slightly," he starts with a hint of frustration in his voice.

"How so?" I inquire, noticing the deep lines etched on his face.

"You remember the Guerras?"

"Yes," I reply, immediately recognizing the name of another powerful family in the city. Their longstanding feud with the DeVille family is notorious and has been known to escalate into violence.

"Well, let's just say our differences with them have exacerbated," Enzo reveals.

"I didn't know you were on bad terms with Guerra," I admit, surprised by this new information. While they may not have strong alliances with other families, their only known conflict was with the DeVilles.

Enzo lets out a grimace.

"I was supposed to marry Gianna Guerra. The contract was all but signed," he confesses bitterly.

"But you chose not to go through with it," I add.

"Yes, and they took great offense to that. They've been boycotting our businesses ever since."

"Why are you telling me this?" I ask, intrigued by where this conversation is headed. My dealings have never crossed paths with the Guerras and Valentino had always maintained a neutral relationship with them.

"Because someone we know is now in trouble with them. Someone who needs protection."

I gesture for Enzo to speak freely as we sit in the dimly lit study. The air is heavy with the scent of cigars and whiskey, a familiar smell that always reminds me of my father. I wait patiently as Enzo hesitates before explaining the situation.

"It has to do with your future marriage," he says, his voice low and grave.

I lean forward, intrigued. "Go on."

He takes a swig from his glass before pushing a letter towards me. I scan its contents quickly, my eyebrows furrowing in disbelief. It seems that the woman I am set to marry has killed a member of the Guerra family, and they want revenge.

Enzo confirms my suspicions, adding that it's even worse because the killer is a woman. They could not fathom that someone of the opposite sex would dare to harm a Guerra man.

"Why did she kill him?" I ask, trying to hide the spark of curiosity in my voice.

Enzo looks uncomfortable as he explains, "He was molesting her daughter."

I nod in understanding. No one could blame her for her actions if that was the case.

"But that's not all," Enzo adds gravely. He recounts how someone had desecrated the corpse and put it on display at the Sacre Coeur convent.

"And your sister helped her?"

I sputter in shock. Did I hear that correctly? My own sister aiding in such an act?

Enzo nods solemnly. "Yes. And now I fear for her safety within the convent walls."

"I'll take care of it," I state firmly, already planning to meet with Assisi to ensure my sister's protection.

"Now, onto our agreement." Enzo shifts gears back to business. "Given the situation at hand, I suggest you marry this woman and offer her your protection under your name."

I nod in agreement, feeling oddly pleased by this turn of events. A woman with a child is not some naive young girl, and I believe we will get along better because of it. Plus, her maturity will understand my boundaries and our marriage will not be a typical one.

"I was hoping you'd say that," Enzo smiles, relieved.

"Who is this woman you're talking about?" I ask, knowing that at this point, it's better to at least have a name to put to the face.

"My sister, Catalina." The moment he utters her name, I freeze. No... It can't be her.

"Your sister?" My voice sounds hoarse as I take a deep breath, trying to compose myself and not give away any emotions. "And she agreed to this?"

"Yes. She knows she's in danger, and she'll do anything for her daughter." Catalina... and she has a child. A small pang of heartache hits me at the thought.

"I'll agree, on one condition. I want to meet with her first, to see if she's truly willing," I say, my pulse quickening with anticipation at the mere possibility of being in her presence again.

Enzo considers my request for a moment before nodding in agreement. As he stands up to leave, he adds one last thing. "If this weren't so important, I would never have allowed her to go through with this."

Alone now in the quiet of the office, I try to steady my breathing. In and out. Catalina... the girl who had captured my heart over a decade ago. Just as her image begins to flood my mind, there's a knock at the door.

"Come in." I try to keep my voice even as she enters the room. Her nervousness is evident as she tucks a strand of raven hair behind her ear. She looks different yet still so familiar. Time seems to have stood still for her. Her face is pale and freckled, and her eyes are just as expressive as I remember. But there's no hint of recognition in them.

"Catalina," I greet her, trying to maintain a calm facade while my heart races at the sight of her.

"My brother must have told you the circumstances," she says, her hands neatly folded in her lap as if trying to hide any nervousness.

"He has," I reply, attempting to focus on the conversation and not let my emotions get the better of me.

But she makes me nervous too. If only she knew how much she still affects me after all these years. I can't help but almost chuckle at the thought.

I try to maintain a cool facade and gauge her true feelings towards the arranged marriage.

"Are you in agreement with this match?" I inquire, and she nods briskly.

"Yes," she responds, but then a crease forms between her brows.

"But first, there's something I must tell you. You can decide if you still want me after." I hide my inner turmoil and wait for her revelation, hoping it's not what I fear it might be...

"I'm not..." She starts to say, but stops herself. "I'm not pure," she confesses, looking at me with hesitance, expecting me to judge her. How could I? My own actions are so monstrous, so abhorrent that if she knew the truth, she wouldn't look at me with such understanding in her big, luminous eyes.

"That doesn't matter to me," I force out the words.

"But that's not all. I have a daughter..." She continues, and my mind flashes back to what Enzo had told me. The priest had violated her daughter. A red haze clouds my vision and I must take deep breaths to remain composed.

"Enzo mentioned that," I state simply.

"I refuse to be separated from her." It would be unthinkable for Catalina to leave her daughter behind. Despite being a monster myself, even I am not capable of such cruelty.

But then... I must ask. "How old is your daughter?"

"She's nine and a half. She's very well-behaved; she won't cause any trouble for you," she explains, and my hand grips the armrest tightly. Nine years old... so grown up. I turn away so she cannot see the emotion in my eyes.

Catalina has a daughter. A nine-year-old daughter. Is that why she disappeared?

"What is her name?" I ask through gritted teeth.

"Claudia." The name echoes in my mind.

"Very well. You and Claudia will have nothing to fear," I assure her. With my name, I will make sure that no one can harm them ever again.

"It's not... a problem?" Did she really think I'd care about that?

"No. I have a younger sister at home. They aren't that far off in age and could get along." She seems relieved at my words.

But I need to take advantage of this to let her know the terms of the marriage.

"However," I start, "I also have some ground rules. That's why I asked Enzo to let me talk to you beforehand." I'd also wanted to see her reaction. But now? How can I in good faith take advantage of her... when there's so much wrong with me?

How I loathe my past, and the baggage that makes me so bad for her. And yet, I could never find it in myself to refuse her. Not her... never her.

"This will be a marriage in name only. I will give you my name, and I will provide for you and Claudia. You will not want for anything. You will be given your own room in the house. How you spend your time is up to you. I will only impose on you if there is an event we are invited to, or if we are hosting one."

"That is fine with me." She seems stunned at my list of requirements, but she immediately agrees with all of them.

"And one last thing. Don't touch me." I need to add this. For my peace of mind. And yet... if only I could bear someone's touch... that someone would be her.

"What do you mean?" she asks, scrunching up her nose in confusion.

"Just that. I don't like to be touched. Even something small, like a brush of a hand. Don't." I know my voice is brusque, but maybe if I establish a cool relationship from the start, then we both won't suffer the *what ifs*. I'll be tortured enough knowing she is in my home, within my reach, and I won't be able to touch her. It's better to keep boundaries.

She nods, almost absentmindedly.

"It's better to lay out our expectations from the beginning. That way, there will be no disappointment," I tell her. She needs to know this will never be more than a business arrangement. But more importantly, *I* need to keep that in mind. Just then, I realize there is one more thing that needs to be addressed. "That does not mean that you can see other men." No one will touch her. She will be mine... even though she won't.

"What about you then?" She narrows her eyes at me.

"Me?" I'm almost tempted to laugh. Did she not hear anything I said so far?

"It will be a marriage in name only, as you said, but I am not allowed to be with anyone else. Then what about you?" She elaborates, and I do laugh. It's just ludicrous. Ah... if she only knew that I've not touched another woman since the first time I saw her, years ago... she'd probably think me deranged.

"You don't have to worry about that, Catalina." I focus on her as

I say the words. "My affliction, so to say, extends to everyone. I'll be true to my vows; of that you can rest assured." I take a big gulp of air, the proximity to her already playing with my head. "If I could..." I trail off. She doesn't need to know.

"If we're both in agreement?" I don't think I can be around her for much longer. My control is already too strained.

Enzo joins us shortly, and we decide to register our marriage by the end of the week. I'm very curt in my replies, and once I realize I'm no longer needed, I bail.

It's only on the drive back home that it occurs to me Vlad had to have known. Yes, what I wanted most will be mine... and not. I give a dry laugh at the thought... and I remember the first time I ever saw Catalina. She'd mesmerized me back then, just as she did now. And I'm marrying her. In another life, maybe I would have thought myself lucky. In this one... it's one more price I have to pay for my sins.

———

BACK AT THE LASTRA MANSION, I try to avoid bumping into anyone as I head directly to my room. I close the door and lock it. Quickly, I take off my jacket and my shirt so I'm naked from the waist up.

I falter for a second before I collapse to my knees. Head hung low, I place my hands on my thighs as I take a moment to myself. The memories are too much. They're threatening to drown me. And no matter how much I try to gasp for air, I can't. My hand clutches at the material of my pants as I grit my teeth in frustration.

Why?

Why did Catalina have to return to my life?

Why?

Kneeling in front of my makeshift altar, I grab the strap from the table, and I wrap one end around my knuckles. Then, using all my force, I whip it back until it makes contact with my skin, breaking it. I wince in pain... but I deserve it.

I'm a sinner.

Once. Twice. Thrice.

The pain is helping dull my senses.

Catalina... my Catalina.

I'll never deserve her.

Whip.

Whip.

Whip.

I can feel the blood trickling down my back.

Whip.

Whip.

Whip.

My breath is ragged as the pain threatens to make me lose consciousness. Just as I am about to reach that pinnacle, I stop.

I have to marry her.

You'd think I would rejoice at the thought.

But I can't.

I'll only taint her. Defile her with my corruption. Damn her soul with my depravity.

She's my one weakness. A beacon of true innocence... My *Beatrice*.

I stagger to my feet, dropping the whip to the floor. With uneven movements, I make it to the shower. Taking the rest of my clothes off, I prop myself under the jet of water and let it wash the blood away. Everything is red.

Blood...

Like that night.

I lose my balance, falling on the shower floor. The water is still running, coursing over my head and mingling with my tears.

I grab onto my knees and I start rocking.

Sinner.

I'm a sinner.

Lord, what have I done?

MARCELLO

"**H**urry, boy!" Father scowls at me as I try to keep up with his big strides. It's been a month since he's started taking me with him to his meetings with the Pakhan. The first time he took me there was also my first time witnessing him interact with someone outside our household.

The Pakhan is very much like Father. He has the same coldness in his eyes. He also has children, but so far I've only met Misha. He's older than me, but I can't say I like him. He's a bully. He likes to pick on me when there's no one else around. He thinks his words impact me, but after living with Father for so long, I think nothing can scare me. I rarely react to his taunts, and I think that annoys him.

We reach a door and Father gives me a shove inside. "I told you to hurry, boy. I don't have all day." I look him in the eyes without blinking and I nod.

One thing that I've learned when dealing with Father is that he will treat me even worse if I show any sign of weakness or fear. He likes it when I look him straight in his eyes. One might even say he is proud when I stand up to him. Inside, Father is greeted by the Pakhan and they hug, kissing each other on both cheeks.

"Giovanni," the *Pakhan* says and motions towards some stairs. "I already have them ready for you." A smile spreads onto his face at this, and my father chuckles.

"It's time to show these boys how it's done, wouldn't you say?" He half-turns towards me, and I have the sudden urge to take a step back. Instead, I just steel myself and try to look impervious to anything they have to say or do to me.

"I have to say, I can't wait to see what your boy is made of."

"Vlad is here today too?" Father asks. I'd heard about Vlad before. He is another one of the Pakhan's children, a couple of years younger than me.

"Yes..." The Pakhan grimaces. "I need to discipline him. He killed another one of my guards. Again." He shakes his head and starts walking towards the basement.

I have to wonder what happened to Vlad. Is his father forcing him to be bad as well? Maybe we could be friends.

We go down the stairs until we reach a basement. There are a few doors, and the Pakhan leads us to the furthest door on the right. He opens it, and we follow him inside.

The room is completely empty but for a table on the side. There is something on the table, but I can't quite make it out since the lighting is extremely poor.

A boy is standing next to the table, his gaze fixated on whatever is on top of it.

"Vlad!" The Pakhan's sharp tone seems to shake him out of his reverie, and he slowly turns his head towards us. He walks casually, with measured steps, until he is in front of the Pakhan.

"*Otets.*" He greets his father with a tilt of his head.

He is slightly shorter than me, with dark hair and black eyes. So black, in fact, they look soulless—empty. His complexion coupled with his features makes him seem like a doll. A lifeless doll that still moves.

I don't know why, but just one look at him and a shiver goes down my spine. Unlike Father and the Pakhan, his eyes don't have that malicious coldness. No, they are just bleak.

The Pakhan seems satisfied with that gesture of subservience and nods to one of the men outside the door. Soon, a man is being brought inside the room by two guards. He is thrashing around, and the guards secure him to a chair. One look at the adults, and I can see they are relishing this. I have an inkling of what is about to happen.

"Giovanni, this one's all yours. For now." The Pakhan mentions, and a smile spreads on Father's face. He goes to the table and picks up something... a knife, I think.

"Felix, you should have known this was going to happen when you spilled our secrets." Father takes a few steps until he is in front of Felix. He holds the knife up so the blade reflects the light, before moving it down Felix's cheek in a caressing motion.

"Let's see what you have to say in your defense." He lowers the gag from Felix's mouth, and he immediately starts saying something.

"It wasn't...." Father takes advantage of this to grab his tongue, and in one swift movement, he slices it. Looking with disgust at the piece of flesh in his hand, he flings it back, and it falls to my feet.

"I think you spoke enough," Father says, laughing at his own joke. The Pakhan joins as well, so do the guards sitting next to the door. Vlad's gaze is focused on the blood dripping from the man's mouth.

"There's no such thing as a pardon here." Father looks at me as he says this. I raise my head higher and try not to show I'm affected by what's happening.

I keep myself calm and controlled as I watch Father maim the man, chuckling every once in a while at a morbid joke.

"That's it." Father throws the knife on the ground and picks up a white cloth to wipe his hands off blood.

The prisoner is writhing on the floor, a few fingers strewn around him, his eye hanging out of its socket. He's still alive, but barely.

Father winks at the Pakhan and settles back, switching the roles.

The Pakhan slowly assesses the situation before picking up a drill from the table.

"Watch and learn, boy," Father says.

I bring my focus back to the Pakhan.

"Some areas on the body bring more pain than others. This isn't just torture. It's a lesson in what happens if you betray us."

With one hand, he grasps Felix's foot and lifts it up.

"See here, the arch of the foot is a very sensitive area." He starts the drill and, locating a middle point in the man's arch, he pushes the drill bit into it. Felix chokes on the pain, making a strangled sound as the drill advances, until the head disappears inside the foot. The pain must be unbearable, because at some point he passes out.

"Fuck!" The Pakhan curses as he realizes that.

"Finish him off and let's eat," Father complains, clearly not impressed with how things turned out. The Pakhan shakes his head in disappointment, and taking a small axe, he severs the head from the body.

"Let's eat!"

Lunch is even worse than watching someone being tortured, if that's possible. Vlad is as quiet as he'd been before, sometimes fixating on something with his eyes. Father and the Pakhan are boisterous, and they just won't shut up. You'd think that at least during a meal they'd shut up about their depraved acts, but it's just another opportunity for them to compete for the title of the most immoral in the room.

Otherwise, I can't explain why they'd talk about the men they've killed, the whores they've fucked, and the money they've made... all illegal, of course. The details are something I have no wish to hear, so I do my best to block everything out and focus on my food. Too bad even my appetite's gone.

After we're done, I'm surprised that we head back to the basement. Even more surprised when I see that there's a new prisoner inside instead of the dead one. This one is pretty much alive and terrified.

The Pakhan explains that the ball is in our court now, specifically mine, since Vlad probably wouldn't bat an eye at killing the man—at least from what I'd heard.

Father lowers his head to whisper in my ear.

"Don't disappoint me, or you'll regret it."

With a slightly aggressive pat on my back, both Father and Pakhan exit the room, leaving me with Vlad, my only audience. I look at the table and then at the prisoner, trying to make my body move and do whatever Father wants me to do. But I can't.

I pick up a knife and stare at it for a second, willing myself to do this, knowing what will happen if I don't. Vlad takes a step forward and tilts his head, studying me.

"You're not going to do it, are you?" His voice is just as empty as his eyes. There's not a trace of emotion in it.

He doesn't wait for me to answer, swiping the blade from my hand and casually walking towards the prisoner.

Whereas before the prisoner had looked terrified, mostly because Father and the Pakhan had been inside too, now he looks smug, probably not intimidated by the sight of two kids with a knife.

But not a second later, blood spurts out from the man's cheek. Vlad is wielding the knife as if he's had years of training. His hand moves and he makes a few more incisions in the man's cheek in the form of a square, effectively cutting a sizeable chunk of skin and revealing both the man's mandible and his maxilla. The rag that had been stuffed inside his mouth to keep him from crying out is also visible now.

Vlad's features are set in consternation as he regards his work. He has the piece of flesh in his hand and he brings it closer to his nose, inhaling the scent. That's just... wrong.

His smile widens suddenly and removing the rag from the man's mouth, he stuffs the flesh in instead.

"Eat," he commands, but the prisoner just looks at him with wide eyes, wildly shaking his head. Vlad's blade trails down the prisoner's torso, stopping at his stomach. The prisoner stills. Vlad goes even lower, and the threat to his crotch makes him grind his teeth against the flesh. The chewing is reluctant at first, but Vlad keeps encouraging him with a nip here, a nip there.

Vlad looks entranced as he stares at the man's jaw work its way around the piece of flesh.

"Haven't you ever wondered..." Vlad starts, his eyes glossy with excitement—the most I'd ever seen from him, "how chewing looks from the outside? We always do it... so naturally. And yet, so many forces are at work."

"Stop!" Vlad commands and the prisoner stops chewing. Vlad looks pensive for a moment, before taking the rag once more and stuffing it inside the mouth of the prisoner.

"What...?" I blurt out, my first words since we've been here.

Vlad's knife is already trailing around the man's throat. He seems extremely focused on the position of the incisions. He tries to cut, but the prisoner moves, so he withdraws his knife, shaking his head.

"You," he points at me, "hold him!"

I hesitate for a moment, but end up walking across the room and planting my hands on the man's shoulders, trying to keep him in place.

A small smile tugs at Vlad's lips, but it's immediately gone. He's once again focused on his incisions, cutting from the man's Adam's apple downward. This time, his cut is the shape of a rectangle.

He removes the skin but scowls as he notices there's still more muscle tissue in the way. He stares at it for a second.

"What are you trying to do?" I have to ask.

"Want to see how he swallows," he murmurs, bringing his bloody hand to his chin. He taps his foot impatiently, and I feel the man flinch. I tighten my grip.

Vlad's eyes light up. He takes the rag out and again gives him a piece of flesh to chew on.

"Eat!"

The prisoner does as he's told, slowly munching on the piece of skin. Just as he's about to swallow, Vlad puts his hand up. "Stop!"

With a sudden swipe of the knife, he tears a hole in the man's throat. "Now!" he commands.

I don't know what's happening, except there's blood coursing from the man's throat. He squirms a few more times before he becomes limp under my hold.

"Shit!" Vlad curses, looking decades older than his actual age. If I didn't know what he looked like... I could have sworn that no child could do something like this.

Vlad's hand tightens on the knife, and his features stretch over his face in anger. I blink. In no time, he's on top of the already dead man, swinging his knife in and out. I take a step back.

He's stabbing and stabbing, blood spattered on his face.

"Vlad!" I call out, but he doesn't answer, digging deeper into the man's flesh.

"Vlad!" I yell, and somehow he snaps out of it. He stands up, throws the knife on the ground, and looks at me as if dazed.

There's blood on his face. He lifts his hand, and with one finger he swipes some red liquid and brings it to his mouth, sucking.

My eyes widen at this display.

He's not normal... he can't be normal.

The door opens, and Father and the Pakhan come in. They take in the scene before them, and they immediately zero in on Vlad.

"Misha, take your brother out," the Pakhan orders, and a teenage boy comes in to drag Vlad away. Before he can grab him, however, Vlad leans in and whispers something in Misha's ear that has him blanch.

Vlad lets himself out, and I'm left with father and his obvious disappointment.

"What did I tell you, boy?" His eyes blaze with fury.

"I don't want to kill anyone," I say, my voice full of false confidence.

"You don't want to kill anyone?" he asks me, narrowing his eyes. He then opens the door, taking one guard by the collar and making him kneel inside the room.

"You didn't want to kill someone who clearly wronged us. Let's see how you feel about someone who is innocent." He kicks the guard to the floor. He drags me by the hand until I'm in front of the guard and places a gun in my hand.

"Kill him!" he commands. "Don't embarrass me!" He hisses before closing my fingers over the gun and pointing it towards the guard.

"Kill!" He yells in my ear, but all I can do is shake my head.

I don't want this. I never wanted this.

"Kill, or else, your mother might not sleep well tonight, nor will that thing inside of her," he says, and I can feel my skin crawl. Mother is eight months pregnant. Surely he wouldn't... he wouldn't kill his own child.

But then I look at him. He would... he would kill anyone.

He still senses my hesitation, so he continues to describe in great detail what he will do to her.

"And when her stomach is wide open, I'll take that thing out..." I can't hear this anymore.

I squeeze my eyes shut and press the trigger. I'm jerked back by the pistol firing, and I see the bullet hit the target.

More blood.

The floor is becoming soaked in red.

"I knew you had it in you, boy."

Do I?

It seems I do...

———

MOTHER IS IN LABOR. It's been a few hours since she started, and I can hear her screams now and then. I don't know what's happening, but father didn't want to send her to a hospital. Instead, he brought a doctor to care for her at home. I don't know how much he's doing for her, though, because she doesn't seem fine to me.

I'm worried. Not because of mother, since at this point I couldn't care less if anything happened to her, considering how much of a presence she's had in my life. No, I'm worried for my sibling. I'm worried something will happen to him or her... I hope it's a boy. A girl could never survive in this house, not under father's thumb.

I'm attentively listening for any noises when a screech reverberates through the house. I open the door to my room and dash towards the first floor where mother is resting. The door is closed. I don't go in. Rather, I move closer to the door and press my ear to it, straining to hear what's happening.

"Push!" someone says, and mother curses at him.

There are more noises before I hear a wailing sound. The sound of a newborn.

I'm still plastered to the door when I see father come. He scowls at me but says nothing as he opens the door and heads inside. I follow.

"It's a girl, signor." The doctor turns to face father.

"Useless," I hear him mutter under his breath, and my fists clench at my side.

Poor babe...

"It's the devil's mark! Take it away from me!" Mother pushes away at the bundle of cloth sitting on her chest.

"It's cursed! It's the devil!" she yells, and against my better judgment, I step forward and take the baby in my arms.

Father is still in the room, sporting a bored expression, but I can see he's assessing my next move.

I look down and see the sweetest face. She's a little red and dirty, but as she opens her eyes to look at me, I feel something tugging at my heart.

I didn't even know I had one.

It's the first time I've felt this... I can't even name it.

My fingers tighten around her small body, wanting to offer her protection, love... Love?

I almost laugh at the thought. I've never loved anyone, and no one's ever loved me. Do I even know what that is?

But as I look into her deep eyes, I think I understand.

She has a big deep red mark that starts just above her eye and extends into her forehead. This is what mother must have meant when she said it was the devil's mark.

But... I suddenly realize.

I look up at mother and see she's holding tightly onto her rosary, saying a prayer—an exorcism most likely. Then there's father, and he just looks at me as if he expects me to slip.

My eyes move once more over the innocent life in my arms, and I realize what I need to do.

I can't let her live through what I did... I know exactly what will come, the abuse she will have to bear at mother's hands, especially because of her birthmark. And father... I don't even want to think of what he could do to her.

I can withstand everything he dishes my way, but if he did that to someone I cared about... to my little sister? And he would.

"She's cursed," I say, repeating mother's words. It takes everything in me to do this, but she's better off without this family.

"She has the mark of the devil. Mother was correct. We should send her away."

"Is that so, boy?" Father leans into the wall, taking a cigarette from his case and lighting it.

"We should send her to a holy place, so they can take out the bad from her." I lift my head and look him dead in the eyes.

"She'll bring us bad luck if she stays," I continue, and mother turns to me, agreeing wholeheartedly.

"Yes! Take her away. The devil... it's the devil trying to tempt us. She's going to bring only bad luck," she cries hysterically.

Father shrugs. "Do what you want. She's not a boy." He throws his cigarette butt on the ground and stubs it with his shoe before turning and leaving.

There are a few maids in the room, and I also spot Amelia. I go to her.

"Where can we send her? Somewhere she'll be taken care of?"

"I... I..." She stammers, "There's a convent. The famiglia has connections there."

"Take her. Take her there." I hand over the baby to her, trying not to look again, knowing that the more I hold her, the harder it's going to be to let go.

"OK," she nods. "But... what about her name?"

"Let the nuns name her," I say and turn my back, leaving the room.

Because if I named her... if I let myself care...

I don't think I could survive.

CATALINA

"**G**o grab your bags!" I tell Claudia as we get out of the car. We'd spent all day shopping since we don't have a lot of things.

After the meeting with Marcello, we'd decided to officiate the marriage in three days. That meant that I had three days to get ready for my future. A shiver goes down my body at the thought. Marcello was not who I'd expected him to be.

Sure, he's good-looking and handsome, and I did dream about kissing him but... It's probably never going to happen, and I will respect his boundaries.

There was this sadness that clung to him. I can't put my finger on it; I felt like he'd been holding himself back. From what, I don't know. I'm trying not to read too much into it, especially given my slight crush on him.

I'd explained the circumstances to Claudia to the best of my ability, and she'd seemed understanding. At least, I think so. She's been very excited about being outside Sacre Coeur for the first time. And given her sheltered upbringing, I don't know how much she understands about marriage and what it entails.

When we'd spoken about the terms of the marriage, I'd asked Marcello to bring in a therapist for Claudia. I don't want what happened with Father Guerra to scar her in the future. And she might benefit from it when adjusting to this new lifestyle too.

We head inside the house, but the moment we step in, I hear a noise. It sounds like a scream... A female screaming.

"Claudia. Go to your room! Now!" She looks at me wide-eyed but does as she's told, running up the stairs.

I take the first thing I see, a lamp, and head towards the source of the noise. What could it be, though? There are so many guards around... When I enter the drawing room, I stop in my tracks, my eyes going wide with shock, my mouth hanging open. That can't be what I'm seeing, can it?

Allegra, my brother's wife, Allegra is naked on her knees. A man is mounting her from behind, pumping his hips in and out of her. There's another man in front of her, and she's putting his member in her mouth, sucking on it. I gasp. What is she doing?

The men grunt, and Allegra moans in a high-pitched voice. She keeps sucking the man, and her eyes wander towards me. She doesn't seem in the least surprised to see me there.

In fact, she winks at me. What? The man behind her steps away, and another man, one I hadn't noticed before, replaces him. What is this? This... depravity? This can't be normal.

"There she is, my sister-in-law," she drawls, and everyone's gaze focuses on me. "Join us, will you?" She says, and I instinctively take two steps back, before running up to my room.

How can Enzo allow that in his house? Does he even know? Lord, his son lives here, and he's only five!

As I enter my room, I try to put on a smile and pretend nothing happened. Claudia doesn't seem to notice how rattled I am. Instead, she's excited about her new dresses that we'd bought, and she tries them on.

I attempt to put the scene I'd witnessed out of my mind and focus on my daughter. But Lord, is that what people do in the outside world? I know I'm not very knowledgeable in these things, but surely that's not normal.

It's much later that I find Enzo in his study, immersed in a book. I softly knock and he lifts his head, a smile playing on his lips.

"Lina."

"Enzo... can I talk to you about something?"

"Of course, *piccola*. What is it?"

"When did you get home?" I start, and he regards me strangely.

"Not too long ago." He looks at his watch. "Maybe half an hour ago, why?"

"I... I don't know how to say this but... I came across your wife today."

"Allegra?" He frowns. "Here?" He seems surprised.

"Yes. She... she was cheating on you." I blurt out. Enzo's expression doesn't change.

"Here?" I nod.

"Damn, I told her to keep it out!" He curses under his breath. He knew?

"You... you know about it?"

"It doesn't matter," he says. "Our marriage isn't a normal one. She's... we're not together." He shakes his head briefly, as if annoyed.

"Who was it this time? Was it one of the guards?" He asks as if this is a common occurrence.

"I don't know," I answer honestly. "But it wasn't just one." I'm almost embarrassed as I say this. Enzo just raises an eyebrow.

"She was with three men... in the living room."

"Fuck! I told her to keep that shit out of my house." He stands up, clearly pissed. "Damn! Claudia or Luca could have seen her." He smashes his fist on the desk and I keep myself still, though the urge to flinch is there.

"That's what I was worried about too. Luckily only *I* saw her, but even for my eyes it was..." I trail off.

"Oh, Lina! Of course!" He comes and takes me into his arms. "I'm sorry you had to see that. I'll have words with her so she doesn't do it in here anymore."

"What happened, Enzo? You were so in love with each other," I whisper, the situation confounding me. I'd met Allegra before. She'd come with Enzo to visit me. She'd been the loveliest woman, and I could see how much they loved each other. It just makes little sense.

"Not everything is as it seems, Lina. I couldn't give her what she wanted..."

I shake my head. "It's not right."

"Don't worry about it, *piccola*." He strokes my hair. "One day, I'll tell you all about it."

"YOU LOOK BEAUTIFUL, MAMMA," Claudia says, resting her head on her hands as she looks at me.

"You think so?" I twirl around a little, examining the back of the gown.

We'd picked up this dress when we'd gone shopping. I somehow didn't want to pass up the opportunity of wearing a white dress at my wedding, considering it might be the only one I'll ever have.

The dress is a creamy white with a high neck and short sleeves. The hem reaches my calves. It's not very skintight, but it molds nicely to my body.

The sales assistant had suggested I try some shorter dresses, and some that emphasized my cleavage too much. Yeah, they hadn't looked bad, but I'd been so uncomfortable in them, feeling extremely self-conscious about myself.

It must be that I've gotten so used to wearing church-acceptable clothing that I've lost the taste for anything on the more daring side.

I smile a little, pleasantly satisfied with my look.

An intruding thought tells me that maybe Marcello will like it too, but I quickly catch myself. It's better to nip this crush in the bud before it's too late. I mean, who knows, maybe he's actually an awful person.

I sigh.

I don't even know if that would be better or worse. Sure, it would be better because then I could dislike him... or at least *not* like him. But then it would be worse because we will actually live with him and his family.

I sneak a glance at Claudia, and she's admiring her own dress in the mirror. I don't think she's ever worn anything as colorful as that. It's a nice dusty pink, with glitter on the sleeves.

Regardless of the circumstances that brought us to this point... maybe it's for the better? Claudia can finally have a normal childhood, and I will make sure she's safe at all times.

That makes me a little worried though... us moving to a foreign house, especially after the whole fiasco with Father Guerra.

I shake my head, trying to dispel those thoughts. It's not worth it to dwell on that. Surely not everyone is like Father Guerra.

"Are you ready?" She jumps from the bed and nods at me. I take her hand and we leave the room. The ceremony is going to be officiated here, and after that, we will leave for Marcello's house. I'd already packed all of our meager belongings.

As we go down the stairs, I can see Enzo deep in conversation with Marcello. There is a significant distance between the two, and it just reminds me of the fact that Marcello can't stand being touched.

It had seemed odd when he'd said that, but who am I to judge? Maybe he has his own demons to grapple with.

Like I know I have....

Our footsteps echo on the stairs as we descend, and when they both look up, I catch my breath. Enzo's smile is warm and welcoming, but Marcello's expression is difficult to read—almost bored, with a hint of something else lurking within his dark eyes.

As my eyes meet his gaze, I suddenly feel self-conscious in my plain dress. My fingers twitch towards the neckline, but I resist the urge to cover myself up. Claudia tugs her hand free from mine and rushes ahead, her long dark hair flying behind her.

"It's you!" she exclaims, pointing excitedly at Marcello.

I hurry after her, suddenly worried that she might try to touch him. How does she even know him?

"Hello there," Marcello crouches down to be on eye level with Claudia. A small smile tugs at the corner of his mouth and my heart skips a beat. I've never seen him smile before... at least not like this.

"How do you two know each other?" Enzo asks, suspicion lacing his voice.

"We met briefly at Sacre Coeur," Marcello replies, straightening himself and giving Claudia a tender look before his face becomes blank once again. He turns to me and nods in acknowledgment. An awkward silence settles between us as we both just stand there, unsure of what to say or do next.

"Well then," Enzo interrupts, breaking the tension. "The priest is waiting for us in the drawing room. Let's get this done."

The ceremony is short and uneventful, and before I know it, we are signing the marriage certificate—officially tying the knot.

I steal a glance at Marcello out of the corner of my eye. There's still an undeniable distance between us despite our new marital status. I can't help but wonder what he's thinking or feeling behind that impassive mask he wears.

He has a brief conversation with Enzo before turning to me.

"Are you ready?" he asks, his voice devoid of any emotion.

I hesitate for a moment, caught off guard by the question. "Yes... let me just grab my bag," I reply, turning towards Claudia. "Go get your backpack from the room."

She nods and runs off, leaving me alone with Enzo.

"I've had someone take your luggage to the car," he informs me, coming closer to offer some comfort.

"It's going to be alright, Lina," he whispers, tucking a loose strand of hair behind my ear. "I'm sorry it had to be like this, but..." His voice trails off, filled with regret and pain.

I give him a quick hug before heading towards the room to gather my things. I can't help but wonder what lies ahead for me now that I am officially married to a man who seems so distant and closed off. But I push those thoughts aside and focus on getting through the day—one step at a time.

Marcello stands in the doorway, his tall and imposing figure casting a shadow over us. My cheeks flush with self-consciousness as I pass by him to meet Claudia by the stairs.

"Time to go?" she asks, her voice ringing with anticipation as I hold out my hand for her.

Marcello catches up with us and leads the way towards the car. The sleek black vehicle sits in front of us, surrounded by a few other cars that I can only assume are for our protection. We quickly settle into the backseat while Marcello takes the driver's seat.

The journey is short, and before I know it, we have arrived at Marcello's house. My mind is still reeling from everything that has happened when Claudia grabs my hand excitedly.

"Come on, let's go see!" she exclaims, her eyes shining with curiosity as she pulls me towards the entrance.

I follow behind her, feeling a little lost in this new world I've been thrust into.

As soon as we step inside, we are greeted by an army of staff members bustling around. Marcello addresses one of them before disappearing down a hallway to our left.

"That's it?" I say, frowning at the lack of explanation or instructions.

Before I can dwell on it any further, Amelia, one of the older staff members, approaches us.

"Welcome," she says with a small smile before turning to me and Claudia. "Signor Marcello has instructed me to show you both to your rooms."

My eyebrows shoot up in surprise. Rooms? As in separate rooms?

Amelia leads us upstairs to the second floor where she opens the door to what she announces as my room. My jaw drops at the sight that greets me – it's like something out of a palace.

The room is enormous, easily bigger than any bedroom I've ever seen. A king-sized bed sits in the center but seems almost small in comparison to the rest of the room. Claudia's gasp echoes my own as she runs towards the bed and jumps on it.

"Is this really our room, mamma?" she asks with wide eyes.

I can only nod, still speechless at the opulence surrounding me. I take a few tentative steps into the room, marveling at the massive closets and luxurious furnishings.

And there's even a bathroom attached! I can't help but open the door and step inside, pinching myself to make sure it's all real. The bathroom is a vision in white and gold, with a bathtub in the center and a shower tucked away in one corner. It's like something out of a dream.

Amelia must have noticed my amazement because she speaks up, "Mr. Marcello wanted to ensure your comfort during your stay."

"Signor Marcello wanted to make sure you have all the comforts."

My heart swells with gratitude, and I turn to Amelia. "This... this is all wonderful. Thank you," I say, voice thick with emotion. She nods in understanding.

"Now for the second room..." Amelia begins to turn and lead us out, but I quickly interject.

"We don't need a second room. I mean... this is too big. Claudia and I can both stay here together."

"Mamma..." Claudia pouts, her eyes pleading with me. I frown, torn between wanting to give my daughter her own space and not wanting to leave her side.

"You want to see the other room?" She immediately nods eagerly.

"But..."

"If they're offering us another room, then I'd like to have my own space," Claudia declares with surprising confidence before glancing down, almost ashamed of her request.

"Baby, there's nothing to be embarrassed about," I start to reassure her, but then I try to put myself in her shoes. She's never had her own room. We've always shared a small space at Sacre Coeur.

I sigh, realizing that maybe she needs her privacy now more than ever as she grows up.

"Fine," I say with a resigned tone. "Let's see the other room."

Amelia leads us across the hall to the second room, which turns out to be smaller but just as luxurious as mine. Somehow, I had assumed our rooms would be next to each other for convenience.

She opens the door and we step inside.

"Wow..." Claudia breathes out in amazement as she takes a step forward into the room. "This is incredible."

The room may be smaller than mine, but it's decorated specifically for a pre-teen girl. The wallpaper is a soft shade of pink adorned with glittery gold illustrations. The bed is also pink, complete with a canopy draped beautifully over it. Actually... the whole room is so pink, it's almost blinding.

"Signor Marcello made sure the room would be ready for Signorina Claudia. He wanted everything to be perfect," Amelia mentions with a half-smile, gesturing around the room.

Truth be told, the effort is visible, and I'm surprised that he took the time and care to ensure my daughter's comfort in just three days.

"I love it, mamma!" Claudia exclaims from the center of the room, her eyes sparkling with delight.

"I'm glad you like it." I smile at her affectionately, feeling grateful for this unexpected act of kindness from our host.

"Your luggage will be brought in shortly."

"What about Marcello's sister? He mentioned a sister." I turn to Amelia with curiosity.

"She... she's on this floor too. A few doors down. I must apologize that she wasn't here to greet you. She's been rather indisposed lately..." Amelia explains with a hint of sadness in her voice.

"I'd like to meet her."

"I'll make sure to let her know," Amelia replies before bidding us goodnight and leaving us to settle into our respective rooms.

———

I DON'T KNOW what I expected from this marriage, or from moving to this house, but it certainly wasn't being this ignored.

I'd met Venezia right before dinner, and she'd been... unpleasant would be an understatement. She'd been downright rude to me. After a tense first meeting, we'd gone on to the dining room, where she'd continued to drop hints about her displeasure, until she outright insulted me.

"Couldn't you have found another wife... you know, one without a child?" she impudently asked Marcello. I'd immediately turned to Claudia, trying to gauge her reaction. I didn't want her to be ashamed of our situation...

Damnation!

She looked just as stunned as I felt, as she turned her hopeful gaze towards Marcello. Their eyes met, and I could see a twitch in his upper lip.

"Venezia, Catalina is my wife, and you'd do well to respect her," he'd said in a stern tone.

Venezia had huffed and immediately left the table, but not before violently throwing her cutlery at her plate.

After the incident, Marcello had offered a short excuse for his sister's behavior, and we'd continued to eat in silence. I'd tried to initiate conversation a few times, only to be shut down. I wasn't sure that he wanted to interact with anyone, so I'd just taken to talking to Claudia. After dinner, Claudia had gone to her room, and I'd stayed a little behind, trying to engage Marcello in conversation, but it had backfired again.

He'd nodded at me, as usual, then he'd turned and left.

And so, here I am, hours later, about to knock on the door of his room. After a couple of hours of deliberation, I'd decided that I needed to see where we stand.

I know he's put in place some boundaries, but surely he doesn't plan on ignoring me for the rest of our lives. We still have so many things to talk about... like schooling for Claudia, booking her therapy. Also about me...

What am I supposed to do with myself? I'm not used to lying around doing nothing, and it's pretty clear my basic cooking or cleaning skills aren't required here as Marcello has an army of staff. That simply leaves me with nothing to do.

I take a deep breath and, closing my eyes, I knock. There's some noise on the other side of the door before a voice says,

"I told you, Amelia..." The door opens suddenly, and my eyes go wide as I take in Marcello's casual appearance.

The Marcello I am facing now is a stark contrast to the man I first met. His appearance is disheveled; his white t-shirt wrinkled and slightly stained, black sweatpants hanging low on his hips. Stray strands of hair fall across his forehead, lending him a rugged and unkempt look.

"Catalina," he says with surprise in his voice as he takes in my presence. I steel myself for the conversation that's about to happen, knowing it won't be easy.

"Can we talk, please?" My request seems to catch him off guard, and he narrows his eyes at me suspiciously.

"Is it urgent?" He keeps the door only slightly ajar, hiding the interior of the room from my view.

"Yes, I think so," I lie. But if this is the only way I can get him to listen to me, then maybe it is urgent after all.

He ponders my words for a moment before slowly nodding his head. "Go to the study and I'll meet you there in a few minutes. It's the second door on the right." He gives me no chance to reply before shutting the door. At least he didn't say no... right?

I follow his instructions and find myself in a lavishly decorated study. Clearly, Marcello has good taste and wealth. A few minutes later, he appears and takes a seat across from me at the desk.

"So? What did you want to talk about?" His intense gaze makes me squirm uncomfortably in my seat.

"My daughter, Claudia. I wanted to discuss her education," I blurt out, trying to appear confident and serious. But it's hard when faced with such a handsome man dressed in nothing but casual clothing. How would his hair feel under my fingers... soft or coarse?

Marcello clears his throat, bringing me back to reality and causing a blush to creep up my cheeks. Damn it, was I staring? I hope I'm not making things awkward.

I straighten my posture and continue, determined to be taken seriously. "She will need a teacher. There was a grammar school at Sacre Coeur, but it leaned more towards Bible study. I'm afraid she's missed out on a proper education."

"I see. You have no reason to worry about that," Marcello interjects smoothly. "I've been searching for a governess for my own sister, Venezia, as she too is behind in her studies." He grimaces slightly. "If you'd like, we can interview potential governesses together and decide on the best fit for them." His offer takes me by surprise, but I can't help feeling grateful for his understanding and willingness to help.

"Really?" My tone is perhaps too enthusiastic, and I notice I unconsciously bend forward. I try to lean back a little before continuing. "That would be great, thank you. I want to make sure she gets the best education, but also in a safe environment."

"I agree." He gives a brisk nod.

"I also want to find a therapist for her. The sooner, the better. I wouldn't like for what happened to her to scar her."

Marcello tilts his head as he regards me.

"How bad was it?" he suddenly asks.

"What do you mean?" I frown at his question.

"What exactly happened with Father Guerra? Did he..." From the corner of my eye, I notice him clenching his fist.

"It didn't go too far, thankfully. When I came across them, he had his hands up her skirt." I shudder, remembering the events of that night. "But he could have... Lord, he could have done so much worse..." I take a deep breath, trying to compose myself. Just the thought of that man doing something to my baby girl...

"You did well, Catalina. You did very well." He praises me, even though what I'd done had been murder.

"I killed him..." I whisper, and close my eyes shut, trying to block the memory of the spilled blood.

"He deserved it. He was a vile human being, and you protected your daughter. What you did was very brave." He adds, and I look up to see his expression. His eyes are *almost* warm.

"He wanted to kill me," I confess. Would I have killed him if he hadn't attacked me? Maybe...

"Stop blaming yourself. It's over."

"It's not... I keep remembering..." I shake my head.

Marcello stands up and starts pacing around the room.

"The first time is certainly the worst."

I whip my head around to regard him. Does he mean...?

"You've killed someone before?" I dare to ask.

He gives a dry laugh.

"Someone..." He muses before chuckling again. "Yes. I've killed someone." He pauses before saying, "I've killed *many* someone."

I'm stunned at his admission, more so because I thought that maybe he was different. I know that my family was... is involved in that type of shady business. But considering what I'd heard from Sisi about him, I thought he might be different.

With one last look, he turns to leave.

"Wait," I call out.

I'm not finished. Why is he always so ready to ignore me? Am I so contemptible?

"I'll have Amelia compile a list of therapists – female therapists. She'll bring it to you. If that's all..." He turns once more and opens the door to leave, and if I wasn't so anxious I might have rolled my eyes.

"There's something else."

He pauses, closes the door and leans against it.

"I'm listening."

"What am I supposed to do?"

Marcello frowns at me. "What do you mean?"

I bring my hands to my lap and I start fidgeting. Marcello doesn't exactly make it easy for me to talk to him.

"What should I do all day? I mean..." I trail off, trying to find the right words. "Venezia and Claudia will have their lessons, but what about me? Is there anything I can do around the house?"

"No. There's not," he replies.

"Then?"

"What do you want to do?" he asks me and I still. What do *I* want to do? I have no clue.

"I don't know," I answer honestly. "At the convent, I did my share of chores and that was that."

"Then let me ask you differently. What do you like?" His eyes glint in the dimly lit room, and I find myself lost in them.

You.

I quickly shake myself when I realize my train of thought. Surely not... no, of course not. That was just a rogue thought.

"Me?" he asks, his tone half-amused and half in wonder.

Damnation!

Did I say that out loud?

My eyes go wide at the realization.

I fake a cough. "What do *you* like, is what I meant." I internally cringe.

"That's not what I asked." He raises an eyebrow at me challengingly.

"Well, I don't know what *I* like." I shrug, trying to immerse myself in this subject and forget my earlier blunder.

Lord, I bet my cheeks must be flaming still.

Focus!

"There wasn't much I could do at Sacre Coeur, I'm sure you realize that."

"What about before?"

Before? That's a strange thought... Can I even remember what I was like before?

I shrug again. "I used to sew sometimes."

"And you couldn't continue at Sacre Coeur?"

"I mended a few of our clothes, nothing creative. I didn't have the materials..."

"That solves it then," Marcello says, sounding almost eager to get rid of me. "Start sewing again." He brings his hand up to check his watch. "Goodnight then."

This time he actually leaves.

What?

As I enter my room, the emptiness feels heavier than usual in the wake of Marcello's sudden dismissal. My heart sinks as I realize that he may not enjoy being in my presence. It's a sobering thought, one that sends waves of insecurity and self-doubt crashing over me.

With a sigh, I undo the buttons of my dress and let it fall to the ground. The fabric pools around my feet as I make my way to the bathroom, drawn to the promise of solitude and warmth. I notice that there are already a few sets of clean towels laid out for me.

In the bathroom, I can't help but eye the deep porcelain bathtub longingly. After a brief deliberation, I decide to indulge in a warm bath, hoping it will somehow ease the weight on my shoulders and clear my mind.

I grab a couple of towels and lay them on the countertop before undressing completely. As I stand in front of the wall-length mirror on the other side of the bathroom, I try to see myself as someone else would. As Marcello would.

What does he see that makes him recoil in disgust? Is it my features, which I know are not ugly? Or is it something deeper, an unspoken flaw that only he can see? Every time I catch him avoiding looking at me, I can't help but feel inadequate and unworthy of his attention.

But when I turn slightly, there is no hiding from my biggest imperfection.

I trace my fingers over the bumpy white scar tissue that covers my back, each bump representing a painful memory from that night. The last time I dared to look at it, the scar had still been angry red and raw. But now, years later, it has faded into a reminder of what happened to me.

The knife slicing into my skin...the unbearable pain...the darkness that consumed me.

I force myself to push those memories aside, but they still linger in my mind.

What would Marcello say if he saw this? What would he think of me?

The chill of the air against my bare skin snaps me back to reality, causing goosebumps to rise on my arms. I turn to the half-filled tub and slide into the warm water, closing my eyes and allowing myself a moment of peace. My hand glides over the surface of the water, droplets clinging to my fingers like precious jewels.

What would it feel like to be touched by him? To be loved and desired?

I try to imagine his hands on my body, his lips on mine, but it's all just a fantasy. A dream that will never come true.

I submerge myself completely, letting the warmth surround me and soothe my troubled mind. But it's only temporary relief. Deep down, I know that I'll never be fine.

Not when I carry another man's initials imprinted on my back as a constant reminder of what happened that night.

And certainly not when I know that Marcello will never love me in return.

MARCELLO

My room envelops me like a warm embrace, but my mind is still racing from what just happened. I shut my eyes and focus on the erratic rhythm of my breathing.

How did I let myself get so out of control? When I agreed to this marriage, I never thought I would struggle to keep my emotions in check. My body had been dormant for so long, I assumed Catalina's presence wouldn't affect me at all.

And yet, here I am. Heart pounding in my chest. Pulse racing through my veins.

I can feel the heat rising in my cheeks as I groan out loud. Fuck! She probably has no idea what she does to me... how just seeing her and being near her can send my body into such a frenzy.

I've been in complete control for so long. But just the sight of her across from me was enough to set my mind racing, conjuring up forbidden scenarios that I know I can't act on. Since the ceremony, I've made a conscious effort to avoid her at all costs. She looked so breathtakingly beautiful... so innocent.

Shit!

The mere thought of her presence ignites a wild desire within me, tempting me to break all of my rules. Shaking my head, I take another deep breath and try to calm my racing thoughts. Avoiding her is the best course of action.

I undress, shedding the clothes that seem to bind me in this internal struggle. The cool tiles under my feet lead me to the shower, where I can finally wash away the physical and mental tension that consumes me.

I'd always thought there was a special place in hell with my name on it. A place in the 7th circle where my punishment would be carried out for an eternity to come. I had come to terms with that, oddly enough. It was what I deserved, after all, and I made no excuses for myself.

But this...

Having Catalina near me is a form of anguish that not even hell could contrive. But of course, a soul so pure like hers would never step foot near that inferno.

I laugh at that, a cynical laugh that almost makes me choke.

That's it, isn't it?

What other punishment could I receive to rival this one? None...

It seems it's hell on earth then...

The realization that Catalina's presence here is the price I must pay for all my sins doesn't stop me from thinking about her... yearning to be with her.

My breath catches at that thought. Droplets from the shower dampen my hair until it sticks to my face.

Ten years and my body feels alive again. *I* feel alive again.

The image of Catalina peering up at me from beneath her lashes, saying she likes *me*, even though I know she didn't mean it...

My cock is already straining against the plane of my stomach, and I grow even harder the more I picture her lips... I take myself in hand, stroking my shaft from base to tip, almost groaning at the sensation.

It's been *too* long.

The skin at the top of my cock is so sensitive that I shudder when my thumb touches the head and skims the underside.

I close my eyes and continue to visualize, all the while pumping my cock faster and faster. What would she look like on her knees? Her tongue stretched out, waiting for my seed?

My breathing picks up.

Would she spit or swallow?

The moment I imagine her swallowing my cum, licking her lips as if it's dessert, I lose it. I feel my balls contracting, and I shoot my load all over the shower stall.

"Fuck!" I mutter, barely able to hold myself still as the intensity of the orgasm hits me. I need to put a hand on the wall to steady myself, all the while dizzy and breathing hard.

It's not long before the euphoria disappears, though, and a deep sense of shame envelops me.

Fuck... how could I do that? How...

How could I defile her like that, even if it's in my mind?

I curse at myself.

On shaky legs, I get out of the bathroom, my mind still foggy and disoriented. The amount of self-loathing I'm feeling right now overwhelms me, and I can do nothing but stumble towards my altar. I trip on my legs and fall, but my single-minded focus doesn't let me stop.

I crawl until I reach the table housing my paraphernalia, and I take my rosary in one hand, and the whip in the other.

I need to stay away from her...

The more I'm near her, the more I risk defiling her with my darkness... more than I already have. I angle the whip and I strike, my eyes squeezed shut, my mouth parted as I experience the pain.

I must pay for my sins.

I do it again.

Whip!

And again.

Whip!

Why?

Whip!

Why must I want her so badly?

Whip!

I'm dirty... vile.

Whip!

Tears are running down my face, but I don't stop. My old wounds have probably reopened, but I relish the extra bite of pain.

Whip!

I need to suffer.

Whip!

I am a sinner...

The pain brings me down, and I crouch on the ground, bringing my knees to my chest and tightening my fist around the rosary. I slowly rock as I say my prayer.

I pray that *she* will be fine.

I pray for strength to keep myself from her.

And... I pray for it all to end.

———

AGE THIRTEEN,

I scrub and scrub. It won't go away.

I can still feel the cheap perfume, that cloying smell that almost made me gag. I bring my hand to my mouth to stop myself from getting sick. I should probably feel proud that I didn't get sick on that girl. It's not as if *she* wanted to be there. It's her job.

I'd never imagined Father would go this far, but he's gotten it in his head that I needed to become a man, and that no son of his would be a faggot.

I'd already learned my lesson, years before, that when dealing with Father, it's best to never show emotion. Never show if I hate something and never show if I like something.

When he'd told me there was somewhere we had to go, I'd kept my poker face in place. I hadn't argued. I'd just followed.

Worst-case scenario, he'd make me kill someone. Been there, done that. After my very first kill, I'd taught myself to become desensitized to death. It happened to everyone, no?

What did it matter how, when death was nevertheless inevitable? That's what I told myself. I was just hurrying along a process that was already in motion. From one kill to another, and another, every new victim became just another face in the sea of myriad faces. I learned to dissociate from the act.

It was me who killed them, and yet... it wasn't me.

Sometimes I felt like I was having an out-of-body experience, watching myself pull the trigger, or stab the knife deeper into someone's flesh.

It was me... and it wasn't.

It's also why I never questioned what Father had in plan.

But then we'd pulled up at a brothel. I'd learned it was a brothel because the soldiers started talking. That, and the naked women parading themselves inside the place. And as we walked around, I realized what Father had in plan.

I did *not* like it.

My introduction to sex had been the sight of Mother being raped by Father on the altar in her room. And it had been enough to turn me off the act completely. After that, I'd been exposed to lewd talk, mostly done by Father's soldiers. It hadn't impressed me or made me change my stance towards sex. Which was also why the thought of doing anything in that dirty place threatened to make me ill – my poker face be damned.

Father hadn't cared to ask for my opinion. He'd demanded that the Madame bring in a woman, and then he'd taken me to a room, forcing me to undress. When the girl had arrived, Father had pulled up a chair and watched as she'd tried and failed to arouse me. Eventually, given the futility of the matter, Father had thrown her out.

I'd really thought the ordeal was about to be over.

But I was wrong.

"You're a faggot, aren't you? That's why you can't fucking respond when a woman touches you." He'd sneered at me. "No son of mine will be a faggot, you got me, boy?"

I could only nod.

He'd left the room for a minute, before returning with a pill, and forcing me to take it.

"You'll become a man today," he'd declared, and two more women had come in. Both seemed to be older... twenties, or maybe thirties? What had followed had been the worst experience of my life. Eyes blank, I'd just sat there, letting them do whatever to my body. Father had joined in as well. Bonding. That's what he'd called it.

Water still pouring on me, I collapse on the tiled floor, shivering from the cold air.

Please make it go away!

I wish I could erase the feel of their hands on my body... the way they'd coaxed a reaction where there wasn't any.

I'd lost more than control over my body that night.

I'd also lost control over my mind.

———

IT CONTINUED.

Father forced me to accompany him to the brothel every time. I've already lost count of how many times we've been there.

He also introduced me to his favorite pastime — orgies.

Every time we went to the brothel, there was an event that entailed a room full of people fucking like rabbits.

I was there... and I wasn't.

It slowly became as normal to me as killing.

It was me, and yet... it wasn't.

My body complied, but my mind retreated somewhere safe.

I can never remember the people. It's like I black out after every single event.

And somehow... I'm glad for it.

Maybe it's my mind's way of dealing with things. I've been doing a lot of reading into the brain and how it functions... especially how it reacts to traumatic events.

Why?

Because I'm afraid. My entire life has been a traumatic event. How much more can one human possibly take? How much more until I snap?

And I'm afraid... Because what if I just... lose myself? Retreat so deeply in my mind that I never reemerge. Yes... That scares me.

———

I COULD HEAR the screams all day, which is odd, given that Father is not home. Although I'm fairly certain Mother must have lost it again.

So many years, and she's gotten worse and worse. At this point, I'm not even sure if anything can help her.

It's a little after six in the evening when the screaming resumes. This time, it doesn't die down. Since I've gotten used to Mother, I know that her hysterical fits usually last a couple of hours, until her throat gets sore. Then there is a break in between when she loses her voice.

The way she's going about it now, I'm pretty sure she won't be able to speak for the coming days.

I try to mind my business and ignore the permeating noise, but when another voice joins in, I frown. That's not Mother. What's happening?

I reluctantly go downstairs to check what's going on. I'm on the top of the stairs when I see Mother on top of one of the cleaning ladies, screaming and kicking.

Going closer, I notice Mother is holding a hammer and nails, and she's trying to hold the hand of the cleaning lady and drive a nail through it.

"Mother!" I call out, reaching out to grab her.

"No! Impure... you... devil!" She stammers when she sees it's me. Her eyes are wild and unfocused.

"Mother, stop," I repeat and drag her off the already bleeding woman. I try to loosen her fingers off the hammer, so she can't hurt anyone anymore, but she takes me by surprise by shoving a nail as hard as she can into my thigh.

"Fuck!" I mutter under my breath, and Mother takes advantage of this to shove me back, running up the stairs to her room.

I take a few stabilizing breaths and, without even thinking, remove the nail embedded in my flesh. I revel in the pain as it gives me the mental acuity necessary to deal with Mother.

I stride determinedly towards her room, intent on removing all weapons from her person. She can hurt herself as much as she wants, but she shouldn't abuse the staff. I reach her room, and I kick it open, hoping the display would intimidate her.

How wrong I am...

Mother is looking at me with terror in her eyes. She's holding a knife in her hand and as I step inside the room, she keeps on retreating towards the altar.

"Mother, give me the knife," I tell her, my voice steady.

"No...no," she shakes her head. "Devil...." She takes a cross from the altar and shoves it in front of me, probably hoping I'd suffer some side effects from the holiness of the cross.

"Mother, stop this. I'm not a devil and you know it. I'm your son."

Her eyes widen for a moment before she frowns.

"My son?" she asks as if this is the first time she's hearing it.

"Yes, now please drop the knife before you hurt yourself." I take another step forward and she does the same, hitting the altar.

"No... my son is the devil..." She keeps on shaking her head, her eyes bleak as she looks at me. It's like she's a shell of a person.

I try to reach out, but she brandishes the knife in front of me, making me retreat a little.

"Let's drop the knife, okay?" I do my best to keep my voice calm. "God wouldn't want you to hurt yourself, right?" I change tactics, hoping it will somehow make her more receptive.

"No... You're the devil... You're trying to tempt me, aren't you?" She snickers, an ugly scowl transforming her features. "Yes... I knew you'd come to test my faith. But you won't win."

She gives me a smug grin before lifting the knife once more. I think she's going to attack me, so I instinctively take a step back.

She's not.

She takes the knife and positions it close to one ear. My eyes widen in understanding, but it's maybe a second too late. I start towards her at the same time that she cuts through her own flesh and drags the knife from one ear to another, grinning like an idiot as the blood flows down her clothes.

I stop.

She's gasping for air as her life's essence leaves her body, and I just watch. The rivulets of blood flow down until there's nothing left. I watch until the last drops of blood have left her body. She's a mess on the floor, her eyes still open and glaring at me defiantly. Her lips still carved in a dark smile.

And I feel nothing but relief.

She's gone...

I turn my back and leave the room, letting the staff know to clean the room.

Death is everywhere. Why should I care about one person more than the other?

We all die eventually.

Mother just precipitated her demise. Like I do to so many others...

Death is everywhere. And I'm finally at peace with that.

MARCELLO

My plan has been going smoothly. For a few days now, I've been able to *mostly* avoid Catalina. And I consider it a feat, seeing that she's been trying to get me alone for another conversation. After the last time, I think I'll pass. Just knowing she's in the house... I'd say that's torture enough.

Luckily, I've also been busy. Since I've gone through all the financial accounts and had compiled a dossier of all the ventures within the Famiglia, I've gotten a better understanding of how it operates, or rather, how it *should* operate to maximize profit. I've made a few notes and have been working to implement them. I've hired a few accountants and stock market specialists to revise the portfolio and to suggest further investments.

I can't afford to be placid, especially when all eyes are on me. I know Nicolo is just biding his time. Francesco has been monitoring the other branches of the Famiglia and he is updating me daily. We've also paid a few people to keep tabs on the suspicious individuals, and I can't wait to see what they uncover.

It's a little over five in the afternoon when I reach the house. I'd spent the entire day at the hospital with my friend – former friend, that is. Adrian had recovered from his brain injury, and I owed it to him to come clean about my reasons for betraying his confidence. I would have never sold him out if the debt I owed hadn't been that big.

Ten years ago, Valentino had saved my entire world, and in return, I'd agreed to do whatever he asked of me. Who would have thought that my choices would bite me in the ass again? I'd confessed to Adrian my darkest secrets. I didn't want his pity, nor his forgiveness, since I know I don't deserve it. But I wanted him to know that I valued his friendship.

I step inside, about to go to my room. As I'm passing by the living room, I see Venezia standing up, hands on her hips, snickering at someone. I move a little to the right, keeping myself out of sight, and I notice Catalina sitting on the couch opposite Venezia.

"I'd appreciate it if you at least respected my daughter. She is innocent in this." Catalina's voice is calm, yet determined. From my hiding place, I notice she is looking at Venezia straight in the eyes, challenging her.

"Why would I do that? She's *your* responsibility." Venezia counters.

"Yes, she is my responsibility. But it's also your responsibility to behave like a human being. I don't understand why you always have to throw a fit." Catalina continues, narrowing her eyes at Venezia. "But that's what you want, isn't it? You want to throw child-like tantrums to get attention." She point-blank confronts Venezia, and she pales at the accusation.

"Shut up!" Venezia screams at her. "You know nothing!"

"I see..." Catalina says quietly. "You want attention, don't you? From your brother?"

"Shut up!" Venezia replies, lifting her hands and blocking her ears so she can't hear anything.

"But he doesn't give you any attention, no matter what you do." Catalina stands up and takes a step towards Venezia.

"No... I won't hear what you have to say!" Venezia throws her hands in the air and makes to leave the room.

Catalina moves even faster and in less than a second, her arms come around Venezia and she tugs her forward in a hug.

"It's ok, Venezia." She says, her voice lower than before and I strain to hear.

Catalina pats her back, and Venezia stands still for a few moments. Her hands are still frozen in the air, her body stiff. It's as if she doesn't know how to respond. Catalina's hand goes to her head, and she pats her slowly.

"It's ok to feel that way. But I'm not the enemy. My daughter isn't the enemy. We will not take your brother away from you. I'm your sister now too, you know." Catalina's words seem to be a balm for Venezia because I hear a few stifled sobs. Venezia's hands slowly come down, but still, they're not touching Catalina.

Catalina, seeing that this is working, continues with her soothing voice. Even I, from the sidelines, feel more relaxed just listening to her melodious tone.

"I..." Venezia starts, but before she can continue, she lets out a loud wail. She then sobs her heart out, finally returning Catalina's hug. She cries and cries, and Catalina continues to comfort her.

I feel like I've seen enough, and I try to stealthily leave before I'm seen. I head to my room and close the door. If I didn't already know what Catalina was capable of, now I knew... After how Venezia's treated her these days, I'm amazed she had such patience with her. She's been nothing but lovely. A smile plays on my lips. She's something else... Catalina... Lina.

Sometimes, in the hidden depths of my thoughts, I like to call her Lina, the familiarity of the nickname warming me up. And once again, I wish things were different. Oh, Lina... in another life... maybe.

I shake my head, dispelling the hopeless thoughts, and I go back to work.

———

THE ABRUPT RATTLING of the doorknob startles me, causing my brow to furrow in annoyance. I had given Amelia strict instructions not to disturb me while I worked in my study.

After a moment, the rattling stops.

I shake my head and return my focus to the pile of documents on my desk. Our merchandise has been facing obstacles at every entry point, resulting in significant losses. I had made a promise to fix this issue, but now it seems the problem goes beyond just lifting an embargo. I must find a way to compensate for our losses as well.

The mere thought of it elicits a groan from me. This is not my area of expertise, and it's causing me a headache.

As I delve deeper into the numbers, the doorknob begins to move again. But this time, it slowly tilts downwards before the door is pushed open. My gaze shifts to the intruder, a small figure peering through the slightly ajar door.

She seems unsure as she looks at me, her wide eyes filled with curiosity and perhaps a hint of fear.

"Please, come in Claudia," I say with a gentle smile.

She hesitantly steps inside, her posture stiff and self-conscious.

"May I?" The slight wavering in her voice betrays her underlying nerves.

I nod, indicating that it is okay for her to join me.

As she takes a seat and folds her hands in her lap, I can see the weight of her worries resting heavy on her small frame. She seems so mature for her age, especially when she talks with Catalina. But now, in this moment, I can see that she is still just a child, trying to make sense of things far beyond her years.

"What brings you here?" I prompt gently, sensing that she is hesitant to start the conversation.

Truthfully, I haven't interacted much with Claudia before now. I've always felt unsure of how to act around children. But seeing her here now, I am reminded of how much she resembles her mother.

"I..." Claudia begins, lifting her emerald eyes to meet mine. "You don't want us here, do you?" Her words catch me off guard, and a frown creases my brow.

"What do you mean?"

She lowers her gaze, her lashes casting soft shadows on her cheeks. "You always seem to avoid us," she admits quietly. Her observation makes me pause. I hadn't realized she was paying such close attention.

"I'm not," I deny quickly, the lie slipping easily past my lips. "I've just been busy."

"Oh," she whispers, looking down at her fidgeting hands. "I thought..." She starts but ultimately shakes her head.

"You thought what?"

"I thought maybe you were only taking care of us because you had to. Because something happened to mamma and she was afraid...especially after Father Guerra..." Her voice trails off, and I can see the tremble in her lip. My heart aches, wanting to pull her into a comforting embrace. To tell her that no one will ever hurt her again.

But I can't.

"Mamma is trying to protect me, isn't she?" she asks, and I struggle for an answer.

"You don't have to worry about any of that anymore, Claudia. You're safe here. Your mother is safe here," I try my best to placate her.

"But... she's not very happy," she finally says. Is this why she came here?

"What do you mean?"

"You don't like her, do you? That's why you avoid her."

"Did she say that? That I don't like her?" I frown. I didn't realize my actions would be construed like that.

"Not exactly... but she thinks she's imposing on you."

"That's not the case, Claudia. I assure you. I like your mother very much, and just like I told you, I'm not avoiding her, I'm busy with work."

"You like her?" Her eyes widen, and a smile stretches across her face. Shit! Did I fall into a trap?

"Erm... Of course I like her." What else can I tell a ten-year-old?

"Yes, I knew it! Mamma likes you too, you know. I think she was sad because she thought you didn't like her." She jumps from her seat. "I have to tell her."

"Wa..." Wait. I'm a second too late, as she's already run out.

Damn!

This is exactly what I needed. I shake my head ruefully at the thought.

I do like her, and that *is* the issue. And I like her too much to get close to her. Our arrangement needs to stay as it is. With me as far away from her as possible.

Seeing the direction my thoughts are taking, I distract myself by going over the documents again. The shipment that had been stopped had cost us over two million in lost merchandise. Since the attack, I've postponed other deliveries to figure out an alternative route.

It's even worse because we still don't know for sure if the Irish were behind the attack, or other organizations. The more I look at the figures, the more frustrated I become. I pull out my phone and dial Vlad, hoping he has some additional information regarding the attack.

It rings twice before I hear him.

"I see that wedded bliss is not all they say it is, is it?" he asks ironically, and I have the urge to roll my eyes.

"Have you heard anything about the attack?"

"No. I must give it to them, whoever they are. They've erased their traces. From the outside, it looks like an Irish attack..."

"But?"

"But it doesn't fit. Quinn's been sighted all over New York since then. You'd think after a declaration of war he'd be more careful about where he shows his face."

"I think you forget the guy is a machine. Maybe he's just over-confident?"

"No." Vlad pauses. "He grew up in this lifestyle. He knows exactly what it entails. He knows, especially when to retreat."

"So what are you saying?" I ask, curious to see what Vlad's getting at.

"I have two working hypotheses. Either his father is working by himself, seeing how he's been in hiding since the attack on Agosti, or..."

"Or it's a setup," I say.

"Yes. To make us turn our focus on the Irish. Honestly, at this point we can't discount any option."

"But who would benefit from this? I mean, sure, many would stand to win from an all-out war."

"If Jimenez were alive, I'd say it's his M.O. But now... I need more information for this. I'm trying to get a hold of Quinn, with no bloodshed that is. I'll let you know what that yields."

The heavy wooden door of the study crashes open, causing me to startle and lower the phone from my ear. Catalina bursts in, her usually composed demeanor replaced by pure panic.

"What..." I begin, trying to process the sudden intrusion.

"It's Sisi," she blurts out, her words coming out in a jumble. "Something happened at the convent."

My mind immediately jumps to the worst possibilities, but I force myself to calm down and ask, "What happened?"

"A murder," she says, her eyes wide with terror. "One of the nuns was killed in the chapel." She shakes her head as if trying to rid herself of the gruesome image.

My heart sinks at the news, and I can feel my hands trembling as I try to wrap my head around it. "Who would do something like that?" I mutter aloud.

"Sisi said..." Catalina cuts off, her voice cracking, "She had a C carved on her forehead..."

"When?" I demand, trying to keep my composure despite the chaos swirling inside me.

"They just found her," Catalina replies, and I immediately stand up from my desk.

"You heard that?" I bring the phone back to my ear as Vlad's voice comes through on the other end with a chuckle.

"Oh dear. Another murder in such a holy place? It seems almost poetic."

"I don't have time for your sarcasm, Vlad," I snap, ready to end the call, but he interrupts me.

"I'll meet you there." And just like that, the line goes dead. Typical Vlad.

"Don't worry. I'm going straight there," I assure Catalina, who looks like she's about to break down any moment.

"I'm coming too," she declares firmly.

"Catalina..." I hesitate, knowing how dangerous things could be.

"I'm going," she insists, meeting my gaze with determination. "Sisi is my friend. And if someone got hurt because of me..." She trails off, and I can see the anguish on her face.

I let out a resigned sigh and nod, but make it clear, "You don't leave my side at any moment. Understand?"

"Yes, yes! Thank you!" She nods vigorously, and I motion for her to follow me as we head towards the car.

———

PUSHING the car to its limit, I speed towards Sacre Coeur with Catalina sitting silently beside me. Worry etches deep lines into her face, and I can't help but think about Assisi and the danger she may have been in.

After what happened with Father Guerra, I had begged Mother Superior for extra protection for Assisi within the convent, but my request was swiftly denied. Even my suggestion of hiring a female bodyguard, since men were not allowed inside, fell on deaf ears.

It has only been a few days since the incident, and yet here we are again, rushing to the scene of another possible attack. Vlad's words ring in my head—he had been right, in his own twisted way. It is highly suspicious that two incidents would occur at a holy place like Sacre Coeur, and so close together. Something is not right.

I pull up to the entrance of the convent, parking the car quickly before both Catalina and I exit and make our way towards the security checkpoint. Just before we reach it, I spot Vlad lurking nearby, a sly grin on his face.

With a regal tilt of his head, he greets me, "Marcello," then turns his attention to Catalina. She regards him with curiosity, and I reluctantly introduce them.

"Catalina, this is Vlad," I say, my voice tight with restraint as he takes her hand in his own and shakes it.

"I've heard many things about you," Vlad says smoothly, a small smirk playing on his lips. My fists clench at my sides, barely containing my rage. Just the sight of his hand on hers is enough to make my vision turn red. He notices this and holds it a second longer than necessary, likely to bait me.

"Shall we go inside?" I quickly interject, trying to defuse the tension between us. But Vlad raises an eyebrow at me, knowing full well that he is provoking a reaction.

The security measures are tighter than the last time we were here, but we navigate through them swiftly. As we enter the building, chaos seems to reign supreme. Nuns scurry about in what can only be described as mass hysteria.

"Let me call Sisi," Catalina says as she pulls out her phone and dials my sister's number.

"I didn't know she had a phone," I remark, frowning in surprise.

"I left her mine," Catalina explains before speaking into the phone. "Sisi, we're here... What about the graph? Okay, we'll be right there." She hangs up and turns to both Vlad and me. We nod in unison.

"Lina?" My sister's voice echoes through the hallway as she spots Catalina. With a delighted squeal, she rushes over and throws her arms around her in a tight embrace. "Oh Lina! I've missed you so much!"

"Sisi, are you all right?" Catalina asks with concern as she strokes my sister's hair lovingly. I never realized their bond was so strong.

Assisi nods, then looks at the two of us with a furrowed brow, clearly sensing the tension between Vlad and me.

"Marcello and...?"

As Assisi's narrowed eyes fix on Vlad, he remains utterly unfazed. His easy smile only adds to his charming facade as he introduces himself with a smooth tone. It's a tactic he often employs to appear harmless, but few see through the guise to the predator lurking beneath.

"Vlad. Pleased to meet you."

Vlad extends his hand, but Assisi barely spares him a glance before turning back to Catalina. The tension between them is palpable.

I sneak a glance at Vlad and can't help but smirk as I sense his bruised ego from Assisi's snub. If only I could hi-five my sister for it.

Without skipping a beat, I redirect the conversation back to Assisi.

"Tell us what happened," I urge her gently. She gives me a small, sad smile.

"I don't know all the details either," she admits, "but I was near the chapel when one of the nuns started screaming. I rushed inside and...you'll have to see it for yourselves if Mother Superior will allow it. It's just..." She trails off, shaking her head in disbelief.

"She'll allow it," Vlad interjects confidently, and we all make our way towards the chapel with a sense of foreboding hanging in the air.

There is a crowd outside, and some elderly nuns are trying to keep the others in order. Mother Superior is also outside, looking contrite as she's talking with a priest. Vlad immediately goes to her, and they exchange a few words. Whatever he is saying to her, she doesn't seem pleased. He returns to our side and tells us we can proceed inside.

"You two should stay here," I address Catalina and Assisi, but they both immediately shake their heads. The determination in their eyes is unwavering.

"No," they say in unison.

I let out a frustrated sigh. "I don't think it's something you should see," I add.

"I already saw it," Assisi retorts, her voice firm and resolute.

"And if it concerns me... I need to see it!" Catalina says fiercely, her chin held high as she meets my gaze with defiance.

I turn to Vlad for support, but he just shrugs nonchalantly.

"Fine..." I relent once again, knowing that arguing with them will do no good. Surely it can't be that bad, seeing that Assisi is alright.

We make our way inside, and Catalina immediately links her hand with Assisi's. It's a small gesture, but one that speaks volumes about their bond.

I'm almost tempted to tell them to wait outside, but there's a steely determination on Catalina's features that makes me proud of her. She may be delicate in appearance, but her strength is unmatched.

Shaking myself from my musings, I focus on the task at hand. As we take a few steps further into the room, my heart begins to race and I come to an abrupt stop. The sight before me is more horrifying than I could have ever imagined.

The chapel is designed in a Gothic architectural style, and the altar has an imposing sculpture in relief that is ceiling high. It depicts the scene of Jesus's crucifixion as its central piece. The high vault allows for almost life-sized figurines.

All around Jesus are his mourners, both earthlings and celestial beings. Or at least, that's what I'm assuming the altar would look like on any other day. The entire wall is painted with blood, some areas smeared with child-like handprints.

The body of the nun had been placed in the middle, on top of Jesus's form. The killer had spread her arms out to mimic the position of the crucifixion, while her legs had been secured together with rope.

She was still dressed in her habit, but the cloth had been ripped in the middle, effectively baring her to the entire world. The white of her coif had splatters of blood all over it.

There is a big C on her forehead, carved seemingly with a nail. Maybe even one of the nails that is now holding her secure to the wall. Her mouth is half-open, her tongue cut. I can't see well from this distance, but I'm suddenly curious to see if she has any teeth left.

I step closer.

The nun's entire torso had been cut open; her organs taken out. Instead, they were laid on the altar table as offerings. The heart was placed on a silver plate.

To the right, a medium-sized cross had the intestines wrapped around its indentations like a serpent. The lungs were next, all cut into small pieces next to a chalice full of red liquid — blood. I have to wonder if this is supposed to emulate the Eucharist.

I hear a gasp behind me. Catalina brings up her hand to her mouth as she looks in disbelief at the scene in front of her.

"Who would do this...?" she whispers.

Assisi is studying the nun's form, her gaze intent on the hollow in her chest cavity.

Vlad is a few steps behind us, keeping a moderate distance. I can see he's trying very hard to avoid staring at the blood.

Why did he even come?

"This looks eerily similar to what happened to Father Guerra," Assisi comments, pointing at the body. "His insides had also been tampered with. Well, not in *this* manner, but quite similar."

"But who would do that? We still don't know who dug up Father Guerra and put him in the graph..." Catalina shakes her head. "And why?" She steps closer. "Why the C?" Catalina is focusing on the nun's face when Assisi narrows her eyes.

"Wait..." She goes towards the altar and stops right in front of the body.

"Assisi, what are you doing?" I ask.

"I think I saw something glint in there..." She frowns and looks closer, almost sticking her head inside the nun's stomach.

"Assisi," I repeat, and I hear someone groan.

Vlad.

Assisi raises her hand and inserts it into the body, her nose scrunching up in concentration. She explores the contents of the cavity, as if searching for something hidden within its depths.

"For God's sake, Sisi!" Catalina's eyes widen. "What are you doing?" She makes to go closer to my sister, but I put a hand up to stop her.

"Assisi?"

"Damnation!" she says. Her hand resurfaces and her fist is full of something.

She stalks towards the altar table, her steps heavy and purposeful. With a sudden release, she unclenches her fist, and a cascade of bloody teeth spills out onto the crisp white tablecloth with sickening thuds.

I recoil in horror at the sight, my eyes wide with shock and disbelief. My gaze shifts to Vlad, who stands beside me, his expression mirroring my own dread.

He reaches into his pocket and pulls out a silk handkerchief, carefully dabbing at the beads of sweat on his forehead before stepping closer.

"Well, well. This is quite an unexpected development." His voice is laced with curiosity as he leans down to examine the teeth before recoiling in disgust.

Assisi rolls her eyes at his dramatic reaction and returns her attention to the body, unfazed by the gruesome display on the table.

"There's something else. I couldn't get it before." She inserts her hand again and rummages through the contents of the nun's stomach.

It's funny how Vlad's looking at her in half-awe, half-distaste.

"Here!" Assisi exclaims, and she withdraws a crumpled piece of material.

She puts it on the table, and we all gather around to analyze it.

"It's vellum... mayhap human vellum," Vlad comments, taking a knife and tossing it around to get a better look. There is some sort of writing on it, and Vlad reluctantly uses his handkerchief to wipe the blood off it.

"Paying for the sins of others," I read out loud, and Catalina gasps.

"It's because of me, isn't it? Whoever is doing this, it's because of what I did..." A tear makes its way down her cheek, and I wish I could just lift my hand and wipe it.

"Catalina," I say, trying to figure out how to tell her it might not be her they're after, but me.

"Whose skin is this?" Assisi asks as she gets a closer look. "Is it hers?" She points to the nun.

"Probably not," I say and grimace at my own words. It's simply how this person works.

She frowns.

"How are you so sure?"

"Because whoever did this," I start and take a deep breath, turning to look at Catalina, "is not targeting you."

"What do you mean?" she asks, her voice a mere whisper.

"This," Vlad brandishes his knife towards the nun's face and the C marring her features, "is the mark of a serial killer. The C by itself could have pointed to you," he turns to Catalina, "but the teeth confirm it's a serial killer we've been looking for."

"What...?" Assisi asks, tilting her head, as if in disbelief.

"Let me get this," she starts. I'm once again amazed by her composure throughout all of this. "You are saying that the person who killed our Sister is a serial killer? Then what about Father Guerra? I don't believe it's a coincidence these things happened almost within a week of each other."

Assisi's hand reaches up to massage her forehead, smearing the blood on her skin. She winces as the pain shoots through her head, but she tries to ignore it.

Vlad's intense gaze is fixated on Assisi's face, his eyes tracing every tiny trail of blood with a mix of morbid fascination. In just two quick strides, he is standing right in front of her.

"Vlad!" I bark out, my heart racing with worry. Will he lose control? Will he hurt her?

But Vlad remains silent, his entire being focused on the red spots on Assisi's face.

I mouth to Assisi, "Don't move," fearing that any sudden movement might trigger Vlad's volatile emotions. The last time he had one of his episodes... it hadn't ended well.

Her eyes widen in surprise, but she gives a slow nod, understanding the gravity of the situation.

Vlad's usually expressive eyes are now vacant as he tilts his head to study my sister's face with an almost otherworldly intensity.

"Vlad!" I call out again, hoping to wake him from whatever trance he's in.

His arm moves up and I'm already in motion, ready to pull him off Assisi.

To my surprise, his hand goes to her forehead, almost tenderly, and he swipes some blood with his fingers. He stares at it for a second before bringing it to his lips. He closes his eyes and takes a deep breath, enjoying the taste of the blood.

"What...?" Assisi looks stunned as she frowns at Vlad.

"Assisi, come here, but slowly. He might be dangerous."

She looks unconvinced but does as asked, moving herself out of Vlad's grasp. He's still locked away somewhere, his face blank.

"What's wrong with him?" Assisi asks when she reaches my side.

"He's not... normal," I say because that's the only thing that can accurately describe this situation.

"Not... normal?" Assisi repeats, continuing to study Vlad's rigid form.

"Stay here, both of you." I slowly make my way in front of Vlad and snap my fingers in front of him.

"Vlad! Snap out of it!"

He raises his gaze to regard me, narrowing his eyes. He twirls his finger in the air, little specks of blood still on its surface.

"More..." He whispers, and I let out a groan. He won't snap out of it, will he?

Knowing what might happen if he lets himself go, I prepare myself to act. I need to knock him out before he becomes too dangerous. Keeping my eyes on his face, I fold the sleeve on my right hand, already dreading the idea of skin contact.

"Marcello, what are you...?" Assisi takes a step forward and I turn sharply to stop her. Catalina's hand also shoots out to deter Assisi, but she brushes it off.

Fuck!

"Assisi, stay back!" I yell, and I am momentarily distracted by Assisi's movements. In a split second, Vlad leaves my side.

Shit!

His hand is around Assisi's throat, pushing her body into the wall and lifting her off the ground.

"Sisi!" Catalina whimpers, and I'm suddenly afraid.

"Lina, stay back," I tell her, putting myself in front of her.

"But..." She starts.

"No sudden movements. We need to snap him out of it!" I tell her.

"Assisi, are you okay?" I ask her, and I notice that she doesn't seem afraid.

"I'm okay... he's not hurting me," she replies, and I have to frown. He has her up in the air by the throat and he's not hurting her?

"Vlad, I need you to focus, all right? You're hurting my sister right now." I speak each word with determination, trying to break through the hazy fog clouding Vlad's mind. His head tilts to the side, as if he's hearing me but not fully comprehending.

"That's my sister you're holding," I emphasize, knowing that simple language is necessary when dealing with him in this state. It's like he regresses to a non-verbal state.

He pauses for a moment.

"Sister?" He murmurs with a guttural sound.

Yes, he's starting to grasp it.

"Yes, she is my sister. And you are hurting her right now."

His head moves once more, his eyes focusing on Assisi.

"Sister?" He says again, the word coming out breathy and confused. "Sister..."

And then, finally, he releases Assisi from his grip and both Catalina and I breathe a sigh of relief.

But instead of moving away, Vlad collapses to his knees and wraps his arms around Assisi's middle.

He's...hugging her?

"Sister," he repeats, almost in awe.

Assisi looks at me questioningly, but I shake my head, signaling for her to stay put.

Vlad's hold tightens around her as he continues to repeat the same word over and over again.

"Sister," his voice grows more urgent each time.

Assisi's hand slowly descends and she gently pats his back in comfort.

Vlad's breathing quickens and he emits low sounds from deep in his throat.

"It's okay. You're safe here," Assisi coos softly, her words having an immediate effect as Vlad closes his eyes.

"I think he's sleeping," Assisi says after a while, slowly disentangling herself from his grasp. Vlad collapses onto the floor, out cold.

"What was *that*?" Assisi asks, but I just shake my head.

How can I explain Vlad without making the currently disemboweled nun seem like child's play?

I'm just relieved things didn't get out of control. I've witnessed Vlad in the throes of his rage before, and all of those episodes had ended with at least a couple of corpses. Whatever clicked in his brain when I'd mentioned that Assisi was my sister must have stopped him from going all berserker on us.

"He..." I try to come up with a plausible explanation, "has some trauma. This must have triggered him." I mean, it's technically true.

Both Assisi and Catalina nod, and I change the subject. Because them finding out more about Vlad would mean finding out more about me...

"Before we leave, I want to ask you something," I tell my sister.

"What?"

"Do you really want to take your vows? If you feel in any way that this life isn't for you, you can tell me. I'm worried about your safety here, and Mother Superior won't let me hire a guard for you."

Assisi's lip trembles for a second, and she lifts her eyes to look at me in wonder.

"You... you're saying..." She stammers. "You're saying I can leave the convent? But where would I go... I..."

"You can come live with us," Catalina interjects, coming towards Assisi. "We'd love to have you, isn't that so, Marcello?"

I nod.

"It's your home too. And you'd be safer there."

"I..." She shakes her head. "Yes, yes, please," her voice is thick with emotion, and she throws herself into Catalina's arms.

"Thank you! I... You do not understand what that means to me," she repeats, and I'm suddenly stunned by her reaction.

"Did you not like it here?" I ask, almost hesitantly.

"It's not that," she starts, but the slow shake of her head belies her words. "I don't think I'm fit to be a nun."

"I think this is the best option. I've always known Sisi wasn't meant for this life," Catalina turns to me, an approving smile playing on her lips.

All this time... It really seems that nothing I do is ever right.

A loud groan resounds in the chapel.

Vlad slowly draws himself to his feet, his eyes unfocused.

"Damn," he curses. He looks as if he's just waking up after a hangover. "What happened?"

"I think you've had your fill of blood for today," I add drily, knowing he will get my meaning.

His features are taut, and he gives me a brisk nod.

"Sorry about that." The transformation is immediate. One moment his jaw is tense, the next a beaming smile appears on his face.

"I'm glad you're fine," Catalina says, while Assisi snorts.

"So what did I miss?" Vlad has the gall to ask, coming around to examine the teeth.

"Are you sure you want to do that, *again*?" I raise an eyebrow, but he ignores me.

"We need to find out why Chimera is targeting a convent. Maybe it's..." He turns and looks at Assisi and Catalina, squinting his eyes.

"We'll talk about that later," I tell him tensely. The last thing we need is for them to think a serial killer is after them.

"Did... did you just say Chimera?" Catalina pales, her voice a mere whisper.

"Indeed," Vlad replies and folds his arms across his chest, observing.

Catalina sways on her feet, and Assisi takes her hand, stabilizing her.

"Why?" my sister asks her.

"Nothing..." Catalina shakes her head, but I'm still skeptical. Is it possible she knows about Chimera? But that would be impossible, unless...

"Can we go back?" Catalina doesn't look too well, so I immediately agree.

"What about me?" Sisi asks, as we exit the chapel.

"You're coming with us too."

"But Mother Superior..."

"I'll settle everything with Mother Superior. Go with Catalina to the car and I'll meet you there."

She doesn't look too convinced, but she nods.

"Your sister was right. It's too much of a coincidence that Chimera would show up here," Vlad mentions after they walk away.

"Whoever it is, it's getting too close. And I don't like it."

"Between the Guerras, Chimera, and your own family, I'd say you have your hands full," he chuckles.

"You forgot the Irish," I add drily.

"Right... we'll see about that."

CATALINA

Restlessness consumes me, causing my body to shift and twist in my bed. I've been trying to fall asleep for what feels like hours, but my mind refuses to let go of today's events. The mere mention of *that* name, after all this time, sends a shiver down my spine.

I shake my head vigorously, trying to dispel the intrusive thoughts that threaten to overwhelm me. I can't allow myself to be consumed by the past again. I've worked too hard to move on.

But still, I can't help but wonder why now...

Why did he resurface after all these years? Sisi was right; it can't be a coincidence that these events have occurred so closely together. My mind races with possibilities and questions, but I push them aside, refusing to give in to their tempting pull.

There is one silver lining in all of this chaos—Sisi is finally able to live with us. For years, I had known deep down that she didn't want that type of life. But back then she had no choice.

Now, her freedom brings me immense joy and relief. We had stayed in touch after I left Sacre Coeur, and through our conversations, I could sense her sadness at being alone there.

But now, she has her family with her. Venezia's behavior towards Sisi—and even towards me—has surprised me. She greeted her long-lost sister with overwhelming happiness, and they immediately hit it off as if they had never been apart.

Perhaps our heart-to-heart conversation from the other day had an impact on her after all.

Finally realizing that sleep is not forthcoming, I decide to go to the kitchen and make myself a chamomile tea. One glance at the clock and I see that it's past four A.M. I purse my lips, frustrated once again that I've not been able to get any sleep. Maybe a hot cup of tea will help me.

I leave my room and try to be as quiet as possible when I make my way down the stairs and into the kitchen. The house is so quiet, it's almost eerie. I rummage through the cupboards until I find some tea and I put a kettle on.

Waiting, I tap my foot and look around. The kitchen is modern and seeing all the appliances makes me think of baking duty. Maybe we could do that again and include Venezia too. I smile. That sure sounds good. It would be like a bonding exercise.

A clicking sound signals that the water is done, so I pour it in a cup. I'm about to take it with me back to my room when I hear an odd noise.

I frown.

It sounds like someone screaming in pain.

Leaving the cup behind, I go towards the direction of the noise. The closer I get, however, the more I realize that I'm heading towards Marcello's room. I take a few more steps and I stop. I hold my breath, trying to focus on the noise.

Maybe I misheard?

But then I hear it again, this time more intense. It's such an anguished sound, like someone being tortured.

In front of Marcello's door, I hesitate. The weight of my decision sits heavily on my chest, unsure if he would appreciate my intrusion.

The chorus of pained cries from inside only deepens my apprehension. My hands clench and unclench as I listen, but ultimately I know I have to check up on him. If he's fine, I'll apologize and leave. That seems like the best course of action.

Taking a deep breath, I reach for the doorknob and push the door open. The room is noticeably smaller than any others I've seen in this grand house. It's also quite bare, save for a lone table tucked away in the corner. But my attention is immediately drawn to Marcello.

He's caught in the grips of a nightmare.

His body thrashes about on the bed, tangled in sheets that cling to his sweating skin. Cries escape his lips as he struggles against whatever demons are plaguing his dreams. With each moan, he pulls at the blanket covering him until it falls down to reveal his naked form.

I quickly avert my eyes, heat rising in my cheeks. This was not what I expected to see when I entered his room. Guilt washes over me for invading his privacy, so I take a step back, ready to retreat.

But then another pained moan escapes his lips and I freeze. "Please no," he murmurs, curled up into a fetal position. My heart breaks for him, seeing him so vulnerable and tormented by whatever is haunting him in his sleep.

What could he be dreaming about?

My heart aches as I listen to Marcello's pained moans. I can't just leave him like this; I have to try and help him. With a deep breath, I gather my courage and enter the room, closing the door behind me. Keeping my distance, remembering his aversion to touch, I carefully sit on the edge of the bed.

"Marcello," I whisper, hoping to rouse him from his restless slumber. "Marcello, wake up."

He stirs slightly, but remains lost in his nightmares.

"Marcello?" I raise my voice, trying to reach him through his troubled dreams.

He trembles and whispers "no" with a pleading tone. My heart breaks at the sight of him; he looks so helpless and vulnerable. Acting on instinct, I gently place a hand on his shoulder and call out to him again.

"Marcello, please wake up." This time, I speak in a softer tone, hoping to soothe his tormented mind. "It's just a dream, please wake up."

I wait for a few seconds before attempting to wake him once more.

"Marcello," I begin, but before I can finish my sentence, his eyes snap open and lock onto mine. Relief washes over me as I see that he is finally awake. "Marcello? Thank God." I let out a sigh of relief and start to stand up.

But before I can move away from the bed, Marcello's hand shoots out and grabs onto my arm tightly.

"Marcello?" I ask tentatively as his skin makes contact with mine. Looking up at him, I see that he is still staring at me with an almost puzzled expression.

"I'm sorry for barging in like this," I quickly apologize, hoping he won't misinterpret my intentions. "You were having a nightmare and screaming; I couldn't just leave you like that. I'm sorry."

He tilts his head to the side and squints at me, his grip on my arm only tightening.

In this moment, he looks almost intimidating and scary.

"Marcello," I plead, my voice shaking as I try to pry his fingers off my arm. My heart races as he doesn't budge, instead pulling me towards the bed with a tight grip.

I stumble and fall onto the mattress, barely missing landing on top of him. Fear courses through me as I look into his eyes, but they are vacant, as if he's not really seeing me.

My mind races, trying to understand why he's doing this. Is he angry with me for coming into his room? Or is he still in some kind of trance?

I reach out tentatively, placing my hand on his arm to test his reaction. He looks at it briefly but seems unaffected.

Gathering my courage, I trace my hand up his arm and to his jawline, feeling the warmth of his skin for the first time. "Marcello, please wake up," I whisper softly, my fingers gently caressing his cheek.

He jerks at the touch but doesn't pull away. His brows furrow, and he stares at me with confusion, as if the sensation is unfamiliar to him.

"Marcello," I continue, mustering my courage. "Could you let go of my arm?"

He frowns again, but instead of releasing me, he pulls me closer until our bodies are touching.

My face is mere inches away from his, our breaths mingling in the small space between us. The intensity of his gaze holds me captive, a heat emanating from his dark eyes that I had never seen before.

Instinctively, I reach for his shoulder and give him a gentle shove, hoping to break free from his grasp. But instead, his hold on me only tightens, causing my body to react with a mix of fear and arousal. A slight tremble runs through my limbs as I struggle against him.

"Marcello, please let me go!" I demand firmly, trying to break free once more.

"Shh," he finally speaks, placing a single finger on my lips to shush me. I gasp in shock at the unexpected touch. What is he doing?

His gaze shifts to my lips, and I feel his fingers tracing their shape, sending a jolt of electricity through my body. As I open my mouth to speak again, he covers it with his own soft lips, silencing me completely.

A wave of sensation washes over me as I try to make sense of what is happening. His lips are gentle yet insistent, leaving me almost powerless under their touch. But as much as I want to give in to the pleasure, my conscience pulls me back, and I push at his shoulders in protest.

To my surprise, his lips part, and I feel the warm intrusion of his tongue seeking entrance into my mouth. Is this really happening? My mind races with confusion as his tongue dances against mine, eliciting a shiver down my spine.

Out of curiosity, I tentatively touch my own tongue to his, and a spark ignites between us that only fuels the fire burning within me. *Lord!*

My hands, once firm in pushing him away, now cling to his shoulders, seeking closer contact. My mind tells me to stop, but my body betrays me as I press myself against him.

His arm wraps around my waist and pulls me onto his lap, our bodies fitting together like two pieces of a puzzle. His fingers dig into my flesh as the kiss deepens, sending shivers down my spine.

Lost in the moment, I can't think straight, so I just hold on to him with all my might. His teeth graze my bottom lip, and I let out a low moan.

Marcello's hands trail lower until they reach the curve of my hips under my nightgown. He cups my bottom, pulling me even closer to him.

I gasp for air, my heart racing as I melt into the kiss once more. But then I feel something hard pressing against me, and panic sets in.

No... Not that!

With a surge of strength that surprises even myself, I push him away and scramble off the bed. My cheeks are flushed, and my breath comes in quick gasps as I try to compose myself.

"I'm sorry... I..." I shake my head, struggling to calm down. "It just reminded me of something and... I didn't mean to..." My attempts at explaining fall short as I struggle to find the right words.

Frustration builds inside me, and I clench my fists.

My voice catches in my throat as I try to speak, turning to face Marcello, who is lying on his side, eyes closed and chest rising and falling with each steady breath. He's sleeping?

My confusion morphs into amusement at the irony of the situation. Here I was, about to open up my heart to him, and he's completely unaware, peacefully lost in slumber. I shake my head with a smile and reluctantly make my way out of the room.

Lying back in my bed, I can't help but replay the events in my head. The touch of his lips against mine, the warmth of his embrace, all so new and foreign yet undeniably... satisfying. I struggle to find the right words to describe it. It had been an experience unlike anything I'd felt before.

And now, lying here alone with my thoughts, I can't help but feel a sense of giddiness at the memory. So this is what it feels like to be kissed...

A soft giggle escapes my lips as I think about it. It hadn't disappointed in the slightest. Maybe there is hope for us after all, if we take things slow. My mind races with possibilities and hopes for the future as sleep slowly takes over me.

———

SISI'S EYES widen in wonder as she gazes at her reflection in the mirror. She is wearing a deep blue gown that reaches her ankles, a stark contrast to her usual habit. I can't help but smile at her, knowing how uncomfortable she must feel in something so different from what she's used to.

"It looks amazing on you," I say with genuine admiration. "Definitely take it."

Sisi turns to me, a hint of uncertainty in her expression. "You think so?"

I nod eagerly. "Absolutely."

Claudia chimes in, mouth full of chocolate and eyes sparkling with excitement. "I agree, Aunt Sisi. You look like a princess!"

Sisi laughs and spins around, admiring herself from every angle. "I should get it in other colors too," she muses out loud.

"Good idea," I reply, already imagining how stunning she would look in various shades of the same dress.

We make our way to the check-out counter, our small group surrounded by discreet bodyguards. After paying for our purchases, we head to another store where we can buy some much-needed electronics for both girls. Marcello had given us free rein with our spending, and I am grateful for his generosity.

As we browse through laptops and phones, Claudia excitedly tells us about the ring she bought from a street stall earlier. She had been obsessed with it ever since. But that doesn't trump her love for chocolate—her newest addiction.

Though I'd like nothing more than to indulge her, we'll need to have a conversation about enjoying everything in moderation.

After finishing our shopping, we head back home with our bags filled with new clothes and gadgets. The girls chat away happily while I try my best to hide my nerves. I hadn't seen Marcello since morning, and we haven't had a chance to discuss what happened between us last night.

As much as I try to distract myself with this shopping trip, my mind keeps wandering back to our conversation, and I can't help but feel a tinge of nervousness. What if he regrets what happened? I push the thought away, not wanting to imagine how that conversation would go.

Once back home, the girls are giddy about their new purchases and they gather to play on the computers. Venezia seems reluctant to join them at first, and I think she feels like an outsider, considering that Claudia and Sisi grew up together.

I gently nudge her, trying to encourage her to join in on the fun as well. She gives me a hesitant smile, her eyes full of longing as she watches Sisi and Claudia.

"I don't know..." She shrugs, but I can see the inner turmoil playing across her features.

"Go ahead. You're family too," I urge her, knowing how much it means to be included in this tight-knit group.

After a moment of hesitation, she finally gives in and joins the festivities.

As I turn to go back inside, Amelia stops me in my tracks.

"Signora Catalina, Signor Marcello wants to see you in his study." My heart skips a beat and I hold my breath.

"Did he say why?" I ask, already dreading the answer.

"No, he did not."

Taking a deep breath, I decide it's best to face whatever confrontation awaits me now rather than let my mind run wild with imagined scenarios later.

With determined steps, I make my way to Marcello's study.

He is sitting behind his desk, engrossed in a document with a pair of glasses perched on his nose. Startled by my entrance, he quickly removes them and folds them neatly on the table.

"Catalina. I didn't expect you so soon," he says, motioning towards the seat across from him. With a heavy heart, I take a seat and prepare myself for whatever is about to come next.

As soon as I sit down, I feel the words bubbling up inside of me, desperate to be released. "I'm sorry," I say quickly. "I shouldn't have..."

"What are you talking about?" He frowns, leaning forward with a look of confusion on his face.

"Last night, I shouldn't have..." I trail off, my heart racing as I wait for his response.

He tilts his head to the side, studying me as if I'm speaking a foreign language. "Catalina, what happened last night?" he asks again, genuine concern now evident in his voice.

Does he not remember our encounter? My mind races, trying to come up with an explanation for his apparent amnesia.

"Why did you call me here?" I quickly change the subject in an attempt to divert attention away from my slip of the tongue.

"I wanted to talk to you about the governess matter," he says and pauses, catching on to my evasion tactics. "What were you sorry about? Did something happen?"

I hastily backtrack, hoping to avoid any further incrimination. "I meant this morning," I amend. "I'm sorry I spent so much money."

His expression softens as he immediately reassures me. "I told you to get whatever you need. You don't have to worry about money."

A pang of guilt hits me for lying. But if he doesn't remember... maybe it was all a mistake? Maybe he was asleep and didn't intend for it to happen? But that makes me feel even more guilty for intruding in his room in the first place.

"What about the governess then?" I steer the conversation back on track, eager to focus on something else. We spend the next few minutes discussing potential candidates and scheduling interviews.

"Today?" I ask hesitantly, caught off guard by the sudden urgency in his tone.

"I've been putting this off for too long," he admits with a heavy sigh. "I didn't realize how bad things were with Venezia before. She doesn't even know how to read."

My frown deepens at his revelation. "She doesn't know how to read?" I repeat, shocked by the news.

"No one showed an interest in her before... And she's fifteen. I never imagined the situation would be so bad," he confesses. "Assisi and Claudia should also benefit from it since they haven't exactly had a normal education."

"Yes. Claudia is still young, but Sisi... I'm worried about how she will adjust to living outside of the convent."

"I didn't know she disliked it in there so much..." He shakes his head. "If you'd like to be present for the interview, I have three candidates coming in a few hours."

I readily agree.

"Great. Meet me in," he looks at his watch, "two hours in the drawing room?"

I nod and go back to my room to change.

When I go down to the drawing room a while later, Marcello is already there, a newspaper on his lap.

"The first candidate should be here in ten minutes," he casually mentions when I take a seat next to him. He seems to be totally indifferent to me, and I curse myself for even contemplating that we could be something more. It doesn't help that now I know what his touch feels like, what his lips on mine can make me feel.

I let out a long sigh, telling myself to forget everything. It's just not meant to be.

The first candidate comes in, and Marcello grills her on her experience. He does the same to the second and the third candidate, and we ultimately agree none of them would fit.

"Why is this so hard?" He groans when we get a small break before the last person is supposed to come in.

"I can't believe how snobbish they were," I'm already frustrated with the process. They'd all scoffed at the fact that Venezia is fifteen with no formal education. Marcello had guided the interview so they could show their true colors, having already had an awful experience with Venezia's last governess.

Amelia announces that the last candidate is ready to come in. She looks to be around mid-thirties, definitely younger than the others before her. She takes a seat in front of us, and we proceed with the standard questions. Her answers are on point, and I give Marcello a slow nod. She even got the tricky questions right.

"One last thing," I add, wanting to be perfectly sure about this. "Since the three of them are in different age ranges and require different curriculums, how would you plan on making lessons cohesive so they also don't feel isolated?" I'm hoping some shared lessons would help them bond with each other. God knows, Venezia really needs it.

"Yes, of course. While perusing the job advertisement, I took the opportunity to draw up a mock schedule." She rummages through her dossier and stands up to hand us a sheet of paper. She goes directly to Marcello, however, when *I* was the one who asked the question. I try not to show my slight annoyance at this, but I feel better when Marcello shakes his head and motions towards me.

The woman's smile is tight as she hands me the schedule. I look carefully, liking what I'm seeing. The shared time would be during art and etiquette classes. The plan is detailed enough that I can get a feeling of what she would teach them.

"Very well." I share a look with Marcello and he agrees.

"When can you start?" He asks, and she beams.

"Anytime."

"Even tomorrow?"

"Yes."

We spend some time sketching out the details, and Sarah, the governess, would get her own teaching room on the third floor, and free rein to use any resources she may need.

After she leaves, I sigh in relief.

"I'm so glad we found someone," I say out loud, to no one in particular.

I turn my head and catch Marcello's intense gaze fixed upon me. His lips are curved into a slight smile, revealing a hint of his dimples. My heart flutters as our eyes meet, but then he suddenly averts his gaze, causing a rush of disappointment to flood through me.

"Indeed," he says and quickly leaves the room.

———

A GENTLE KNOCK on my door startles me from my morning routine. Amelia's voice rings out, announcing a delivery for me. Confused, I make my way to the doorway and watch as a few men lug two colossal boxes into my room, their muscles straining under the weight.

"Do you know what this is?" I ask Amelia, but she simply shakes her head and leaves me to tend to the mysterious delivery.

With growing curiosity, I grab a pair of scissors and carefully cut through the top layer of the first box. As soon as I catch a glimpse of its contents, my breath hitches in my throat. It's a sewing machine, complete with all necessary accessories—needles, thread, scissors... everything. My mind reels at such an extravagant gift.

Eagerly, I turn to the second box wondering what other treasures it holds within its tightly packed walls.

"Oh my goodness," I gasp in awe as I peer inside. Yards upon yards of fabric lie before me, each one carefully folded and arranged by color and type. It's a seamstress's dream come true.

After unloading all items from the boxes, I discover a note tucked away amidst the fabrics.

It's from Marcello. "I hope this allows you to pursue your passions," it reads simply.

Overwhelmed with emotion, I bring a hand up to cover my trembling lips. He remembered our conversation...and he went above and beyond to surprise me with this thoughtful gesture.

I can hardly believe it as I begin assembling the sewing machine and examining all of its accompanying tools. With each passing moment, my heart swells with gratitude for such a kind and generous gift.

Tears prick at the corners of my eyes as I stare at the beautiful gift in front of me. No one had ever given me something so thoughtful and meaningful before. Growing up, my parents had made it clear that I was not a priority in their lives. I found solace in my teachers and the staff, but they were far from being a real family to me.

My only true companion was Enzo, my father's heir, but he had his own responsibilities and I rarely saw him. He would visit a few times a year, while the rest of the time he was off in Sicily fulfilling his duties.

Feeling overwhelmed with emotion, I wiped at the tears with the hem of my dress. I knew I had to thank Marcello for this incredible gift.

Quickly getting to my feet, I rushed down the stairs and headed towards Marcello's office, hoping to find him there. But he's nowhere to be found.

Turning to make my way back upstairs, I run into Sarah.

"Mrs. Lastra," she greets me, and I give her an absent smile.

"Sarah," I incline my head, not really paying much attention.

"I just finished the lesson with Claudia. She's such a bright young lady," she comments, and I instantly become alert.

"She is, isn't she?" I say affectionately. "Thank you for doing this. I'm sure she's going to learn a lot from you," I add. But then I get a better look at Sarah, and I have to blink twice.

She's wearing a low-cut top, and her breasts are practically hanging out of it. I have to snap my eyes to her face and force myself to keep them there. Is that how people dress these days? I mean, it's getting warm outside, so maybe this is summer fashion.

It doesn't help that she's paired the top with a very short skirt.

Although I'm a little surprised by how little clothing she's wearing, I try to pretend that I don't notice. She can wear whatever she wants, but I might have a talk with Claudia so she doesn't get any ideas from it. I don't think I'm ready for my daughter emulating that quite yet.

"I'll see you tomorrow." She takes her leave, and I go back to my room.

I install everything nicely, and when Claudia comes by, I ask her to model for me. I think Marcello noticed her love of pink because a lot of the fabrics are different shades of that color.

We spend the rest of the day playing with fabrics, and Assisi and Venezia join us a little later.

Over the next few days, I continue to invite them so we can spend time together bonding. Venezia seems to have thawed towards Claudia. Sisi, being Sisi, has gone a little crazy over her computer, and she rarely takes a break from it.

She's been reading up on everything and anything. The lessons have helped them, and I've even noticed Venezia make an effort to learn her letters. After her hours with Sarah, I try to go over the material again with her. She needs all the help now until she can grasp the basics.

I have to admit that Sarah is doing a magnificent job with the girls, even if her clothes seem to become shorter and shorter. Maybe it's just me, but sometimes I can't help but stare at her. I'm glad Marcello is mostly away because wouldn't it be embarrassing for him to see her like this? I shake my head at the thought.

I've seen little of him lately. I thanked him for the gift, but his response had been perfunctory at best, and he'd hurried to leave the house.

The entire week passes in a blur. The girls are either at their lessons or keeping me company while I try to make a dress for Claudia.

I'd been hoping to show my progress to Marcello too, but he's always absent. Well, today I know for sure he is at home. I sigh deeply and look at the bodice I'd sewn together. It looks nice for a first attempt. I remove the safety pins and take it with me downstairs.

I'm about to knock on the door of his study when I hear voices.

"The girls are doing great. Thank you, Sarah," Marcello tells her in his usual monotonous tone.

He's busy... It wouldn't be right of me to eavesdrop. I take a step back, intent on leaving them to chat and coming back later. But then I hear Sarah speak.

"There are ways to thank me," she says, and I still. Her voice is completely different from the one she's used with me or the girls. It's high-pitched and...

"I think your salary shows my wife's and my appreciation," Marcello replies drily. I blush at his words. I like it when he calls me his wife.

Sarah bursts out laughing at his words.

"Your wife," she starts in between laughing, "you mean the one with the frumpy clothes?" I look down at my dress, frowning. I don't think it's frumpy... why would she say that?

"I can't believe a man like you would actually find *that* attractive," Sarah has the gall to say, and I gasp. What?

"Sarah, please refrain from talking like that about my wife," Marcello tells her, and it gives me a little hope. Still, the jab hurts. Mainly because maybe he doesn't find me attractive...

"Why? I'd be offending her tender feelings? Don't worry, she won't hear anything from me," she says, and I hear movement. I can't help but glue my ear to the door, wanting to know what's going on.

"Sarah, I'd appreciate if you did not come into my personal space. This is inappropriate," Marcello tells her off very professionally.

"Please, Mr. Lastra. I know men like you," she replies, and there's a pause.

"Sarah, please put your clothes back on and leave." He emphasizes the word *leave*. Why is he telling her to put her clothes on? What's happening?

My heart is racing, and I don't know if I should just barge in or not. I can't hear anything anymore, and I start fretting.

Is Marcello... no, he wouldn't do that.

My hand is on the doorknob, and I debate with myself whether to open the door. I...

A loud sound jerks my attention, and I push the door open, consequences be damned. Sarah turns towards me, her mouth wide open. She's missing her top, her breasts bare. I quickly shift my gaze towards Marcello and gasp when I see him on the floor, a blank look on his face. His hands are wrapped around his knees, and he's rocking very slowly, almost out of it.

"What happened?" I ask Sarah.

"Nothing... I... I just touched his arm and then he was like that," she stammers, but I don't care. She touched him. Marcello doesn't like to be touched. And now he's...

"Out!" I say, my voice firm.

"But..."

"Get the hell out before I throw you out myself. And don't think about coming back!" Her eyes are wide with fear, and she nods slowly before leaving the room.

I close the door after her and kneel on the floor next to Marcello.

"Marcello," I call out, my voice soft.

He's shaking, his whole body shuddering as he's rocking faster and faster.

"Marcello, you're safe," I try again.

I'm so scared. Just looking at him like this is enough to bring tears to my eyes. She touched him. She fucking touched him and now he's... he's shut down, hasn't he?

"Marcello," I lower my voice, "look what I have here. I made this with the materials you gifted me." I pull the bodice I'd made in front of him and start talking. Maybe changing the subject could help him get out of whatever place he shut himself in.

I tell him all about the process and how I'd worked on it.

"I want to make a princess dress for Claudia. You remember Claudia? She's my daughter." His rocking slows down a little, and he raises his head to look at me. His gaze is still blank, but one word escapes his lips.

"Claudia?" he croaks, and my heart bursts with emotion in my chest.

"Yes, Claudia is my daughter. You've met her. She's almost ten, and she's a little troublemaker." I tell him stories about Claudia scaring the nuns off at the convent, about her little stunts and her newly found love of chocolate.

"Catalina?" His voice is hoarse as he says my name, and I eagerly nod.

"Yes, it's me. Do you recognize me?"

His eyes look straight at me, and he furrows his brows, as if clearing the fog surrounding his mind.

"Catalina?" He blinks twice. He then leans forward, dropping his knees to the floor.

"Are you alright?" I move as close to him as I can without making him uncomfortable.

"Now I am," he whispers, "thank you."

"What for?" I ask, baffled.

"You made them go away..." he responds, looking above my head.

"Who, Sarah?"

"No." He shakes his head and takes a deep breath. "The demons. You made the demons go away," he says in all seriousness.

And then he does something that surprises me. His hand hesitantly reaches out and, with the tip of his finger, he strokes my cheek with the ghost of a touch.

"You always chase the demons away," he whispers, and a tear falls down his cheek.

Marcello

In that moment, it felt as if every nerve in my body had suddenly become a razor-sharp needle, each piercing into my skin with relentless force. Sarah's hand on my arm was barely a touch, but it sent me spiraling into a state of agony. It was the familiar feeling of being trapped and helpless, like I was drowning in a sea of pain that threatened to swallow me whole.

But then, just as quickly as it came, I retreated into my own mind. It was a place I had created long ago, a sanctuary from the outside world and all its horrors. It was a white room with no windows or doors, just an endless expanse of emptiness and silence. A place where the monsters couldn't reach me, where I could be alone... but at least I was safe.

Yet even here, in the safety of my own mind, the monsters sometimes found their way in. The room would suddenly feel too big, too vast for me to control.

That's when I would downsize. Imagining myself as small and insignificant, I would squeeze myself into a tiny box that held only me inside. It was a coping mechanism that helped me feel like I had some sense of control over my own mind.

But this time was different. As I sat in my small box, humming a quiet prayer to myself, I could sense something shifting. The air around me grew heavy and oppressive, like there were countless unseen eyes watching my every move. And for the first time, instead of waiting for the false sense of safety to come, I knew I needed to fight back. This time, I wouldn't let the monsters win.

As I retreated deeper into myself, a persistent voice from the outside world grew louder. It was gentle and soothing, speaking of simple things like taking measurements for a dress.

The melody of her voice washed over me, calming my nerves and providing a sense of security. She said a name... Claudia, and my heart tightened with a foreign feeling. Then she began to tell me about this young girl, her adventures, her journey through life.

Inexplicably, my walls started to crumble. The box that I had locked myself in started to expand beyond my control. I wanted to cling onto it and keep it contained, but it unraveled before my eyes until I was once again back in the room.

Only now, I was not alone. In my white room, there was a beautiful angel whispering comforting words. The more I listened, the more captivated I became by the sound.

But then a door appeared.

No!

I did not want to face the demons that lurked beyond that door. They would take me away from this safe haven.

Desperately, I tried to hide, but her lovely voice refused to let me. It permeated every atom of the room and reverberated through my entire being. She extended her hand towards me, but I could not bring myself to touch her. She was too pure... too good for someone like me.

"I'll protect you," the angel reassures me with a gentle smile, and I lift my head to meet her gaze with tear-filled eyes.

A blinding white light suddenly engulfs me, and in my panic, I reach out and clasped onto her hand for comfort and security.

"Catalina?" My eyes struggle to adjust to the brightness of daylight. Catalina crouches down in front of me, her face etched with concern.

"Are you alright?" she asks softly, inching towards me.

"I am now," I manage to say through my trembling voice. "Thank you."

She has no idea just how much she saved me.

"What for?" Her brow furrows in confusion.

"You made them go away..." The words falter as I try to explain. "The demons. You made the demons go away."

It wasn't the first time either.

For the past decade, her face had been my only anchor to reality. The only thing that could break through the darkness that consumed me.

I don't know if it was the love and gratitude that overwhelmed me or some other force, but before I know it, my hand is reaching out to caress her cheek.

I brace myself for the inevitable pain, but to my surprise, there is none.

"You always chase the demons away." My tears flow freely now as I looked into her eyes.

Despite my internal doubts and fears, I am unafraid to show any perceived weakness in front of her. Just being in her presence fills me with a sense of strength.

"Marcello, you..." Her eyes hold an expression of awe as she gazed at me. Bolstered by an unknown bravado, I take her hand in mine and let out a loud groan at the sensation. Tentatively, I wrap my fingers around hers and have to pause to regulate my breathing. It has been over a decade since I felt human contact that was not accompanied by pain. This is a new experience for me.

"Lina," I rasp, attempting to convey the overwhelming emotions coursing through me, yet unable to find the words.

"Shh, it's okay," she coos, intertwining our fingers. The warmth and gentleness of her touch soothes me.

I stare at our joined hands, as if trying to commit this moment to memory forever.

"I can touch you," I murmur incredulously, mostly to myself.

Am I still trapped in my own mind? The thought brought on a wave of disappointment. It wouldn't be the first time... Every night, thoughts of her consumed me. In my dreams, I reached out and touched her, kissed her.

"Is this real?" I whisper, lifting my gaze to meet hers and silently pleading for confirmation.

"It's real. I'm real." Her body inches closer until our knees almost touched.

I want to say something profound or meaningful, but all that came out was a jumbled mess. She is dazzling. That inner beauty radiating from deep within her takes my breath away. Unable to express my feelings adequately through words, I squeeze her hand instead. If only she knew how much she means to me.

But she doesn't need to know.

I don't deserve her compassion or comfort. Yet here I am, weak and unable to resist her pull.

Her gentle voice breaks through the silence, pulling me out of my thoughts.

"Are you okay?" she asks, her voice full of softness and concern.

For *me*.

A monster who doesn't deserve an iota of compassion.

I can only nod in response, unable to find the words to express the turmoil inside me.

I bring her hand to my lips and press a tender kiss against her skin, grateful for the small comfort she offers.

"Thank you," I whisper, my voice heavy with emotion.

She smiles softly, shaking her head. "There's no need to thank me. We're family."

The word catches in my throat, foreign and unfamiliar. Our definitions of family are worlds apart—for me, it has always been synonymous with pain and suffering. But for her, it seems to hold so much more meaning.

As she continues to hold my hand, she moves closer until we are both leaning against a bookcase. She stretches out her legs in a relaxed pose, and I follow suit, mirroring her movements.

"Can I ask why you hate being touched?" Her voice is gentle and understanding, like a soothing balm for my troubled soul.

I take a deep breath before answering honestly, "My childhood was... difficult. There were things that happened..." I trail off, unable to reveal the full extent of my past trauma.

"It's okay," she whispers, placing a comforting hand on my shoulder. "You don't have to tell me now. But just know that I'm here for you, if you ever need anything."

Her words bring tears to my eyes, and I clasp her hand tightly in mine. "Thank you," I choke out.

We sit in a comfortable silence for some time, and I realize that in this moment with her by my side, I feel more at peace than I ever have before.

Catalina shifts nervously, her cheeks flushed with embarrassment as she looks down at the ground. "I have a confession to make," she begins, struggling to find the right words.

My heart races with worry. What could she possibly have to say that would make her so flustered?

"There's nothing you could say that would make me mad, Lina," I assure her, trying to ease her nerves. A small smile eventually tugs at the corners of her lips.

"I like it when you call me Lina," she whispers almost sheepishly.

"Then Lina it is," I reply with a warm smile.

She takes a deep breath before continuing, "A week or so ago, I was in the kitchen late at night and... I heard you."

Those words send a chill down my spine. She heard me? She knows about my nightmares?

"You heard me," I manage to choke out, feeling vulnerable and exposed.

"You were having a nightmare," she explains softly, and I close my eyes in shame.

It's true. I've suffered from horrific night terrors for as long as I can remember. Most nights, strong medication helps me fall into a dreamless sleep, but even then... The thought that Catalina would have heard me at my worst makes me feel sick to my stomach.

"I didn't mean to intrude, but I was worried about you. So I entered your room. I'm sorry," she adds earnestly.

My mind races with fear and guilt. Did I hurt her? Did I do something unforgivable while lost in the grips of terror?

"Did I... Did I do anything?" I ask, desperate for answers. My lack of control during these episodes haunts me.

"You..." Catalina hesitates before finally confessing, "You kissed me." Her voice is barely above a whisper.

"I kissed you?" The words leave my mouth in disbelief. I kissed her... and I don't remember a single thing about it.

I let out a muffled curse.

"I'm so sorry," she quickly tries to placate me, her voice gentle and soothing.

"Don't... I'm not angry because it happened. I'm mad because I don't remember it," I explain, taking a deep breath to calm myself. It's frustrating to have dreamed about this moment for so long, only for it to happen and for me to have no memory of it. "Was it good?" I ask, almost afraid of the answer.

"Yes," she nods, a small smile playing on her lips. "I think so. It was my first kiss," she confesses, and my eyes widen in surprise.

Catalina seems ashamed of this fact, so I try to comfort her by sharing a secret of my own.

"Mine too, even though I don't remember it."

"You're kidding." She turns to face me, her expression incredulous. "You mean you've never kissed anyone before? But how?" She furrows her brow in confusion.

"I've never wanted to." I shrug, but don't elaborate. It's better that she doesn't know about my troubled past, the things I did just to survive under my father's watchful eye. But even then, I drew the line at something as intimate as kissing. It had never felt right.

"Oh," she seems unsure of herself now. "We can do it again, if you want. Since you don't remember it..." Her words trail off, and for a moment I say nothing, too shocked by what she just suggested.

"If you're willing... and want to," she quickly amends, turning towards me with uncertainty in her eyes. I turn my head towards her and meet her gaze.

"I'd like to try."

Reluctantly, I release her hand and tentatively cup her cheeks. She trembles slightly under my touch, her breathing becoming harsher. My thumb lightly traces the soft curve of her lips, savoring the feel of her skin against mine. No amount of dreaming or fantasizing could have prepared me for this moment... For the rawness of her naked flesh under mine.

Despite my initial fear, there is no pain. Only a growing sense of comfort and belonging as I explore every inch of her breathtaking face.

I feel... at home.

My fingers trace over her cheek, memorizing every contour and detail of her face. "You're exquisite," I manage to say, though my throat feels thick with emotion. "So beautiful."

Lina's eyelashes flutter down at my praise, a delicate blush staining her cheeks. "I didn't think you liked me," she admits in a low voice. "You always seemed to avoid me."

"Only because I like you too much," I confess, unable to hide my feelings any longer. "To be near you and not be able to touch you..." I groan in frustration. "It's pure torture."

A shy smile plays on Lina's lips as she meets my gaze. "I like you too," she murmurs, and my heart swells with joy. The words I'd always longed to hear...

As I lean closer to her, our breaths mingle together in a warm embrace. Her eyes are wide open, and she bites her lip, sending a shiver down my spine. She may not realize it, but every move she makes sets me on fire. I hover over her lips, hesitant but unable to resist any longer.

And then I do it.

My lips gently cover hers, like the soft touch of a feather. I take in her essence, savoring the taste and feel of her. She opens her mouth eagerly, inviting me in. I can't help but pull her closer, turning our sweet kiss into one filled with urgent desire. Her hands remain stiff at her sides, a clear sign that she's trying hard not to touch me. My heart swells at her thoughtfulness.

We kiss for what feels like hours, losing ourselves in each other's embrace. And when we finally break apart, we are both left breathless and wanting more.

"Where does this leave us?" Lina asks, hope lacing her voice.

"Wherever you want." With her, I have no boundaries or limits. She's breaking down even the walls I thought were impenetrable.

"Can we take it slow? Have a proper marriage?"

"Slow... I think I can do slow," I answer honestly.

Maybe all is not lost.

Maybe there is still hope for me after all.

CATALINA

We all meet together at breakfast, after which Marcello declares that he's taken the day off to spend it with me.

As we step out of the car and make our way towards the mall, I can't help but voice my doubts once again. "Are you sure it's okay for us to take the day off?"

"It's more than okay," he replies with a wink, his eyes full of confidence. "I make the rules, remember?"

I avert my gaze, feeling a flush of heat rise to my cheeks. How can he be so effortlessly charming? Sometimes I wonder if he's even real.

Ever since that unforgettable afternoon in his office, I've found it nearly impossible to get him out of my mind. The fact that I have a chance at a real marriage with him still feels almost surreal, something I never thought possible in the past.

And as we grow more comfortable with each other, perhaps romance will blossom too. The physical attraction between us is undeniable—though I'm still apprehensive about what that might entail. But knowing that he shares my fears brings me some peace of mind.

A driver takes us to a nearby mall, a few discreet cars following behind to ensure our safety. Once we arrive, I turn to him and ask curiously, "So where are we going?"

"I know you went shopping with your Assisi and Claudia, but I heard you didn't get anything special for yourself," he explains.

"You...heard?" I frown in confusion.

"I asked Claudia." He shrugs nonchalantly.

"That little traitor," I mutter playfully under my breath. "But I don't understand what you mean by 'something special.' I bought everything I needed."

"Perhaps too little," he remarks with a teasing smile.

I blink in surprise and look up at him quizzically.

"Just remember, I have plenty of money," he adds confidently. "You don't have to worry about being frugal."

"But I don't need much," I protest. "I've always been used to wearing the same clothes for years."

He suddenly stops.

"And that is the issue, Lina. You shouldn't have suffered like that."

I'm still not sure why he's insisting on this topic. I like clothes. What girl doesn't? But I would rather get a few quality pieces rather than a lot that will get destroyed at the first wash. And I have everything that I need thanks to Enzo and Marcello's generosity.

"I lived in a convent, Marcello. They're not known for their extravagant attires."

He purses his lips thoughtfully. "You should have never been sent there in the first place, Lina," he adds, a hint of regret in his voice.

"It is what it is." I shrug. "I'm happy I'm not there now."

At that, he smiles.

"And because you're here now, you get to be extravagant. So today we're getting you something special." With that, he tentatively reaches for my hand. His fingers twine through mine, slowly.

He blinks and gulps down hard as he gets used to the touch. I don't move, letting him go at his own pace and become comfortable enough to hold my hand.

The mere fact that he's trying is a wonder in itself. And when he succeeds in holding tightly onto my hand, I can't help the beaming smile that spreads over my face.

He gives me a small nod and we proceed toward the entrance of the mall. Behind us, a group of men dressed in dark suits follow closely, their watchful eyes scanning the crowds around us.

As we walk through the bustling mall, the sound of chatter and footsteps fills the air. The glittering displays of countless shops catch my eye, tempting me to stop and browse. My gaze lingers on a dazzling jewelry display, but I quickly avert my eyes. I don't want Marcello to spend exorbitant amounts of money on me.

Just one glance at the prices and I am shocked—when did a simple pair of earrings start costing tens of thousands of dollars? Perhaps it's because I've been sheltered for so long, but this sheer extravagance astounds me.

"Oh shit." Marcello suddenly stops in the middle of the mall. My brows furrow as I look up at him.

"I'm such an idiot."

"What do you mean?"

"I never got you a ring, did I?"

My mind reels at the words he just spoke. I had never considered wearing his ring on my finger, but as I imagine it, a warmth spreads throughout my body.

His eyes sparkle mischievously as he catches my bashful expression. "That can definitely qualify as something special," I stutter, feeling my cheeks flush with color. "But please, nothing too grandiose."

He raises an eyebrow at me and gives me a knowing smile. With a firm grip on my hand, he leads me back to the extravagant jewelry shop we had passed by earlier. My heart races as I remember the exorbitant prices of the rings displayed in the window. Did he see how much they cost? But then again, he did say he has money...

"I'm sure there are other stores where we can find more affordable options," I mutter, trying to hide my unease. But he seems determined to go inside.

"This one," he declares confidently, pushing open the heavy door.

I follow behind hesitantly as his security detail surrounds us, drawing attention to our presence. The sales assistant, a young man around my age, greets us with a smile and asks how he can assist us.

"Can you show us your diamond engagement rings?" Marcello asks directly, not wasting any time.

The assistant's eyes widen slightly at the request but quickly recovers and heads to another display case. He carefully selects several glittering rings and presents them to us.

"Diamonds?" I murmur in disbelief. "Those must be incredibly expensive..."

"And incredibly beautiful," Marcello interjects smoothly, sending me a wink that makes my heart skip a beat. "Like you."

I blush furiously and lose all train of thought regarding the prices of diamonds. Although I'm wary of receiving such a gift from him, haven't I always dreamed about it? Every girl dreams about her fairytale wedding, and growing up, I certainly did my fair share of daydreaming even knowing my marriage would be an arranged one with someone my parents chose for me. But it was only after I entered the convent that those dreams intensified. Perhaps it's because I never thought they could materialize, so every time I'd go to sleep, I would imagine I met the love of my life who fell for me at first sight and decided to marry me—and take me and Claudia out of the convent. I always pictured a handsome man with a kind smile who would not only love me but also my daughter. And so far...I'm almost afraid to admit to myself how close Marcello is to that face-less man I once pictured.

The sales associate shows us more available rings. They don't even have a price tag attached to them, so I assume they must not be too expensive. That makes me more comfortable in browsing them.

"What do you think of this?" Marcello asks as he picks out a rose gold ring with a big diamond set in the middle.

He takes my hand and slides it over my finger. We're both surprised how well it fits without any adjustment.

"This is beautiful," I breathe out.

"That one is a five-carat natural diamond set against an eighteen-carat rose gold band. A wonderful choice."

"Do you like it?" Marcello asks, almost unsure of himself.

I'm speechless so I can only nod meekly.

The sales associate takes my silence as indecision, so he starts endorsing all the features of the ring.

"May I see that one?" I ask as I take the diamond ring off and point toward an emerald one a few rows down.

"Certainly."

The sales associate gives me the ring and Marcello places it on my finger. It's a white gold band with the most stunning emerald set against a row of small diamonds.

I am speechless as I stare at the beauty of it.

"It goes well with your eyes," the sales associate mentions.

Marcello gives him a harsh stare.

"Indeed, it does," he adds tensely.

"How much is this?"

"The price doesn't matter," Marcello swiftly says. "We'll take it."

"But—"

"You like it. We'll take it," he interrupts me.

"It is a good choice," the sales associate chimes in. "A beautiful ring for a beautiful lady." He smiles at me as he reaches out to take the ring and pack it.

Before he can touch me, Marcello snatches my hand away.

"My wife," he emphasizes, "will keep the ring on."

The sales associate blinks. "I can—"

"You can ring it up for us," Marcello counters.

"Of course," the man adds with a feeble smile.

I look at Marcello questioningly. Why is he suddenly so tense? He has a menacing look on his face that I don't think I've seen before.

I'm still wondering about that as he quickly pays and leads me out of the store.

"You were rude," I tell him honestly. "He was only trying to help us, as is his job."

His fists are clenched by his side and he mutters something inaudible under his breath.

"What?"

"He said you were beautiful," he says through gritted teeth. "I didn't like how he... looked at you."

"I don't understand. How?" I frown.

He takes a deep breath and scrubs his hand over his face. "He looked at you the way only I can look at you, Lina," he says slowly.

Is he... is Marcello jealous?

"He was just doing his job," I add again in an effort to diffuse the situation.

"Then perhaps I should be the one to do my job better." He turns to look at me. "You are beautiful. The most beautiful. And I am lucky to have you with me," he tells me sincerely.

His words touch my heart and I take a step forward, raising myself on my tiptoes and placing a kiss on his cheek.

"Thank you. And thank you for the ring too. It's gorgeous."

His cheeks redden and he looks away, suddenly uncomfortable.

"I think I saw a pink dollhouse over there. Maybe Claudia will like it," he suddenly says and changes the subject.

With a smile, I follow him. He's right, Claudia does like it. But I like it more, because even when he wants to give me something special, he doesn't forget about my daughter.

Marcello, Marcello... Can I allow myself to fall for you?

MARCELLO

The afternoon sun casts long shadows across the deserted streets as Vlad and I reach a secure location to discuss the case. He parks his car with a screech, and as we get out, he tosses a file my way.

"What's this?" I question, catching it before it can touch the ground.

"Forensic report for our lovely nun," Vlad smirks.

I open the file and scan its contents swiftly. There isn't much to work with. The cause of death is blood loss, but the coroner has noted some lacerations on the left ventricle of the heart. It appears that the nun might have been stabbed through her heart, leading to her bleeding out.

"I don't see why this is important." I hand back the file to Vlad.

"The coroner's remarks are quite intriguing though, aren't they? To stab someone through the heart takes precision and skill. Our copycat must be familiar with anatomy."

I raise an eyebrow at Vlad's observation. He's right; stabbing someone through the heart is not an easy task. It requires not only a sharp blade but also a perfect angle and just enough force to penetrate layers of fat and muscle.

"So our killer is not only intelligent but physically strong as well," I muse, already strategizing our next move in this perverse game of cat and mouse.

"I've been running some scenarios in my head," Vlad starts pacing in front of me.

"Do tell."

"The coroner only mentioned lacerations, not holes or anything that might singularly identify it as a stabbing event. That means the wound wasn't too big to begin with."

"Or she didn't get stabbed through the heart," I point out the obvious.

"But if she *was*," Vlad continues, "then our copycat purposefully used a narrow blade to perforate the heart, but ultimately delay death."

"What are you trying to get at?"

"So she bled out. But she did *not* bleed out immediately. It takes time. You and I both know that."

"And?"

"Look again at the report. There's a list of all her injuries. But you know what there's not?"

I wait, knowing he will enlighten me.

"Defense wounds. None. The toxicology report came back clean too, so she wasn't drugged. If the wound was shallow, she would have had enough time to fight."

"So there wasn't a struggle." I frown, processing the information. "That would mean..."

"The perpetrator was someone she knew."

"You're reaching," I say. There could be a million other reasons she didn't fight him, right?

"Am I? I spent the entire night running through all the possible scenarios. It's all right here," he points at the file, "no defensive wounds and no restrictive wounds either. So her hands were free, yet she did not so much as scratch her killer. Her fingernails were clean. And I don't mean clean as in someone cleaned them on purpose. There was simply no foreign tissue underneath."

I can see that Vlad is getting excited, so I just wait for him to continue.

"There are two likely outcomes. One, she was too shocked to react. Possible, but not entirely probable. It's reflexive to react, especially in self-defense. Two..." He pauses and turns to me. "She was a willing participant." His face is serious as he says this, and I can't help but burst into laughter.

"So she wanted it. Do you hear how absurd that is? Who would willingly agree to be chopped up and displayed on an altar?"

"Someone brainwashed. Someone who believes there's a higher purpose to their death?" Vlad shrugs. "Humans have given their lives for less," he says in a bored tone.

"You say *humans* as if you're not one," I retort drily.

"I might as well *not* be." He smirks and then walks to the back of his car and opens up the trunk, revealing a sleeping man.

"What is this?" I groan, knowing exactly what Vlad has in mind. So this is why he wanted to meet here. I shake my head.

"As I said, so far it's only a theory, but I'd like to put it to the test."

"Couldn't you do this by yourself?"

"You know I can't. I need someone to keep me in check."

Vlad then tells me that the man in question is a rat and he would have received a similar punishment anyway.

I reluctantly agree, and we set up all the variables for Vlad's experiment. He sure thought of everything.

When the man is awake, Vlad proceeds to stab him with a long, narrow knife. The man struggles in Vlad's hold, his hands flailing about, trying to latch onto Vlad.

I'm on the sidelines, observing.

After Vlad removes the knife, a trail of blood starts falling slowly. He takes a few steps back and assesses the situation.

Sure enough, the man is in shock, and he stumbles a little, clutching at his wound. But he doesn't go down. He charges at Vlad, trying to get the knife away from him.

"You've proven your point. End it," I yell at Vlad, already seeing signs that he's struggling with his control.

I think my warning came one second too late because Vlad has the man on his back, his knife slashing and slashing.

I sigh, the scene in front of me too familiar. I get into my car and close my eyes for a moment. It will be a while before his rage has run its course.

Moments later, a knock on the window startles me awake, and I turn to see Vlad covered entirely in blood. I roll down the window and hand him some napkins. He wipes the blood off his face. His suit is dripping, and I can only imagine the state of the body if Vlad looks like this.

"Thanks."

I get out of the car and survey his handiwork. The man is completely butchered, his body a mass of mangled flesh and bone.

"So, did that prove your hypothesis?" I ask ironically, and Vlad chuckles.

He crouches down and takes the man's hand – or what's left of it.

"I'd say I proved my point. If you want to believe it, it's up to you." He shrugs, showing me the residue under the man's fingertips and some scratches on his own skin.

I help him dump the body in the trunk of his car, and then he's on his way.

Vlad's theory sounds crazy. Hell, it *is* crazy. Why would anyone willingly let themselves be murdered by a serial killer? But if there's any chance that he may be right... Then the nun knew the copycat. It's a starting point. And I can't afford to leave any leaf unturned. Not when I have someone to protect.

I get back in my car and drive home, noting how late it has gotten. It must be a little after midnight when I get back to the house. My first thought is to go get cleaned up since I must be a bloody mess too.

"Marcello?" I hear Catalina's voice.

"Lina? What are you doing up at this hour?" She comes towards me and gasps when she sees the state I'm in.

"Are you hurt? God, what happened?" She frowns as she takes me in, her face full of worry.

"Not my blood," I say, and I attempt what I think is a smile. "I need to wash this off." I go towards my room and Lina follows behind me.

"Did you..." she starts, and her lower lip trembles.

"Did I kill someone? No. Did I help get rid of a body? Yes." I give her the short version of the story and unbutton my dress shirt. The blood has seeped through the material and is now staining my skin, the stickiness making me feel uncomfortable.

"Do you need any help?" Lina asks, shocking me. I look at my bare torso, and then back at her, lifting my eyebrows in question.

"If you want help, that is," she quickly rephrases and lowers her gaze, clearly embarrassed.

"And if I did..." I take two steps until I'm in front of her. "How would you help me?" I tip her chin up ever so slightly, reveling in the simple touch. Catalina may be the only woman in this world I can touch without a problem... and I don't know if it's a blessing or a curse.

"I can help wipe your chest." Her eyes are looking anywhere but at me.

"Really?" I drawl, enjoying seeing her like this. She just nods.

"Follow me." I show her to the bathroom and hand her a towel. Then I take off my pants, stripping down to my boxer briefs.

Catalina immediately averts her face.

"Is that necessary?" she asks in a small voice, her hand lightly covering her eyes.

"I wouldn't want to wet my pants now, would I?" I challenge.

"True." She accepts my explanation. "What about the shirt then? Shouldn't you take it off too?" Her question is innocent enough, but I'm not ready for her to see my back yet. Not soon.

"I can do it myself if..." I change the subject, but she cuts me off.

"I'll do it."

She takes the towel and dampens it before coming in front of me.

"Can I?" She seeks my approval before touching me, and my heart threatens to burst in my chest.

"Please," I guide her hand until it's resting over my ribcage. She dabs at the blood, her movements soft and tender.

"Thank you," I say. I could have easily just showered, but having her do this? It's like a dream come true.

She's so focused on her task, she doesn't realize she's going increasingly and dangerously lower. When she's past my belly button, I have to stifle a groan. Does she even know what she's doing to me? Just a little lower and she'd see just how much she affects me.

But I don't want to scare her. Not yet.

I grab her hand and bring it over to my mouth for a soft kiss.

She must have noticed all right... judging by the pink stain on her cheeks.

"I can't help it, you know. Not when I have a beautiful woman touching me." I lean forward to whisper in her hair. She giggles slightly, and the sound is pure music to my ears.

"I... Thank you," she replies, the red spreading to the roots of her hair.

After the blood is off my body, I try to get her to go to her room and get some sleep.

"Can I stay with you?" Lina asks, and I wish I could say yes but...

"Not now, Lina. You saw how I can get during the night. What if I hurt you?" I shake my head, knowing full well how bad my night terrors can get.

"You won't!" she immediately says. "You didn't last time."

"I don't trust myself. Maybe in the future. But now? I won't take any risks." I move closer to her, intent on showing her this isn't me rejecting her. It's me protecting her. Even if it's from myself. I caress her cheek with the back of my hand before leaning over and brushing my lips over hers.

"Go," I whisper.

She looks at me for a moment, her eyes full of yearning, but she does as she's told.

Damn it!

I need to get a hold of myself. Even if that means therapy again. I need to do this for Lina.

Everything I ever wanted is within my grasp. I just need to be brave enough to take it.

CATALINA

Claudia pouts at me, her arms crossed tightly over her chest. "I didn't realize how long this would take," she complains, shifting impatiently in front of the full-length mirror. I continue to focus on pinning her dress properly, trying not to let her attitude get to me.

"It takes time to create a masterpiece from scratch," I reply, my fingers deftly adjusting the hem of the skirt.

Finally satisfied with my work, Claudia steps in front of the mirror and gasps in delight. A pleased smile spreads across her face as she turns and twirls, admiring her new dress.

"I love it!" she exclaims, beaming at me.

"See, it was worth all that time and effort," I say with a smirk.

She looks at me teasingly and says, "Given that's the only time you can spare for me..."

I can't help but laugh at her suggestive tone. "Hey now, that's not fair. You have your lessons during the day," I remind her.

Ever since the incident with Sarah, we had been on the hunt for a new teacher. After weeks of searching, we finally found Mrs. Evans. She is an elderly woman with over thirty years of experience teaching young girls. And despite our initial doubts and reservations, she has proven to be a great fit for us. Even Venezia, who is notoriously picky about people, seems to like her.

With a playful lilt in her voice, she replies, "And you have

Marcello," but I can tell from the glimmer in her eye that she's joking. I never would have thought she'd feel jealous of me spending time with him. But then again, we have been spending a great deal of time together.

We've been taking it slow, one day at a time. We've been getting to know each other better and exploring his newfound tolerance for touch.

Sometimes, as we sit together, I catch a look of wonder on his face as if he can't quite believe he's touching someone.

And the more time we spend together, the more my heart falls for him. It's inevitable when you get glimpses into someone's soul. He always wears a mask, afraid of being hurt. It gives him an air of aloofness and sternness to those who don't know him well. But I've also seen his tender side.

A contented smile spreads across my face as I think about our newly established routine. Since Marcello is constantly working from his study, I had asked if I could keep him company and read a book while he tended to his business.

To my delight, he had welcomed the idea with open arms, and now for weeks we have met almost daily in the study. The silence between us is comfortable and companionable, though I do catch him stealing glances at me every now and then.

"You have no idea how hard it is to focus with you here," he would groan.

"I can leave if I'm distracting you," I'd offered, not wanting to ruin his workflow.

"Don't even think about it. I enjoy having you here," he'd replied, going back to his work.

There are days when he's away. I know it's mob business, so whenever he is out, I can't help but worry. This life is too dangerous.

Despite the countless moments we've spent together, our physical intimacy has never progressed beyond kissing. Yet every time his lips touch mine, my body sets ablaze with desire. And yet, just as things start to heat up, Marcello always pulls back. It's like a tantalizing game of cat and mouse, and I long for more.

I can feel it in my bones—I am ready for more. I've devoured articles and books on the subject, seeking guidance and knowledge. But I have no idea if Marcello is ready for the next step...

It's strange how I used to believe I was different from other women, incapable of experiencing these intense desires and pleasures. The fear and hesitation had consumed me for so long.

But when I'm with him, all those doubts vanish. That night from years ago feels like a distant memory now, fading into the background as I focus on the present and the future with Marcello by my side.

I not only have a beautiful daughter, but now I also have an amazing husband who might one day come to love me.

Maybe it was all worth it.

Claudia's voice cuts through my thoughts like a sharp knife. "Mamma!" she exclaims, raising an eyebrow as she catches me lost in my reverie.

I snap back to reality and see her smirking at me mischievously. I playfully pinch her arm as I scold her, "Don't tease me, young lady!"

She puts on a mock pout and replies, "Fine, I won't. But know that I'm onto you." She points two fingers at her eyes and then towards me, indicating that she's watching my every move.

I shake my head at her with a fond smile, and we return to working on her dress together.

Later in the afternoon, Marcello knocks on my door. He places a huge box in my arms and tells me to get ready because he's taking me to dinner. Too flabbergasted to respond, I just nod.

I put the box on the bed and lift the top. Inside is a gorgeous off-white dress and a pair of sandals. I'm immediately touched by his gesture, and I take off my clothes, ready to try it on.

Marcello must have noticed that I prefer to wear mid-calf dresses, because he's chosen the perfect length. The shoes also fit. I'm entirely too amazed by this and can't help but wonder how he could have known. Maybe Amelia looked through my things and told him?

I shake my head, a smile playing at my lips.

He wants to take me out. I'm almost too giddy at the thought.

I try my best to look put-together, not wanting to embarrass him. I look into the makeup bag I'd gotten the last time at the mall, and I apply some foundation to cover my freckles and a little mascara to lengthen my lashes.

Satisfied with the result, I head downstairs. Marcello is waiting for me by the stairs, already dressed in a suit – not that he's ever wearing anything else.

"Lina... you look amazing." He takes my hand, tugging me closer. I blush at his compliment.

"Thank you. You too," I add gingerly. He leans in closer, inspecting my face with a slight frown.

"What did you do to your face?" My hands instinctively fly to my cheeks.

"I just put on some foundation and mascara," I reply, confused by his concern.

He shakes his head, his eyes searching mine. "Your freckles are gone. I don't like it."

His hand finds mine and leads me to the kitchen. He gently takes a damp napkin and begins wiping away the makeup from my face.

"There, that's better," he says with a satisfied hum. I feel a blush creeping up my cheeks as I lower my gaze.

"Hey, you're beautiful no matter what. But I love your freckles, and I love looking at them." He lifts my chin to meet his gaze. "All one hundred thirty-nine of them."

"One hundred thirty-nine...?" I blink in surprise. "How do you—"

"I counted." He smiles proudly. "I've been watching you so much it's become a habit," he adds, a little self-consciously.

His fingers trail softly against my skin, causing shivers to run down my spine.

"Seventy-two on your left cheek," he says as he gently caresses my left side. "And sixty-two on your right cheek."

I stare deeply into his eyes. "That's only one hundred thirty-four."

His lips curl into a fond smile before pressing a quick kiss to the tip of my nose.

"Five small ones on your nose," he whispers.

I blush furiously and avert my eyes, my heart beating so fast in my chest I'm afraid it's going to leap out any moment now.

"You're perfect and so are all of your freckles. Never hide them from me," he murmurs. "Now let's go before we're late for our reservations."

The restaurant Marcello booked for us is a stunning Italian place with an outside garden.

"You mentioned that your favorite food growing up was *arancini*. This place is famous for their Sicilian food."

"You remembered that?" I'm shocked at his thoughtfulness. But then again, Marcello has this special ability to surprise me every single time. "This is amazing. Thank you," I tell him sincerely.

We are shown to our seats in the heart of the garden. After we peruse the menus, we settle on a full course meal, with appetizers, soup, and a main dish.

"I love this," I say as I gaze around me. The garden is housed between two buildings, but there's an in-built ceiling full of roses.

"I'm sorry I haven't been around as much, but things have been hectic," he apologizes.

"You have enough on your plate right now." I know he's been having issues with some businesses, even if I don't know any of the particularities.

"There have been some rogue groups that have been targeting our merchandise, and we aren't any closer to catching them." He sighs and brings his hand to massage between his eyes.

"That's why you agreed to marry me, wasn't it? For my brother's help?" I feel compelled to ask this, mostly because I'd been wondering for a long time.

Marcello grimaces but nods. "That, and that I needed to bring something to the table to make the famiglia trust me as capo."

"I see."

"The last few months have been nothing but trouble. There are a lot of new players in the city, and we still don't know who we are dealing with exactly."

The appetizers arrive, and we both dig in.

"Is it okay if you talk to me about..." I look around before whispering, "*that*?" I'd seen enough in my family to know that men didn't talk business with their wives.

"Why not?" He leans in. "You're my wife." He gives me a smile, and I feel my stomach contracting. Butterflies... I'm having butterflies in my stomach. Lord! Now I understand the origin of the idiom.

"Men in the famiglia aren't usually as... accommodating," I add.

"There are a lot of things the famiglia and I don't agree on, and it's high time some of them changed."

"What do you mean?"

Marcello sighs. "I never wanted to become capo. I wanted out... as far away from the famiglia as possible. But now that I am here, I have a responsibility, so I might as well make the best of it. I've been trying to change a few things in how we run our businesses, but some things are so entrenched in people's mentalities..." He shakes his head.

"How do you plan on doing that?"

"By setting an example," he gives me half a smile. "That's why my wife should be privy to what's happening around us."

"That's... I don't know what to say." I'm surprised by his statement. Growing up, I'd been told countless times that I was an accessory, and that my value depended on the man I attached myself to. When I got pregnant with Claudia, I lost all my value for the famiglia. I was suddenly persona non grata.

"I don't want my sisters, or our children to conform to this anachronistic type of thinking. I don't care how much of a tradition it is for a woman to be nothing else but a stay-at-home mother. They should be their own person," he adds, and I can feel a little moisture forming in my eyes. I quickly blink it away.

"You have no idea how much that means to me. I was never seen as a person, rather as an opportunity for my family. I witnessed my sisters being sold into marriage like cattle, and then I had to wait around until it was my turn." My lip curls in distaste. "When I got pregnant..." I feel a knot forming in my throat as I recall how I'd been treated by my family. "If it weren't for Enzo back then, I would have been homeless. My father said I'd brought shame to the family and that..." I take a deep breath. "That I was not his daughter anymore. My mother didn't dare intervene."

A whimper escapes my lips, and Marcello takes my hand in his, squeezing it in comfort.

"You can do whatever you want, you know that, right? Maybe not right now because it's so dangerous, but once that's over..."

I give a nervous laugh.

"I don't even think I'd know what to do," I muse. The thing with freedom is that it's great... until you get it. So many times I dreamed about what I would do if I were free. So many plans, and so many scenarios, and here I am. Free, but still trapped. Trapped in my head and in the endless possibilities. What if I make the wrong choice?

See... freedom is a dangerous thing.

"You'll find out," he says with a confidence I lack.

"You mentioned children," I change the subject, a little uncomfortable being put under the microscope like that. "Would you like children?"

"Would you?" he fires back.

"Yes," I say and look anywhere but at him. Having children with Marcello... I think I'd like that. Very much so, in fact. I blush at the thought.

"Then I would too."

"I haven't yet thanked you for the way you've treated Claudia. I know not all men would be as accommodating with their wife having another child and—"

"Lina, stop."

My eyes flutter in surprise at his tone.

"She's part of you. That's enough for me."

I stare at him, unable to believe how I became this lucky. Not only is my husband handsome and powerful, but he is also so understanding and kind. I don't think anyone's been this nice to me...ever.

The server comes to clean the table and then he brings the soups.

"Have you heard anything about Father Guerra?"

Marcello shakes his head.

"It's odd, but so far they haven't reached out. Considering the letter they sent to Enzo, I find it a little unsettling."

"You think they're biding their time with something?" I'm a little afraid at the prospect. Not as much for myself, but for Claudia. I don't want her to become a target just to get back at me.

"Yes. And I don't like it."

I turn my attention to the soup. I take a spoonful, and I almost choke on a foreign object. Marcello rushes to my side, worried, and I immediately spit it out.

"Ugh," I heave, feeling a scratch down my throat.

"What..." Marcello looks at my hand where the object is, and I curse.

It's a ring. Claudia's ring.

"No..." I frown, shocked at what I'm seeing. How could it be here?

I turn my attention back to the soup and move my spoon around. Marcello grabs my hand, pulling it back.

"Lina..." He shakes his head, his attention on the bowl of soup. That's when I notice it. The tip is just above the liquid, but there's no mistaking it. It's a finger... a human finger.

With a cry, I jump back, falling down. No... this can't be...

"Claudia..." I whisper, a hysterical cry escaping my lips. "That's Claudia's ring... no..."

People are already gathering around us, whispering. Tears running down my cheeks, I grab onto Marcello.

"Call home. I need to speak with Claudia..." I'm yelling, all my common sense out the window. I need to make sure Claudia's fine.

It can't be...

The more I think about it, the more hysterical I get, despair taking over.

"Yes, your mother wants to talk to you," I vaguely hear Marcello say into his phone before passing it to me.

"Claudia?" I rasp out.

"Mamma? What's wrong?" she asks.

"Are you hurt anywhere? Are you okay?" My words are hurried, but I just need to know she's fine.

"Of course. Why wouldn't I be?" I release a breath.

"Good... good. Where is your ring?"

"Ring? I don't know... I must have forgotten it somewhere. But how did you know?" Her answer helps me calm down a little, so I just assure her that everything is fine and that I will see her at home.

I hang up and look to see Marcello's grim expression.

He gathers me into his arms, and I let myself go.

"I've got you," he whispers in my hair, his arms tightening

around me. He swoops me up and carries me out of the restaurant, leaving everyone behind staring at us.

———

AFTER I CONVINCED myself that Claudia was fine, Marcello took me to his room and left me here.

He's been interviewing the staff for a couple of hours now, because someone must have been in the house to take the ring. But more than that... they must have known where we were going. That someone knows our movements and has personal access to us makes me sick to my stomach.

"Lina." Marcello opens the door and comes towards me. "I have people looking into the restaurant right now. We'll get whoever did this, I promise you."

"It's all my fault..." I shake my head. "If I hadn't killed Father Guerra... They are probably trying to get even, and now they are threatening my daughter." A sob catches in my throat at the thought. "It's all my fault."

"Don't say that, sweetheart." He kisses my forehead. "You did the right thing. You were so brave, Lina."

I succumb to the comfort of his embrace.

"When will this end?" I whisper.

"I'll keep you and Claudia safe. I promise you. As long as I'm alive, I won't let anyone hurt you."

"Thank you. Thank you." I keep murmuring.

I cry myself to sleep, with Marcello holding me so close I *almost* believe that nothing can harm me.

I wake up a while later and look around me, feeling disoriented. I take a couple of seconds to remember everything that happened and the fact that I'm in Marcello's room. He's not anywhere in sight, though.

I frown.

Getting out of bed, I go to look for him in his study.

"I gave her to you to protect her, and *this* happens?" My brother's voice booms from inside the study.

"I'm on it," Marcello replies, his voice clipped.

"Sure looks like it," Enzo replies sarcastically.

"Might want to check the basement," Marcello retorts. What does he mean by that?

"It's a declaration of war if I've ever seen one. And now they want us to go to their fucking banquet and pretend nothing happened?" Enzo curses, and my hand freezes on the doorknob.

"Which is why I'm not even considering bringing Catalina there." I open the door.

"Where?"

If it's anything concerning me, then I should know it.

"Lina..." My brother groans, and Marcello purses his lips.

"What banquet?" I ask.

"You shouldn't have heard that."

"Didn't you say you'd discuss things with me?" I turn towards Marcello. "I have a right to know."

"Lina, it's not that simple," he replies, but I'm not having it.

"What banquet, Enzo?"

"The Guerras are having a banquet for the five families. The core leadership is expected to attend from each famiglia." He brings his glass to his lips and empties it.

"Why? Why now?"

"Keep your enemies close." Enzo goes to the liquor cabinet and fills his glass again. "It's a matter of perspective, really. They want a show of force, but they also want to gauge the competition. Both our families," he inclines his head towards Marcello, "have experienced a rather abrupt change in leadership. Marchesi is basically dumpster diving for power and DeVille..." he pauses. "They are as they've always been. Closed off."

"What happens if we don't go?" I ask, afraid I already know the answer.

"A personal affront," Marcello shrugs at the same time that Enzo says, "War."

"Okay, so we need to go."

"No, we don't."

"But that's the thing, isn't it? They expect us not to go. And that's one more reason for them to formally go against us."

Enzo smirks and tips his glass in my direction.

"And that's why you're my favorite sister."

"If we go," Marcello starts, "and that is a big *if*, we won't know what to expect. We're on their territory."

"I want to go," I say, suddenly determined. "I can't let them bully me anymore. Tell me, how long do you think until these little games turn serious and they end up really targeting me, or even worse, Claudia? If we don't go, it's just like telling them they've succeeded with their threats."

"We still don't know if the Guerras were involved with the restaurant," Marcello notes.

"You might not know, but I do. I can feel it. And it's only going to get worse."

They are both silent for a moment before Enzo remarks,

"I'll be there."

I look at Marcello, and he doesn't seem at all pleased by the turn of events. He reluctantly agrees.

After Enzo leaves, I ask Marcello why he's so willing to risk a large-scale conflict just to spare me some discomfort. His answer, though, floors me.

"I never want to see you hurt again, Lina. And I know these people... They will hit below the belt."

"I can take it."

"I'm not sure I can..."

MARCELLO

As I button up my shirt, I glance over at Lina, who is engrossed in a file detailing the attendees of the upcoming Guerra Banquet. "Lina, have you noticed that Assisi has been acting strangely lately?"

She looks up, surprise evident in her features. "You've noticed too?"

I know I won't win any awards for being a great brother, but even I can see that something is off with Assisi. It started with her missing a few family dinners, and now she spends most of her days locked in her room except for when she has lessons. Even Mrs. Evans mentioned that Assisi seemed distracted.

"Have you tried talking to her? Maybe it's trauma from seeing that nun like that," I say, though Assisi had appeared composed during the entire ordeal. But perhaps that only masks deeper issues.

"I don't know. I'm worried about her too. I've been giving her space to adjust to life outside of the convent, but she's shutting us out. All of us. Even Claudia has noticed the change in her behavior. It's like she's hiding away from the world." Lina sighs, clearly troubled by the situation.

"Maybe we should make an appointment with Claudia's therapist," I suggest. It's not healthy for her to close herself off from the world. Maybe it's the guilty part of me that's saying that, but I want her to be happy... normal.

"If she wants. I'll try to bring it up with her, but she can be very stubborn."

"You know her best." Catalina's told me about their friendship, and I can't help but be extremely grateful for her presence in Assisi's life. She truly is an angel.

"This is a lot of people." Lina groans and closes the file.

"You need to be on your guard tonight, and it's better if you can recognize everyone."

"But we only have to worry about Guerra, right?"

"I'm not so sure. We don't know who they might work with." The Guerras have always been insular. While their conflict with the DeVille family is legendary and goes back many generations, their allies have always been a little harder to peg. Generally, it's whoever hates DeVille too. I'm almost afraid to entertain the notion that they might be connected with this so-called Chimera.

"Ready?" I turn towards Lina, shaking myself from my musings. Her beauty, though, blows me away. She's wearing a classy black maxi dress that clings to her body. Her hair is slightly curled at the edges, giving her an elegant vibe. She seems rather self-conscious as she nibbles at her lip and pats her dress down.

I stop in front of her and breathe her in.

I don't deserve her.

Hell, I don't deserve any of this.

But she's here, in front of me. And I can touch her.

With two fingers, I tip her jaw up and I see the apprehension in her eyes.

"You're the most beautiful woman I've seen in my life. Don't be embarrassed." Heat travels up her cheeks and she gives me a timid smile.

"Thank you," she whispers.

If I have it my way, she'll be hearing that every single day for the rest of our lives. But I know deep down that I don't have that much time with her. And I'll take all I can get.

Oddly enough, the banquet is hosted at the St. Regis Hotel's ballroom. Everything about the affair points to a peaceful event, seeing that it's taking place right in the center of the city. But appearances can be deceiving.

We arrive at the hotel and are escorted towards the ballroom. There's a routine security check that we have to pass through, but then we're good to go.

We're about to enter the ballroom when someone calls out my name.

"Marcello!" Catalina's hand tightens on my arm.

I school my features and turn to greet my uncle. This wasn't the way I wanted to see him again. I'd been in touch with my under-bosses, but not with him. I'm sure he's taken offense at that, with him being the Consigliere and supposedly my right hand. I almost snort at the notion.

"Uncle," I greet him.

"Is this lovely lady your new wife?" He starts in a saccharine voice that's uncharacteristic of him.

"Yes," I respond, and tug Catalina slightly behind me, putting my body in front of her.

"Marcello," Nicolo shakes his head as if disappointed. "You didn't think to invite your family? Imagine my surprise when I find out my nephew," he pauses, "my capo got married and no one in the famiglia was invited." His criticism doesn't get past me. I'd known from the beginning that a small ceremony would raise eyebrows in the famiglia, given their penchant for extravagant weddings. But I couldn't... wouldn't subject Catalina to something like that. Not after what she'd been through. Besides, expediency had been paramount.

"It was rather sudden," I reply, closing the subject. Catalina is off limits. To everyone.

Nicolo narrows his eyes at me but doesn't comment further.

"I'm glad you could be with us tonight." He fakes a cough and walks past us.

"So that was your uncle..." Catalina frowns at his retreating figure. He's come alone tonight, it seems.

"Stay away from him. He's dangerous."

"Why?" She peers at me from beneath her eyelashes.

"He doesn't think I should be capo," I answer grimly. And because of that, I don't know what he's capable of.

"Lina!" Enzo comes to our side. He's looking immaculate as always, dressed in a white suit and a black shirt.

"Enzo." Catalina releases my arm to give him a hug.

"And your wife?" I ask, noting he's alone.

"She'll be here at some point," Enzo shrugs.

Dropping the topic, we head inside the ballroom.

There must be around fifty people inside, all of them highly ranked within the five families. Or four... I scan the room and see that DeVille hasn't shown up or sent anyone on their behalf.

"DeVille's not here."

"Did you expect them?" Enzo raises an eyebrow.

"Not really, but stranger things have happened," I remark, my eyes focusing on the crowd once more.

I zero in on Benedicto Guerra, the current capo. He's in his late forties but still looking fit. I remember him from back in the day, but I can't say we've had many interactions. Next to him is his brother, Franco, Antonio Guerra's father. He's the one holding my attention because he's the first one who'd like retribution for his son's death.

My gaze moves further, and on each side of Benedicto are his sons, Michele and Rafaelo. I'm entirely surprised to see them calm in each other's proximity. I'd met both of them when I was younger, and their enmity was palpable even then. When Francesco had updated me with relevant information about the other families, he'd noted that the brothers' feud had only amplified over the years.

They are less than a year apart in age, but they have different mothers. Michele's mother died in childbirth, but she hadn't yet been cold in her grave before Benedicto wed Rafaelo's mother. That probably contributed to the conflict, though it didn't help that Benedicto wants to name Rafaelo as his heir, even though he isn't the firstborn.

"He looks like Father Guerra." I feel Catalina's slight tremble, and I tug her closer to my side.

"He can't hurt you," I tell her, and she gives me a tight nod.

At our entrance, all eyes are on us. Franco's lips immediately curl in disdain, and he leans in to say something to Benedicto, who puts his hand up in a stop sign.

Maybe he will keep his brother in line.

"They definitely look surprised," Enzo remarks ironically. He turns his head and notices the Marchesis with his wife in tow. He doesn't look too pleased by that fact, and he signals to us he's going to their side.

"Easy," I whisper to Lina as we step further into the room. She's trying hard to keep her calm, plastering a fake smile on her face.

"We can do this." She takes a deep breath. Just in time for Benedicto to come greet us.

"Lastra. Heard about your brother. My condolences." He extends his hand to me. My body immediately tenses.

"Pleased to meet you, Signor Guerra." Catalina grasps his hand before I can react.

Benedicto seems surprised, but he shakes her hand.

"And you, Signora Lastra. I've heard about your nuptials. Too bad it was such a small affair," he adds.

"We didn't want to involve too many people. Just friends and family. Besides, I've heard about your tragedy. Condolences for your loss." I hope my message is received. By being the first to bring up the subject, I can control the direction it will take.

"Indeed." Benedicto narrows his eyes at me, at the same time that his brother makes a go for me. Benedicto's arm shoots out, stopping Franco from advancing.

"We are all friends here, right *fratello*?" His voice is tense as he addresses his brother, and he nods. Franco's eyes are still murderous as he looks at me, then at Catalina, and I know this is far from over. It's just too public right now.

"Right," Franco reluctantly agrees.

"Why don't you let your wife join the other women, and we can talk some business?" Benedicto nods towards the gaggle of women chatting at a nearby table.

I don't want Catalina anywhere out of my sight, so I try to respectfully decline.

"I'm not sure she would be comfortable."

"Bah!" Benedicto exclaims, and yells at one woman.

"Cosima, come here."

A woman in her forties joins us, sticking herself to Benedicto's side.

"What's wrong, *amore*?"

"Why don't you take Signora Lastra and introduce her to everyone?"

Cosima narrows her eyes at Catalina, and she doesn't seem too interested. But she puts on a smile and addresses her, anyway.

"Catalina, I'm Cosima."

My wife gives me a reassuring nod and moves to go to Cosima.

"Will you be ok?" I whisper in her hair, afraid to let her go.

"I'll be fine," she answers confidently.

"You know what to do if anything happens," I remind her. We'd gone over every possibility in preparation for this evening, and I'd given her a panic button. If she felt threatened in any way, she should push the button and it will make enough noise to alert everyone in her vicinity.

Already I have to grit my teeth and let her go, but I know that we need to follow a certain etiquette.

Just as Lina leaves with Cosima, a drunk Michele stumbles towards us. He's carrying a half-empty bottle of Jack.

"Look at them love birds. He can't bear to be separated from her," he slurs and puts his hand on his father's shoulder.

Suddenly I can feel the tension in the air.

"You should take lessons, *papa* dear."

"Michele," his brother hisses from behind him.

"Oh, there's the retard. I have to wonder why you organized this, capo." Michele's words are full of venom. "Did you perhaps want to showcase to the world that your eldest is a drunk," he smiles sarcastically, "while your *heir* is a fucking retard." His emphasis on heir doesn't escape me.

"D-d-don't sss... sp..speak t-to fa...father l-like that," Rafaelo stammers as he grabs onto Michele.

"Both of you, cut it out!" Benedicto finally intervenes.

"Yes, Raf, stop talking. You'll show everyone you got dropped on your head at birth," Michele says in a mocking tone, and his brother's head is hung low in shame. Surprisingly enough, he takes the insult without so much as batting an eyelash.

"I'm s-s-sorry," he replies, and I realize he might have a stutter. That doesn't make someone a retard.

Odd, though. When I'd known them years ago, Rafaelo hadn't had a stutter. Or maybe I'm not remembering correctly.

"See," Michele laughs, and pats his brother on the shoulder. Rafaelo squares his shoulders and lowers his gaze in a submissive gesture.

"Enough!" Benedicto removes Michele's hand and bends it awkwardly.

"Afraid people might think less of you when they find out your heir is touched in the head?" He laughs in derision and extricates himself from his father's hold.

"Fucking assholes. *Porca Madonna!*" Michele yells some expletives but removes himself from the situation, simply by going to the next available table and grabbing more alcohol.

"You must excuse my son. He has a problem with alcohol. You know how it is," Benedicto explains.

Franco is still shooting daggers at me, while Rafaelo has a timid, almost cowering demeanor.

I keep my expression in place, accepting his explanation, but inside I have to wonder how much of this is a show and how much of it is real.

"So, Lastra," Benedicto starts, "I've heard your last shipments were busts."

"Right," I respond skeptically. Word sure got around.

"I'm sure that together we can work something out. I've been in your position. Young capo, just starting out. You'll need all the support you can get."

Franco snorts at Benedicto's words.

"You would allow my son's murderer in our midst?" Franco spits out, but Benedicto rolls his eyes, a bored expression on his face. He makes a waving sign with his hand and gives Franco a threatening look. I don't know exactly what that's supposed to mean, but Franco immediately shuts up, not too pleased about it.

"I think you might be needed elsewhere, *fratello*," Benedicto says suggestively. Franco seems to hold it together, but barely. With a tight nod, he disappears, losing himself in the crowd.

"You must excuse my brother. He's still grieving."

"I can imagine." I don't know what he wants me to say. Admit guilt? I'd sooner finish Franco off than let anyone say a word against Lina.

"Now, back to our topic," he says and takes out a cigar from an inner pocket in his blazer. He lights it up and takes a few puffs. "My transport lines are entirely secure. You could easily make up for the lost revenue." He explains that he has transports twice a week, but could squeeze another one for me.

"I see. And what would that cost me?" I'm rather curious what Benedicto could possibly want in exchange. Simply because his actions are a little... suspicious. So much enmity between our families right now, and he wants a partnership? There has to be more to it.

"Bah! I'll have none of that. Consider it a gift. For better future relations." Yeah, well, I don't buy that. So I continue to probe.

"I could never in good conscience accept such a thing from you."

"If you put it like that..." He pauses and regards me, narrowing his eyes. "My son here is my heir." He tugs a still cowering Rafaelo to his side, slapping his back and making him stand straighter.

"But I have still not found him a nice bride. He needs a good woman to take care of him and the house. Hard to find these days," he sighs, "with these feminist notions, all women are suddenly independent." He shakes his head in disgust and starts a tirade on how women's places should be at home taking care of their husbands and children. I'm half-listening at this point, and I note Rafaelo's tormented expression.

"I...I d-d-don't w... w-w-ant a www...ife." Rafaelo musters with great difficulty, and I feel for him.

"But you *need* a wife," his father remarks and moves on, disregarding his son's opinion. "I've heard about your sister," Benedicto suddenly says, and I see where this is going.

"With all due respect, my sister is too young."

"Not *that* sister." He frowns. "The one who grew up in the convent." I have to carefully mask my features. How is it that he knows Assisi's no longer at Sacre Coeur? "She would be perfect for my boy. I'm sure the nuns must have instilled in her traditional values." He says this with such conviction, as if he has everything figured out.

"I don't think Assisi would be ready for that anytime soon. And should she decide to marry someone in the future, I'll leave it up to her," I try to explain. I will force none of my sisters into marriages they don't want. I'd meant what I told Lina last time. It's time things changed a little within the *famiglia*.

"Come on, Lastra. You can't mean that!" He starts in an outraged tone, but immediately catches himself. "Of course she wouldn't be ready just yet. But why don't we let them meet and see where it goes?" He insists, and I have to wonder *why* exactly he's so set on a union between our families. "If they decide they suit, then who are we to stand against their happiness, right?"

The way he's phrased this has me a little backed into a corner. I can't overtly refuse him, so I just nod. "Maybe something can be arranged." It's best to be vague.

"Good. I knew you'd see reason." Benedicto nods, satisfied. But then Rafaelo starts trembling next to him.

"I...I..." He stutters, and I hear a trickling sound. I look closer and see that a wet spot is forming on the front of his trousers and down his leg.

Rafaelo just pissed himself.

His father notes this immediately, but he doesn't react in any way. Rather, he excuses them both and leaves the room.

Maybe Michele was onto something... Maybe Rafaelo does have some mental issues. It's hard to associate his physical appearance with it. He's a big man, if not for his slumping shoulders and craning neck. His posture alone makes him look more like a child than an adult.

Shaking my head at what I'd just witnessed, I scan the ballroom for Catalina.

I frown.

Where is she?

I can't see her anywhere, so I check with the women she'd been with. One of them tells me she must have gone to the bathroom. But I'm not mollified.

She can't be alone. Not here, with so many out to harm her.

I immediately zone in on Enzo. He's by an alcohol station, a bored expression on his face. He's staring into the half-empty glass he's holding, while the people around him are chatting away. His wife is next to him, but she's busy talking with her father.

"Catalina's missing." I go straight to the point when I see him. I have his attention right away, and he puts down his glass.

"We need to find her," he says, and we plan to cover the entire area.

"Where are you going?" His wife, Allegra, clings to his arm and pouts.

"I'm looking for my sister." His voice is tense as he tries to shake her off.

"*That*," Allegra's voice is full of venom as she refers to Catalina. "I'm sure she's off with someone." Before I can react, Enzo pushes her off.

He grasps her jaw in his hands, and in a callous voice he tells her, "Stop running your mouth if you want to keep this pretty face." He thrusts her backward, and with a scowl, he signals me to get moving.

After checking every single corner of the ballroom, I feel like I'm losing my mind. Where is she? The things crossing my mind are not helping one bit.

I check the bathrooms, a few women screaming at me and calling me a pervert, but I don't care.

I need to find Catalina.

Now.

I'm hyperventilating.

Minutes pass, I'm running around, and still no sign of her. I even check outside the hotel and in the parking lot, and she's not there.

"No luck?" Enzo looks as grim as I feel. I nod, and we enter the ballroom again. I'm ready to jump on Franco, convinced he's done something. After the aggression he'd displayed earlier....

I make a beeline for him, ready to shed blood.

But that's when I hear the whispers.

"*What did you expect? She willingly gave birth to a bastard.*"

"*Of course she'd lift her skirts for anyone.*"

"*But can you believe she'd actually try to seduce Michele? Such a slut.*"

"*Whore!*"

"*Slut!*"

The words are being thrown around so carelessly. A group of women is gathered around the other end of the ballroom, and everyone is busy gossiping.

Some are commenting on her lack of morals, others are just repeating what they'd heard or seen.

I block it all out.

All I see is Lina. My beautiful Lina is alone in a corner, her cheeks tear-stained. Her dress has been torn at the hem, and she's trying her best to stay strong.

Catalina's eyes meet mine, and a sob escapes her lips.

In two strides, I have her in my arms. I hold on to her, trying my best to comfort her.

"What happened?" I croak, barely in control of myself.

"He... He tried..." She starts, in between hiccups. Lina tries to explain how Michele had caught her in the bathroom and she'd fought him off. My hand is on her hair, caressing her lightly and trying to assure her she's safe now.

But I failed her.

It's like someone's squeezing my heart with an iron fist. I'd promised myself to never fail her again.

It's all my fault.

I hold tighter, hoping she'll tune out the vicious tongues wagging all around us.

"Don't listen to them," I whisper, ready to take her home. I quickly remove my blazer and place it around her shoulders, turning her towards the exit.

But then the loudest voice of them all has the gall to intervene.

Franco, preening like a peacock, steps forward, bringing new accusations with him.

"You see, everyone? You see how she's trying to ruin men? She's a Jezebel, I tell you. Driving good men to their doom!" He points his finger at her.

I place Lina behind me, intent on shielding her.

Franco continues.

"That's what you did to my son too, didn't you? You seduced him and then you fucking killed him. She's a murderess, everyone! A murderess Jezebel!" His voice gains in decibels, and more people join in, denigrating Lina with every word.

"I didn't!" Lina's voice surprises me as she responds. At first she's timid, but she steels her tone and continues. "He was a pedophile... He was touching my daughter." I look at her with awe in my eyes. What must it have taken for her to be able to make this claim?

Franco laughs ironically. "Aw, really? Like mother like daughter then. She's starting young."

Catalina gasps next to me, and I lose it.

No one. Absolutely no one speaks like that about Catalina or Claudia and gets away with it.

Before I know it, I grab a fork off the table.

CATALINA

osima takes me to a nearby table where a few other women in their thirties and forties are. They don't seem too pleased to see me. I become a little self-conscious when they just ignore me and start talking with one another.

I purse my lips and paint a pleasant smile on my face. I'd wanted to come here, so now I have to be strong and show them they can't bully me.

"Is that your son?" one of the women asks Cosima, pointing towards a drunk man.

"He's my stepson," Cosima grits her teeth.

"Oh, I forgot about that. What, with them being so close in age." Another woman joins in and jokes. I remember reading about their family, and that Benedicto Guerra has two sons by two different mothers. I'm assuming they are alluding to the fact that Benedicto had married Cosima barely a few days after his first wife had died.

"If only he saw me as his mother." Cosima feigns a sigh and proceeds to recount how hard she's tried to be a mother for Michele. "But he just hates me."

The other women start comforting her in an obviously fake manner, and I have to ask myself what I'm doing here.

"If you'll excuse me, I need to go to the restroom." I give them a tight smile and go towards the exit.

Inside the restroom, I turn on the faucet and splash some water on my face.

"I can do this," I look in the mirror and tell myself. I need to be strong...

Hard to do when I've never been in a situation like this before.

I take a deep breath, and I'm about to leave when the door bangs open, the drunk man from before striding inside.

"This is the women's restroom," I tell him, thinking he's just made a mistake.

"Is it?" His lip curls in a cruel smile. He advances inside, closing the door behind him.

"You should leave," I say with a little more conviction. I don't have a good feeling about this.

When I see that he's not moving, I decide to get out myself.

"Easy, there," he says mockingly, his fingers digging into my flesh.

"Let me go!"

"Now, why would I do that?" His manner is casual, but I can't help the shudder going through my body.

"Let go!" I try to get my arm out of his grasp, but he shoves me into the wall, crowding me.

"You know who I am, don't you?" His mouth is too close to me and I can smell the alcohol on his breath.

"Michele Guerra," I answer, moving my head to the side.

"Hmm." He pinches my chin between his fingers and turns it forcefully towards him.

I try not to show the fear I'm feeling. Instead, I look him in the eyes, all the while searching for the panic button Marcello had given me. It's a small device that will release a deafening noise if activated. He'd been so worried about our presence here that he'd thought about everything, bless his heart.

His fingers are rough and bruising on my face, but I try not to cry out. My hand is in my bag, searching for the panic button.

"Is this how you got my cousin? With this innocent look of yours?"

I don't reply.

"Answer me!"

I purse my lips.

"Bitch!" His movement is so sudden I can barely react. His hand shoots out and wraps itself around my throat. Instinctively, my arms go around his hold, trying to loosen the grip. My purse drops to the floor, all the contents spilling out.

No!

"Let go!" I groan, my hands kicking at his chest and face. He seems amused by my efforts, and he smirks.

"You poor thing," He coos derisively. "I wonder if one night between your thighs is really worth dying for."

Still choking me with one hand, he starts pulling at my gown with the other.

No! Not this! Not again!

My heart is racing, my mind almost blanking. Tears gather around the corner of my eyes.

"No, please. Don't do this to me!" I beg him, trying to push him off me.

He doesn't budge.

The back of his hand connects with my cheek so hard I'm seeing stars. I struggle to keep my balance, and he's once again tearing at my dress, his fingers skimming the inside of my thigh.

No!

I don't know what happens next. I start yelling like a banshee, limbs flailing and kicking.

I won't go down! I'm not letting him do this to me!

He seems momentarily surprised by me fighting back, but it's short-lived. He thrusts me towards the sinks, and my back hits the steel.

I reel from the pain.

He's struggling with his belt when the door opens, and some women gawk at us.

"Help..." My voice is hoarse as I try to call out, but they just giggle and leave.

No!

"You really think anyone's going to help you?" He mocks me as he holds me down.

He's trying to pull the dress over my hips when I see my chance. With as much force as I can muster, I bring my knee up and hit him. He groans, stumbling back and releasing me. I don't waste any time running out of the bathroom.

I need to find Marcello. I need him.

Just thinking about the *what-if* has me hysterical, tears running down my face.

I reach the ballroom and I desperately look around, trying to spot my husband.

And then I hear them.

Slut

Whore

Tart

My hands are trembling, but I try to hold my head high.

Everyone's talking about me, and what those women think they saw in the bathroom. How I'm so cheap I'm willing to lift my skirts for any man.

So many feelings threaten to overwhelm me – panic, embarrassment, fear.

But then I see him.

We make eye contact and I can finally breathe again.

He's here.

His eyes move around my body and I can only imagine what he's seeing... the state I'm in.

Marcello runs towards me and tugs me to his chest, holding me tight.

"What happened?" His voice is low and gruff.

"He... He tried..." I start. I can barely speak, but I tell him everything.

His hands tighten in my hair. The warmth emanating from his body makes me relax... He's here, that's all I need to know. When I'm with Marcello, I just know I'm safe. As he holds me, people continue to run their mouths, calling me all types of names.

I'm so embarrassed for Marcello. What must he think of me?

"Don't listen to them." His voice is for my ears only, and the pain in his eyes mirrors my own.

He drapes his blazer over my ruined dress and takes my hand, ready to leave.

But it's far from over.

Like the Red Sea, the crowd parts to reveal Franco, looking extremely smug.

"You see, everyone? You see how she's trying to ruin men? She's a Jezebel, I tell you. Driving good men to their doom!" Franco targets me directly, almost shoving his finger in my face.

Marcello places me behind him in a protective gesture.

"That's what you did to my son too, didn't you? You seduced him and then you fucking killed him. She's a murderess, everyone! A murderess Jezebel!" Why is everyone so against me? What did I ever do to them? I look around, and all I can see are accusing faces... hear derogatory words.

I close my eyes briefly, trying to escape the pressure building inside of me. But why do I bother? They've already branded me a whore and a murderess.

"I didn't!" I find my voice, surprising even myself. If they want a scandal, they will have one. I'll just state the truth.

"He was a pedophile... He was touching my daughter." People are quiet all around at my confession, but then Franco laughs.

"Aw, really? Like mother like daughter then. She's starting young."

I take a step back, my mouth hanging open in shock. He... Did he just... Tears are running down my face at this point. How can he say that?

I'm so shocked I barely register Marcello leaving my side. I immediately look for him, needing his presence.

He's maybe two steps away, his hand on a fork.

With inhuman speed, he flings the fork towards Franco, sharp side forward. Both the aim and the force must have been incredible because the fork embeds itself into Franco's right eye.

Everyone is staring in horror at the unfolding scene.

Franco is wailing in pain, clutching his bleeding eye. His knees give out, and he's on the floor, his body quivering.

Marcello looks at him without an ounce of empathy in his gaze. The change is so sudden, I can hardly believe my eyes.

I've never seen that expression on his face before. He turns slightly towards me and gives me a comforting nod.

What is he doing?

Marcello casually takes a glass of red wine from a nearby waiter and swirls the liquid inside.

"What did you say? I didn't hear you?" He plants himself in front of Franco and stoops down so he's on the same level.

"What did you say about my wife?" He asks again, his voice hard and unyielding.

Franco, like a fool, doesn't know when to stop.

"That she's a lying whore. And I bet her daughter's the same."

"Is that so..." Marcello narrows his eyes at him. "Should I remind you that the daughter in question is also *my* daughter?" Him claiming my daughter as his warms my heart in a way I'd never thought possible.

He doesn't wait for an answer as his hand grips the end of the fork and pulls hard. In one fluid motion, the fork comes off, together with Franco's eye. The blood pools down his face, and his screams echo in the room.

Marcello swirls the fork up in the air, looking at it with a bored expression.

"Anyone else have anything to say about my family?" He turns to face the crowd and dares anyone to say something.

There are hushed voices in the background, but no one outright intervenes. In a shocking gesture, Marcello drops the eye into his wine glass. He tips the glass up.

"Cheers," he says before downing the contents.

Some women are passing out, others are heaving and emptying the contents of their stomachs. Even some men look a little bit yellow in the face.

But no one says anything.

Marcello stops again in front of a bawling Franco and tells him something that I can't quite make out. Whatever it is, it's making Franco look even more ill than before.

"Did you say anything? I didn't hear you," Marcello says out loud.

A bloody Franco, still on his knees, does his best to crawl towards me.

"I'm sorry." His head is hung low, his voice laced with pain.

"Still didn't hear you," Marcello echoes, and Franco grits his teeth.

"I'm sorry." This time it's loud enough for everyone to hear.

Benedicto emerges from the back of the crowd, clapping.

"Bravo!" He shakes his head in admiration. "Bravo!"

He takes the glass still housing the eye from Marcello and comes towards his brother.

"What did I tell you, *fratello*?" He makes a tsk sound.

"How... how can you let him do this to me?" Franco stammers, his face taut with shock.

"I didn't. You did." He shrugs and then flips the glass so that the eyeball falls out on the ground.

Franco immediately makes a go for it, but Marcello is one step ahead of him – literally. There's a soft sound as the eye gets squished under Marcello's shoe, and Franco becomes hysterical.

I don't even have time to process as I'm being whisked away by my husband.

"What was that?" I whisper in confusion. The entire episode had been... I'm simply shocked.

"I may have implied that he can get his eye reattached, if some conditions are met."

"He can?" I ask in wonder.

"Not anymore."

We get inside the car, and the entire ride home, Marcello doesn't let go of my hand.

As he drives, I sneak glances at his profile, and I fall for him a little more.

For some people, his actions may seem too cruel, but for me, they meant the world. No one's publicly stood up for me before.

Marcello doesn't know it yet.

But he's just become my guardian angel.

———

THE MOMENT we make it home, he swoops me into his arms and takes me to my room.

"Shh, don't speak," he whispers in my hair as he lays me down on my bed, his wild eyes assessing my torn dress and my bruised flesh.

He turns his back to me and goes into the bathroom. I can hear the sound of water, and I think he's drawing me a bath.

"Marcello?" I ask tentatively.

He reemerges, coming towards me slowly. With an anguished look, he falls at my feet and puts his head on my lap.

"I'm so sorry. You have no idea how sorry... It's all my fault," he cries, his voice full of emotion.

My hand goes to his hair, and I slowly run my fingers through it.

"It's not your fault, love. It's not." How could he have prevented that man from assaulting me? In the women's restroom of all places.

"What you did for me... how you defended me." I shake my head, my eyes sparkling with unshed tears. "No one's ever done that before. No one's stood up for me like that. And because of that, you're my hero," I tell him tenderly.

"I'm no one's hero," he speaks after a brief pause. "Hero... me," he gives a dry laugh. "If you only knew..."

His hands come around my middle, and he hugs me.

"So sorry," he keeps mumbling.

We stay like that for a while, and I revel in the warmth of his body next to mine. I feel safe... so safe. Taking me in his arms once again, he enters the bathroom, placing me next to the almost-filled tub. Marcello looks conflicted as his gaze moves from me to the tub and back to me.

"I..." he starts but shakes his head. "I'll be outside." He visibly swallows before turning to leave.

"Wait, please!" The words are out of my mouth before I can overthink it.

"Stay." I don't know where this courage is coming from, but as I look into his eyes, I know I can do this. I can show him my most vulnerable self.

With shaky fingers, I pull at the side zipper of my dress and shimmy out of it. I'm now standing only in my bra and underwear. Marcello's gaze darkens as it moves over my form, and a shiver goes up my spine.

I can do this!

Before I chicken out, I stretch my arms behind me and snap the clasp of my bra, letting it fall.

"Lina," Marcello groans, and my cheeks heat up in embarrassment.

With what courage I have left, I quickly take off my underwear and climb inside the tub.

The scorching temperature of the water gives me goosebumps, and I grit my teeth at the painful heat.

It doesn't take me long to get accustomed to the water. I gaze up and see that Marcello is still standing in the doorway, his eyes fixed on me.

"Can you help me?" I lift up a sponge and hold it to him. I don't know where this is coming from... this forwardness... but I don't want him to leave.

He comes towards me, folding the sleeves of his shirt. When he's next to the tub, he kneels down and takes the sponge from my hands.

He lathers a good amount of liquid soap onto the sponge and then starts to tend to my arm. His movements are slow, the feel of the sponge soft on my skin.

He moves up to my collarbone, and I have to swallow hard at the sensation. I sneak a glance at him, and he's not unaffected either. Marcello tends to both of my arms before getting ready to move to my back.

I grab his hand, suddenly remembering what he's about to see.

"It's not pretty," I whisper, but slowly turn my back to him.

I'm afraid of his reaction. I can't see it, but I can tell he's shocked by his immediate intake of breath.

"Lina..." his voice is soft, his breath almost touching my skin. Then I realize how close he is to me.

"Mar..." I trail off when I feel his lips on my back, right where my scar begins. He starts tracing the contour of the scar with his lips, and my eyes tear up.

"You're beautiful, Lina. So, so beautiful." His voice is like a balm to my heart. There's this warmth... I don't think I've ever felt like this before. This emotion, bigger than life, expands in my chest and seeks to get out. I tense, painfully gripping the edge of the tub.

Dear Lord, what is this feeling?

The sponge touches my skin again, and Marcello continues with his ministrations. By the time he's done, I'm breathing hard, and I don't know whether it's from the steam in the water or...

He brings me a towel and helps me out, cocooning me. He takes me back to the bed.

"Thank you. For this." He takes my hand and brings it to his lips for a light kiss.

As I look into his eyes, I find myself hypnotized.

"Don't leave. Stay with me, please."

"Lina, you have no idea what you're asking."

"I do... I want this. I want you."

For the first time, I want to be in control of what happens with my body. And God, do I want him. He's all that's kind and good, and I don't even know what I've done to deserve him.

He's simply everything.

My fingers caress his cheek, and I lean forward to lay a kiss on his lips, wanting to show him how much I want this.

"Are you sure?" he asks me, his voice barely above a whisper.

I nod.

"Please."

His hand comes up my neck, and he cups my jaw, drawing me into his kiss. I part my lips to allow him inside, my tongue seeking his.

I fall back on the bed, taking him with me. My towel's hanging open, and I try to fit my body to his, wanting to feel closer.

His hands start tracing down my ribcage, and I shiver from the feather-like touch.

"Do you have protection?" I suddenly remember to ask. I know he's said he wants children in the future, but I don't want to assume he meant in the near future.

He lifts his head for a fraction, his pupils so dilated his eyes are almost black.

"No." He pauses. "But I'm clean. I haven't been with anyone in over a decade." His words surprise me. I'd never imagined a man like Marcello would be celibate for that long. But given his problem with touch... I see how that might impact things. And it makes me feel incredibly honored he's sharing this part of himself with me.

"Me neither," I reply. "I've never made love before." I blush at the words and instinctively lower my head in embarrassment. Technically, I can't even say I've had sex before... not with how my first and only time went, or how little I remember of it.

"Hey." He tips my head up. "I've never made love either. I may have been with others before, but it wasn't... my choice." A small grimace appears on his face. "So this is a first for both of us, okay?"

"Okay." I barely breathe the word out before his mouth is on mine once more. He kisses me for what seems like forever before he moves up, trailing kisses all over my face – my nose, my temples, my forehead.

"I can pull out. I know there is still a risk but..."

"No, don't. I want you, all of you." I want to be his, and I want him to be mine. Any children we may have would be nothing but a blessing.

His expression softens at my words, and he regales me with the most precious smile I've ever seen. My heart is about to burst in my chest.

With a determined look in his eyes, Marcello lifts himself up and swiftly removes his shirt. My gaze lingers on his exposed torso, taking in the defined muscles and smooth skin that I had tried so hard not to stare at before. But now, with permission, I can admire him to my heart's content. He takes my hand and gently guides it onto the plane of his stomach, urging me to explore further.

My fingers tentatively trail over the hard ridges of his abdomen, tracing the curves and dips with fascination. His skin is warm and firm under my touch, a stark contrast to my own softness. Just as I begin to gain more confidence, he stops me and presses a tender kiss to my knuckles before guiding me back onto the bed.

His lips are everywhere, igniting wave after wave of sensation throughout my body.

A whimper escapes my lips when he reaches my breasts, skillfully teasing and sucking at one nipple while gently massaging the other with his hand. Is this how it's supposed to be done? The thought quickly disappears from my mind as he continues to play my body like an expert musician. Every touch elicits a response from me, driving me closer to the edge.

But then he goes lower, leaving a trail of kisses down my stomach until he reaches the apex of my thighs. Heat rushes through me as his breath fans over my most intimate place. I shiver in anticipation as he carefully parts my thighs to accommodate his shoulders, bringing himself even closer.

"Marcello!" His name on my lips starts as a question, but as his tongue meets my flesh, it ends on an exclamation.

A mixture of scandal and intrigue floods through me as Marcello groans against my skin, his tongue sending waves of pleasure through my body. Every touch, every kiss, feels like a miracle as I gasp and writhe beneath him.

"You're my fucking miracle," he rasps, his words igniting a fire within me that only he can quench. My hands find their way into his hair, urging him on as he continues to explore every inch of my body with slow, deliberate movements.

With each nibble and suck, he brings me closer to the edge until my limbs start to spasm in pure bliss. And then it happens—an explosion of sensation that leaves me gasping for air. My eyes are wide open in wonder.

I think I heard angels sing!

As I come down from the high, my hands are still gripping onto Marcello's arms for support. As I catch my breath, I can't help but ask.

"What was that?" I huff out, feeling both exhausted and amazed at the same time.

"The most beautiful thing I've ever seen in my life," he replies with tenderness in his eyes.

He moves back from me, his body glistening with a light sheen of sweat. With fluid movements, he raises himself and undresses, peeling off his pants and underwear to reveal his naked form.

My cheeks flush with heat as I instinctively try to shield my eyes. But Marcello's touch on my face is gentle and reassuring.

"We can stop if you want," he offers, sensing my reaction.

But I shake my head vehemently. No, I don't want to stop. It's just... the first time I'm seeing him like this.

Slowly, I force myself to look at him. It's Marcello. My beloved Marcello. There's nothing to be afraid of. I focus my gaze on his chest, taking in every ridge and muscle, before letting my eyes wander downward towards the v of his stomach and finally settling on the hard length between his legs that twitches eagerly in my direction.

"That... can't possibly fit!" The words escape my lips without thought, horror evident in my widened eyes. I know how this works, and there is no way that thing will fit inside of me. Memories of the painful experience last time flood my mind, and I unconsciously start to back away.

But Marcello is quick to reassure me. "It will fit, I promise you." He takes my hand and guides it down between my own legs, pressing it against the slick folds already damp with arousal. "Feel how wet you are for me?" His fingers replace mine and begin stroking up and down in a mesmerizing rhythm.

I can feel the embarrassment rising within me at how easily he can make me wet with desire, but his next words erase all thoughts of shame from my mind. "You're so soaked, you're going to take me in like you were always meant to, Lina." His voice is smooth and commanding, and I can't help but nod in response.

In a trance-like state, I open my arms and legs to him, inviting him closer. He covers me with his body, his hardness pressing against my center.

"Relax, don't be afraid," he whispers in my hair, brushing his fingers along my cheek in a soothing gesture.

I swallow down my anxiety as his words wash over me. "I'm not afraid... Not with you." And in that moment, I trust him completely.

Never with you.

As he enters me, a wave of pleasure washes over me. He surges forward slowly, stretching me bit by bit, and there's no pain, only the feeling of being filled and completed by him.

I wrap my legs around his back, pulling him closer and tilting my pelvis to take him even deeper inside of me. The sensation is incredible.

"Fuck!" He mutters, his voice strained with desire. "You feel so good, Lina. You're mine," he rasps against my ear, sending shivers down my spine. "You were made for me, angel. Only for me." He pauses, fully seated in my body, as we both relish in the moment of being connected.

"Tell me I can move," he pleads, his voice laced with urgency and need.

"Please!" I urge him, wrapping my arms tightly around his back and pressing our chests together. The added friction ignites a delicious fire between us as we begin to move together.

My hands roam over his back, and I can feel some indentations that mirror my own. But before I can dwell on it too much, he retreats and then thrusts back into me.

A moan escapes my lips at the delicious sensation.

"I never knew..." I start to say but am cut off as he groans and kisses me hungrily. Our bodies continue to move together in perfect rhythm.

He picks up speed, and I feel something building inside of me. It's similar to before but somehow different.

"Ah!" I cry out as he moves one hand between us, lightly stroking my clit. The pleasure intensifies, and I find myself clenching onto him as everything overwhelms me at once.

"It's too much," I gasp.

"I've got you," he whispers, knowing exactly what I need as he continues to move his hand between my legs.

And then it happens, the most intense release I've ever experienced. He comes too, filling me with a warm liquid before he collapses on top of me.

"Fuck!" He curses and quickly rolls us over so that I'm on top of him. "I didn't crush you, did I?"

But all I can focus on is the tenderness in his eyes as he looks at me with love and adoration. And I know in that moment that we are perfect together.

"Perfect... so perfect," I murmur, feeling completely fulfilled in every way.

My lids feel heavy, and the safety of knowing Marcello is by my side lulls me to sleep.

So perfect...

MARCELLO

My eyes flutter open to the warmth of a body pressed against mine. For a moment, I am disoriented and filled with panic at the unfamiliar sensation of another person so close to me. But as my mind begins to clear, I remember exactly who is lying next to me and what happened between us last night.

Lina's head is nestled in the crook of my shoulder, her soft breaths tickling my skin. Her hand rests on my chest, moving up and down in a gentle rhythm, while one leg is draped over mine. She looks like an angel in her peaceful slumber... so beautiful and serene.

I take a deep breath, savoring the moment and all the emotions that come with it. Just a few months ago, I never would have believed that I could be this intimate with another woman. And yet here I am, having spent the night with someone special.

And she's not just anyone. This is Catalina... the woman who has captured my heart for the past decade. The one who got away... until now.

Gently, I reach out and caress her hair, inhaling her sweet scent. I wish time could stand still forever. If only we could live in this blissful state for eternity...

But then she stirs in her sleep, turning towards me and pressing her backside into my groin, rubbing against my leg unconsciously. My body responds immediately, aching for her touch.

With great effort, I bring my hand up to my forehead to stifle a groan. Last night was beyond anything I could have imagined... the passion, the desire, the raw connection between us. I never dared to hope that she would welcome me into her bed... or into her body so soon.

I'd been completely honest with her when I told her I'd never made love to a woman before.

Everything had been just as new for me, too. From the feel of her skin against mine, to the sound of her moans and the look of her coming. I felt like an addict being introduced to a new substance. Her lips slightly parted, her pussy gripping me tight. The way she'd tentatively touched me.

I shut my eyes tightly, feeling the guilt of my actions assault me.

I didn't deserve it... any of it. And yet I took what was not mine to take. So greedy, so insatiable I'd been for her touch that I made myself forget everything. In that moment, there had been just us. No past, no mistakes. Just two people feeling deeply for each other.

At least I assumed that's how she feels. Catalina is not the type of person who'd go to bed with someone she didn't care for. And that's the biggest gift of them all—her affection. I don't dare call it love because...

I shake my head slightly at the thought, melancholy setting over me. I'm not someone she should love, but I'll take any scraps she can spare.

If she only knew how deep my feelings run for her. I turn my head and take in her sleeping form. Lina has no idea just how much I love her. She doesn't even remember me. Yet, I do. That one act of kindness is forever etched in my soul.

"Mhmm..." She murmurs sleepily, stretching next to me. Slowly, she lifts her head, a dreamy smile on her face. She seeks the warmth of my body, her face nuzzling my cheek.

Fuck!

My body is on fire, my cock aching and throbbing with desire. Each touch from her innocent hands ignites a new wave of heat within me, making it harder and harder to control myself. I try to focus on something else, anything else, but Lina's soft curves pressed against me are impossible to ignore.

Her delicate hand brushes against my chest, her breasts pressing into me with each breath she takes. My mind is spinning as I struggle to keep my composure.

"Lina," I groan, the sensations overwhelming me. My hand instinctively goes to her thigh, intending to move it away from my throbbing erection. But once it's there, I can't help but let it trail higher towards her round ass.

"Lina?" I breathe out, my fingers creeping closer and closer to her center. Her voice is barely audible as she whispers my name in response.

"Mhmmm..." She whimpers when I cup her ass, a shiver running through her body as my touch sends electricity through her veins.

"Are you sore?" I ask softly, my finger dipping between her cheeks and towards her wetness. She moans as I enter her lightly, pushing herself onto my finger and taking me deeper inside.

"No," she gasps, her voice breathy and filled with need. I use my thumb to glide over her clit, circling it faster and faster until she begins to tremble. Her walls tighten around my finger and I turn my attention to her face, watching as she surrenders to her orgasm.

"I..." She stammers as she comes down from her high, a beautiful smile spreading across my face at the thought of giving her pleasure.

Her small hand starts to move down my chest, wrapping around my now fully erect cock. The feeling of her tiny hand grasping at my girth only adds fuel to the fire that's been consuming me since the moment I woke up.

"Is this okay?" She looks up at me, her eyes wide and full of innocent interest.

I part my lips to respond to her, but before I can speak, she tightens her grip on me and moves down. A strangled sound escapes from deep within me.

"Lina..." I manage to choke out, unable to form any coherent thoughts as she takes control.

"What do I do?" Her voice is laced with uncertainty.

I gently cover her hand with mine and guide it up and down, from base to tip. Her focus is solely on getting it right, her teeth nibbling at her bottom lip and her brows furrowed in concentration.

The more she teases me, the harder it becomes for me to hold back.

With great effort, I stop her.

"Did I do something wrong?" Her question comes out small and hesitant.

"No, no. I just...want to be inside you when I come." I turn towards her and tuck a stray strand of hair behind her ear. "I *need* to be inside you," I all but beg.

"Okay." She gives me a tentative smile, and I have to resist the urge to flip her over and ravish her like a wild animal.

Instead, I guide her on top of me, one leg on each side of my body. Confusion flashes across Lina's face as she settles against my hard length. The wetness between her legs makes it easy for me to slide against her as she grinds against my pelvis.

Gripping my cock with one hand, I position it at her entrance. She lowers herself onto me slowly until I'm fully buried inside of her.

"Oh." A soft whimper escapes from her lips as she leans forward, placing her hands on my chest for support.

Lina begins to wiggle her hips slightly, causing a jolt of pleasure to shoot through me. My head falls back at the sensation.

"Yes, just like that." I praise her, my hands guiding her movements as we find a rhythm together.

Soon she finds her own pace, and she starts riding me as if we've done this a thousand times in the past.

I like watching her like this. In control. Taking me.

My arm snakes around her waist and I bring her closer to my torso, my mouth seeking her neck. I trail wet kisses all along her jaw before I take her mouth, kissing her again.

She increases the speed, her hands clutching tightly at my hair. She's about to come. I can feel it in the urgency of her movements, the intensity of her kisses.

Her walls clamp down on my cock and I hold her as she shudders.

"Fuck!" I mutter and I turn her on her back, my hands on her ass as I thrust faster into her, chasing my own orgasm.

"Marcello," she moans, her head thrown back, her mouth agape.

"I..." She trails off and she comes again as I empty myself inside of her.

———

AFTER WE'VE BOTH SHOWERED, we head down to breakfast. Surprisingly, Venezia and Claudia are already in the living room. Venezia is sitting down dutifully on the edge of the couch and Claudia is playing with her hair.

"And what are you doing there, little troublemaker?" Lina stops next to the pair, observing Claudia's work.

"I'm trying a style I saw on the internet. I'm not very good though. I don't know how you always do it, mamma." Claudia frowns, her hands moving in Venezia's hair, folding and twisting.

"Show me what you're going for."

Claudia takes out her phone and gives it to Lina.

"Hmm, I think you should have parted it this way." She moves in and takes a comb, helping them.

They are both focused on what they're doing. Venezia patiently withstands their ministrations as they go about trying and failing and then trying again.

As I take a seat in front of her, I can't help but notice the subtle change in Venezia. Her posture is more relaxed and her expression less guarded. She bites her lip hesitantly, before admitting with some reluctance, "It's... nice."

I'm surprised by her easy surrender and realize that she has slowly changed since Catalina came to live with us. Gone is the bratty and rude girl, replaced by someone who is coming out of her shell.

"Mrs. Evans praised your progress," I mention, watching as her expression changes from shock to pleasure.

"She did?"

"Yes, she said you are taking your lessons seriously, and that you'll catch up in no time if you continue."

"That's... nice of her," Venezia responds, lowering her head. But Claudia interrupts, pulling on a strand of her hair and causing her to yelp in pain.

"Sorry," Claudia quickly apologizes.

I expect Venezia to snap back at Claudia like she used to. But instead, she just gives a brisk nod and remains calm.

"I want you to know that as long as you put in your effort and get your GED, you're free to go to any college you want," I tell her sincerely.

"You mean that?" Venezia seems genuinely surprised, and it makes me feel guilty for not properly communicating my expectations.

"Of course. You can become anything you want," I add, glancing at Catalina who gives me a nod of approval.

"Thank you... wow. That means a lot," Venezia says gratefully.

"Me too!" Claudia chimes in enthusiastically.

I raise my eyebrows at her.

"And what do you want to become?" I ask.

"A lawyer," she beams, her smile radiant and full of ambition. "Like you."

My heart flutters painfully in my chest.

"Like me?" I repeat in wonder.

"Yes, Mamma told me about how you put bad guys away," Claudia says, her voice filled with enthusiasm. "I want to do that too!"

My gaze turns to Catalina, who seems slightly embarrassed.

"I hope you don't mind that I told her about your job," she says, two pink dots marring her cheeks.

I'm suddenly overwhelmed with humility and gratitude toward both of them.

"Not at all," I hurry to reassure them. "What kind of bad guys would you put away, Claudia?"

Her eyebrows furrow as she purses her lips in deep thought. She looks so cute in that moment.

"Those bad nuns, like Mother Superior or Sister Celeste," she answers finally. "They were always mean to me, Mamma, and Aunt Sisi. One time..."

"I don't think Marcello wants to hear that, sweetie," Catalina interrupts gently.

"No, let her speak," I insist.

Claudia shrugs before continuing. "They would call my mother horrible names and give her more chores than the other sisters.

And when she got sick, they wouldn't even allow her to see a doctor."

"Claudia!" Catalina gasps in shock and dismay.

I turn to look at her, needing confirmation that these accusations are true. My heart clenches at the thought of anyone mistreating them.

"Is that true?" I ask Catalina softly.

"It is! I understand more than you think." Claudia looks at her mother with sad eyes.

And it hurts. It hurts to know how badly they've been treated, and there was no one there to defend them.

"You don't have to worry about your mother ever being mistreated again, Claudia. I promise you," I assure both of them.

She regards me with hopeful eyes and sticks out her hand, her little finger in the air. "Pinky promise?"

I look at the raised finger, and then I look back at her. She's smiling, and I can't find it in me to refuse her.

I hold my breath and slowly wrap my little finger around hers.

"Yay!" She jumps up, removing her hand from mine.

My finger is still in the air. The contact had been so brief... but I did it.

I look up and Catalina is gazing at me with such tenderness... I almost want to think it's love.

"I want to be a policeman then," Venezia suddenly intervenes and crosses her arms in front of her, almost put off that we hadn't included her in the conversation. "They *catch* the bad guys," she says smugly.

"But..." Claudia frowns. "You're not a man."

"Why would I be a man?" Venezia suddenly turns.

"Well... it's policeman, right? So it's a job for a man."

"Women can be police officers too. Think of policewomen if you want," I explain. "I told you, you can be whatever you want. Your gender shouldn't stop you. Just replace the 'man' in the profession with 'woman' and you can do it."

Both Claudia and Venezia look pensive but agree with my observation.

In the meantime, Amelia comes in and informs us that breakfast is ready.

The girls race towards the dining room, while I stay behind and offer Lina my arm.

"You were great, you know?" She rises on her tiptoes to give me a kiss.

"I meant everything I said."

"I know. You're the best." Her eyes are sparkling with warmth, and I take her mouth for a quick kiss.

"Damnation!" A voice curses out.

I look to see Assisi on top of the stairs shielding her eyes.

"Sisi?"

My sister casually comes down the stairs, ignoring Lina's question.

"Sisi, wait!" She says as Assisi makes a left for the dining room.

"What?" She huffs out a breath.

"What's that?"

Lina's hand goes to Assisi's neck and she moves her hair aside to reveal a red spot.

"Are you ill?" She asks, worried about her friend.

"What? No... something must have bitten me." She stammers, her eyes looking anywhere but at Lina. "I'm hungry. I'll see you in the dining room."

"Odd..." Lina remarks once she's back by my side.

"I agree." I frown. I'd noticed for a while now that Assisi's behavior had changed. I don't claim to know her well enough to comment on her personality, but she's completely different from what she'd been like in the beginning.

And there's also the matter of her being extremely secretive, even with Lina. She's taken to not getting out of her room, and that worries me.

"Guerra wants Assisi to meet his son," I tell her, grimacing at the thought. I explain our conversation and that I'd tried to refuse.

"Where does that leave us?" she asks, nibbling on her bottom lip.

"I agreed to a casual meeting, nothing more. I couldn't refuse and risk a confrontation. Or I should say *another* confrontation. But don't worry. I told him it would be Assisi's decision in the end. Nothing's going to happen."

"I hope so," she whispers, but clearly she isn't convinced.

"Think of it as keeping our enemies close," I add.

Because certain things just don't add up. And I mean to discover who exactly is terrorizing my family.

———

"I DIDN'T THINK I'd be sitting in a room with you two again." Adrian crosses his arms as he regards me and Vlad.

We moved to the study to discuss things of a more confidential nature. Catalina, Claudia, and Venezia are still in the living room, chatting. Assisi had been rather abrupt in her departure, but given her behavior lately, it wasn't entirely too surprising.

"I didn't think so either," I reply drily. In all honesty, I didn't think Adrian would ever forgive me for what I'd done. After visiting him in the hospital, he'd dropped by to tell me he's had some time to think things through, and while he doesn't know if he can forgive me, he's willing to try. It had been such good news, considering he's my dearest friend.

"Come on, boys, don't be so pessimistic." Vlad makes a tsk sound, getting up from his chair and pacing around, his eyes perusing the stacks of books in the library.

"Why don't we just get to the point?"

"The point." Vlad twirls around, raising an eyebrow. Adrian groans out loud.

It's well known they don't get along. Adrian has a strong dislike of Vlad because of his close relationship with his wife, Bianca.

For all our old acquaintance, not even *I* knew about Vlad and Bianca's partnership. They've known each other for some ten years, being partnered up for assassination jobs. Vlad is somewhat of a loose cannon with his rage issues, so Bianca ended up being the perfect partner for him with her cool temper. Not to mention that she literally had his back in missions. Vlad prefers reckless close-range killing, whereas Bianca is addicted to her pistols and rifles.

I glare at Vlad, my patience wearing thin. He always seems to be on the move, never able to stay in one place for too long. "You said you had news," I remind him sharply.

"News? Oh, indeed." He nonchalantly pulls a pack of gum from his pocket and pops a piece into his mouth. Lazily, he takes a seat on the edge of my desk, stretching out his legs in front of him.

I narrow my eyes at him as Adrian speaks up, curious about this so-called news. "How did you get in touch with Quinn?"

"The normal way." Vlad's tone is dismissive, as if resorting to violence is just another mundane task for him. "I dropped by his gym."

My gut tells me there's more to this than he's letting on.

"As I was saying," Vlad continues, unfazed by our skepticism. "Quinn wasn't behind the recent attacks. He believes it wasn't his father either. Things have been chaotic since Jimenez's death."

"Chaotic how?" I press, wanting more information.

"They've lost their backing and resources. They may even need to leave New York and return to Boston." Vlad chews thoughtfully before adding, "Quinn was surprisingly cooperative when I spoke to him. It's unusual for him."

"After Jimenez's death, all the cartels under his control started vying for power," Vlad explains further. "Even Ortega is making moves to strengthen his position and bring others onto his side. The empire that Jimenez built is already crumbling."

"That makes sense with the data I have too," Adrian adds. "I've spoken with some people. I thought I should take advantage of this while I'm still *alive*." He jokes, referring to his plan to fake his death. "As Jimenez's son and designated heir, I would be the first target if anyone wanted to recreate Jimenez's reach. There have been a lot of petty crimes reported in the last month. If you compare that with previous months and previous years, it's definitely an outlier."

"So you think that because they suddenly found themselves sans leadership they just went crazy?"

"It would make sense. The issue is not the crime rate. It's the fact that these people are ripe for plucking. Anyone could come along and give them a purpose. And *that* would make them danger-ous," Vlad comments, his eyes suddenly focused.

"Well, whatever happens, I'm out of this particular issue." Adrian raises his palms, imitating a surrender gesture.

"It's something I'm monitoring," Vlad gives him a look. "After all, it's my job to make sure the market remains in equilibrium." He winks at me. "But I don't think it's going to happen right *now*, which gives our shipment problem priority. That and the fact that whoever did it tried to blame the Irish." He shoves some more gum in his mouth before continuing. "Although, there is one thing that I've noticed."

Both Adrian and I look at him expectantly. There's no denying that for all his instability, Vlad is brilliant – and even brilliant might be an understatement.

"There's suddenly a lot more clamor within the five families. Your new involvement notwithstanding, I don't think there's been so much traffic in New York since..." he bites the inside of his cheek, trying to find his words, "the '90s. You only have to look at who's present. When was the last time that the Marchesi stepped foot in the city? What about Guerra? I don't for one second buy that the banquet was to threaten you. I bet Benedicto doesn't even care that his wastrel nephew died."

He takes a deep breath, and I can see he's getting excited. Of course, Vlad always gets excited when it comes to chaos and mayhem, and this seems like the perfect recipe for him. "And lastly, we have DeVille. They've been the most active. If I were Benedicto, I'd watch my back."

"You forgot Enzo."

He dismisses my words with his hands.

"And you forget I have ears in his office." He chuckles. "He's floundering, although nothing to do with business. There are a few things I found that are... titillating. I would have never guessed that about him." He smiles sheepishly, and both Adrian and I are waiting for him to reveal what he knows.

"He's not going to tell." Adrian shakes his head, already resigned.

"I won't have to. It's going to come out sooner or later." Vlad shrugs.

"Anyway," I start, moving away from that particular subject. "From what you're describing, I'm getting the sense that you suspect one of the five families."

"Bingo." His hand shoots out, and he points at me with a fake smile. "Although," his smile immediately falls, replaced by a slight frown, "they made a mistake in that they involved me too. Now I feel compelled to intervene." He says in all seriousness.

"As if you wouldn't have otherwise," I reply drily. He's always involved in other people's business.

"You might be right on that, but not with so much pathos. I'm already losing sleep over this."

"I think you're losing sleep for other reasons." Adrian chuckles.

"Hastings, did you just make a joke?" Vlad turns to him, scandalized. "You might be saved still." Vlad leans towards him to whisper, not too quietly. "P.S. though, it wasn't *that* funny."

"Anyway," I clear my throat again, sensing the impending conflict. "If it's one of the families, then that changes things. I'll try to be more vigilant," I say, already going through everything that happened at the banquet and cataloguing everyone who was in attendance.

"Good, because you have a bigger problem on your plate. I've had someone run an analysis on this Chimera's work." He tosses a file on the desk.

"I see." I frown as I go through the reports. Every single Chimera incident had happened at the same time I'd been in the area. It's uncanny.

"It's personal," I utter out loud what I've been thinking for a while now. "And Catalina's being targeted because whoever it is knows what she means to me."

Vlad nods, his gaze intense.

"It has to be someone around you. Who else would know Chimera's M.O. to a T? Another question is why *now*?"

"See, the ones that we *know of* started two years ago. I think they're trying to play with me."

"Mind games. Could be."

"The only other person who would be so intimately aware of Chimera is dead," I add, knowing both of them will catch my meaning.

"And dead people don't go around killing other people," Adrian replies drily. "I asked around, and the FBI is seeing the cases as top priority. They've brought in some famous forensic psychologists and criminal profilers, and they had a few things to say."

"Go on," I nod at Adrian, curious for any insight.

"There was more care given to females. And they were always accompanied by some sort of religious symbol. There was one instance in which the female had a cross carved in her palm, another where the cross was physically present next to the corpse.

The opinions are split, really. One profiler said it might be some internalized misogyny, going on about how the woman is inferior to the man in different religious interpretations. Then another suggested the opposite, that the killer is giving special care to females, and that it might be a case of recreating a certain type of death all over. Conversely, the males are always subjected to the worst treatments, and their corpses are the ones desecrated."

"That's..." I frown, thinking back to the nun. I turn to Vlad and see he's thinking the same.

"Theoretically speaking, the nun wasn't desecrated. It was almost like an offering, with how the organs were put on display. The religious symbols are certainly most prevalent in this instance."

"You're right. And the position of the teeth inside her cavity... her womb," I add pensively.

"I think it's a man," Vlad suddenly says, standing up. "If my previous theory is right, then the nun offered herself up, exactly as an offering. Why would a woman do that for another woman? Now, I'm sure it could be a case of sapphic love, but what are the odds, really? My bet is on a man though – a very charming man. And you're right about the placement of the teeth. We have to think about this as the killer would – every detail is intentional. The teeth could be interpreted as some symbol of fertility; he's laying his seed in her body."

"Was the nun also sexually assaulted?" I don't remember reading that in the forensic report.

"No, she wasn't. But then none of the other victims were either."

"Right, purity not profanity," I say, going back to the very basic concepts that religion and Chimera both have in common.

"Yes, the women are treated almost reverently, and the men oppositely."

"I think we're going off the deep end," Adrian puts a hand up. "You're looking into this too much. Do you really think everything is a symbol?"

"That's the thing. The original Chimera's M.O. was to appeal to the baser instincts. He would intentionally use any personal references to elicit a strong reaction," Vlad mentions, giving me a side glance.

"Then why don't we try to look at the clues through Marcel's lens? If he is the target, then the symbols are directly connected to him."

"A woman with strong religious connections?" I give a dry laugh. "I think I know a few of those."

"Right," Vlad suddenly says, pursing his lips. "Well, let's take them one by one."

MARCELLO

AGE FIFTEEN

With one last slash, I throw the knife to the ground and grab a cloth to wipe the blood off. I head to the bathroom and look at myself in the mirror.

Damn, the blood really got everywhere this time. Even my blonde hair is now splattered with red. I turn on the faucet and splash some water on my face.

When I return to the room, Father is already there inspecting my work.

There are four lifeless bodies on the floor. This had been one of my more intensive torture sessions, since they didn't seem to fear a teenager as they would an adult.

I'd set to prove them wrong.

It had taken me two hours to break the first man. The others had quickly followed, which proved my theory that they would be more malleable if they were to see what happened to their friends.

Father stoops low and inspects the mortal blows, his brows furrowed.

"Are you sure you got everything?" He moves over to the next corpse and does the same.

"Yes, sir," I answer, addressing him with his due.

"That was fast." He stands up, looking pensive. "I have to say, boy," he pauses and I mentally cringe at his use of *boy,* "I am impressed." He doesn't look like it. In fact, his expression shows how much it cost him to admit this. After all, I am always the disappointment.

I don't reply. Even his praise can't affect me anymore. If anything, I find myself growing colder.

"I think it's finally time for the next step." Father narrows his eyes at me, almost reluctant for what's to come.

I simply nod.

In the last years, I've learned that the less I talk, the less I reveal of myself to the world. This way, no one will find any faults or weaknesses in me.

I simply am.

My existence is to serve the famiglia and to do Father's dirty work. I've come to terms with the fact that I can be nothing more.

I am, but I am *not.*

Even the notion of pain can't faze me anymore. Physical pain is just that – physical and as such ephemeral. I can close my eyes and dissociate.

Emotional pain... That doesn't go away. So I do the only thing I can. I stop feeling.

"I'll have someone clean this up." He points to the dead bodies before adding, "Let's see how you'll fare in the position I have in mind." He turns to the exit.

I give him a brisk nod, following.

"There is a reason people don't mess with us." Father continues as he leads me towards an area of the basement I haven't been to until now.

"Not that they don't want to, but that they don't dare." He smirks, pride reflected in his gaze.

He opens the door, and inside I see a man strapped to a chair.

The room is much smaller than any of the others, but I've never seen so many instruments of torture in one place before.

"There's a tradition in our family. The younger sons are trained to serve their capo, which is what I've been doing with you until now. Every test I've given you has been for this." He motions me towards the center of the room.

"You've proven yourself to be beyond my expectations." Father muses, and it's the first time he doesn't scowl at me. "But now you must pass your biggest test yet."

"Yes, sir," I confirm. What can be worse than what I've been through so far? I almost want to laugh at that thought.

Yes, Father's done something alright, and that's erasing what little humanity I had left.

"You see," he starts as he surveys the instruments of torture, "there's always one eminent student who gets to do *this*." Unexpectedly, Father is excited about something.

"When someone wrongs the famiglia, we have to give back retribution. But our kind of retribution is a little different."

He takes a long knife, testing its sharpness by running it along his forefinger.

"We hit where it hurts the most, and we let them know *why* and *who* did it."

Father saunters to the prisoner and using the tip of the knife he removes his gag.

"Romero Santos. Want to tell my son about your crime? You have your chance to confess your sins." Father's lips are drawn in a sardonic smile.

I move my gaze to the prisoner and regard him as he's breathing deeply, sweat falling down his face.

"I didn't know, I swear. I thought she was eighteen." His voice is pleading, and his eyes jump between me and Father before settling on me. In a pleading tone, he addresses me.

"Please, please! I have a family."

"Exactly!" Father interjects, slapping the man behind his head. "And your family will know what you've done. This should show people what happens when you mess with someone in our famiglia."

"What happened?" I finally utter, aiming the question at my father.

"Nothing, I swear. She wanted it!" Eyes bulging, shoulders slumped, the man is trying his best to profess his innocence.

Annoyed at the outburst, Father places the knife, sharp edge inward, in Romero's mouth.

"Now he's quiet." He shakes his head, exasperated. "This man, who by the way is twenty-eight, seduced and impregnated the daughter of one of our soldiers."

I tilt my head, taking in the information.

So?

I don't voice that question, as Father continues.

"She's twelve."

My expression changes immediately, my eyes blanking.

"Rape?" I turn to Father.

"Does it matter?" he asks, shrugging his shoulders. Of course it wouldn't matter to Father. For him, rape isn't that bad of an offense in the first place. It's not as if I don't hear his new wife screaming all the time in the house.

No, this is about pride. Romero dared to touch a daughter of the famiglia and he must pay for it. Funny, but if Father had done the same thing, and I know he's done it before, it would have gone unnoticed.

I school my features once more, focusing instead on the rapist in front of me.

Twelve. She's twelve. That's even younger than I was when... I stop that train of thought. It always makes me ill thinking about that encounter, or any of the subsequent ones.

"What do you want me to do?" I ask.

"Get the message across. Personalize it. Make it a punishment and a warning at the same time."

I nod.

Father regards me for a second before turning to leave.

"You have two hours."

I see. This is a test too.

Once I'm left with Romero, he blabbers, begging me to save him. I don't even listen to his cries for help as I survey the tools at my disposal.

Rape.

He's a rapist.

A small smile tugs at the corner of my eyes, looking forward to this for the first time.

I put aside a few instruments. Turning, I take the knife out of his mouth. I look over his form, my mind coming up with novel ideas.

Personalize it.

I might have just the thing.

I place the gag back in his mouth, not wanting to hear his screams.

I grasp the handle of the knife with trained ease, bringing it at an angle. Holding the tip of his nose, I cut through skin and cartilage. I ignore the trembling of his body as I saw through the material, cutting as efficiently as possible.

The only remaining skin is attached to nasal bones. I will need that a while later.

For a second, I stare at him, blood pouring down his face, his nose a wide-open orifice surrounded by red. If Vlad were here, he would have been overjoyed to inspect the inside of his olfactory system. Momentarily, I'm struck by a thought – how well can he smell now? All my time spent with Vlad has spoiled me. Now I think like him.

I throw away the piece of flesh and remove his gag. Romero sobs immediately, his eyes glued to his nose on the floor.

"Did you really not know?" I deadpan ask him.

"No... no, I swear." He shakes his head, tears falling down his face. Fool, it's probably going to sting when they touch the wound. Not my business.

"Really?" I ask, continuing my inspection of his body.

Father wants something inventive. My mind goes back to the needles and thread I'd seen among the other tools.

My eyes crinkle with hidden merriment. I have just the thing. The knife descends towards his crotch. Romero becomes visibly more terrified.

"I knew, OK? I knew. She told me," he blurts out.

"Hmm. Is that so?" I raise my eyes so he can see that nothing can sway me.

I am what I am. And because of that, he has no chance.

"Yes... I convinced her... Please let me go. I'll marry her, OK?"

"But Romero," I start, my voice the epitome of fakeness, "She's twelve." I say in a high-pitched voice, as if to emphasize my stance.

He pales, realizing there's no way out.

I bring the knife to his crotch and I cut out the material until I reach his wet, flaccid cock. He's pissed himself.

I look up at Romero, raising my eyebrows in question. He's still trembling. Waiting two more minutes to make sure he won't piss on me, I position the knife at the root of his cock and dig in. It's a clean cut, his screams music to my ears. One easy swipe and his cock falls down, separated from his pubis. Using two fingers, I take it and fling it to the floor.

Now for his balls...

His entire pubis is a mess, blood pooling down rapidly and mixing with piss from his severed urethra. I get over my disgust soon enough, as I cut his balls, making sure I also separate them through an incision in the middle. And just so he can experience more pain, I do it before cutting them from his body.

He screams and wails until his throat is sore.

I won't lie, that was my intention all along. I know that father is monitoring me closely.

With the entire genitalia separated from his body, I'm suddenly afraid he's going to bleed out.

No, that wouldn't do.

I take a step back and think on my options. Weighing in everything, I nod to myself and head back to the instruments. I pick up the sewing kit and I return to Romero's side.

I take off his gag and stuff it between his legs, lest he die on me before it's time. Then I start to painstakingly sew his dick to his nose. The flanges on what's left of his nose are slippery, so I use a smaller knife to detach some skin from the bone. I then hold the organ and thread the needle through the skin. It's not exactly easy to pace my stitches with all the blood still leaking from his dick, but I make do.

Romero stops moving.

Frowning, I check the pulse, and he's still alive. He must have passed out from the pain.

I shrug and continue to focus on my task. When the last stitch is done, I draw back to examine my work.

Still, while having a dick for a nose will definitely signal his crimes, it still doesn't feel enough. My gaze moves past the abandoned balls, and I get an idea.

Since they are already separated, it's easier to work with them, and I attach each ball to an ear. They hang low, like earrings, their weight pulling on the ear.

Romero looks exactly like he acted – with his dick instead of his brain. His penis is slumped down his face and over his lips, almost like an elephant trunk. Another brilliant thought crosses my mind and using my fingers I spread his mouth open and stuff the head of his cock inside.

Nice. I feel satisfied with this work.

But still. There is one more issue.

He's not dead.

Careful to keep my masterpiece, I use a thick axe for a swift decapitation. Leaving the headless body behind, I take the newly adorned head and place it on a tray.

And that's how father finds me.

Going by his hum of approval, I'd say I pass this test.

Romero... not so much, as his family will soon find out.

AGE SEVENTEEN,

"Really?" I lean against the wooden door, raising an eyebrow at the carnage before me. "You really couldn't control yourself?" I shake my head, not too keen on the work I have to do.

"I snapped," Vlad wheezes, spitting some blood. He wipes his mouth with the back of his hand, a frown on his face. He feels his face for a few seconds. "Oh, it's not mine." He breathes in, relieved.

"Want to tell me how blood that isn't yours ended up in your mouth?" I ask sardonically.

He grins at me, showing white teeth stained with red. "I might have gotten *too* into it." He jokes, even though I'm sure he can't remember what happened.

Ever since we started working together, I've noticed that about Vlad. He becomes a killing machine, but he loses his mind at the same time. It's not exactly... reliable. Which is where I come in.

I take a step forward, my lip curling in disgust.

Severed limbs, shredded organs, disemboweled torsos.

"You know I have to clean up after you, no?"

"Isn't that the whole point of this?" Vlad waves his finger between the two of us. "I destroy and you repair? It's your art."

"It would be easier if you didn't... go berserk on the targets." I survey the remains, trying to come up with a plan to put them back together. After all, we were supposed to send a message through the crime scene. The only message you'd get from this is that a feral animal had escaped the zoo and had paid these people a visit.

"Sometimes I wonder if you're some human-animal hybrid." I muse out loud. Vlad snickers at my comment.

"You're jealous." He sticks his tongue out at me. Sometimes I forget that he's a teenager.

"Jealous of what? Of getting intestines stuck between my teeth? I think I'll pass."

"It was one time, OK? I have enough nightmares about that, don't remind me." He puts one hand up, the other massaging his forehead. *Drama queen.*

"Or," I pause, a smile tugging at my lips, "not realizing I have a rib in my hair and going out like that?"

"That was one time, too," Vlad sighs. "And it was a floating rib. Those things can be tiny."

"Sure. From now on, make your victims take a blood test. You know, just in case you end up swallowing other parts."

"I do, in fact," he says nonchalantly, focused on the mirror in his hand and trying to clean his teeth.

"Sure," I repeat ironically.

"I'm serious. I never take an assignment if they have any blood disease." He peeks his head from behind the mirror. "I'm not *that* reckless."

"You're serious?"

"Uhm." He nods and starts whistling, ignoring me.

I huff out a breath, and I raise my sleeves. Well, it's time to get started.

There are three men in total. Part of the distribution network, they'd been caught stuffing their pockets with money that wasn't theirs.

Greed

That's their sin, and what they're going to be remembered for.

I look around, already picturing the finished product.

"How long will it take you?" Vlad interrupts my thoughts. I turn my head slightly and he's making himself comfortable in a corner.

"Go ahead, sleep," I say flippantly, knowing that's exactly what he wants to do.

"Gotcha. Wake me up when you're done."

I grunt, returning to my task. I take my backpack and pull out my kit. Vlad did not make my job any easier.

One man is cut in half, his organs spilling out. Another has his limbs severed, while the third is relatively whole, aside from his head that's lying some feet away from the body.

I decide to use the third one as the main canvas. Removing the medical staples from my bag, I lay them on the floor next to my sewing kit. Then I assemble the pieces.

I take the empty torso from the first man and lay it next to the headless body and the one that's missing the limbs. I already have enough experience to know what's going to appeal to the senses – what's going to terrify and horrify.

Before anything else, I take out all the organs, laying them aside for future use. Then, I ensure the limbs are completely severed.

Finally, I take out a handsaw and hammer at the ribs, removing the right side from the first torso, the entire rib cage from the second, and the left side from the third. I make sure the spine is still in place for each body. Then, taking the flapping skin of the first torso, I staple it to the second, and then the third, ensuring a Frankensteinian continuation.

Still loose, the three torsos are now bound together, emulating Siamese triplets.

The middle is empty, since I removed the whole rib cage from that particular body. To make the transition seamless, I use the discarded ribs to build a larger replica of a ribcage. I take a hammer and some nails and I connect the right side to the left with the left-over ribs.

It takes me a good half an hour to fit the pieces together. But at the end, the torsos look like they share a chest cavity.

Using some tape, I secure the spines in the back, before moving to the necks. I cut and discard any unnecessary skin to create a larger diameter from all three necks. I then tape them together, making sure they will hold for the final piece.

Returning my attention to the chest cavity, I retrieve the organs and stuff them inside the vacant space. I put the hearts, lungs, livers, bladders, kidneys, and stomachs to the back, using them for volume more than anything. Then I turn my attention to the intestines, and I staple them all together, converting them into a long organic hose.

Starting from the bottom, I strew the intestines around in a labyrinthine manner, interspacing them with the other organs. When I reach the end, I let them fall for a moment.

"Are you done?" Vlad asks in a bored tone.

"Not yet. You might as well help me if you're awake."

"Ugh, fine." He blabbers something but comes to my side.

He surveys my handiwork, reluctantly acknowledging it.

"What now?"

"The heads. I need to break the skulls."

"What do you want to do?" He narrows his eyes at me before realizing. "No way! You're serious?"

"Yup. Should be feasible."

"You can't possibly control how they're going to break," he adds.

"I'll just put them together. I need the skulls broken; it doesn't matter how."

"Fine." He shakes his head before proceeding to violently smash the skulls to the ground. Yeah, I didn't expect *that* many pieces. That's a lot of reconstruction.

"You did that on purpose!" I accuse him, especially after I see his uplifted mouth.

He shrugs.

"I don't know how no one's renamed you so far, *Berserker*." I give him a look, knowing he hates the moniker. "So wild, no wonder no one wants to date you." I pretend to shake my head in despair.

Vlad merely raises an eyebrow, unaffected.

"I wouldn't want to date me either," he says, tongue-in-cheek.

"Right, Casanova, either help, or go back to sleep."

He pouts, looking between the smashed pieces and the torsos. His eyes narrow before he gives a deep sigh.

"Fine, I'll help."

A smirk threatens to appear on my face, but I school my features. There is one thing that I can be sure of with Vlad – he's incredibly easily bored. He needs something to challenge him constantly, or he becomes a pain in the ass.

"Help me glue the pieces you smashed into the shape of a chalice, but with no bottom."

"Hmm." He brings a finger to his chin as he processes the information. "You want to make it like a funnel?"

My eyes widen in surprise at his quick thinking.

"Indeed," I respond.

Before we get to work, I gather the brains and separate them from shards of bone, putting them aside.

Then the painstaking work begins. We glue the shards until the funnel-shaped chalice starts to form. It takes us hours before we complete it to a satisfactory degree.

"I'm done." Vlad wipes a hand over his forehead, leaning back on his elbows. "This is boring."

Yeah, can't say I didn't expect that.

"You can go," I dismiss him. The bone sculpture is almost done. I don't need him anymore. Yet, he doesn't move.

"I want to see the finished thing." I shake my head at him, but I continue to focus on my task.

Once the newly built bottomless skull is done, I attach it to the enlarged neck. There's still hair and scalp on the outside, which betrays the seamless transitions I'd worked so hard on, but alas, I did not have any flesh-eating beetles on hand.

When the pieces are connected, I put the brain inside, crowding it towards the narrow part of the funnel to make sure it won't collapse. Then, I reach inside the chest cavity and with some difficulty I connect the intestines to the neck and then staple it to the brain matter.

Done, but....

This masterpiece will require an audience before it's complete.

"We need to move this carefully. Can you manage that? And I'll meet you at the warehouse in an hour?"

Vlad sighs, exasperated, but I know that for all his immature display, he is very meticulous in his work. So much so that I know the exhibit will be untouched at the destination.

"Fine. Where are you going?"

"I need the last piece. It needs to be an interactive exhibit," I explain.

Greed.

They'll see greed.

One hour later, and I'm at the warehouse, a bag full of furred friends, and not of the domestic variety.

Vlad is on the other end, standing next to the exhibit, his expression clearly annoyed.

"You're late," he notes when he sees me, raising his hand to show me his watch.

"Two minutes," I groan.

"Two minutes too late. Let's do this. I have things to do," he says in a clipped manner. Yeah, I doubt he has anything to do. Much like myself, Vlad is a loner. Even more than I, no one would willingly associate with him. With his volatile nature, you never know when he'll snap.

I give him a look before unveiling the top part of the artwork. Reaching inside my bag, I grab the rats I'd brought – New York rats – and I drop them on top of the brains. When they start eating away at the organic matter, I give Vlad a nod, and we take the entire sheet off it.

People from both the Bratva and the Famiglia are inside the warehouse, together with workers and other essential staff. And they are all present to witness.

Greed.

It doesn't even require an introduction, as people stop to stare, some getting ill, others fainting.

The rats make excellent work of the brain matter before reaching the intestines, and then, like Hansel & Gretel, they make their way through the organ maze. Everything is visible from the outside.

"What would you call this?" Vlad suddenly asks.

"This? I don't know. Art?" I joke, but he's not even cracking a smile.

"You know, if I'm Berserker, then you should have your own name too. Let's see..."

"Frankenstein?" I chuckle at the thought.

"No." His expression is serious. "Too man-made. We need some-thing more powerful. Mythical."

"Hmm," I muse, but I don't exactly take him seriously.

"Chimera," he suddenly says.

"Chimera?"

"A creature of amalgamations. Not whole, but not lacking. And most of all – terrifying." Vlad turns to me, awaiting my reply.

"Chimera," I repeat, testing the name. In Greek mythology, it was a fire-breathing animal hybrid that instilled fear in people.

Not bad... not bad at all.

Because so would I become. A name so feared, almost mythical in reputation.

CATALINA

An overwhelming sense of dread churns in my stomach, causing me to toss and turn in bed. I know what's coming—I can feel it in the air, even in my half-asleep state.

My fingers grip the sheets tightly as I try to push away the inevitable. But no matter how hard I try, I am transported back to that room. The room where I am always face down, strapped to a cold metal table.

My heart pounds loudly in my ears, drowning out any other sound. I strain to hear voices, but they are muffled and distant. All I can focus on is the searing pain ripping through my backside. It's a pain that has become all too familiar, one that never seems to go away.

I thrash against my restraints, a desperate attempt to escape the agony. But it's no use.

Then suddenly, there is someone by my side. A gentle hand strokes my hair and offers me water. Even in my hazy state, I can see his eyes—a piercing amber, like a flicker of hope amidst the darkness. The liquid soothes my parched throat, but most of it ends up spilling on my face and in my hair due to my position.

As I take deep gulps of water, struggling not to choke, everything around me starts to blur together. It feels like the world is spinning with me.

What did they give me?

In a daze, I feel someone unbinding my restraints and pulling me off the table. My dress is lifted over my hips and someone touches me intimately—a violation of my body that leaves me feeling vulnerable and helpless.

My body feels like a heavy weight, too sluggish to move. I barely struggle when something invades my body, tearing me apart. The pain is sharp, so sharp that it slices through my foggy mental state. My eyes sting with unshed tears, my mouth opens in a silent scream of agony.

And then it stops.

A wave of relief washes over me, but it's fleeting. Cold metal presses against my skin under my chin, and I try to make sense of what's happening around me. But the metal keeps digging into my flesh, a threatening reminder.

Is this how I die?

Amidst my internal panic and hyperventilation, I can't even muster the strength to move a finger. The gun remains trained on me, its cold presence never wavering.

And then the pain returns.

In and out.

I jolt awake, gasping for air as beads of sweat coat my trembling body. It was just another nightmare... the same one that has haunted me since that fateful night. Tears blur my vision as I realize I haven't truly moved past it; it still lingers in the depths of my mind.

"Lina?" Marcello asks groggily, sitting up on the bed. "What's wrong?"

"Nothing." I shake my head and attempt a placating smile. He frowns, not quite buying my explanation. His hand goes to my neck, feeling the moisture clinging to my skin.

"Lina, what happened?" He tugs me closer to him, his arms wrapping around me.

"I dreamed about that night again." A soft whisper escapes my lips as I lie next to Marcello, the memories of that fateful night flooding back in fragments. He stiffens beside me, sensing my unease. His warm lips brush over my forehead, trying to comfort me.

"Do you want to talk about it?" he asks gently.

I hesitate, the pain and hazy memories still fresh in my mind. But then I feel his comforting presence and snuggle closer to him, seeking solace in his embrace.

"I don't remember much. Just some impressions and... pain." I shudder at the memory of the agony I endured. Marcello doesn't press for more information, understanding my need for silence.

I am grateful that he has never asked me about what happened or about Claudia's father. Enzo must have told him the abbreviated version, and Marcello has been kind enough not to bring it up. He has never once made me feel ashamed for what occurred.

"You are safe now. I will always protect you," he assures me with unwavering sincerity. His words send a shiver down my spine, and I turn to kiss him, wanting to forget everything else.

He senses my need for escape and lays me on my back, covering me with his body. "Make me yours," I plead with him, surrendering myself completely.

"You already are mine, Lina," he whispers against my lips before claiming them in a passionate kiss. His hand caresses my face tenderly, his eyes gazing at me with an intensity that both scares and excites me. "You will always be mine."

"AND you really think Sisi will go with it?" I frown and start pacing. Marcello had suddenly gotten a call from Benedicto, who invited himself over.

"I had a brief talk with her and I explained that we need to monitor the Guerras to see if they had anything to do with the nun's murder. She wasn't too against it and said she would be on her best behavior."

"Did you also warn her about their son?"

"I told her to be kind to him," Marcello says and moves over to put on his tie.

"I'm still worried. I don't want Claudia around when they get here."

"Agreed. We'll see if Mrs. Evans can stay for a while longer."

"Signor Lastra, Signor Guerra and his family are here," Amelia knocks to announce.

Marcello gives a tight nod and offers me his arm.

In the drawing room, we greet the guests, and I watch awkwardly as we try to engage in conversation. The topics are very mundane, but I can't help but feel out of my element. The only thing I can think of is the finger I'd found in the soup and the threats... to have these people in my house is a little unsettling, to say the least.

Marcello doesn't seem too enthusiastic about this either, as he listens to Benedicto talk with half an ear.

A short while later, and after some more tedious discourse, Sisi comes down.

"Good afternoon," she says, and Marcello proceeds with the introductions.

"My son, Rafaelo, is a little shy. But I hope you can get along," Cosima chimes in, giving her son a pat on the back. The poor boy seems to shrink away at the contact, focusing his attention on Sisi instead.

"P-p-pleas... pleased t-t-to m... m-meet you," he extends his hand, and Sisi shakes it with a kind smile.

"Lastra, why don't we let the women and the children do their thing and we can discuss some business," Benedicto interjects, rising to his feet.

Marcello reluctantly nods, but he doesn't seem too happy about the notion. He gives me a brief, sad smile before leaving.

"Assisi, what a lovely name you have," Cosima starts, her voice a grating, saccharine tone. She looks Sisi up and down, a little frown marring her features. She quickly schools her expression and continues with pleasantries.

"Thank you," Sisi replies, her pose and manners without reproach. Still, this is not the Sisi I know.

"Now, tell me, what are your thoughts on marriage?" Cosima probes further.

"M-M-mother," her son interrupts, "S... stop."

"Nonsense, Raf," she waves her hand and turns again to Sisi.

"I haven't thought about it since I was supposed to take my vows before I left Sacre Coeur," she replies cordially, even though I see she's not pleased with this line of interrogation.

"There's enough time for that, dear," Cosima glibly remarks.

"Why don't you two go over there and get to know each other better." She fakes a smile as she points to the other couch at the end of the room.

"But—" I'm about to intervene, not liking this. Cosima, though, speaks again.

"Don't worry, Catalina, they will still be within our sight. Nothing improper will happen." She tries to joke, but I'm not amused. Mostly because I don't trust anyone in their family.

I reluctantly agree and Sisi and Rafaelo take a seat in a farther corner.

"Now we can also talk uninterrupted, no?" She smiles knowingly, as if this was what she intended from the very beginning.

"Right," I say, wariness in my tone.

"I have to ask. I've been curious ever since I met you. Why did you marry Marcello? Couldn't you have found yourself someone else? I mean," she studies me. "You're a pretty girl. I'm sure you could have found someone else to disregard," she pauses, as if she's looking for the right words. "Whatever they needed to disregard." She smiles awkwardly. Yeah, that is definitely the best euphemism I've heard so far.

"I wanted to marry him," I answer with as much confidence as possible. Truth be told, I don't know if there were any other options. But the moment Enzo had mentioned Marcello, I'd jumped at the chance. I don't know why I'd wanted him so much, but I think he left a deep impression on me when I'd seen him at Sacre Coeur.

"Really?" She leans back, horrified.

"Yes, why?" Now it's my turn to frown. What would she have against Marcello? Any woman with two good eyes could see what a catch he is.

"Well, aside from his looks, which granted are quite superior, his reputation is one of the most stained I've ever heard of."

"What do you mean?"

"You haven't heard?" She tilts her head, an eyebrow raised.

"I don't know what you mean. I'm aware he's been living outside the famiglia for the last ten years," I start, but she cuts me off.

"Oh dear, I mean before that. Marcello and his father had the worst type of reputations. No self-respecting woman would have been caught having any connection to them."

"Why?" I'm confused. On the one hand, I am curious to hear what she's talking about, but on the other, I don't know whether to believe a word she says.

"Oh my," She raises a hand to her mouth. Then, she quickly looks around, as if what she's about to impart is of utmost secrecy.

"You didn't find this out from me but," she leans in to whisper, "they used to attend brothels and engage in the most despicable acts." She looks towards the door again, before adding, clearly scandalized, "In groups!"

"I don't understand." My brows furrow in confusion.

Cosima looks frustrated at my question.

"They went to orgies. Everyone knew. They were the most debauched events; the things people would say about what went on inside those events..." She shakes her head.

Orgies? I don't think I've heard that term before. I'd ask her what it means, but I don't think my question would be received well, so I just nod and let her continue.

"They would have even ten women in a night. Sex, drugs, alcohol. Every debauched thing in the book. Some rumors say they even had animals." Her face is horrified as she recounts this.

I'm a little disturbed at her descriptions that I even tune out some words.

"Sodomy and the likes." She shudders. "I'm extremely surprised your brother accepted the match. He must have known."

My face is blank at this point, and I remember snippets of Enzo's disapproval of Marcello. At the time, it made little sense... But what if... No! I shake myself. I can't just trust whatever she's saying.

"I see," I simply reply. She continues chatting away, regaling me with more lurid tales about the Lastra family.

"Why, his mother killed herself. The second wife ran away. And then there's that third wife. She killed herself too. I wonder if there might be a curse."

I'm so shocked by what she's saying that I just smile and nod.

Finally, she changes the subject.

"Look at them. Don't they look good together?" Cosima gushes about Sisi and Rafaelo.

I turn in their direction, and they seem cozy. They are sitting a little too close together, and Rafaelo's head is tilted towards Sisi intimately. Sisi, too, is smiling and talking animatedly with him.

I'm stunned by this development. Blocking everything Cosima told me out of my mind, I take a moment to focus on the two of them.

They are around the same age, with Rafaelo only two years older at twenty-two. But considering his problems, I wonder if Sisi isn't just being kind to him.

When the visit draws to a close, I take Sisi aside to ask her how it went.

"I like him. He's sweet," she replies and blushes.

"Sweet," I repeat, a little taken aback. "That's great!"

"I'd like to keep seeing him, if that's possible." She seems enthusiastic about this, and I'm happy for her. If she likes Rafaelo and wants to befriend him or more, why shouldn't she?

"Of course! I'll talk to Marcello."

After I assure her I will put in a kind word for them with Marcello, I retire to my room.

———

SITTING ALONE WITH MY LAPTOP, my curiosity gets the better of me and I find myself typing in the word "orgy" on the search bar. I'm not quite sure what to expect, but I definitely wasn't prepared for what came up.

My eyes widen as I read the first definition from an urban dictionary: an orgy is defined as five or more people engaging in sexual acts together. I furrow my brow, trying to wrap my head around how that even works.

Determined to learn more, I continue scrolling through various websites until one catches my eye. Without a second thought, I click on it and a loud moaning sound erupts from my speakers. Panicked, I quickly shut down my laptop, praying that no one heard the explicit noises coming from it.

Feeling embarrassed yet still intrigued, I cautiously open my laptop again and mute the volume this time. The video shows multiple individuals, all passionately entangled in sexual activities together. In a way, it's not too different from what I had witnessed Allegra doing before.

A realization hits me like a ton of bricks—is this what Marcello enjoys? My stomach churns at the thought. The idea of him participating in such acts makes me feel sick to my core. Am I uncomfortable with the actions themselves or just jealous that he has been with others before me? Perhaps it's both. But then again, could I ever bring myself to do something like that for him?

Shaking my head, I scold myself for even entertaining these thoughts. They are dangerous and only serve to fill me with self-doubt and insecurity.

Despite my initial reservations, I continue to browse the web, reading various articles and slowly becoming more familiar with this intimate business. To my surprise, I even stumble upon tutorials for beginners.

Lost in this new world, I'm only faintly aware when Marcello enters my room. I try not to show my interest as I nonchalantly close my laptop.

"Finished?" I ask with a casual smile.

He nods absentmindedly. "I'll go take a shower first."

As he disappears into the bathroom, I quickly return to the tutorial video I had been watching, studying each step intently. Once I feel confident enough, I make my way to the bathroom.

I give a hesitant knock on the door.

"Can I come in?" I ask, hoping for his permission.

"Yes," he responds loudly from inside, and I push open the door.

I cautiously step inside. Marcello is standing in the shower stall, the clear glass leaving nothing to the imagination. His expression is one of surprise at seeing me.

"Is something wrong?" He furrows his brow and starts to step out of the stall.

"No," I reply quickly, fumbling with the zipper of my dress. Damn, why didn't I undress before coming here?

His gaze is fixed on me, watching my every move intently. With determination, I strip off my clothes and walk towards the shower stall, ready to put what I've learned into practice.

I try to maintain the same level of confidence as the girl in the video, even though my nerves are threatening to betray me. The steam from the newly turned on water envelops my body the moment I step into the shower stall.

"Lina, what are you..." Marcello starts to ask, but I interrupt him by standing on my tiptoes and pressing my lips against his. A deep groan escapes him as our mouths meet, and he pulls me closer by wrapping his arms around my waist.

I can feel his arousal, hard against my stomach, which only fuels my plan further.

Breaking away from the kiss, I sink down to my knees. Marcello's eyes darken with desire as he watches me take him in my hand. I mimic his movements, moving up and down his length. His head falls back and a small whimper escapes his lips.

"Lina," his voice is breathy and it only gives me more confidence as I continue to explore his pleasure points with my hands and mouth.

I tilt my head to the side and open my mouth wider, taking him inside without hesitation. He's soft yet firm, and the taste is surprisingly not unpleasant. My tongue glides over the tip of his erection, eliciting a moan from Marcello as he runs his fingers through my hair, urging me on. I stretch my mouth wider to accommodate all of him, but I can't help gagging when I'm only halfway through.

He must have heard me, because he lets go, taking a step back.

"Lina... what are you doing?" His expression is horrified.

Gazing up at him from my knees, I whisper, "I want to please you." His sudden outburst catches me off guard, and I can see the confusion in his eyes.

"Why would you do this?" He shakes his head, water droplets falling from his hair. Turning off the shower, he moves to leave the stall.

"Did I... did I do something wrong?" I ask, feeling a pang of unease. I stay on my knees, afraid that if I attempt to stand, my legs will give out beneath me.

"This isn't like you. You don't have to do this... Damn it." He mutters under his breath, reaching for a towel and wrapping it around his waist. Despite his obvious arousal, he seems agitated.

"But you enjoyed it before." My words spill out before I can stop them, desperate to keep him from leaving.

"What are you talking about?" He stops in his tracks, his eyes narrowing as he looks down at me. Suddenly, I feel exposed and vulnerable.

"It doesn't matter." I mumble, embarrassed that Cosima's words had planted seeds of doubt in my mind, leading me to believe that Marcello wanted this when he clearly didn't.

"No, tell me what you meant." He kneels down beside me.

"Cosima told me about your past," I confess hesitantly. "About the orgies. And I thought..."

"Orgies." He gives a dry laugh. "And what did you think?" He raises an eyebrow.

My head hangs low as I answer him, the weight of my shame dragging me down. "I can't fulfill that desire for you... but perhaps there are other ways I can please you." I try to explain, but he stops me.

"Lina, please look at me." His voice is gentle and coaxing, so I lift my gaze to meet his. "Whatever Cosima may have told you... there are always multiple sides to any truth. Yes, I have done things in the past that I am not proud of, but they are behind me now. It's been over a decade since I have been with anyone else. Does that sound like someone who craves orgies?"

I shake my head in response, but then another thought crosses my mind. "But... what if you were able to touch others? Would you have had those experiences?"

His answer is swift and resolute. "No."

"No?" I press, needing to be sure.

"No," he repeats firmly. "Because they were not the woman I loved." The words strike me with a force that nearly knocks me off balance, and I end up falling on my backside.

"The woman you loved," I echo hollowly. "Who was she?" My question spills out without hesitation, though my heart aches at the thought of him loving someone besides myself.

Do I even stand a chance against such love?

There is a deep sorrow in his eyes as he turns away from me. In an instant, he is standing and preparing to leave.

"Perhaps one day, I will tell you," he says softly before walking.

My mind is still reeling from the sudden revelation. Marcello was in love with someone else, maybe he still is. And I am already in too deep; my feelings for him intensifying with each passing day.

As I rise to speak, I catch a glimpse of his retreating figure. Shock and horror surge through me at the sight. His once smooth skin is now marred by countless scars, crisscrossing his back in a chaotic pattern—some old and faded, others fresh and raw.

I gasp, my hand flying to my mouth in disbelief.

Good Lord! What happened to him?

It dawns on me then that in all our intimate moments, I have never seen his back. He had purposely kept it hidden from me.

But why?

Another realization hits me like a ton of bricks. I know next to nothing about my own husband, do I? The man I thought I knew has become a stranger before my eyes.

MARCELLO

With a heavy heart, I retreat to the safety of my room before I can do any further damage to my fragile relationship with Catalina. The air is thick with tension and my fists clench at my sides, ready to release the built-up frustration.

My fingers form a tight fist and I punch the wall, welcoming the sharp sensation of pain that briefly takes over my mind. It's a welcome distraction from the swirling thoughts that threaten to consume me.

But perhaps I deserve this pain. After all, what was Catalina thinking, trying to please me in such a way? Sweet, innocent Catalina, on her knees before me. How many times had I fantasized about just that? But seeing her there, struggling to choke down my cock out of some misguided sense of inadequacy...I couldn't let her continue.

And then she had to mention the orgies. A bitter laugh escapes my lips at the absurdity. Did she truly think I would be interested in those depravities? If only she knew...

I shake my head, feeling a strange mix of amusement and disgust at the irony of it all.

Most of my past experiences are nothing more than a blur in my mind now. I'm not proud to admit it, but at some point, drugs and alcohol became necessary tools to make it through those hedonistic gatherings. Whatever memories weren't blacked out by overindulgence were surely buried deep within my subconscious.

My lip curls in disgust as I recall unwanted hands roaming over my body.

No, I refuse to dwell on those memories.

But despite everything, I owe Lina an apology for my harsh words earlier. I know I was too brusque with her. In fact, I almost revealed the truth about my decade-long infatuation with her.

This day has been filled with one complication after another—from Lina's nightmare to Benedicto's unexpected visit, and now to the discovery of some questionable paperwork. I'd managed to calm myself down a little regarding the first two, but the document I'd found had made me restless.

Restless enough that I'd almost snapped at the only person I'd *never* snap at.

I take a deep breath and close my eyes, trying to calm the tension that is already building in my body. My hand reaches for the drawer where I keep my stash of burner phones, and I pull one out and start dialing Francesco's number.

He answers after a few rings.

"Yes?"

"Did Valentino ever mention anything about visiting an asylum?"

There is a brief pause on the other end.

"Yes, he used to visit one a few times a year. Why do you ask?"

"Do you know who he was visiting there?"

"No, I accompanied him a couple of times but I never went inside."

"I see," I respond grimly. "I need to go there too. Meet me at the asylum tomorrow at ten."

"Understood."

I hang up, feeling even more agitated than before.

"Damn it!" I curse under my breath.

Quickly getting dressed, I make my way to my study. I grab the document I had found earlier and read over it again.

Male. Fifty-seven years old. Born on November second.

Just like my father.

The same man I thought I had killed.

The man who had turned me into a monster; who had taught me everything about torture and murder.

The man who was closely familiar with Chimera.

"Damn it! Damn it! Damn it!" Frustration boils within me as I throw the document onto the table. How did I not consider this before? Yes, I left him to die, but I never received confirmation that he did. When Valentino took over, I just assumed that was the case.

"Fucking hell!" My teeth grind together as anger courses through me, directed mainly towards myself. Because of my recklessness, my family is now in danger. Again.

Of course.

My father would be first in line to want revenge against me, and his expertise lies in psychological torture. Not only did I betray him, but I also attempted to end his life. If this man is truly my father...

I shake my head, feeling a wave of fear wash over me at the thought. But I need to be certain. I need to see with my own eyes if this man is indeed my father. And if he is, then I will make sure he stays dead – this time for good.

The following day I meet Francesco at the asylum.

As we make our way inside, I turn to him and ask, "And you never knew whom he visited?"

"No," Francesco answers, a hint of regret in his voice. "Valentino was very secretive about this. It's why I was the only man he'd take with him." My suspicions are confirmed. There's no way the famiglia would have turned a blind eye if their beloved patriarch was still alive.

Tino, Tino... it seems you did betray me.

I try to mask my emotions as I fill out the paperwork and provide details about my relationship with the patient. In truth, I am bluffing, as I have yet to confirm his identity. But time will tell if this is the truth or just another lie.

"He's been making great progress," a nurse informs me cheerfully. "He's been eating all his meals without any issues." She continues to chatter away about mundane details that hold no interest for me. Tuning her out, I focus on the man behind the closed doors.

"Here we are. Let me know if he feels unwell or experiences any discomfort."

I nod in response and enter the room, leaving Francesco waiting outside.

As I approach the window, I catch sight of a man in a wheelchair facing away from me. Reluctantly, I step closer and notice that his head is tilted at an odd angle.

Flashbacks of that fateful night come rushing back, but I push them aside and steel myself for what lies ahead.

When I finally stand in front of him, I can hardly believe my eyes. My father, alive and breathing before me. His eyes widen with recognition when I lower myself to his level, but his mouth trembles wordlessly. His hands shake on the armrests as though willing his body to move, but it remains frozen in place.

The doctor in charge had filled me in. Paralysis likely caused by brain injury. It seems I did some damage after all. He'd also told me that although father can't move or communicate, he can understand me.

"So we meet again, father." My voice is full of the hatred I have for the man – hatred that's festered even more in the last ten years.

His pupils move wildly from right to left, knowing this will not be a friendly visit.

"Finally, it's not me who's afraid," I casually comment and lean on the windowsill, blocking the light.

I wonder what it's going to take for him to break free of this ruse. I *need* to know he's definitely incapacitated. Regardless, his fate will be the same.

"How would you feel..." I pause, observing the pulse at the base of his throat. "If I put to work everything you've taught me." The only reaction I'm getting is the quick fluttering of his eyelids and his sudden intake of breath. Nevertheless, it's telling me all I need to know.

"Remember when you suggested I use teeth for the mark of the Chimera? I wonder, will you even feel if I pull your teeth out one at a time?" I remove a pair of pliers from my coat. I'd come prepared.

Drops of liquid hit the floor. I turn my gaze downwards.

"So this is how you react when you're on the receiving end. You piss yourself." I make a tsk sound, opening the pliers and moving them closer to his face.

"Let's see, if this makes you piss yourself, what will it take to cause a heart attack?" He pales even more at my words, and I don't know whether to cry or to laugh at this. I'm finally confronting the man who's made my entire life hell, and I can't even do it properly. What satisfaction will I get from killing a man in a wheelchair? None.

But kill him I must.

Disgusted with the situation, I go outside and signal Francesco.

"It's done," he says. I give him a tight nod, and then I grab onto the wheelchair's handles, leading father out of the room.

While I'd been getting reacquainted with him, Francesco had been settling the paperwork to release father into our care.

We leave as the picture of family happiness, and I instruct Francesco to make a few turns until we are close to a secluded forest.

As we get father out of the car, I'm struck again by a pang of regret at this pity kill. How many times had I imagined paying him back for everything he'd done to me? How many times had I prayed for a chance to put him in his place?

And now, as I look upon his pathetic self, I can't even muster the hate anymore.

One bullet and he's dead. His head shoots back with the velocity of the bullet, and his body spasms once more before his eyes turn blank. This time forever.

With a sigh, I nod to Francesco to get rid of the body and the wheelchair. I return to the car and, putting my head in my palms, I cry.

I let it all go— three decades of torture at the hands of this man. And the sad truth is that I don't think I'll ever get rid of the mark he's left on me.

Pulling myself together before Francesco returns, I direct him to take me home. There's only one thing I need right now – her.

When I open her door, I find her on the bed, focused on a piece she's sewing. She jumps up a little, startled to see me.

"Is there something wrong?" Lina turns to me, a little frown forming between her brows. She holds herself still, her entire body stiff.

We'd slept in separate beds the night before. Mostly because I'd been so ashamed of myself, I couldn't bring myself to face her.

But now it's over. It's finally over.

And my past will remain just that – *the past.*

"Can I come in?"

She gives a brisk nod, her eyes still regarding me suspiciously.

As she sees me walking towards her, she puts away her work on a nearby chair. I take this as an invitation to sit down.

Her hands are tightly folded in her lap, her chin slightly lowered.

My heart races as I reach for her hands. My palm covers hers in a gentle gesture of comfort and understanding.

"I'm sorry," I say, my voice soft and contrite. "I should have said this sooner."

Lina's eyes meet mine, filled with a mix of emotions. "I'm sorry too," she murmurs. "I shouldn't have just assumed..."

"Hey, no more of that," I interrupt firmly. "I realize you don't know a lot about me, and of course you'd be curious."

Lina shakes her head, her gaze dropping to our linked hands. Her fingers intertwine with mine, as if seeking reassurance.

"I shouldn't have let Cosima's words get to me," she continues, her voice strained. "I should have thought before I acted."

I can see the weight of her apology in her eyes, and without thinking, I pull her into a hug. She stiffens at first but then relaxes into my embrace.

"I know that we were both thrown together into this marriage by circumstances," she whispers against my shoulder. "But I think...never mind."

"Lina, you don't have to hide from me," I urge gently. But it's clear she's not ready to open up yet.

A strained smile tugs at her lips as she turns to face me again. "It's fine, really. We just had our first disagreement," she says lightly.

"Am I forgiven?" I ask tentatively.

She tilts her head to the side, considering me for a moment before surprising me with a quick peck on the cheek.

"I quite liked that," she teases with a hint of playfulness in her tone. "Do you think I can get a repeat?"

I chuckle at her cheekiness and wrap my arms around her once more. This time, when she leans in for another kiss, I'm ready for her. Our lips meet in a gentle, tender embrace, and I can feel the warmth of her body against mine as she molds herself to my chest. My hand moves up, cupping her neck before settling on her cheek.

Her eyes flutter open, the green of her irises so intense it's almost blinding. How many times had I dreamed of this? Of her lovely eyes staring into mine? Of holding her in my arms, our skin touching, our breaths mingling?

My thumb glides gently over her lips, parting them in anticipation. She responds by flicking out her tongue, barely grazing the tip of my finger. But then she surprises me by taking my thumb into her mouth, sucking on it lightly. Her eyes widen with curiosity and innocence as she gazes up at me.

I can't help but groan in response to her bold move.

"Oh, the things you do to me, Lina," I rasp out.

"Good things, I hope," she quips back playfully.

"The best." Leaning in for a kiss, we are interrupted by a knock at the door.

Damn!

"Come in," Lina calls out, pulling away from me and composing herself.

Claudia peeks her head through the door, interrupting our intimate moment.

"Why aren't you with Sisi?" Lina asks with a slight frown as Claudia steps inside the room.

Claudia rocks back and forth on her heels, wearing a sheepish expression.

"Aunt Sisi has a visitor."

"A visitor?" I repeat, surprised by this news.

"Yes. Her friend Rafaelo. She told me to go to my room, but I'm so bored," Claudia shrugs nonchalantly, looking like a spitting image of Catalina.

"Did you know about the visit?" I ask Lina, but she shakes her head.

I get up, intent on seeing what this is all about, but Lina stops me.

"Let's give them some time. I'm sure nothing untoward will happen. Besides, the staff is downstairs."

"But..." I trail off as she bats her eyelashes at me, making me lose myself in her gorgeous eyes.

She's not playing fair.

"I'll just inform Amelia to monitor them," I relent a little.

"Will you play with us, Marcello?" Claudia comes by her mother's side, picking up the piece Lina had been working on. I sneak a glance at Lina, and she gives me a small nod.

"I guess I am."

"Cool." Claudia's beaming smile swallows me whole, and I return the gesture.

I find that I've smiled these past few months more than I've ever done in my entire life.

And there's only one reason for it. Well, now two.

CATALINA

Watching Marcello's interactions with Claudia warms my heart. He's so gentle and patient with her, his eyes bright and attentive as she chatters away.

As I watch them, I feel a fluttering in my chest that I can't ignore. It's a warm, comforting sensation that spreads through me, and suddenly everything becomes clear.

I am deeply and completely in love with Marcello Lastra. This overwhelming feeling is unfamiliar yet strangely comforting, like a puzzle piece that finally fits into place in my heart.

Deep down, I think I always knew it would come to this. From the very first moment I saw him, there was something about him that drew me in. It wasn't just his striking looks—although they certainly didn't hurt—but it was something deeper. A tingling sensation in my chest that hinted at a connection between us.

At the time, I had dismissed it as mere physical attraction. After all, he was undeniably eye candy. But now I realize it was more than that. There was an unspoken understanding between us, a sense of trust that I rarely felt towards anyone after the incident.

Perhaps it was the hint of sadness in his eyes or the way he looked at me with such wonder and disbelief, as if he couldn't believe someone like me existed. Or maybe it was the fact that he showed me kindness when no one else did.

With him, I feel cherished—truly seen and appreciated for who I am. And for once, I allow myself to bask in this feeling without any doubt or hesitation.

I observe as his eyes crinkle around the corners, filled with amusement and adoration as Claudia meticulously describes her vision for the perfect princess dress. In that moment, I can feel my heart opening up to him completely. Knowing that he will treat my daughter with the same kindness and love he shows me only solidifies my feelings for him.

A small smile tugs at the corners of my lips as I watch them interact. It is a gentle reminder that this man before me, whom I have fallen deeply in love with, would also make an amazing father figure for Claudia.

And with that thought, I decide it's time to tell him how I truly feel. Even though there is a possibility of rejection, I cannot deny the strong pull towards him any longer. Yes, I will not give up on us. Whoever he may have loved before holds no hold over him now; he belongs to me and I to him. My cheeks flush at the intensity of my thoughts, but I know deep down that I will do whatever it takes to keep him by my side.

As Claudia excuses herself to finish her homework, Marcello pulls Amelia aside to inquire about Sisi.

"They were simply conversing, sir. I made sure there was nothing inappropriate happening," she explains.

"Do you think they have feelings for each other?" He turns his attention to me, taking my hand and pressing his lips to it in a tender kiss.

"Perhaps. That would be lovely, wouldn't it?"

"I don't know. I don't trust Guerra, and Sisi's barely had time to get used to life outside Sacre Coeur. It might be too fast." Marcello frowns, and I get the urge to kiss his worries away.

"She's old enough to decide for herself. Besides, she's extremely strong-willed. No one could pressure her into doing anything she didn't want. That's why I think there might be something between them."

"We'll see." It's all he says.

"You called her Sisi." I stifle a smile. "That's a first."

"That I did. I must be getting more familiar with her." A smile tugs at the corner of his mouth.

I finally give in. Raising myself on my tiptoes, I place a kiss on his lips. Given our height differences, I have to almost jump.

"You shouldn't start what you can't finish, Lina." There's a seductive quality to his voice as he winds his arm around my waist and pulls me into him.

"Who says I can't?" I raise an eyebrow at him. I can't very well scream *RAVISH ME;* it wouldn't be quite proper.

"You have one second to change your mind before I throw you over my shoulder and take you to my lair to have my way with you." His words always have the ability to make me blush to my roots.

"Hmm, that doesn't sound bad at all." I flutter my eyelashes at him suggestively.

"That's it!" He says a second before he scoops me up and actually throws me over his shoulder.

"Marcello!" I gasp, shocked he'd do that in the open. His hand comes down on my butt and he pats my dress so it stays in place. He doesn't waste any time as he takes a few steps at a time, quickly reaching my room and depositing me in the middle of the bed.

There's something different about *this* Marcello. He's more carefree, more playful. It's like an entire weight has been lifted off his shoulders.

I recline against the soft sheets, propping myself up on my elbows as I gaze at him through lowered lashes. My breath catches in my throat as his hands ghost over the buttons of his shirt, his eyes never leaving mine. Desire burns in his glazed gaze as he slowly reveals the toned muscles and taut skin beneath.

My heart races with anticipation, the heat between us palpable and making me tremble. I remember a night when he was away from me, the emptiness and longing tearing at my heart. In the short time we've been together, he's become my every thought, my every desire.

He approaches me on the bed, his knees sinking into the soft mattress as he moves closer. Without hesitation, I part my lips slightly and guide his hand to my chest, placing it over my racing heart. I want him to feel how much he means to me, how his touch sets me on fire.

The scars on my back may forever bear witness to the darkness that once consumed me, but it is this man in front of me who has brought light back into my life. He has imprinted himself on my very being, filling me with hope and love that I never thought possible.

My fingers lightly graze against Marcello's rough stubble, and for the first time, I see him less than perfectly groomed. Perhaps he had a hard time like I did? He turns my palm over, kissing the center before bringing it to rest against his cheek. His eyes close as he nuzzles into my hand.

"It's over... It's finally over," he whispers, his voice filled with relief and emotion. "What is it?" I ask, but he simply shakes his head.

"Sometimes I still can't believe you're here," he says with a sad smile.

"Me neither." I draw him closer, my dress acting as a barrier between us. I gaze into his eyes, trying to commit every detail to memory—the way they light up when they look at me, the flecks of green in their deep brown depths.

"When I'm with you, I feel like I can be a good man. Someone worthy of you," he confesses, his words laced with pain and reverence. His thumb gently traces along my cheekbone.

"You are. You are," I repeat, yearning for his lips on mine.

They say love can happen in an instant, but it feels like every moment spent with Marcello has led me to this point. Every second in his presence ignites a fire within me that has grown into an inferno.

But that's just it—I would willingly burn for him.

His other hand skims up my leg, tugging at the hem of my dress until it falls off me. I stand before him in a simple white bra and cotton underwear. Even though he has seen me naked before, I can't help the heat that flushes my face as Marcello leans back to take in my body, his eyes roaming hungrily over every inch of me.

With a playful swat, I try to push him away, feeling slightly embarrassed to be the center of his attention. Instinctively, I cross my arms and turn my head to the side.

"Lina, don't hide from me," he softly admonishes, gently untangling my arms and leaving a sweet kiss in the center of my chest, between my breasts.

"You're the most beautiful thing I've ever laid eyes on. If I could capture this image in my mind forever, I would." His warm breath caresses my skin as he speaks, slowly trailing upwards towards my neck with his touch tickling and delighting me all at once.

"Thank you," I whisper shyly, feeling overwhelmed by his proximity. "You're really handsome too."

His chest rumbles with laughter and he leans in to whisper in my ear, his lips nibbling and teasing before taking my lobe between them. "I'm glad you think so."

As he reaches under me to unclasp my bra and slide it off my arms, he continues to murmur soothing words in my ear. My eyes flutter closed as I revel in the feel of his bare skin pressed against mine. Soon enough, my underwear follows suit.

Driven by an unfamiliar urgency, I pull at his belt, desperate to be even closer to him. He helps me unzip his pants and I use my feet to tug them down. And finally, when we are both fully naked, I wrap my legs around him, needing him to fill the void within me.

"Not yet, love." His hand sneaks between our bodies, touching me, feeling how much he affects me. "You're not ready," he says, and my brows furrow at his words.

"I'm ready, so ready. Please." How can he not see how ready I am, want dripping from my very being?

He chuckles and shakes his head, giving me a quick kiss before lowering himself between my legs.

I just want him inside! My mind is screaming, but as his tongue makes contact with my flesh, I can't be mad anymore.

I fall back onto the mattress, eyes wild, legs on his shoulders and hands in his hair.

He's killing me.

My breathing picks up, my body responding to every touch.

"Marcello," I gasp, that elusive feeling nearing ever so slightly.

My thighs clench, tightening around his head. His hands on my butt draw me closer, his movements increasing, his tongue wringing every bit of pleasure from my body.

Until it all collapses.

"Mar-cello!" I moan out loud, feeling my body go limp.

Marcello's lips press gently against my stomach, his head resting on the slight curve. My fingers tense as I remember the stretch marks that adorn my belly from pregnancy, but he stops me from pushing him away.

"Don't," his voice is filled with tenderness and a hint of awe. His hand rests on the most prominent scar, tracing it delicately.

"It's not pretty," I try to stop him, placing my hand over his.

"But it is," he interrupts, dropping another kiss on the marred skin. "Because it gave life. Never be ashamed of it, Lina."

His words wash over me like a warm embrace, causing tears to well up in my eyes. He sees the scars as symbols of strength and sacrifice, not flaws or imperfections.

"You gave up everything for your beautiful baby girl when others wouldn't. This is your badge of honor, Lina."

"Thank you," my voice catches in my throat. It's the first time someone has acknowledged my sacrifices for Claudia, the first time anyone has seen them as anything but shameful.

"You have no idea how much that means to me," I whisper, running my fingers through his hair in gratitude and love. He truly understands and appreciates what I've been through as a mother.

With a fiery fervor, he moves up my body, his lips finding mine in a scorching kiss. All other thoughts dissipate as I surrender to the overwhelming sensation.

He settles between my legs, slowly entering me with each deliberate thrust. My arms wrap around his strong form, holding onto him as he lavishes attention on every inch of my body. With each touch and stroke, he worships me like I am the most precious thing in the world. I can do nothing but gaze into his intense eyes, feeling the waves of pleasure wash over me.

But it's almost too much to handle.

"Faster," I plead, unable to contain the building pressure inside of me. Marcello responds by increasing his pace, his length retreating and then plunging back into me until I am stretched to my limits and gasping with delight.

Just a little bit more!

I clench around him, every nerve in my body electrified with pleasure. The intensity pushes me over the edge, tears streaming down my face as I release all control. And moments later, I feel him join me in bliss, filling me completely.

"Lina," he groans, resting his forehead against my shoulder as we both catch our breaths. He lifts his head slightly and sees my tears.

"Fuck! Did I hurt you? Are you all right?" He tries to move, but I keep holding onto him.

"No, you didn't hurt me. It was just... too much. Too much feeling," I confess, biting my lip. His eyebrows crease in confusion.

"You're sure?" he asks again.

"Yes, everything was perfect." My hands glide across his back, and I'm once more reminded of the horrific sight I'd seen.

We settle in bed, and he drapes the sheet on top of me. We sit in silence for a while, and I muster the courage to ask.

"What happened to your back?"

"You saw," he slowly says. I turn around to face him. His expression is tight, and he's looking anywhere but at me.

"Who did that to you?" His shoulders slump at my question. He shouldn't feel embarrassed about it. Not knowing is something I can understand very well.

"I..." He pauses, taking a deep breath. "I'll tell you someday," he finally says, not meeting my eyes.

Someday. Why is it always someday with him? Before I can control myself, I blurt out,

My voice trembles as I struggle to form the words, my heart pounding in my chest. "Like the woman you loved?" The question hangs between us, charged with a mixture of fear and jealousy. I can feel my hands ball into fists, itching to neutralize any competition.

Marcello's gaze meets mine, his expression pleading for me to drop the subject. But I need to know. "Can't you tell me?" I continue, feeling a surge of desperation. "I want to know who I'm competing against. Is she still in your life?" But what I really want to ask is if he still loves her.

"It's in the past," he replies, his voice tinged with regret.

"Marcello," I start again, struggling to find the right words. "I think we should lay everything on the table."

Confusion clouds his features as he frowns at me.

"I'm in love with you," I declare, my heart racing with every word. "I've been falling in love with you from the very beginning. That's why... I need to know if there's still someone else in your heart." Now that the truth is out, I don't know if I should rejoice or weep. Moments pass as he simply stares at me, his mind racing.

"You... love me?" he repeats incredulously.

I nod, tears welling up in my eyes. "Of course I do."

He pulls me into a tight embrace, his arms wrapped around me so tightly it feels like he wants to never let go.

"You love me," he whispers against my hair, his voice filled with disbelief and wonder.

"I do," I reply without hesitation. "I love you."

He continues to hold me close, repeating those three words like a mantra as if trying to convince himself that this is real.

After a while, he finally lifts his head from the crook of my neck, his eyes shining with unshed tears.

"Marcello?" I tentatively break the silence, feeling a lump form in my throat.

His eyes meet mine, and I can see the emotion swirling within them. And then, I hear it—a small sob slipping from his lips as he pulls me even closer, sealing our love with a passionate kiss.

"Marcello," I say again.

"There isn't anyone else," he finally speaks against my skin. "There was never anyone else."

"But... that woman..."

"It's always been you."

MARCELLO

With a deep breath, I gather the courage to tell her the truth, knowing that it could change everything between us. "It's always been you," I whisper, my eyes locked onto hers.

She pulls away slightly, her arms pushing at my shoulders as if trying to create a physical distance between us. "What do you mean?" Her voice is laced with confusion and a hint of vulnerability. "How is that possible?"

I take a step back, giving her the space she needs. "I've only ever loved one woman—you."

Her eyebrows furrow in disbelief. "You don't have to lie to me, Marcello," she says softly, almost pleadingly.

"I'm not lying," I assure her. "Not about this." My heart races as I prepare to reveal something I have kept hidden for too long. "I fell in love with you ten years ago."

"Ten years ago..." Her voice trails off as she tries to make sense of my words. "But... how?"

"It was at one of your father's banquets. You were in the garden, trying to sneak in through the back gate." The memory is crystal clear in my mind, like it happened just yesterday. "I knew then that I wanted to marry you."

A look of confusion crosses her features again. "We've never met before," she insists.

"We did meet," I reply gently. "Just outside your house." And with that, I proceed to recount every detail of the encounter that has stayed with me all these years. The moment she had captured my heart completely and irrevocably—whether she had known it or not.

Since that day, I have been hers without hesitation or question.

———

AGE TWENTY-ONE

Agony rips through my insides, a searing pain that threatens to consume me. My hand is desperately clutching at the wound on my abdomen, trying to stem the flow of blood. I know I won't die from this injury, but that doesn't make it any less excruciating.

I keep my head low as I trudge forward, the hood pulled over my face providing some relief from the relentless beating of father's fists.

Do I even look human anymore?

My eyes are swollen shut, one eyelid completely busted and useless. The other is barely functional, allowing only a sliver of vision through the swelling. My cheek throbs with each step, likely fractured from the repeated blows. And as for my nose...well, it probably won't ever be the same again.

But the knife wound is what catches me off guard. It's a new level of punishment from father, one that I didn't see coming. I guess I went too far this time.

Farther than I ever have before.

I had stood up to him, refused to go along with his weekly visits to brothels and engage in his depraved activities. Why should I lower myself like that? All because he is my father? No, I needed to get my life together if I ever wanted to be worthy of Catalina.

Rocco was well aware of my father's illicit activities, and by association, mine. This meant he would never agree to give me his daughter's hand in marriage. Among made men, there was one thing that was strictly forbidden: frequenting bordellos. Of course, this wouldn't matter to my father, but for any other self-respecting capo, it would be disgraceful to have his daughter married to a notorious philanderer who could bring shame upon her and their family name.

While Rocco himself was no saint, his preferences leaned towards kept women rather than paid ones. Though the distinction was minuscule, some might argue it made a difference. But when you took into account my father's penchant for debauchery... I couldn't imagine any man willingly offering his daughter's hand in marriage to someone involved in such scandalous activities.

It was clear I had my work cut out for me. Not that giving up those vices was a hardship for me – I had never truly enjoyed them. However, if I'm being completely honest with myself, the main reason I wanted to change was for Catalina.

I wanted to be worthy of her love and respect. Someone she could proudly stand beside without fear of judgment or embarrassment. Perhaps even someone she could learn to love in return...

The streets were quiet as I wandered closer to the Agosti home. My father had grown increasingly angry with me for refusing to accompany him week after week, until he finally snapped and resorted to violence. He claimed to be teaching me a lesson, saying that my actions reflected poorly on him and made him appear weak.

But his "lesson" had been anything but gentle. His soldiers held me down while he mercilessly pummeled my face with his fists, the pain nearly causing me to lose consciousness. And when that wasn't enough for him, he grabbed a knife and thrust it between my ribs, inflicting a wound that would cause maximum agony without causing any permanent damage.

As I groan from the throbbing ache in my side, I realize that deep down I must have been hoping to catch a glimpse of Catalina. Seeing her again would bring some relief to the pain, even if only temporarily.

But I know better than to approach the front of the house. Doing so would only result in another beating from my father, and I've already endured enough for one day. So I continue to wander aimlessly through the streets, lost in my thoughts and trying to push away the physical and emotional pain that consume me.

A dizzying sensation washes over me, likely from the blood loss. I stumble towards the back of the imposing house, its high fence blocking any chance of entry – not that I have the strength or desire to enter in my current state.

My vision blurs as I spot a small corner nestled in the nook of the fence. From this angle, I can see into the back garden of the house. It's enough for me as I collapse against the fence, struggling to catch my breath. Every movement sends sharp pains shooting through my body, but I try to find a comfortable position against the cold metal bars.

To any passerby, I must look like a homeless man with my torn and bloody clothes, huddled against the fence with my face hidden under a hoodie. But right now, that doesn't matter to me. All I care about is drifting off to sleep and maybe even dreaming of her...

I lose track of time, but suddenly something prods at my shoulder, startling me awake. My first instinct is to defend myself or run away. With great effort, I lift my head and squint my good eye, trying to make sense of my surroundings in the harsh light.

"Fuck!" I curse as everything remains blurry. I pray there isn't any permanent damage to my eyesight as I struggle to focus on my unexpected visitor.

"Are you all right?" A soft, gentle voice breaks through the silence, and I slowly turn around. My heart flutters as I see her standing on the other side of the fence, her hand reaching through the gaps in the pickets. Catalina. She's like a vision, too perfect to be real.

"I..." My words catch in my throat as I take in her appearance. The way sunlight dances across her features, making her seem almost ephemeral. It's hard to tell if she's just a figment of my imagination or if she truly stands before me.

"You're hurt!" Her gasp of concern brings me back to reality, and I lower my head in embarrassment.

Why did I even come here?

I try to stand up, wanting to leave before she can see me in this vulnerable state, but it takes all my strength to do so.

"Wait, please! Don't go," her voice pleads, holding me in place with its magnetic pull.

I turn towards her fully now, taking in every detail. The way the sun illuminates her yellow dress, making it seem almost ethereal against the lush greenery surrounding us.

"Do you need anything?" Her eyebrows furrow with worry as she looks at my battered face.

I shake my head slightly.

"Please, just... wait here. Wait for me." She pauses as if waiting for my confirmation before dashing towards the nearby house. The sound of her footsteps fading away echoes in my ears as I wait for her return.

I stand rooted in place, my mind racing as I try to make sense of the figure before me. Is this a dream?

But then she's back, her presence palpable and undeniable.

"You didn't leave," she huffs, her breaths coming in ragged gasps. "Can you come closer?" Her hand beckons me towards the fence, and I move towards her like a loyal servant.

"Here," she says, slipping a small bag through the gap in the fence.

As our fingers brush against each other, a current of electricity jolts through my body.

"Oh!" she seems taken aback but doesn't recoil from my touch.

I peer into the bag and find a sandwich, some pieces of ripe fruit, and a small bottle of water. I look back at her in disbelief.

"Why?" My voice comes out hoarse, still raw with pain.

"You need to take care of yourself." She smiles, a gentle expression that reaches deep into my soul.

"Thank you..." My words catch in my throat as I struggle to comprehend this act of kindness – something so foreign to me, especially from a stranger.

I don't think anyone has ever given me anything before.

With trembling hands, I look in disbelief at the contents of the bag, feeling tears well up in my one good eye. A sob escapes me as I try to hold back overwhelming emotions.

"Thank you," I whisper again, my voice barely audible.

"You don't have to thank me. Anyone would do the same."

No one has ever done the same for me. Not until now...

"Could you possibly come a bit closer?" she whispers, pulling out a white cloth from her pocket with delicate fingers.

Curiosity piqued, I inch forward and peer at the cloth in her hand.

"It's for cleaning your wounds," she explains gently, gesturing for me to come nearer.

I press my face between the pickets, feeling her soft touch as she tenderly wipes away dirt and debris from my injuries. A sharp sting makes me flinch as she applies disinfectant, but she giggles and continues her diligent work.

Lost in her careful ministrations, I watch her with awe and reverence. Never before has anyone shown such care towards my wounds – and I've had more than my fair share.

Without thinking, I stop her hand just as it nears my injured eye. Bringing it to my lips, I place a kiss on her knuckles in a simple gesture of gratitude.

"Thank you," I say again, not caring how many times I repeat myself or how vulnerable this action makes me feel. In this moment, I am thankful to her in a way that I never thought possible.

She blushes but doesn't pull away from my touch.

We sit there for a while longer before she finally tells me that she must leave. But before she does, she surprises me with an unexpected question.

"Will you return?" Her words shock me to the core.

I can't find the words to answer her, and thankfully she doesn't press for one.

For the next couple of days, I religiously make my way to our designated meeting spot at the same time, every day. She arrives bearing medicine and food, as well as her comforting presence. We spend our time together discussing mundane topics, but for me, it's a welcome escape from reality.

She has no clue of my identity or the profound impact she has on me. Her innocent ignorance is a blessing and a curse.

Little does she know, I am about to face the consequences of yearning for something that will always be just out of reach.

———

PRESENT-DAY

A trail of tears cascades down her cheeks as I recount the painful details to her. I hold back the more vulnerable parts, like the bruises and scars that were inflicted upon me that day, or the fact that my love for her had made me seem weak in my father's eyes. And how he had taken advantage of that weakness in the worst way possible.

"I... I don't know what to say," she whispers, using the back of her hand to wipe away her tears. "Why didn't you come for me?"

"I didn't think I was worthy of you. My past... it's not pretty." It's a half-truth, but if she knew the real reason... I can't even imagine what would happen. But even though I stayed away, she never left my thoughts for a single day.

"Marcello..." The sound of her saying my name is like a balm to my soul. She has the power to heal me, but also the power to destroy me.

"Are you angry?"

"Angry? Why would I be angry?"

"Because I kept this from you." Her forgiveness means everything to me.

Her head shakes from side to side, her soft gaze never leaving mine. "No... no," she repeats, her voice gentle and full of understanding. "I could never be angry with you. But I do have some questions." She nestles in closer to me, resting her head on my chest. "How is it that you fell in love with me based on just a few brief interactions? It's just... unexpected. Not that I'm complaining, of course. I couldn't be happier to know you feel the same way." Her last words are spoken softly, almost shyly.

"It was simple, really. When all you've ever known is cruelty, the one person who shows you kindness becomes your entire world. And that person was you, Lina. From the moment you gave me that small bag of food and tended to my wounds, I started to believe that there was good in the world beyond the darkness. You gave me hope again." Even though that hope would eventually be shattered, she had still shown me a different way of living. And for that, she became my everything—my muse, my ultimate desire.

"What happened to you, Marcello?"

"More like what didn't happen," I reply wryly. "But I'll tell you..."

"Someday," we say in unison with a laugh.

"It's not that I don't want to, Lina. But it's difficult to talk about it." And because part of me doesn't think she'd look at me the same if she knew the things I've done.

"I'm here. Whenever you want to talk." She lays a kiss on my chest, her face nuzzling my side.

"So, you love me." I subtly change the subject, even though I still can't believe she loves me. It's simply too good to be true, considering I'd dreamed of hearing her say these words for so long.

"And *you* love me." She shoots back, arching an eyebrow, her lips twitching sheepishly.

"So much it hurts." I tip her chin up with my finger, wanting to show her the sincerity in my eyes. "There's nothing I wouldn't do for you, Lina. Tell me to die tomorrow, and I will. Tell me to live, and I'll be your servant. Forever."

She blinks twice, a smile spreading on her lips. "Fine. As my servant, I command you to never stop loving me."

"Easy."

"And I want to have many, many children."

"Done," I immediately say.

"Really? How about ten?" Lina raises her eyebrow in a challenge.

"Ten works for me, but I'm worried about you since you'll be doing the hard work."

"I don't mind that. I want a big family." She tilts her head pensively. "A big *loving* family."

"Then I'll give you everything you want."

I gather her in my arms, my head resting atop hers.

And I silently pray.

That her love will be enough.

When the day comes...

———

GENTLY PLACING a kiss on Lina's lips, I whisper "Love you." It's become a ritual for me—ever since mustering up the courage to confess my feelings, I've made it my mission to let her know just how much she means to me at every opportunity. Some might say I do it in excess, but after ten years of keeping my longing hidden, I have some catching up to do.

I hurry to finish all of my meetings in time so I can return home. Guerra had made me an offer that I couldn't refuse, even if it was only temporary. While my trust in him is still shaky, the famiglia's concerns about our transportation issues are becoming impossible to ignore. Ever since the inauguration, there has been a clear divide among the members—one faction supporting me while the other stands behind Nicolo. It's something I had anticipated, but now it's crucial for me to convince everyone that I am the most capable candidate for Capo.

My doubts about Benedicto linger, as his true loyalties towards his brother remain uncertain. And with Franco's simmering resentment towards Catalina growing stronger after her public shaming, he seems like the most likely suspect in all of this chaos. But deep down, I know it's not him who's been terrorizing Catalina. All evidence points to the copycat Chimera, yet I'm no closer to uncovering their identity.

The entire situation is too messy. I just hope that for now the famiglia will be satisfied with Guerra's routes for transport and Enzo's clubs for distribution.

I spend most of the day going through warehouse to warehouse to make sure the next transport is secure enough. After I feel that everything is in order, I leave it up to Francesco to oversee the details.

It's almost dark when I get back home. I find the girls in the drawing room; Claudia and Venezia are doing their homework while Catalina is focused on drawing a new piece. I frown when I notice Sisi is missing. She's been doing that a lot lately.

"Marcello!" Lina drops everything to jump in my arms.

"Easy, love." I kiss the top of her head.

Venezia and Claudia acknowledge me with a nod, but they seem to be engrossed in whatever they are working on, so I don't want to disturb them.

"They have a quiz tomorrow," Lina whispers and waves me towards the stairs.

"How was your day?" she asks when we get in our room.

"Good, I think. Not sure yet," I admit, and I give her a quick summary of what I'd planned.

"If Guerra holds his end of the bargain, this could work." Lina helps me out of my shirt.

"Your brother's help is also a bonus. I've done the math and we could recoup our losses in a month, max two."

She purses her lips, her face strained.

"I've never liked what Enzo does. I mean, I don't like *any* of this. But he's knowingly and intentionally exploiting women." She shakes her head. "I just can't reconcile that with the image I have of my brother."

"There's one thing you need to understand, Lina." I turn to her, softly stroking her hair. "Mafiosi always have two faces: one that they show to their family, and one that they show to the outside world. You can't succeed in this cutthroat environment without ruthlessness and a compromise on morality. You might know him as a loving brother, but to everyone else, he's a capo and a made man."

She seems pensive for a moment.

"I know who you are with me," Lina says, poking her finger in my chest. "But what's the face you show to the outside world? The one you used to punish Franco?"

"No. It's much, much worse," I tell her honestly, hoping she won't probe for more.

"What do you mean?"

"I pray that you never find out." I lift her finger to my lips. She looks like she wants to say something more, so I silence her with a kiss. What she'd seen me do to Franco had been tame. If she knew what I'm capable of... I really hope she never finds out.

Before we can take things further, Amelia interrupts to let me know I received a package which she'd left in my office.

"Do you have to go now?" Her hand trails softly down my arm before intertwining our fingers.

"I won't be long," I say, reluctant to leave her side. "After that, I'm all yours."

"I'll wait for you."

Anticipation already building inside of me, I make a run for my office, intent on getting this over with quickly. As Amelia said, there is a big box on top of my desk.

Odd that Amelia didn't mention who it's from. A cursory glance tells me it doesn't have any labels.

I shrug and set about opening it. Grabbing a pair of scissors, I cut through the tape holding the box at the top.

I hadn't felt anything before, but the moment I open the box, the smell of death assaults me.

"Fuck!" I mutter, scrunching my nose in disgust. Is this another bad joke? Carelessly, I tear through the cardboard to see what is inside.

And then I still.

Severed at the neck, Father's head is placed face up inside the box. The skin is a blue-yellowish, a mix of pus and blood lingering at the decapitation line. The bullet wound is infested with maggots, as are his eye sockets—or what's left of them.

"Fuck! Fuck! Fuck!" I take a step back, staring in shock at Father's rotting head. Who could have sent this?

But that means...

Taking a deep breath, I rummage through the box, looking for some clues as to who could have done this. It doesn't take me long to find a note.

NICE TRY!

My hand clenches around the piece of paper.

I've been played.

Trying to calm myself, I take a seat and replay the recent events in my head. There's only one conclusion to be drawn.

It's someone close to me.

This is all a joke for whoever is doing this. And putting things in perspective makes me think that everything's been a game so far. From me finding the asylum papers when I did – considering I'd gone through all of Tino's files before – to finding Father and killing him, hoping he was the source of my torment.

A manic laugh takes over. I can't even help myself as I bend forward, my belly hurting from laughing this hard.

And then I stop.

They think they won, huh? But now I have one invaluable clue. Whoever it is has unrestricted access to my house. But more than anything, they *know* about my past, and my work for Father. That narrows the list even more.

It's someone within the famiglia.

But this is more than that. It's personal. And I can't think of anyone I've offended. Sure, there's Nicolo and his cronies, but I've barely interacted with them. There is more to this than meets the eye, but I simply don't have enough information.

I call one soldier and instruct him to get rid of the head.

If they're so close... I might just need to plant a red herring.

I get back a little later to the room, and Lina is already tucked in bed. She smiles when she sees me, opening her arms. I slide in and cuddle her.

One thing is for sure. This is war. I can't let anyone take away my happiness. Not when I finally got her.

CATALINA

The sun has just begun to peek through the windows of my home when I hear the familiar rumble of the delivery truck. Excitement bubbles in my chest as I rush to answer the door, eagerly awaiting my weekly shipment of fabrics. I had ordered quite a few this time, determined to surprise Claudia with her dream princess dress for her upcoming birthday.

As the driver unloads the large boxes from his truck, I can barely contain my grin. The girls are still sleeping, and Marcello has already left for work, leaving me alone in the quiet house. It's the perfect opportunity to unpack the materials and start planning out the design.

I carry the boxes to my room, eager to see all the different textures and colors. Carefully, I line them up on my bed, arranging them for better visualization. As I make a mental note to throw away the empty boxes later, a small scrap of paper falls out. My first thought is that it might be an invoice, but as I pick it up, I realize it's something much more unsettling.

DON'T YOU WANT TO KNOW WHO THE FATHER OF YOUR CHILD IS?

My heart races, and I feel a chill run down my spine. Who would leave such a haunting message? Frantically, I search through all the boxes, but there's nothing else inside except this one piece of paper. With trembling hands, I take a seat on my bed, still clutching the note.

No, I can't let this rattle me. Everything is in the past now, and whoever is behind this couldn't possibly know what happened that night. But as hard as I try to push away these thoughts and focus on my work, I can't shake off the feeling of unease that lingers in the air.

I take a while to compose myself. I rip the note into pieces and throw it in the trash. Then, I just focus on my project.

I won't let this bother me.

"Signora Catalina, this came for you." Amelia's voice interrupts my thoughts as she approaches me on my way to breakfast the following day. I frown but take the letter from her. It's written on thick parchment paper, sealed with red wax and a crest that I don't recognize.

I find a secluded spot under the stairs and carefully open the letter. Inside is another note, similar to the one I received yesterday. My fingers tremble as I unfold it, dreading what words will meet my eyes this time.

He's closer than you think.

My heart pounds in my chest as I read those chilling words. Who is doing this? Who is trying so hard to torment me with the worst thing that ever happened to me? The mere thought makes my stomach churn with fear and anger.

Quickly stuffing the note back into its envelope, I ask Amelia to bring breakfast to my room and excuse my absence by saying I am feeling ill. As soon as she leaves, I rush to my room, needing the safety and solitude it offers.

What is happening? I can't make sense of it. I admit that over the years, I have occasionally thought about Claudia's biological father. But not because I wanted to know his identity – it was more out of a desperate need to see if there were any signs of him in my daughter. Thankfully, she has inherited all of her physical character-istics from me – except for her hair.

Shaking my head in disbelief, I refuse to entertain the idea that the note might be right. The thought of my rapist being near me fills me with an overwhelming sense of dread and nausea.

A loud knock on the door startles me. I quickly shove the letter under the mattress, hoping that Marcello won't notice.

"Lina? Are you alright?" His voice is filled with concern as he enters the room. I try to compose myself before he sees me.

"Just a headache, love. Nothing to worry about." I offer him a small smile and reach for his hand, seeking solace in his touch.

But he isn't convinced. He crouches down in front of me, feeling my forehead with the back of his hand.

"You feel warm. Maybe you should rest." His brows furrow with worry.

"It's fine, really. I just needed some water." I try to sound nonchalant, but I can see the doubt in his eyes.

"I can't help but worry about you, Lina. You mean everything to me." His tender words bring tears to my eyes as I wrap my arms around him, holding onto him tightly.

"I love you," I whisper, burying my face in his chest. If only he knew the truth...but I can't bear to tell him.

"I adore you, Lina. Never forget that." He pulls back slightly, his expression still clouded with concern.

Feeling guilty for causing him worry, I hurry him back to the dining room.

"I'm feeling much better now. Let's go together." I stand up and lead him towards the door.

"If you're sure..." He studies me carefully, trying to gauge if I'm telling the truth.

I nod and force a smile onto my face.

He already has enough on his plate. He doesn't need to worry about this too.

The daily barrage of messages is overwhelming. Every morning, like clockwork, a letter arrives at my doorstep. They come in different envelopes with no return address, but I know they're from the same person. It's been a week now, and the notes never fail to taunt me with the secret of Claudia's father's identity.

At first, I tried to open them, hoping for some closure or answers. But after the first few days, I couldn't bear it anymore. The pain of not knowing was too much, so I started burning them instead.

I thought that throwing away the letters would make it all stop. And for two days, there was nothing.

But then, just when I let my guard down, a pop-up appears on my computer screen as I'm browsing the internet in my room. At first, it's blank, but soon words start appearing in the same sentences as the letters I had been receiving.

SILLY GIRL, IF YOU ONLY KNEW.

THE MAN YOU PROFESS TO LOVE – DON'T
THINK I HAVEN'T HEARD.

I panic and try to exit out of the window, pressing every key on my keyboard frantically. But it's no use; the pop-up won't go away.

THE MAN WHO RAPED YOU IS CLOSER THAN
YOU THINK.

YOU'RE MARRIED TO HIM.

My heart drops as I read those words. My computer suddenly crashes, leaving me staring at a blank screen in shock. Could he be implying that Marcello is the man from that horrific night? The mere thought of it makes me laugh bitterly. This whole charade is just an attempt to make me doubt my husband and tear our marriage apart.

Whoever it was should realize just how far-fetched the idea that Marcello could be Claudia's father is...

I shake my head, determined to put this out of my mind forever.

When dinner is announced, I go downstairs and notice that everyone but Assisi is already at the table. Marcello is deep in conversation with Claudia, and they are discussing some text she'd had to read as part of her homework.

"But it's not very logical," my daughter notes, eyebrows knit together in consternation.

"I think you're just advanced for your grade, Claudia," Marcello nods. "Have you tried telling that to Mrs. Evans?"

"Yes, but she wants me to go the traditional route. She says I shouldn't miss out on a *normal* education." She sighs, clearly disappointed with her teacher's approach.

"Lina, there you are." Marcello gives me a bright smile as I take my seat. I nod at them, urging them to continue.

As the courses come and go, I can't help but stare at the two of them, looking for any similarities. Damnation! Now that the idea was sown into my head, I can't help but think about it.

There isn't much to go off. The only thing they have in common is their lightly colored hair. In fact, the more I stare, the more I realize that it's the same shade of blonde.

Lord! I must be going crazy.

"Lina?" Marcello calls my name, frowning.

"Yes, sorry I didn't hear you."

"You've been lost in thought for a while now."

"Just thinking about my design," I quickly lie, forcing a smile. Good Lord, if he knew what I've been thinking about...

The next course is served, and I see Marcello looking a little disconcerted.

"Something wrong?" I ask as one of the staff members places a plate in front of me.

"I've given specific instructions to avoid seafood," he notes, picking at his food.

I look down into my plate and see that it's a seafood medley.

"Ew." My daughter makes a face, pushing the plate away from her.

"Why?" I ask, my eyes still on my daughter.

"I have a seafood allergy." He shakes his head, rising to go to the kitchen to inquire further.

"Wow. I have a seafood allergy too," Claudia exclaims. Marcello stops in his tracks and half-turns towards Claudia, his expression inscrutable.

"I'll tell them not to make this mistake again." His voice is tense, and my doubts suddenly double.

Surely it's just a coincidence?

The following days are even worse. I watch Marcello and Claudia even closer, studying their interactions and their behaviors. Suddenly, I see a pattern in everything.

This is getting to me too much. Especially when I search the internet for types of evidence that two people could be related. Short of a DNA test, another far less reliable method is to compare blood types of the parents.

I pause for a second to think. My blood type is O and Claudia's is B. I study some charts and the father can only have a B or AB blood type. Okay, so there's not much to go off. But because I'm so paranoid, I end up asking him late at night in bed.

"Where did this come from?"

"Oh, I've been reading some wellness tips and they take blood type into consideration." The lie rolls easily off my tongue, and I feel a twinge of guilt. I'm going crazy, but if he says O or A, then I can put my worries aside.

"Hmm, that's interesting." He turns towards me, his face mere millimeters away. "It's B, I think."

"Oh." It's all I can say.

"Any tips for me?" He jokes, tugging me closer.

"I'll read up and tell you?"

"Deal." His mouth comes down on mine and I lose track of everything else.

Because this is the man I love.

———

"LINA, PAY ATTENTION." Enzo snaps his fingers in front of me.

"Sorry. I've been a little distracted lately."

I'd asked Enzo to meet me at a nearby cafe. I needed someone to confide in, and for all our friendship, I knew Sisi wasn't the best option in this case. Not only because it was her brother I wanted to talk about, but also because she's been too distant lately.

"I see that." He leans back in his seat, studying me.

"Is he mistreating you? You can tell me anything, Lina. I'll make him rue the day he was born if he did anything..."

"No, not at all." I cut him off. "It's not that. He's been nothing but wonderful," I quickly say. I've noticed in the past that Enzo doesn't have the greatest opinion of Marcello, and I have to wonder why.

"You've lost weight, and you look gaunt. What am I to think?" He arches an eyebrow at me and waits for me to talk.

"I..." I start, not even knowing where to begin. "I love him. I love him like I never thought I would." I clutch the cup of coffee in my hands, lowering my gaze. "He's amazing, thoughtful and oh, so kind. He's everything I could have asked for and more."

Enzo snickers at my words, and I raise my head. "Which is why I don't understand why you hate him so much."

"Have you heard anything about his past?"

I shake my head. "Only a little... not much."

"Did he tell you he asked for your hand years back?"

"He did mention that."

"Rocco accepted the match. It was a few weeks before..." He trails off and I know he means *the incident*. "After that, his father suddenly died and Marcello went missing."

"Why did Papa never say anything?" I frown. I hadn't realized how serious the marriage talk had been.

"It was too late by that point." Enzo grimaces. He means I was already damaged goods by then.

"Is that why you're so against him? Because he left the famiglia?"

"No." Enzo's lips curl around the corner sardonically. "It was because of what he did before he left."

"If you're talking about the orgies, then I've heard about that," I suddenly say.

Enzo blinks twice, taken aback by my comment, but he continues. "The orgies were but a small part. The Lastras were infamous ten years ago. Marcello and his father were always together, engaging in the worst, most debasing practices." Enzo pretends to spit to emphasize just how disgusting he finds those practices.

"I see." I turn to my coffee once more, not knowing how to answer. The man I know and the man he's describing are two different people. But that's the whole point, isn't it? He's a two-faced mafioso.

"Why did you call me here, Lina? And be honest. I can see that something's eating at you."

"I've been getting some harassing messages. At first, it was letters, and then they started showing up on my computer too."

"What does Lastra say about that?"

"I didn't tell him."

"Lina..." Enzo groans, slapping his hand over his forehead. "Why would you not tell your husband? I only agreed to the match because he was supposed to keep you safe."

"Because the messages are about him," I whisper, finally getting to the real reason I'd called him here.

"What do you mean?"

"The messages keep saying he's Claudia's father." I recount from the beginning what each message had contained, and then my ever-increasing doubts and observations.

"So your evidence so far is that they have the same hair, allergy, and blood type?" He's pensive as he asks, and I just nod.

"It's not exactly evidence. That would imply I already believe he is guilty. I just can't help being paranoid. I keep looking at every single thing they have in common, and I have these doubts..."

Enzo is silent, his jaw locked tight.

"It's crazy, right? It's too crazy to even contemplate." I shake my head. I just want Enzo to tell me I'm seeing too much into this. I want him to confirm that I am going off the deep end.

"I don't know if it's too crazy."

My head snaps in his direction, my eyes wide.

"What do you mean?" I ask, almost horrified.

"Lina, I told you he wasn't a good man. The Marcello I knew... the Marcello everyone knew was a monster. Fuck! I don't think I'll ever be able to forgive myself for agreeing to this marriage." He presses his fingers to his temples in a light massage.

"What do you mean by monster?" My words are a mere whisper.

"Every bad thing you could think of, he was guilty of," he says with a sigh.

"But it's just rumors, right? You can't know for sure."

"Lina, there was a time that absolutely *no one* dared to go against the Lastras. Everyone who wronged them ended up dead – killed in the worst manners possible. When his father died and Marcello went missing, no one mourned them. Like a stain in the five families' history, they were promptly forgotten."

"But... that doesn't mean he'd do something like that to me." I try to explain to him, but even to my ears, it sounds fake. "He wanted to marry me, right? Why would he...?"

Enzo places a cigarette in his mouth and lights it up. He inhales a few times before blowing a cloud of smoke. He shrugs.

"I'm not saying that he *did* it. I'm only saying he's capable of doing it."

His casual manner doesn't help with my already increasing panic. No, I'm sure Marcello wouldn't do that. I know him, don't I? I know how gentle and how kind he is. How could such a person... I shake my head, not even wanting to go there.

"If you're so preoccupied by what a stranger said, you can always do a DNA test to confirm your doubts."

"That would mean I strongly suspect him."

"No, that would mean you get a result, confirm it's not him, as you clearly believe, and then move on. You're so stressed right now about the possibility that it *might* be him you can barely function." Enzo aptly points out everything I'd been thinking about, and I have to agree with his line of reasoning.

"You're right. I don't think it's him. But I'll do it just to be sure."

"Good. I'll take care of it. You just need to collect some hair samples from Claudia and your husband. I'll have someone drop by to pick them up."

"I'm scared," I admit for the first time.

"Lina, as much as I don't like your husband, if you believe he didn't do it, then I trust your judgment. It is possible someone is just trying to drive a wedge between the two of you."

"I've thought about that. But I'm still..."

"You need to be certain. I can respect that. I'll make sure you have the results as soon as possible."

CATALINA

My hands tighten over the unopened envelope. Enzo had sent one of his men to deliver it to me. It had taken less time than I'd imagined, less than a week.

But now I face the biggest decision. Open it and find out the truth, or discard it, forget about the entire thing, and trust my husband. It doesn't help that Marcello and I are closer than ever. Last night he'd gotten one of his night terrors, and I'd comforted him throughout the night as he'd shared some things about his monster of a father.

So many pieces just don't fit in this story, and it's making me more confused than ever. With a sigh, I put the envelope in a drawer.

I'll do it later.

Maybe I'm afraid of what I'm going to find out... I shake my head, telling myself there's only one likely outcome, and that is a *negative* result.

Pushing it out of my mind, I leave my room and head downstairs. The girls are in the drawing room as usual, playing a game. Even though there is a five-year difference between them, Claudia and Venezia have quickly become best friends. Sisi is present too, sitting in the far corner of the room, book in hand.

"So you've decided to join civilization again?" I joke as I take a seat next to her.

Sisi looks up at me, a guilty smile playing on her lips.

"I know I haven't been around much. I've been trying to find myself." She sighs. "It's weird being free to do whatever I want for the first time."

"I know what you mean. But tell me, does that include a certain Guerra boy?" She lowers her head, and I can spot a blush. So that's how it is.

"We're friends. I think we understand each other. Tell me about you and Marcello." She turns towards me, changing the subject.

"We're good," I confess. "More than good. He's wonderful." Sisi's eyes widen for a second before she bursts out laughing.

I frown, not understanding her outburst.

"So I'm wonderful." Marcello's amused voice echoes from behind me. I whip my head around, and there he is, smirking.

"You shouldn't eavesdrop," I raise an eyebrow at him.

"How can I not when I hear gems like this?" His lips curl up. "Lina, can I see you for a moment?" I nod, and he takes me back to the room.

In the center of the bed is a big white rectangular box.

"What's this?"

"Open it."

I lift the top off to reveal a white dress – a wedding dress.

"What... What is this for?" I stammer as I unfold the dress. I'm shocked as I stare at the most beautiful dress I've ever seen.

"I've been working on a little something for you. I know you didn't get your fairytale wedding, and I'd like to remedy that." His expression is hopeful, and my chest tightens with emotion.

How could I have even entertained the thought that *this* man could be capable of anything as heinous as what I experienced that night? How could I have even suspected him?

"I have no words," I say, my eyes moving from the dress to the wonderful man in front of me.

"Come on, try it on," he urges me, and I gladly accept.

The dress is a dream come to life. With a bodice that hugs my curves and ends in a delicate v, and a full skirt that flares out in true princess fashion, it's everything I could have ever wanted. As I spin in front of the mirror, watching the skirts swish and sway around me, I can't help but feel like a fairytale princess.

"It's perfect," I exclaim to Marcello, who stands behind me with a proud smile on his face. He steps closer and places his hands on my waist, drawing me even closer to him. "You look absolutely breathtaking, Lina." His lips graze over my forehead before trailing down to my ear. "And you're all mine."

"Yes," I whisper, feeling my heart race at his closeness. "All yours."

But then he reaches under the bed and pulls out another box. My eyes widen as he opens it to reveal a pair of stunning white satin pumps adorned with glittering embellishments.

"Wow," I breathe out in awe.

Taking one foot in his hand, Marcello gently slides on the first shoe, leaving a trail of kisses along my ankle and calf as he does so. He repeats the same motion with the other foot, and when he finally steps back to admire his work, I can't believe how lucky I am to have him by my side.

"Come see for yourself," he says, gesturing towards the wall-length mirror. As I approach it, I can't help but feel like Cinderella admiring her glass slippers for the first time. This truly is a fairytale moment, and I never want it to end.

Marcello comes and embraces me from behind, laying his head on my shoulder.

"This is what I see when I look at you. Something so ethereal sometimes I find it hard to believe you're real."

"Marcello," I whisper in awe. Looking at myself in the mirror, wearing this stunning gown, I can't help but see myself through his eyes. And I feel beautiful. "Thank you."

"I love you, Lina." He comes around, cupping my face in his palms for a kiss.

"I love you too," I reply, and I instantly feel guilty about what I've been keeping from him.

He's probably going to be so disappointed in me for even contemplating that it might be true. But I have to tell him. I owe it to him.

"I need to tell you something." I take a step back. His eyebrows furrow in question, so I let the words flow out of my mouth before I lose the courage. "A couple of weeks ago I received an anonymous note. After that, more notes started coming in, almost daily. Until I got a message on my computer."

"What did it say? Lina, you should have told me earlier. It might be the same person who's been harassing you before."

My eyes lower to the ground as I begin to speak, the heaviness weighing down on my chest. "The notes were about Claudia's father," I say, my voice barely audible. "And the last message...it said that you're Claudia's father." My words hang in the air, thick with tension and disbelief. I take a deep breath, trying to steady myself. "It's absolutely insane, I know that now. I'm so sorry I didn't come to you before." I finally look up at him, hoping he won't hold it against me for keeping this information from him.

But Marcello's face is drained of all color. He takes a step back, his expression stricken and his movements slow and deliberate.

"Marcello?" I call out to him, my heart racing with fear. His reaction is so immediate and intense that I can feel it reverberating through my body.

He shakes his head ever so slowly, his eyes wide with horror. I watch as his features contort with shock and pain, unable to comprehend what's happening.

"It's not true, is it?" I ask, desperation creeping into my voice. But instead of denying it, he pales even more at my question, making my heart drop to my stomach.

Surely, no...

"Marcello, tell me it's not true," I plead, but all he does is continue shaking his head. No words come out of his mouth, leaving me feeling helpless and scared.

Why isn't he saying anything? Why is he not denying it?

"Marcello..." My voice trails off as realization dawns on me. No...it can't be true... He keeps retreating until his back hits the mirror behind him. But still, he remains silent.

My breathing becomes erratic as panic swells in my chest. Why is he not saying anything? Why is he not denying it? The silence is deafening, and all I can do is stand there, frozen in shock and disbelief.

My desperate plea hangs in the air, my voice cracking with emotion. But he remains unresponsive, a stone statue in front of me. I can't take it anymore. My hand trembles as I reach for the drawer, pulling out the envelope that holds the truth.

"Lina..."

I can feel myself trembling, but I continue on, tearing through the paper until the results are staring back at me.

99.9% match.

I slowly raise my eyes to meet his. There's a glimmer of recognition in his gaze, but it quickly disappears as he falls to his knees and crawls towards me. He grabs my hands, forcing me to look down at him.

"Lina, please, listen to me. I'm so sorry..." His words fade into a buzzing in my ears as the reality sinks in.

Marcello is Claudia's father.

That means... A sob catches in my throat as the implications become clear as daylight.

Marcello was the man who raped me.

I look down at him and no longer see the man I thought I knew. Instead, all I see is the man with amber eyes who stole everything from me.

A wave of revulsion and anger washes over me, and I flinch at his touch, pushing him away.

"You..." My voice is barely a whisper as I struggle to find the right words. "You raped me." The tears are falling freely now, hot and stinging against my cheeks. "You tortured and raped me." The pain is suffocating, overwhelming every inch of my being.

It hurts.

With a sharp slap, I knock his hands aside and take a step back.

"You raped me," The words come out like a wounded animal's growl, filled with heartbreak and disappointment that threaten to consume me.

"Lina, please," he croaks, his face ravaged with agony. "I can explain, please. I love you more than anything."

A hysterical laugh escapes my lips, the mere idea of his love for me seeming ludicrous.

"You say you love me, but you've caused me the worst pain I've ever experienced. How can that be love?" I yell, watching as he shrinks back from my outburst. My entire body is trembling with anger and betrayal.

"I can't... I can't do this." My voice cracks as tears begin to well up in my eyes. "You knew how much I suffered, and you never once thought to tell me the truth?"

"No." His whisper is barely audible, but it cuts through me like a knife. "I did everything for you, I swear." With each word, it feels like he's twisting the blade deeper into my heart.

"For me?" I choke out, unable to comprehend his reasoning. "You raped me for me? I'm sorry if I find that hard to believe."

"Please, just listen to me, Lina. It's not like you think."

"Stop! Just... stop." I struggle to control my emotions, taking deep breaths to calm myself down. "This paternity test proves that you're Claudia's biological father. How can it not be like that?"

I turn away from him, ready to leave and never look back. But suddenly, he grabs onto my waist and pulls me towards him.

"Please. I love you, Lina," he pleads, but every time he says those words more pain reverberates inside of me.

Was it all a lie?

My voice is laced with outrage as I spit out the words, "What kind of monster are you?" I watch as his expression shifts from shock to hurt, but my anger doesn't dissipate. "If this is how you love someone, then I don't want to know what happens when you hate them."

He starts to speak, but I interrupt him. "I lived with this pain for ten years, Marcello. Ten years. And you think a simple apology will make it all disappear?"

His eyes plead with me, begging for forgiveness. "Please don't leave me. I was wrong not to tell you, but I'll do anything for you to believe me."

"Anything?" I turn away slightly, contemplating his words.

"Anything," he nods, tears streaming down his face and staining his cheeks.

My resolve starts to waver as he pulls me closer, his grip tightening on my arms. "I never want to see you in front of me for as long as I live."

"Anything but that. I can't live without you, Lina." His hands are tangled in the delicate tulle of my dress and he's pulling me towards him, desperation evident in his actions.

"Let go of me," I say through gritted teeth, trying to break free from his hold. But he only clings tighter.

In a moment of fury and fear, I shove him with all my strength. He stumbles backward and hits the mirror behind him, causing it to shatter into pieces. Shards of glass rain down around him as he falls to the ground. His eyes widen in shock as he lies still amidst the broken fragments.

I rush towards him, my first instinct to help him despite everything. But then I stop myself, remembering the pain he has caused me. Blood trickles down his face from a small cut above his eye, mixing with his tears. There must be other cuts from the broken mirror, as blood stains the previously pristine carpet beneath him.

"I-I'm sorry," he stammers, reaching out a hand towards me. But I can't bring myself to help him. My hands tremble with anger and hurt as I stare at the man who has betrayed me. "Let me go." My voice is barely above a whisper, but it carries all the weight of my emotions.

But I can't.

With a heavy heart, I turn to leave. His grasp on my dress is quick and strong, his bloody hands leaving irreparable stains on the once pure white fabric. I look down at him, and my shattered heart breaks even further, just like the mirror that lies in pieces on the floor.

Because no matter how much I despise him, I cannot deny that deep down, there is still love for him within me. It is a cruel paradox; the hate will always overshadow the love as long as I live. And so, with one last ounce of strength, I push him away and tear at the dress he clings to so desperately. The sound of ripping fabric echoes in the air.

Without looking back, I turn and run.

MARCELLO

For generations, the Lastra and Agosti families had enjoyed a strong bond of friendship. However, there was one exception —Father and Rocco Agosti. While Rocco was known for his lavish lifestyle and extravagant feasts, he paled in comparison to Father's debauchery. Interestingly enough, Rocco preferred higher quality bed partners while Father preferred quantity.

Rocco's parties were the talk of New York, attracting the crème de la crème—actors, musicians, and politicians all mingling together. It was at one of these parties that I first laid eyes on Catalina.

As usual, I attended the party and made an effort to socialize. But these events never appealed to me as the company was always lacking. However, as the Capo's son, it was my duty to attend.

I stood in the crowded mansion, nursing my drink and waiting for an opportunity to greet Rocco before making my departure. The crush of people was suffocating, and I longed for a moment alone. I slipped out into the garden, searching for a secluded spot to light a cigarette when she caught my eye.

Catalina wore a simple white dress that did nothing to showcase her figure. Yet, it was far from boring—it exuded elegance and grace. Her face held me captivated. Midnight black hair cascaded down her back, reaching her hips. Her pale complexion was dotted with freckles on her nose and cheeks. But it was her eyes that truly mesmerized me. Slanted like a cat's, they were a vivid green that seemed almost otherworldly.

I wasn't.

She wasn't a dream.

As I took a step towards her, my heart raced with nervous anticipation. But before I could reach her, someone else approached—Enzo, Rocco's son and heir. His voice, carrying the same Italian accent as his father, echoed through the night.

"Lina, what are you doing out here? You know you're not allowed at these parties." Enzo's tone was stern yet concerned. Lina's voice, in contrast, was soothing and melodious, fitting for such a beautiful girl.

From my spot in the shadows, I watched their exchange unfold like a scene from a play. Enzo guiding her towards the entrance of the house while Lina protested, wanting to experience the forbidden world of underground parties.

"You're too young, Lina. You know Father won't like that," Enzo reasoned.

"I'll be eighteen soon, Enzo. I'm not that young, you know." Lina's words were laced with determination and defiance.

"I know, piccola. Do you really want to grow up so soon? Father is already looking for a match." And with those words, they disappeared into the depths of the mansion, leaving me in a state of confusion and longing.

It wasn't until later that I realized Lina must be Rocco's youngest daughter, Catalina. A strange feeling overcame me as I put two and two together—she could marry no one but me.

But how could someone like me ever deserve her? She was like a ray of sunshine in my otherwise bleak life. But perhaps I could try to deserve her...to be a good man for her.

———

TWO MONTHS LATER

As I approach the fence, she leans against it and peers at me with curiosity. I quickly pull up my hood, hoping to conceal the extent of my injuries. My face is still swollen and discolored from the beating I received a few days ago—a sickly mix of purple and yellow around my eyes and nose.

"I thought you wouldn't come." Her voice is tinged with relief.

"I thought so too." I reply gruffly, the pain in my voice betraying the severity of my wounds. My stab wound has become infected, forcing me to drain it on my own this morning. But I keep this information to myself—there's no need to worry her. The idea of someone caring about my well-being is foreign to me, but it's also comforting.

Looking up at her from beneath my hood, I can't help but admire her ethereal beauty. Her shy smile washes away all thoughts of pain and danger.

"I can only stay for a little while." My father has been keeping a watchful eye on me, especially after losing his men who were tasked with following me. But I won't take any chances when it comes to Catalina.

I've come to accept that no matter how much I want to be with her, it may never be possible. Being with me would put her in danger, and I would never forgive myself if anything happened to her.

After many sleepless nights, I've made the decision to distance myself from her. Even though I have already spoken to Rocco about our potential union, it's for the best that I take a step back.

"Are you sure you're alright?" She studies me closely, concern etched across her features.

"Yes...thank you for everything." My words fail to convey the depth of gratitude and admiration I feel towards her. She is like a beam of sunlight in my dark world, and I will carry the memory of her with me always.

Taking a deep breath, I feel my throat tighten and my eyes start to water. It's strange how the worst physical pain couldn't bring me to tears, but the thought of never seeing her again has me on the verge of bawling.

The hardest part is knowing that I will never have the chance to meet her again – not even in death. She belongs with the angels while I am destined for a life in the gutter.

"Hey, are you okay?" Her voice breaks through my thoughts and brings me back to reality.

"I won't be able to come again," I confess sadly. "It's... complicated."

Her expression falls, and I can see the sadness in her eyes at my words.

"Are you in trouble? Maybe I can talk to my father or brother and they could help." Catalina offers eagerly, but I know that there is no one who can truly help me. No one except myself.

But at least she offered.

I stand up, not wanting to stay any longer as it would only make things harder.

"Lord!" She gasps suddenly, pointing at my chest. I look down and see that my wound from earlier has reopened and is bleeding once again.

"It's nothing," I shrug it off, already turning to leave. But before I can take another step, she reaches behind her neck and unties her scarf.

"Can you come a little closer?" She asks softly. A part of me hesitates, knowing that being this close to her will only make my desire for her stronger.

But just like a man on the brink of starvation, I go. I don't think I could ever say no to her. When I'm next to the opening in the fence, she reaches between the pickets to wrap her scarf around my torso. She struggles a little, so I try to help her, getting one last feel of her soft hands.

"Thank you," I say once again, and I bring both her hands to my lips. What I wouldn't give to worship this woman for the rest of my life... But *I*, better than anyone, should know that we seldom get what we wish for.

With a last parting gaze, I leave, holding a piece of her with me forever.

She's all that's pure and good, and I want her to remain like that. I would only taint her with my bloodstained hands; hold her down with the weight of my sins. She deserves better; for I wouldn't wish myself upon my greatest enemies. She deserves the heavens and above, but I can only give her hell and below.

So I let her go.

And with her, I'm also leaving my heart behind — or what little I had left.

———

A FEW DAYS LATER

As I slowly wake from my slumber, a dull ache lingers in my ribs. I groan and stretch, trying to find a more comfortable position. My hand instinctively reaches out for the silky scarf next to me, still warm from Catalina's presence.

Breathing in her delicate scent, I am lost in dreams of her until an urgent knocking on my bedroom door shatters the peaceful moment.

"Tuo padre ti sta chiamando," a soldier yells from outside. When my father calls, I have no choice but to answer.

Reluctantly, I fold the scarf that Catalina had left behind and place it in a safe spot before getting dressed and leaving my room. The soldier informs me that my father has a surprise waiting for me in the basement.

I can't help but feel anxious at the thought of what kind of surprise awaits me down there, especially after the last beating I received.

Trying to keep a cool demeanor, I make my way down the stairs and into the basement. As I open the door, I am greeted by darkness, making me blink several times to adjust my eyes.

"Marcello, just who I was looking for," Father's cheerful voice echoes through the dark space, his enthusiasm contrasting with his usually stoic nature.

"Father," I reply with a forced smile as he beckons me further into the basement.

"Come, come. Let me show you what I got you."

Confused by his words, I furrow my brow. My father has never once given me anything before.

"What you got me?" I ask hesitantly as we reach another door deeper within the basement.

"Consider this a gift for your years of service." He opens the door and gestures for me to step inside.

I take a tentative step forward and stop, my eyes widening in disbelief. The scene before me is real, not just some twisted nightmare playing tricks on my mind.

The table, usually reserved for inflicting pain and suffering, now holds a new captive. Her wrists and ankles are shackled at each end, her body stretched out in the shape of a human X. Her torn dress barely covers her body, revealing a mass of bloody skin and wounds, fresh crimson liquid still seeping from her battered form.

Catalina.

My heart sinks as I realize who the victim is. Before I can even process what has happened, Father speaks up.

"What do you think? Do you like my gift?" He glances at Catalina with an air of satisfaction. "It wasn't easy to obtain her, but I know how much she means to you."

My blood boils as he continues to gloat about how they abducted her from her own home. My fists clench at my sides, anger coursing through every part of my being. But then he points to something on her back, and I feel bile rise in my throat.

Father's cruel handiwork is etched into her flesh—an M encased by a large C. The raw edges show that it was done without mercy or hesitation.

Catalina...

Tears well up in my eyes as I take in the sight before me. What horrors has she endured at their hands?

"What is this?" I choke out, struggling to keep my voice steady.

"A gift for the Chimera," he sneers, admiring his work with perverse pleasure. "I thought it was quite fitting."

Fury consumes me as I look at Catalina's broken body, strapped to that table like some kind of sacrifice. I want nothing more than to unleash all my pain and rage onto those responsible for this unspeakable act. My hands shake with the urge to take their lives, to avenge Catalina and make them pay for what they have done to her.

My voice falters as I try to keep calm in front of my father. I can't let him see how much this conversation is affecting me.

"You think I haven't heard the rumors about your obsession with this girl? You haven't exactly been discreet," Father scoffs, his eyes leering over Catalina's figure.

I clench my jaw, struggling to keep my composure. I won't solve anything by lashing out at him now. More soldiers will come and restrain me before I can even make a move.

"I'm right, aren't I? She's the reason you've been neglecting your duties." His words feel like daggers piercing my skin.

A moan escapes Catalina's lips, and I close my eyes in shame. This is everything I feared and more.

But I can only hope to minimize the damage now.

"I haven't been neglecting anything," I reply through gritted teeth. Technically, it's true—I've killed just as efficiently as always, without letting my emotions get in the way.

"Is that so?" Father raises an eyebrow skeptically. I know there's no use in trying to explain myself further. "It's simple really. I brought her here for you to enjoy, to get her out of your system. She's a virgin, isn't she? The best kind." He nods approvingly, and I feel sick to my stomach listening to him speak of her like an object. "You'll be the first to taste her charms. Now that's a perfect gift." He lets out a whistle and shakes his head in amusement. "Her blood coating your cock. Top quality right here, son."

"You forget she's Rocco's daughter. We can't do that." I bring up my best argument as I try to reason with him. Surely even *he* can see how dangerous this is.

"As if I care." He shrugs, taking out a cigar and lighting it up. "I need you to get your head in the game, and it won't happen until she's out of your system. So go ahead. Fuck her." He motions dismissively to her feeble form.

"I will *not*." For the first time, I'm saying no. I've had no limits before, but I find that Catalina is where I draw the line.

Father takes a deep drag of his cigar, his eyes intent on me.

"You are pussy-whipped, aren't you? He was right," he notes thoughtfully.

"Who?"

He shrugs. "If you don't want her, I'll just give her to the guards. I bet they'll love it."

My eyes widen as I understand the enormity of the situation. It's my fault. All my fault...

It only took one interaction with her. Everything I touch turns to dust... I turn my head slightly towards the table, and I know what to do.

I'll give Father something he's always wanted but never got.

My knees buckle under the weight of my fear and desperation, slowly bringing me to the ground until I'm at his feet. I bow my head in submission, pressing my lips to the worn leather of his shoes.

"I'll do anything. Please... just let her go." My voice is a desperate plea, the ultimate act of subservience.

Father's laughter reverberates through the room, echoing off the cold stone walls. He throws his head back in amusement, a sinister gleam in his eyes.

Still on the ground, I keep my gaze lowered to the floor, trying to hide the tears that threaten to spill from my eyes.

"Please..."

"Oh boy, this is exactly what I was talking about," he muses, gesturing towards Catalina with a dismissive wave of his hand. "You're weak. This girl is making you weak. How can I trust you to do what's necessary for our famiglia when you'd do anything for her? Would you even die for her?" His tone is mocking, knowing full well that I would lay down my life for her without hesitation. "I thought I beat those emotions out of you a long time ago," he sighs, shaking his head in disappointment. "But it seems you need one last nudge to let them go." With a twirl of his fingers, he removes his gun from the back of his trousers and aims it at Catalina. Panic swells inside of me, my mind frantically searching for a way out.

"I'll do whatever you want." My voice trembles with fear as I make my promise. Anything for him to spare her.

"You have two choices, boy," Father says with a sadistic grin, enjoying watching me squirm as he holds all the power. "Either you fuck her out of your system, or you watch as each of my soldiers takes a turn with her." The thought of anyone touching her, violating her, sends a shudder through my body. "What do you say?"

His mouth twists into an evil smile, knowing he's got me backed into a corner.

"I can't do that to her," I choke out, my heart breaking at the mere thought of hurting her. "She'll..." I can't even bear to finish my sentence.

"Yes." A satisfied grin spreads across his face. "She'll hate you. She will despise you for the rest of her life. Either you do it or..."

My heart races as I try to reason with my father, but his cold stare reveals that my words are futile. He has never been one to listen to reason when it comes to matters of power and control.

"She's innocent," I plead, desperation creeping into my voice. But he just chuckles, dismissing my plea with a wave of his hand.

"Innocence is a myth, boy. You made the mistake of putting her on a pedestal, letting your emotions cloud your judgment. Now it's time for you to learn the hard way." His words carry a sinister edge as he lays out my options.

"Take her and defile her, or watch others do it instead. Either way, you'll be consumed by self-loathing." My father's psychological games always hit their mark, and he knows I'll be tormented no matter what choice I make.

I can feel tears stinging my eyes as I choke out a feeble "no," hoping against hope that he'll show some mercy. But he just shrugs and orders one of his soldiers to go first.

"No!" I cry out, dropping to my knees in desperate protest. "Please, don't do this."

But my cries fall on deaf ears as my father spits at me in disgust. "Just like your mother. Always begging on your knees," he sneers. And then he delivers the ultimate blow: "Will you suck my cock like she did? Maybe then I'll spare Catalina."

I feel sickened and disgusted by his words, knowing that there is no escape from this nightmare. I can only pray that Catalina will forgive me for what will happen next.

His words stun me into a momentary paralysis, but something deep within me compels me to nod in agreement.

"Anything." My voice is strained with determination. There is nothing I wouldn't do for her. I am already gone.

My father pauses, his inscrutable expression giving nothing away. Then he chuckles darkly.

"Damn boy, I should have known you were a homo." His sinister smile sends shivers down my spine as he looks down at me. "I'll make you a deal." His eyes gleam with excitement. "Get me hard, and I'll let her go. Fail and..." He trails off, whistling ominously.

God...is this really happening? Is this what it's come to? But I cannot afford to hesitate or question, not when Lina's life is on the line. So I nod again, steeling myself for whatever humiliation is to come. I can take it. But Lina...she won't be able to handle it.

With a crooked smirk, my father unbuttons his pants and takes out his flaccid penis, waving it in front of my face.

"Let's see how well you put that mouth to use." His tone is mocking and condescending, as if he expects me to fail before even starting. But I cannot afford to disappoint him or lose Lina.

And so, with a sense of numb detachment, I close my eyes and empty my mind of everything except this one task at hand.

I can do this!

Taking a deep breath, I tentatively take his limp member in my hand and bring it to my mouth. Bile rises in the back of my throat. I open wide and take him inside, fighting every instinct that revolts against this act. But desperation drives me on as I work my tongue around him, trying everything in my power to elicit a reaction from him. Praying silently that it will be enough to save Lina.

Father is sporting a bored expression, his hands crossed across his chest as he watches me choke on his cock. As I lick him, a small twitching of his dick gives me hope. Just as I'm about to apply more suction, he pushes me off, his foot nabbing me in the forehead and shoving me to the ground.

I can see he's semi-erect by now, but he quickly tucks himself in.

"You wouldn't even be a good whore." He spits on me, the tip of his shoe making contact with my ribs and making me wince.

Shit! My wound!

Father shakes his head callously.

"It seems that you failed, boy." He raises an eyebrow at me. He only did this to test my limits, shaming me in the process. "Now, what will it be?" He tips his head towards the table, raising one hand in the air, ready to signal Silvio.

"I..." I gulp. My eyes wander wildly around the room. There isn't any way out, is there? "I'll do it," I finally acquiesce.

"Let's see." Father nods at me, taking a seat on the chair next to the wall.

I scramble to my feet, my gaze set on Catalina.

"Let me give her some water," I say as I watch her writhe in pain, her limbs trying to move against the shackles holding her firm.

"Make it fast," he grunts.

This is the one moment that I thank the heavens for my sleeping pill addiction. I carry them with me everywhere. If I can't spare her the pain... then at least I can spare her the memory.

With my back to Father, I pour a glass of water, quickly dissolving a pill inside. Then I move to the table, crouching down in front of Catalina.

Her lips are chapped and full of small lacerations. She must have bitten them when the pain had been too much. Just seeing her like this is killing me. I lift my hand and lightly stroke her hair, knowing I have no right to do so.

"Aghh..." A small moan escapes her lips, and I will myself to be strong for her sake.

"Shh, I got you," I whisper in a low voice so that Father won't hear. I help her drink from the glass, glad to see most of the liquid going down her throat.

"It will all be over... soon," I vow to her. Somehow, I'll make sure she gets out of this alive.

"What's taking so long?" Father complains.

I straighten my spine, putting on my best poker face. If he knows how much she means to me, he'll kill her immediately; a fact of which I'm painfully aware. I need to buy some time so the pill knocks her out.

"I can't do it," I start.

"Silvio!" Father yells, but I stop him.

"I didn't mean that. I can't get hard. I need one of those pills." He knows exactly what I'm talking about as he scowls at me; it's not as if it's the first time I've needed them.

"Sometimes I wonder how you came out of my loins. Can't even fuck properly." He opens the door and spews some commands. "Fucking useless," he mutters under his breath, but I ignore the jibe.

I fix my eyes on Catalina, monitoring her movements.

Dear Lord, she's innocent. Please spare her.

I continue praying, even knowing it's too late.

As expected, Father is back too soon. Swallowing the pill, I can only wait until it starts working.

"So?" Father asks flippantly, nodding towards my bulge. "Let the show begin."

I reluctantly close my eyes, trying to shut out the heaviness in my heart. This has become routine for me now, attempting to dissociate from my body and this horrific situation. But tonight, it's not working. My mind is too consumed with guilt and shame.

With shaking hands, I unlock the shackles on her ankles and wrists, releasing her from their cruel grip. Carefully, I pull her towards me so that only her torso is lying on the table. She lets out a soft whimper, and tears prick at my eyes. What am I doing?

My loathing for myself intensifies as my trembling fingers reach for the hem of her dress, lifting it up over her hips. My heart pounds wildly in my chest, a combination of the pill I took and my own anxiety. Trying to remain detached, I unzip my pants and push them down just enough to give me access.

I try not to touch her more than necessary, not wanting to defile her any further than I already have. But as I position myself at her entrance and push inside, all rational thoughts flee from my mind. The pain on her face breaks my heart, and I can only pray that she's too drugged up to feel it fully as I break through the barrier of her virginity. Once I'm fully inside, I freeze, the weight of what I'm doing crushing me.

I can't do this. It's not mine to take but hers to give willingly. Dear God...

In that moment, I plead with any higher power that will listen. The guilt of stealing her innocence weighs heavily on me, and it only amplifies as the pleasure surges through me. How could something so wrong feel so good? How could I be capable of such monstrosity? This is by far my biggest sin.

Lost in a fierce battle with my inner demons, I'm jolted back to reality by Father's voice.

I should have known you couldn't do it." He spits at me, his gun pressing into the tender skin under Catalina's chin. "How's this for motivation, boy?"

Like a caustic substance, the sight of the gun aimed at Catalina's head burns my insides and imprints itself in my head. Father's insidious smile stretches even wider across his face as he sees the turmoil in me. I can't even hide it anymore.

He jabs the butt of the gun menacingly into her chin a few more times before I give up. I move—in and out. All while begging all the gods out there to make this fast.

For once someone listens to my prayers and I come, the staggering guilt an echo of ephemeral pleasure.

Sick. Twisted. Depraved.

Am I anything but?

I pull out, lightheaded, a heavy weight resting on my chest.

Damned... I just damned myself by defiling an angel.

Father starts clapping, a hand coming down my back in a congratulatory slap. He's saying something, but I can't hear him. Eyes blank, heart shattered, I turn away from the wretched body I've just corrupted.

Looking down, my cock is stained with red, the evidence of the innocence I'd ruined glaring back at me. It's the last drop, and I stumble to my knees, heaving and emptying the contents of my stomach.

Father makes a disgusted noise before leaving the room.

He already got what he wanted.

For what seems like forever, I sit alone in my puke, staring at the dark walls. Catalina is still out—a small grace. But I realize where this is all heading... Father's next step. She'll be dead by tomorrow, and I can't allow that. I'll take on the entire famiglia if I have to, but Catalina will survive this. It's a solemn vow I make to myself.

One day, this will all be but a distant nightmare for her, but at least she'll be alive.

And I'll stay away—forever.

———

THERE'S ONLY one person who can help me get her out. The only other man besides Father who has unrestricted access to the house and the basement—my brother Valentino. Asking him for this favor and implicitly making him go against Father for my sake will cost me heavily.

I don't dare leave her side, even for a moment, as I plan the next move. I call my brother and explain what I need—someone to return Catalina to her family while I stay behind and face the music.

After I'm more in command of my body, I stumble to my feet, and taking my shirt off, I clean her with it.

I'm very gentle with her back, the wounds so raw it's like they're screaming at me. Even with the mangled flesh, the initials are clearly distinguishable. It makes me feel even more despicable, for she will forever carry this with her.

I swallow a sob as I reach lower. A trickle of blood is running down her thighs. I tenderly clean the area, even more disgusted when I see red mixed with white and the evidence of what I've done to her.

"I'm so sorry... so sorry." My voice breaks as I keep repeating, knowing she can't possibly hear me.

I've killed and maimed in my life; tortured, and desecrated, and never have I felt such a torment deep within. I'd gotten used to my lot in life, never thinking I could reach rock bottom, because how can you when you've always lived under sea level? But this... what I did to her...

I know I'm going to spend the rest of my life repenting, seeking some nonexistent absolution.

I finish cleaning her up and I try my best to cover her with what's left of her dress. Softly, I lower her from the table, cradling her battered body in my arms. I swipe my hand over her pale features, taking her in one last time.

"I'm sorry..." I whisper again in her hair, rocking slightly with her and letting the tears fall. "So, so sorry." I brush my lips against her temple, trying to memorize her features.

That's how Valentino finds me.

"That her?" He nods at Catalina.

"Yes." I stand up, carefully depositing her in his arms. "Please take care of her. Make sure she gets home safe."

"You're lucky she's Romina's sister, otherwise I wouldn't be doing this."

"I know."

"You owe me, Marcello. And when I come to collect, you better be ready," he notes. Tino might not be Father, but that doesn't mean he is any less of a self-serving bastard.

"Thank you." I incline my head in respect. As long as he delivers her safely back to her family, I'm willing to do anything for him—should I live.

"Good luck with Father," he says before leaving.

I watch his retreating figure, saying goodbye to Catalina one last time.

It's time to end this.

When Father comes in, I'm the only one in the basement. He quickly scans the room, his upper lip twitching in displeasure.

"What did you do, boy?" he spits out, backhanding me. I take it, because that's all I deserve.

"She's safe," I say, keeping my composure.

"Fucking useless," he sneers, pacing around. "You know what your punishment is, boy." I lower my head, already accepting my fate. I knew it from the moment I stayed behind.

"Do it fast," I say as he raises his gun to aim for my head.

"You think this is over, don't you? The moment you're dead, I'll take that whore you seem to love so much and I'll make her my bitch. And when I've had my fill, I'll have every one of my men take a turn. She'll wish she was dead, and she *will* die, but not before she despises you so much she takes her last breath cursing out your name," he laughs, mocking Catalina and my feelings for her.

The switch is instantaneous. I'd been resigned to dying, since death would be the greatest comfort considering what I'd done—and a mercy at the same time. Yeah, I'm a coward. But as he gloats about everything he would do to Catalina, with me powerless to stop it, I can't. Before he can pull the trigger, my hand shoots out, knocking it out of his hold.

Father may think he's superior just because I'd been at peace with dying. But in a physical struggle, he won't come out the winner.

A rage unlike anything I've ever felt takes over me, and my fingers wrap themselves around the side of his neck, forcefully shoving his head into the wall. The first impact elicits a cry from Father, and it only spurs me on. Over and over, I smash his brain against the concrete wall, watching blood and brain matter stain the surface. I only release him when he stops struggling.

It's done.

——————

IT'S BEEN months since I've seen the light of day. Stuck in a tiny apartment, a prison of my making, I can only wait for Valentino's next update about Catalina.

That's the only thing that's been keeping me going. The knowledge that she's doing well, and the hope that she will heal.

But it all comes crashing down one day.

"What do you mean?" I croak. "How can she be missing?"

"I'm sorry. Romina said Rocco disowned her. She's probably..." He trails off, and I get what he's hinting at.

"No. It can't be. Why wait so long? It's been months and nothing happened... There must be a mistake." I'm panicking, the sheer thought of a world without Catalina filling me with unimaginable dread.

"You realize the chances of her being alive are slim, don't you?" His voice is somber, and I fall back, shocked to my very core.

I'd refused to believe her own family would turn against her. I'd refused to think she would be anything but safe back home.

But I should have known better. No mafioso would allow a dishonored daughter to continue bearing the family name. And if Rocco has one predominantly deadly sin, it's hubris. A pride that wouldn't let him overlook her lack of virtue.

No...

I hang up, my mind blanking.

I killed her. I did it. I should have known that someone like me can't touch something as pure as her without tainting her. And I did it... I condemned her to hell.

I fall to my knees, my eyes tearing up. Without even thinking, I wrap my hand around the whip lying by me, and with all the strength I can muster, I fling it back, flinching at the biting contact.

I deserve it. I need to feel what she endured on that table. I need to hurt for her.

The more I think about her, the more force I apply.

Whip.

Whip.

Whip.

I'm cursed.

Whip.

Whip.

Whip.

I hit and hit, but it's not enough. Blood and sweat mingle down my back, sticking to my flesh like a second skin.

Still not enough.

All reason leaves me as I numbly move around the room, exerting one last effort. My mind is foggy as everything else fades away, my only remaining goal to join her.

I use an old cable, making a sturdy knot and securing it to the light fixture on the ceiling. Stepping on a small chair, I place the noose around my neck, immediately kick the support away, and wait for death.

My eyes close, my breathing slows, the cable digging into my skin. Lightheaded, I feel myself slipping. And there she is. She's smiling at me, her eyes twinkling with affection.

Lina...

"Am I dead?" I whisper, holding on to the mirage of her.

"No, silly, you're not." Her hand reaches out to touch my face, tenderness emanating from her entire being.

"How can you not hate me?" I sob, and she draws me into her arms.

"I don't hate you. I could never hate you," she reassures me, sharing her warmth with me. "But it's not your time yet, Marcello." She chides softly. "Go out into the world and do good. Show me how much you repent by helping others."

"I don't want to leave you." I hold on to her tighter, begging her to let me stay with her.

"We'll meet again." She draws back and places a sweet kiss on my lips.

I open my eyes, pain emanating from my entire back and head. I blink twice, realizing I'm on the floor staring at the ceiling. Still alive.

I won't let you down, Lina.

It takes me a few more months to get myself together, but I enroll in college. I devote all my time to study, all to achieve my new goal—help the other Catalinas of the world. I accustom myself to being alive while she's not, but I dedicate everything to her memory. As much as I strive to be normal though, some things have irrevocably changed.

Like my ability to sleep. Not that it was great before. Or my ability to withstand touch. The first time someone brushed their hand over mine, I'd gotten such a terrible panic attack someone had called an ambulance.

I'm vile. Disgusting. A monster.

And no one should be tainted by my touch.

CATALINA

PRESENT-DAY

Enzo's persistent knocking echoes through the bathroom, breaking through my thoughts for what feels like the hundredth time today. My heart sinks as I realize he's come to check on me again.

"Go away, Enzo," I yell back, my voice muffled by the door. Can't he understand that I don't want to see anyone right now?

"Lina, I'm not leaving until you open this goddamn door." His words are harsh and determined, causing a knot to form in my stomach. I can hear him knocking harder now, and I fear he might break down the door.

My eyes squeeze shut as I take a deep breath and try to gather myself. After a moment of hesitation, I finally give in and open the door.

"Lina..." Enzo's voice is filled with concern as he takes in my red and swollen face. "It's been a few days already," he comments with a shake of his head. "I'm worried about you."

Since the confrontation with Marcello, I had taken Claudia with me and left immediately. She had asked countless questions, disappointed that we were leaving so suddenly. But what had hit me the hardest was when she mentioned how much she would miss Marcello.

Good Lord! He has known all along that Claudia is his daughter, but how am I ever supposed to tell her that? Or explain how she was conceived...

As hard as it was for me to process all of this, Claudia seemed to have fallen back into her normal routine of playing with Luca. Meanwhile, I spent my days locked away in my room, crying.

"You shouldn't be worried about me," I add half-heartedly. Enzo already knows about Marcello's betrayal, and it took everything in him not to go after him.

Worry etches deep lines into his forehead as he looks at me, his eyes full of concern. It's the first time I've noticed how much I've been pushing everyone away, consumed by my own pain.

"You don't look fine," he says softly, his voice laced with worry and understanding.

"I just found out the man I fell in love with was the same man who brutally raped me ten years ago. I think I'm doing fine, all things considered," I snap, my tone sharp and defensive. Immediately, I feel guilty for lashing out and quickly add, "Sorry."

Enzo turns to face me, his expression hardened with determination. "I'm going to kill him," he declares.

I grab his arm, panic rising in my chest. "No, please stop. Don't make this more difficult than it already is."

"I'll make sure you get a divorce," he says tensely, but I can only let out a bitter laugh.

"A divorce? You think anyone's going to let that slide? There's no divorce in our world, Enzo."

"There can be," he insists, though there's little conviction behind his words. We both know how things work in our society.

"No... We'll just live separately," I suggest weakly.

"It's all my fault, damn it. I practically offered you up to him," Enzo mutters, anger flashing in his eyes.

"You only wanted to protect me," I say, placing a comforting hand on his arm. "Who could have known, really?"

An uneasy silence falls between us before Enzo breaks it with a hesitant question. "Lina, I know this is awkward, but I have to ask. Are you...?" His gaze drops to my stomach, and I understand what he's asking.

"No. I'm not." The tension drains from his face, and he lets out a sigh of relief.

I understand his perspective. A child would make it incredibly difficult to cut ties with Marcello. While I know that, there had been a deep sense of disappointment when I got my period yesterday. Did I want a baby—his baby? I don't know, and I can't explain why it had hurt me the way it had when I'd seen the first signs of spotting.

Because you love him. As much as you hate him.

The mere thought of him brings a bitter taste to my mouth. The once nameless person with piercing amber eyes now has a face and a name, haunting me in my nightmares.

I try to put on a brave front for Enzo's sake, assuring him that I am fine. But as soon as I close the door to my room, I can no longer deny the truth. How could I be fine when the one person I trusted above all else betrayed me in the cruelest manner? Every time I close my eyes, I am met with the image of him among shattered glass, his expression desperate and lost. It is incomprehensible how he could deceive me and still play the victim.

Taking a deep breath, I push aside these thoughts. I need to compose myself for Claudia's sake.

With determination, I make my way to the bathroom, determined to wash away the remnants of this painful memory with a shower. But as soon as I catch sight of myself in the mirror, my resolve falters. With trembling hands, I slip off the dress from my shoulders and turn to face the mirror. My gaze travels down my back, following the angry scar that forms two distinct letters.

The M undoubtedly stands for Marcello. But what about the C? My mind races through possible names or initials until it hits me like a bolt of lightning.

Chimera.

My heart stops at the realization. The man who abducted me had mentioned Chimera, said that I was a gift for them. Could it be that...

Turning off the water, I quickly fasten my dress and make my way to Enzo, drawn in by the sound of his heated argument with Allegra. As I approach, his eyes meet mine, and he tells her something that visibly shakes her. With a brief urging from Enzo, she retreats, shooting me daggers with her fiery gaze. Though I can't recall ever crossing her, there is no time to dwell on it now.

"What is it, Lina?" Enzo's brows furrow as he takes in my flushed face and disheveled appearance.

"Chimera," I say breathlessly, causing his eyes to widen in surprise. "Have you heard of that name?"

Without hesitation, Enzo guides me towards his study and shuts the door behind us.

"Why do you ask?"

"You know about the C and M tattoos on my back. I believe the C stands for Chimera."

Enzo falls deep into thought at my words.

"Please tell me why you think that."

With Marcello's cryptic mention of Chimera in connection to the nun's murder still fresh in my mind, I recount all the details from that fateful night.

"That bastard..." Enzo growls, clenching his fists in anger.

"Enzo?"

"He's obsessed with you, Lina. Fucking obsessed. It all makes perfect sense now..."

Confused by his sudden outburst, I press for more information. Threading a hand through his dark hair, Enzo continues.

"Think about it. He came to me seeking a marriage alliance and then suddenly you were forced to leave Sacre Coeur because you were being threatened by the Guerras."

A frown tugs at my lips, my stomach turning with unease at his implications. Can Marcello really be capable of such malice?

"Isn't the timing a little too convenient?" His voice drips with sarcasm as he gives a harsh laugh.

"But that would mean..." My words trail off, but he continues to spell it out for me.

"He terrorized you on purpose, so you would turn to him for comfort. He became your savior after every traumatic event." A disgusted look crosses his face, and I take a step back in shock.

It all makes sense now.

Father Guerra's strange behavior... The mysterious nun... And then the missing finger.

Only someone who had access to the house could have taken Claudia's ring, just as Enzo said.

"Dear Lord!" My hand flies to my mouth as I try to process everything, blinking rapidly to hold back tears.

"He's a monster, Lina. He manipulated you into thinking you needed him. It's not love you're feeling." Enzo's words are like a punch to the gut, and I can feel the tears threatening to spill over.

But as much as I want to deny it, his reasoning rings true. Marcello's actions were calculated and cruel. How could I have been so blind?

"You need to let everything sink in," Enzo says, shaking his head in disbelief as he pours himself a drink from the cabinet.

"Can I have some too?" I blurt out suddenly, hoping maybe the alcohol will numb the pain. Enzo pauses for a moment, looking at me with a mixture of concern and understanding before pouring me a glass as well.

I hold the glass with both hands, staring at the amber liquid.

Was Marcello really behind everything?

All those reassurances, the kind words, the tender touches. Were they all a lie?

I feel my eyes tearing up, so I quickly tip back the glass, swallowing the contents. The fire traveling down my throat makes me choke.

"But why? Why me? What did I ever do to him?"

"Some people are just unhinged, Lina. It's not your fault. But it worries me. Someone like that is capable of anything."

"You're right. That's why I'm scared for Claudia. What if he uses her against me?"

"You shouldn't go anywhere for the time being. At least until we figure out what we can do."

"Don't do anything dangerous, Enzo," I add, knowing he has a tendency of putting himself in the line of fire for others.

"I don't like this, Lina. I don't like it at all. I'll double the number of guards. Just stay put, okay?"

I nod, assuring him I'll follow his lead when it comes to safety. The last thing I could ever do would be to put my daughter in danger.

It takes me another few days to come to grips with the shocking realization that Marcello had been behind everything. The betrayal cuts deep, and I struggle to believe that someone I trusted could be capable of such manipulation. But as I reflect on his actions and my own gullibility, it becomes clear that he was a master of deception. He preyed on my vulnerabilities, taking advantage of my past as an abandoned outcast fueled by the desire for acceptance.

As angry as I am at myself for falling for his lies, I'm even more devastated by the fact that it was all a facade. Pulling myself together, I push back the tears that threaten to fall once again. Claudia, who had finally found a sense of normalcy in our makeshift family, is now confused and hurt by our sudden departure.

"What was it you wanted to ask me?" I look down at the textbook she's clutching in her small hands. Her features are drawn back in hesitation, unsure if she should voice her thoughts.

"I was reading this problem." She points to the text and explains her disagreement with the formulation.

After carefully considering her perspective, I respond, "I don't see any issue with it." She lets out a frustrated sigh.

"Of course you don't!" Claudia pouts, her tone laced with bitterness. "Marcello would have agreed with me." She crosses her arms defensively.

Her words hit me like a punch to the gut. Marcello may have been a manipulative liar, but he had also been a source of comfort and support for Claudia. Now that he's gone, she feels lost and alone.

"But Marcello's not here," I say calmly, trying to defuse the situation.

"And whose fault is that?" Claudia snaps before storming out of the room.

"Claudia!" I call after her desperately, but she's already out of sight.

Damnation! This is exactly what I didn't want to happen. She's already bonded with him, and suddenly I'm the bad guy for separating them.

What would she do if she knew he's her father?

She'll understand... She must.

I'm still ruminating about how to best handle Claudia right now when someone knocks on my door.

"Come in."

Allegra peeks her head inside, a shy smile on her face. Shocked would be an understatement for what I'm feeling as I see her walk inside, her countenance completely different from before.

"Am I bothering you?" she asks in a voice that I don't recognize. Too saccharine and lacking her usual bite.

"No," I frown. "What did you want?"

"Enzo called. He said the house's been compromised."

"What do you mean?" I draw back, panic overtaking me.

"He wants us to go to a safe house. It's urgent. Get some things; a car is waiting for us."

"Let me get Claudia." I stand up, grabbing some clothes on my way.

"She's already in the car with Luca."

"Why didn't she come to me?" I ask. It makes little sense. Claudia would have come to me first...

But then I remember our argument and I sigh. Okay, maybe not this time.

"Never mind, lead the way."

In front of the house, a big SUV is waiting. Allegra is the first one to get in the front seat. I don't even think as I get in the back.

"Allegra? Where are the children?" I ask, noting there's only one other guard in the car, but no sight of either Claudia or Luca.

Allegra chuckles, shaking her head in amusement.

"You really fell for that."

"What?" I frown, immediately making to open the car door. Just as my fingers touch the handle, the man in the other seat presses a cloth to my mouth.

My eyes go wide and I start struggling. It's only for a moment, though, as I lose consciousness.

———

I WAKE up with a massive headache, my eyes barely opening.

"Wake up, bitch." I think I hear Allegra's voice before she slaps me across the face.

The blow is strong enough to make me see stars, but also to get me more alert.

"Claudia... where is Claudia?" Good Lord, did she harm my daughter? The mere thought of something happening to her has me trembling wildly with fear.

As I regain my awareness, I realize I'm lying on the floor, my hands and legs bound. Allegra is pacing in front of me.

"I don't care about your daughter." She shrugs her shoulders. She stoops in front of me, a disgusting smile stretching on her face. "But you... you're finally going to get what's coming to you."

"What do you mean? Why are you doing this?"

"Why?" She laughs hysterically before slapping me again. A ring catches in my lip, and I feel a rip. Damn! "It's all because of you." Her eyes are manic, her nostrils flaring with anger.

"What did I do to you?" I never understood her attitude. I can even count on one hand how many times we've interacted before, and never was I anything but courteous to her.

"You stole Enzo from me. Don't think I don't know. He's been visiting you *weekly* at that fucking convent. No brother, not even a concerned one, would do that. You think I don't know you've been fucking him?"

What is wrong with her?

She keeps on going with her delusions, implying that I'd been staying at Sacre Coeur so I could have illicit assignations with my own brother. What in God's mercy is that reasoning?

The more she talks, the sicker she sounds.

"Enzo is my brother. How can you even say that?" I ask, repulsed by the very thought.

"You..." She spits out, coming closer and jabbing her finger in my forehead. "You are the reason he rejected me. You... you..." Her words are hurried and incoherent. "You made him hate me."

"Allegra, do you hear yourself? Enzo is my brother, for God's sake! There's been no impropriety between us." I try to reason with her, but she becomes even more volatile, her grip bruising as she wraps her fingers around my neck. She's sputtering so much nonsense that I become lost.

"... after he's done with you, I'm going to enjoy breaking you." Her mouth turns into a twisted smile, and I can only see a deranged person acting on delusions. Good Lord, does Enzo know? But then I suddenly catch what she's saying.

"Who's he?"

She chuckles, falling back on her butt and laughing.

"He's going to play with you first. And I get to watch." I don't understand what she's saying, but the more time I spend in her presence, the more afraid I get. She's mad, and that means she's unpredictable. Does anyone know I'm missing? What about Claudia and Luca? Are they at home, or did she take them somewhere too?

Both Allegra and I turn our heads as footsteps echo down the hall. Soon, the figure of a man dressed in a suit appears in the doorway. Allegra jumps to her feet and dashes to his side, wrapping her hands around his neck and peppering him with kisses.

"Enough!" He raises his palm to stop her.

"Why?" Allegra pulls a face, but the man simply pushes her aside, heading straight for me.

"And the girl?"

"I don't care about the brat." Allegra shrugs, her expression bored.

The man turns towards her, his expression murderous.

"What did I tell you, Allegra?"

She straightens herself, probably realizing the displeasure in his voice.

"To get Catalina and Claudia." She lowers her head in subservience, a first.

Who is this man?

"And?"

"I couldn't be bothered looking around the house for her. She was easy to get." She points at me, puckering her lips like a spoiled child.

"You disobeyed me." The man simply states, unbuckling his belt.

"I'm sorry, Master." Allegra suddenly says, getting on her hands and knees.

"You need to be punished." The man's steps are calm and measured. He reaches behind Allegra, and in a smooth swipe, he slides the belt over her back. There's a piercing sound as the leather meets her back, but she doesn't even whimper. In fact, if I look closely, I can see her purring.

What?

"You did it on purpose, didn't you? You wanted me to punish you."

"Master..." She moans.

What seemed an erotic dance suddenly turns gruesome as he grabs her by her neck and smashes her face against the floor. A whooshing sound escapes her lips, her eyes rolling back in her head. The man seems disappointed by that, so he kicks her in the stomach with his foot.

"You must excuse me." He turns to me, shaking his head in disgust at Allegra's pitiful form on the ground. "Where are my manners?" He dusts the sleeves of his suit before regaling me with a smile.

"Long time no see, Catalina. Let me introduce myself."

MARCELLO

As I slowly awaken, my eyes flutter open to the blinding brightness of a hospital room. My head throbs and my body is heavy with exhaustion.

Where am I?

Slowly turning my head, I take in my surroundings. The sterile white walls and beeping machines confirm my suspicion—I'm in a hospital. A sharp pain shoots through my thigh, causing me to wince and notice the IV drip attached to my arm.

"Officer, there seems to be a misunderstanding. He didn't mean to harm himself. The mirror shattered and he accidentally got injured," I hear Sisi's voice arguing with someone outside my room. Still groggy, I struggle to sit up, the pain in my leg intensifying.

Peering down at my thigh, I see a clean white bandage covering a wound. It takes me a moment to remember how it got there.

She left.

Watching her walk away had sent me spiraling into a dark mind-set. All I could think about was making the pain stop. I never intended to commit suicide, but in that moment, all I wanted was peace—even if it meant inflicting physical pain on myself.

Surrounded by broken shards of glass, I acted impulsively—grabbing a large piece and plunging it into my thigh. Closing my eyes and leaning back against the wall, I relished in the agony, letting it consume me and block out everything else—including her horrified expression.

I remained there among the shards for what felt like hours, each stab of pain bringing me closer to the numbness I craved. Eventually, I pulled out the glass and waited for the cold air to make the sting even more potent.

With a deep breath, I wake up to my reality. Catalina is gone. Claudia is gone.

"Marcello?" Assisi calls my name, noticing I'm awake.

"I'm fine," I croak, my throat dry.

"What happened?" Her brows are drawn together in a frown as she looks at my leg. I don't answer. What can I tell her? How despicable I am? She probably suspects anyway.

A nurse stops by to check on the IV, and she mentions how lucky I'd been that my sister had called the ambulance on time because I'd lost a lot of blood. Eyes blank, I stare into nothingness, an empty void forming inside my chest.

I'm alive—again. And she's gone—again.

The nurse keeps talking, but I register nothing. It's only when she reaches for my wound, probably to redress it, that I snap out of it.

My body recoils at the touch of the nurse, my voice echoing through the room as I yell for her to stop. Sisi quickly steps in, apologizing before directing her attention back to me.

"Mr. Lastra, I need to check your wound," the nurse insists, but I can only shake my head, disoriented and desperate for an escape. My eyes scan the room for a way out, my heart pounding with fear and urgency.

With my one good hand, I pull the IV from my arm, feeling a sharp sting as I jump out of bed. Gasps fill the air as I rush towards the exit, ignoring all attempts to stop me. Shouts and cries follow me as I stumble and push through anyone in my way.

I vaguely register someone calling for security, and then I see Vlad's face.

He raises an eyebrow at me with a hint of disappointment before shaking his head. My legs give out beneath me and I fall to my knees, feeling blood trickling down my thigh. Vlad's gaze flickers momentarily, but he holds up a hand in a firm stop gesture.

"Please kill me," I rasp out, overwhelmed by agonizing emotions clawing at my chest.

"Now, Marcello, what did I tell you before?" Vlad's voice is calm and collected as he kneels in front of me. He glances over my shoulder and nods.

Despite my pleas for death and escape from this Tartarian torment of my own making, I cannot help but feel a tinge of guilt and regret. With every fiber of my being, I knew that marrying her would lead to this moment—her betrayal and hatred towards me once she found out. But in a moment of selfishness and desire for something just for myself, I had chosen to ignore the consequences. And now here it is—the reckoning; and like a coward, I am unable to bear the inferno that I myself ignited.

"If you ever die, it won't be by my hand." He snaps his fingers in front of me, trying to get my attention. I frown at him, my comprehension lagging.

"Pl..." I'm about to say when someone sticks a needle in my neck. The effect is almost immediate, as my limbs become light.

I'm still conscious though as hands grab at my body.

"How come you're here?" Sisi asks.

"Let's just say I heard through the grapevine that someone was in trouble," Vlad remarks.

Their voices become a mere echo as I finally lose consciousness.

———

———

A WEEK LATER

"Nice to see you all chipper," Vlad slides into the seat next to me. "Did you rent out this whole church, or what?" he says as he scans the empty rows.

"Hello to you too, traitor," I reply tensely, closing my fist over the rosary I was holding.

I'd barely gotten myself out of the hospital and managed to dissuade the doctors from committing me. Instead, I'd agreed to have weekly therapy sessions. No matter how much I'd tried to tell them, they hadn't believed that it wasn't a suicide attempt.

Just yesterday I'd had my first appointment, and it had gone as well as it could, all things considered. I'd merely scratched the surface in what I'd told the therapist. At the end of the session, the doctor had point-blank asked me if I even wanted help, because my deflection wasn't helping anyone. On my way out, I'd told her that if I was any more truthful, then I'd have to kill her.

She'd laughed.

I wasn't joking. Not really. I'd had several therapists over the years and just when I opened up a little more, they had to report me to the authorities. Good thing I wasn't too trusting to begin with, and I'd been able to take control of the situation before it came to blows.

But now I am to be monitored by close family, Assisi being the one tasked with making sure I don't harm myself further.

Funny, because if I'd been just a little more selfish, I would have taken the plunge. But I know what awaits my sisters should that happen. Or Lina... There's still someone out there gunning for me, and by extension anyone who means something to me. Even if she continues to hate me for the rest of her life, I'll still protect her.

The incident with the glass had been... well, a slight lapse in judgment. I'd just wanted the high I know I can get every time pain floods my senses. For the first time, I might have taken it too far.

"You should thank me instead of whining," Vlad says, raising his legs and propping his feet on the row of benches in front of him.

"Stop it! It's a church," I grit. Even if no one's inside, it's disrespectful.

"Don't get your feathers ruffled, Marcello. I didn't come here to commit sacrilege, or God forbid, *sin*." He shudders visibly as he utters the word God, and I roll my eyes at him.

"So why did you come?"

"Your sister's worried about you. She says you don't come out of your office for days on end."

"I won't kill myself, don't worry." I purse my lips. "Since when do you talk to my sister?" I narrow my eyes at him.

"Since she's the only adult in that house," he fires back, and I hold back a retort.

"Well, as you see, I'm doing fine."

"There's another reason I stepped inside this..." His mouth curls up in disgust. "dump." He motions to the church. I raise an eyebrow at him, but he continues. "Hastings has been working on our copycat's case. He's been going over every single crime scene again."

"And?" Seeing how thorough this Chimera has been so far, I doubt Adrian found anything.

"He found something," Vlad says and I whip my head around to look at him.

"What?"

"A partial fingerprint. It's not much but..."

"How partial are we talking about?"

"We might get a match if we have something to compare it to. Which is why I'm here. I need you to make a list of everyone you suspect."

"What if it's intentional? Throw us off?" It's not that I don't trust Adrian's work, since I've worked for years with the man and I know how thorough he is. But this copycat killer... everything *is* intentional.

"Might be," Vlad shrugs. "Still worth a look."

"There aren't that many people that could have done that. I would say there are a few in the famiglia who would be capable of doing it. But motive? That's what throws me off." I sigh. It's not as if I hadn't wracked my brains thinking who could have been, my uncle and his cronies being at the top of the list. But why?

"What have you heard from Enzo's side?" I ask after a pause. Enzo still hadn't realized his office had been bugged, and that Vlad is privy to all the confidential information coming out of there. I still don't know why he did that, but now I'm grateful for it.

"Enzo antagonized you further. She thinks you were behind everything so you could comfort her afterwards. On the bright side, the young one's missing you."

"Claudia?" Her name comes out as a whisper. I don't even deserve to utter her name.

"She's quite taken with you, isn't she?" he remarks, almost ironically.

I've conditioned myself not to think about her. How could I when I've failed both her and her mother?

When Catalina had confirmed her age, I felt like I'd been struck by lightning. That incident had resulted in a life—a lovely little girl that looked exactly like Lina but had my personality. While getting to know her, I'd noticed her logical mind and the way she approached problems, not unlike me. For the first time, the evidence of what I'd done was staring me in the face. And for the first time, I didn't find it in myself to regret it, because that meant regretting the beautiful girl I'd come to love so much. That makes me even more of a hypocrite, doesn't it?

"She'll hate me too," I add quietly, knowing I can never claim her as my daughter.

"Maybe. Maybe not." Vlad stands up, straightening his suit. As he pulls on his sleeves, I catch a glimpse of his tattoos. I've always wondered why his entire body is covered in ink.

"You've never told me what those mean." I point at the designs, trying to change the subject. It's already too painful as it is.

"And I won't." He smirks at me. "Wouldn't want the mystery to go away." He shrugs and turns to leave.

I stay a while longer, lost in prayers. By the time I get home, it's already dark outside.

Amelia is the first to greet me.

"Signor Lastra, someone is here for you." She motions to the drawing room, and I give her a small nod. I don't even get to step foot inside the drawing room before Enzo comes blazing at me and punches me straight in the face.

"What..." I momentarily lose my balance. But it's enough for him to pin me to the floor and continue pummeling away.

"Where the fuck is she, Lastra? Where did you hide her?" He keeps yelling, and I still.

What is he talking about?

My hand shoots out, and I stop his incoming fist. I push back and, using my entire strength, I shove him off me.

"What are you talking about?" I ask, spitting blood. He'd done some damage, all right.

"Catalina. Don't pretend you don't know what I'm saying. Where did you hide her? I know she must be here somewhere." He then yells, "Lina? Where are you? I'm here to take you home!"

"Catalina isn't here. Obviously," I add drily, going to the table and taking a napkin. I dab at my mouth, noting he split my lip. I move my mandible a little, pleased the teeth don't feel loose.

"Where is she?" He turns towards me, his face full of worry.

"You should know, since she went to *your* home."

"She's not there. Claudia is still at home, but there's no sign of Lina."

I'm suddenly alert. Catalina would never leave Claudia alone.

"What are you talking about? Where could she be?" My pulse starts racing.

"Don't you dare act innocent, Lastra. You're the only one who could have taken her, you sick bastard. Didn't you do enough already? Didn't you hurt her enough? Just let her go."

"Look, Enzo," I put my hand up. "Catalina is not here. I swear. But if she's missing..."

"You actually want me to believe that? When you were so obsessed with her, you fucking raped her and then married her with no remorse? What kind of sick fuck does that?" He spits out, and I take it. Because he's not wrong.

"What is he talking about?" Assisi decides to grace us with her presence at that precise moment.

"Oh, Assisi. Did you know that your brother here is Claudia's father? Not only did he rape and torture Lina, but he left her to face the consequences by herself."

Sisi's face falls, and she looks at me in horror.

"Is that true?" Her voice is almost a whisper. I turn my head, shame filling me.

"Lord! It is true," she exclaims, her hand going to her mouth.

"And now Lina's missing. And your brother should know exactly where she is," Enzo adds smugly.

"I don't. I swear I have no idea where she is." I pause, immediately realizing that if she's not with Enzo...

"No..." I whisper. "No, it can't be..."

"What?" Enzo asks abrasively.

"Chimera." The words are out of my mouth.

But if she's missing... Lord, please let nothing happen to her.

"You mean *you*?" Enzo laughs derisively.

Then I remember what Vlad said, that they think I was behind everything.

"No, damn it. Not me. Look, I don't profess to be innocent. I know what I did to Lina, and it's not something I'll ever forgive myself for. But *this* Chimera isn't me. Someone's been impersonating Chimera to torment me."

"Convenient, isn't it?" He snorts.

"I swear I had nothing to do with it. I love Lina too. I wouldn't be able to hurt her."

"Right, you already did."

"Damn it! Listen, Enzo, if Lina is missing, then we need to focus on that."

"Lina can't be here," Assisi finally intervenes, giving me a look that conveys just how disappointed she is in me. "I've been watching Marcello closely for the past week. He had an incident." She pauses. "He's under supervision so he won't take his life."

Enzo's eyes widen, and he turns to me, opening his mouth to say something. But he doesn't.

"You're sure it isn't him?" he eventually asks Assisi.

"Positive." She takes a deep breath. "We need to find her, Enzo." Her tone has a slight desperation to it, and then she looks at me. "Marcello. Please."

"I'll give you my word, Agosti. I'll find her. Even if it's the last thing I do," I say solemnly.

"You'd better. Because if anything happens to Lina..." He shakes his head. "I'll kill you."

"And I'll let you." Because how could I live with myself thinking I'd failed her again?

———

I'VE BEEN PACING my study for the last hour like a madman. After Enzo had left, I'd submitted a comprehensive list of people for Adrian to test. It's still going to take time... Time we may not have, damn it. The fingerprint technician has to go through each print and manually match it to the one on record.

Fucking hell!

I don't even want to consider that something might have happened to Lina. According to Enzo, the entire video feed at his home had been off when Lina had gone missing. I'd suggested an inside job, because really, who else would have had access to his house? But Enzo had refused to believe someone from his circle would have sold his sister out.

I feel close to a mental breakdown. Who could have done this?

"Signor," Amelia knocks on my door and comes inside.

"Someone left this for you." I nod absentmindedly and prompt her to leave the package on the desk.

After she's gone, I'm still lost in thought, my mind playing tricks on me and showing me all possible scenarios, all of them ending with Lina dead.

No!

I need to focus. I can't allow myself to go down the rabbit hole.

Dear God, why? Why her?

My prayers are ineffective, not that they've ever been.

I shake my head and turn my attention to the package. I grab it, noting it's very light. Curious, I take a knife and cut through the cardboard. Inside, there's only a letter and a piece of material. I frown.

I carefully open the envelope to find a picture and a small note. I turn the picture around and I gasp.

Lina!

Her back is bare, her scars on view. The gown she'd been wearing is pooling at her waist. The same gown I'm now holding in my hand. My fingers clench around the material, despair threatening to overwhelm me.

With clumsy movements, I pry the note open.

PLENTY OF ROOM FOR ANOTHER LETTER.

I close my eyes briefly, grief threatening to spill over.

What have I done? What have I brought upon her?

I scrunch the piece of paper in my hand, flinging it at the wall.

"Wait for me, Lina," I whisper, even though there's no genuine conviction behind my words.

Pocketing the photo, I head directly to my room, to my inner sanctuary. I lock the door behind me and I kneel in front of the altar. I turn my eyes towards the centerpiece, the statue of Mary, and I supplicate her.

"Please, I'm begging you. Let her be alright. I'll do anything. I'll stay away from her for the rest of my days. Just let her be alright." I keep on repeating the same prayer, hoping someone will hear me.

Lina, my beautiful Lina... a most innocent soul.

It's all my fault.

I'm almost tempted to grab the handle of the whip, craving the medicinal bite of pain. But as I'm battling those thoughts, my phone beeps. It's Adrian.

"Yes?"

"We have a match. You did great by ranking them."

"Who is it?" I rasp out.

"Your first choice..."

MARCELLO

"Your first choice..." Adrian pauses, and the anticipation is killing me. "Nicolo."

"Are you sure?"

"Positive. The technician identified a small scar on his thumb that is also present on the partial print."

"Fuck!" I mutter, rage building inside of me. "Thank you. I'll deal with it."

"Tell me if you need anything."

After I hang up, I take a moment to calm myself. It won't work to anyone's advantage if I dive into this with my mind clouded. Nicolo has played me enough as it is.

But why?

I still can't imagine why he'd go to such lengths to get to me. Does he want my position? It seems a little extreme to do this for years just to become capo. Something doesn't add up.

Time is of the essence now. I can't dwell on the reasons when Lina is in danger. I fumble with my phone and call Francesco, instructing him to assemble all the high-ranking members of the famiglia. He soon confirms they will be here within the hour.

There are around ten of them that hold significant positions. More than half are Nicolo's men, so they should have *some* type of information.

After gathering some tools from the basement, I ask Amelia to lead the guests to the drawing room when they arrive.

Wait for me, Lina! I'll find you!

I arm myself with a couple of guns and knives, knowing that none of the men will have weapons as it is disrespectful to enter armed in the Capo's home. When Amelia lets me know that they are here, I steel myself. I need to make this quick.

Entering the drawing room, the men are deep in conversation. When they see me, they stop and greet me. I keep a nondescript expression, and I turn to lock the door.

"You're probably wondering about the urgency of my message." I explain, taking a seat on the couch. "My dear uncle, Nicolo, has gone rogue. I want any information you may have on him. Now."

They start clamoring, some expressing disbelief, some professing his innocence. I focus on the latter.

"Mateo, you are a close friend of my uncle's. Why don't you start?" I tilt my head to the side, a bored expression on my face.

"I know nothing, capo. I'm not his keeper." He shrugs his shoulders, and I raise an eyebrow at him.

"Then how is it you've been following him *everywhere*?" I counter.

"That's not true. I don't know who told you that, but I've done nothing wrong." He immediately deflects, and I shake my head slowly.

"Who said anything about accusing you, Mateo?" I stand up and walk towards him. His head is bent low as he sees me advance. He's trying to seem meek, but I see the slight pull of his mouth, the way his body itches for a challenge.

One slim blade in hand, I tug it under his chin, lifting his head to look in his eyes.

"Mateo, Mateo... What should I do with you?" I ask hypothetically, wanting to gauge his reaction.

He laughs nervously. "You can't do anything."

I push the sharp edge of the blade just under his Adam's apple, and I watch as he gulps anxiously.

"So you have nothing to say? I'm giving you one chance." I say, my eyes on Mateo.

"No." He replies, raising his gaze to meet mine, trying to show a strength that's lacking. I can see the fear in his body slightly shying away from me, the barely there tremor of his lips, and the tiny trickle of sweat on his brow. He's scared.

"Ok. Good." I nod, taking a step back as if moving to another target. Just as he breathes out a sigh of relief, I move. So fast he barely has time to react, I open his mouth and grab his tongue. One slice and the muscle falls down, blood pouring down his face. "Since you have nothing to say, then you shouldn't say anything."

His hands cup his mouth, trying to stop the blood.

"Let's try again. Do you know where my uncle is?" The room atmosphere changes immediately, and a few men remove guns from the inside of their coats, all aiming at me.

"So that's how it's going to be." I muse, taking a step back and raising my hands up, feigning surrender. At the same time, I click on the remote control I'd been holding.

The large TV in the room springs to life, the screen split into tiny windows, all showing men holding families hostage.

"One click, and they're all dead." I shake my hand, showing them what I mean.

While I'd known some would respect the rules and come unarmed, I couldn't take any chances. Especially with Nicolo's people.

"I require just one thing from you. Nicolo's location. As long as you tell me that, truthfully that is, your families will escape unscathed."

This is more potent than any type of torture, and they promptly put down their weapons.

One man steps forward, his knees giving out.

"He's at the cemetery. Please don't harm my wife."

"What cemetery?"

"The Lastra crypt. Please." He puts his hands together in a prayer, and I just nod.

"See, not that hard."

Just then, my phone rings. Nicolo's number is displayed on the screen.

"Hello, nephew. I see you've found my little secret."

"Nicolo," I reply tensely.

"A little too late, wouldn't you say? When you surround yourself with hyenas, don't be too surprised when you're betrayed." He laughs.

"What do you mean? How is Catalina?"

"Wouldn't you want to know?" he chuckles. "Take care, boy. Sometimes the very hand that feeds you can turn against you." He says cryptically, changing the words of the original saying.

He hangs up.

Damn it!

Still no word on Lina.

I drop my phone to the ground, and grabbing both my guns, I aim. First the ones with weapons, and then one by one the others. As I lower my weapons, everyone is lying on the floor.

Dead.

With one click of the button, I ensure that their families meet the same fate.

I unlock the door to find Amelia in the hallway. Her eyes widen when she sees me, and she stumbles on her words.

"I... I heard the gunshots and..."

Interesting. Usually people run away from gunshots, not towards them. But then I replay Nicolo's words in my head. *The hand that feeds you.*

"Of course." I smile at her. "Can you come help me?"

She nods, following me back into the drawing room. She comes face to face with the dead bodies, but I can see she's trying very hard to control herself.

"Tell me, Amelia, why is it that you left my father's employ?"

She lowers her head, her almost silver hair falling over her forehead.

"He forced himself on me, sir," she confesses, and for a moment I feel a twinge of guilt. Yet another victim of my father's. But then I think about Lina.

"And where did you go after that?" She suddenly looks at me in panic.

"Amelia, Amelia. You know, you were my favorite growing up. You were always the kinder one to me. But now?" I make a tsk sound with my tongue, and she pales. "Why did you do it? Why Nicolo?" I ask, half-bluffing.

"I..." She stammers, and I can see the guilt on her face.

"Why, Amelia, why?"

"I love him," she bursts out, more emotion coming out of her than I've ever seen before.

"You love him," I repeat, tilting my head and studying her.

"I was pregnant and alone and he helped me. He was so kind, so thoughtful. Even when I miscarried he was there for me, supporting me. He even confronted your father on my behalf. And you know what Giovanni did? He laughed." She curls up her lip in disgust. "He laughed for raping me and ruining my life!" Her eyes are tearing up and she lifts a hand to catch the tears. "Nicolo was so good to me... so good."

"So good that you basically served my wife on a platter to him. You were the one planting those messages, weren't you?"

"He won't harm her. He promised."

"Amelia, Amelia." I shake my head, seeing that there's no reasoning with her. In her mind, Nicolo is a character larger than life — her savior.

"The moment you targeted Lina, you lost," I say, regret swamping me as I turn on the only person who made my childhood a little more bearable.

But no one messes with my Lina. No one.

———

JUST A FEW MONTHS AGO, I stood at Tino's grave. Now, I find myself in the same cemetery, but this time, Nicolo has chosen a different spot for our meeting. I can feel the weight of my family's history as I approach the towering crypt that serves as our resting place. It's like a double-story house, an imposing structure meant to showcase our wealth and status.

I enter through the screeching door, hoping that I'm not too late. My heart races as I think of Lina, waiting for me inside.

Please let me be on time.

The interior of the crypt is reminiscent of a grand mansion, with various rooms leading off from a central space. As I check each room on the ground floor, I can't help but feel anxious. Finally reaching the basement where the tombs are located, I hear my uncle's voice booming with excitement.

"There he is!" Uncle exclaims as I descend the narrow stairs. At the bottom, the basement opens up into a vast room supported by four thick pillars. Nicolo stands in the center, his arms wide open and a malicious grin on his face.

My eyes scan the room until they land on Lina's delicate form. She's bound to one of the pillars, her head drooping against its icy surface. The sight fills me with fury.

"Lina?" I call out, taking in her disheveled appearance and the way her entire being shrinks away from my presence.

Does she hate me that much?

I turn back to Nicolo, hurling the present I'd been holding towards him.

Amelia's head rolls on the ground, her eyes wide open and staring at my uncle.

"So you figured it out. Pity. She was a good lay." He shrugs, kicking the head further with his foot. Catalina shrieks when it rolls past her and stops at a close distance.

"I think your wife may be more disappointed in this than me." He chuckles as Lina's eyes widen with fear. Even when she turns to me, her entire being seems to be revolted by my presence.

And it breaks my heart.

"Let her go. She has nothing to do with this."

"Ah, see, there you're wrong. She has everything to do with this. She is your main trigger, isn't she?" Nicolo asks, amused.

Lina's eyes turn to me, and the pain I see reflected in them makes me want to take on the king of hell himself.

I try to convey with my gaze that I will take care of this, but I'm not sure even I believe myself at this point.

"What do you want, Nicolo? You want my position so bad you'd resort to this? Take it, it's yours," I state, my eyes moving from him to Lina.

Nicolo's eyebrows shoot up a second before he throws his head back and laughs.

"You'll give me your position?" He jeers at me, still laughing. "See, this is why you were never fit to be capo. You always put *her* before everything." He remarks in derision. "Don't worry, your position *will* be mine by default after you die." He shrugs his shoulders and casually walks towards the end of the room to pick up a rusty knife.

"Why don't we try this..." He twists the knife around, testing its strength. "I may let her go, if you submit to me."

"What?" I blurt out, a maniacal smile appearing on his face.

"Submit to me. It's the only way she'll go free."

"Fine. I'll do it. Just let her go."

"Not yet," he shakes his head and motions towards another pole. "Go and handcuff yourself."

I pause for a second, and my eyes meet Lina's. Her eyebrows are drawn together in confusion. Just seeing her there... I walk, and sitting down, I secure my hand to a metal pole. One half of the cuff is wrapped around the metal for support while the other is now circling my wrist.

"Why? Why are you doing this?" Lina's voice is but a whisper as she asks.

Nicolo smiles slowly, and I suddenly see Father in him.

"Blame it all on your husband. He is, after all, the reason for all your misfortunes," he happily tells her, delighted when her face falls. She turns to me slightly, and her expression is one of fear mixed with disappointment.

I've failed her. Repeatedly.

Nicolo strides confidently towards me, the glint of a knife in his hand catching the light. He jabs it playfully towards my face before squatting down in front of me, the blade dangerously close to my skin.

"It's time to settle the score, boy." With one swift motion, he slices through the fabric holding my shirt together, and it falls away, exposing my bare chest. The cold metal of the knife trails teasingly down my skin as Nicolo tests my reflexes. Then he cuts.

I clench my jaw against the pain, a familiar sensation that I've learned to endure. Beside me, Catalina gasps at the sight of blood starting to trickle down my torso.

But I can't let myself focus on the pain. My eyes are fixed on Lina, my reason for fighting and staying strong through this torture.

Nicolo continues to make small, deliberate cuts all over my body, but I refuse to give him the satisfaction of seeing me flinch. Only determination and love for Lina keep me going.

Eventually, he gives up, realizing that I won't break under his torture. Standing up with a frown, he surveys my bleeding form with a look of confusion and uncertainty in his eyes.

"It seems this isn't working," he muses, narrowing his eyes at me.

"What did you expect? That I'd be wailing in pain?" I quip ironically.

"I should have known torture wouldn't do much for you. Not with Giovanni as your father." He chuckles, as if he's just realized something important.

Maybe Father had a hand in my increased tolerance for pain, but only when it comes to myself. He'd tried so hard to kill my emotions that the only thing he'd done had been to kill my need for self-preservation. I don't care what happens to me – not anymore. But Lina? She's the only one that matters, and not even the worst torment could make me give her up.

"Don't you worry," he taunts, "I have many tricks up my sleeve."

Nicolo steps away from me, and with a hand motion, he signals someone else to come in. His smile only increases as he watches Franco saunter in, eye-patch on.

"What?" I breathe out, confused at the connection.

"Franco here has a little quibble with you, don't you Franco?"

"And that bitch," Franco adds, his eyes roving over Lina's form with a leer.

"If pain won't break you," Nicolo starts, deep in thought. "Then maybe the sight of your beloved in pain will."

My eyes widen at his implication, swinging from Nicolo to Franco.

They both laugh, and Nicolo gives Franco the green light to proceed.

"Marcello, Marcello, let's see how it feels to be so helpless... to watch your wife get fucked by another while you can't do anything to help her."

My pulse is racing, my breathing labored.

God, no!

"Lina..." I whisper, and I see her back away, as much as her bounds allow her to. Franco is upon her in seconds, his hands grabbing at her legs and pulling them towards him.

I can't watch this! I try to tug my hand free from the cuff, but it's in vain. The pole is highly secured, the cuff tight around my wrist.

"No!" Lina yells, trying to kick at Franco. One hand clumsily works at the front of his trousers, while the other keeps on tugging at her dress.

No!

I turn back to my restraints, knowing time is of the essence. I will my mind to work and think of all the possibilities. I can't uproot the pole... I can't break the handcuffs, but... I can break my own hand.

Lina's cries intensify, and they only spur me on. I hold on to the pole with one hand, and fold the other within the cuff, my thumb directly parallel with the other digits. Then I pull. So hard my eyes tear up, I pull and hit the cuff at the same time. I do it until I hear the sound of bones cracking; until my hand becomes a limp mass of crushed bones. Until it slips free.

Swallowing the pain and using it to feed my anger, I'm up and upon Franco in a second. There's only a slight relief at seeing that he didn't get to Lina before my good hand and what's left of the other wrap themselves around his neck. Using the strength in my wrist, I curb his struggles and twist his neck at an angle, effectively snapping it. The adrenaline must have kicked in, because I have no notion of time as I kick his lifeless body to the side and kneel in front of a scared Lina.

Her eyes are wild as she sees me, but I note a hint of relief in them as well. I hesitate as I reach for her, and when she doesn't shy from me, I pull her closer, holding tight.

"I'm so sorry, Lina. So sorry," I breathe out a sob. "I'll get you out of here. You have my word, I swear."

She doesn't speak, her body shaking with fear. I reach behind her back and with uncoordinated movements; I attempt to untie her hands.

"What a touching scene," Nicolo's voice mocks from behind. I turn around, and I watch as he comes closer, a hint of annoyance on his face as he takes in my limp hand.

"You know, I never thought a monster like you would be capable of such deep emotions. I used to praise your father all the time for the training he put you through. You were really the perfect killer. Until her."

He removes a gun from the back of his trousers and points it at Lina. I react instinctively, putting myself in front of her, shielding her.

Nicolo's laughter echoes in the room right before he presses the trigger. I let out a gasp as the bullet embeds itself in my shoulder. Lina's hands reach out for me, her expression mirroring the pain I'm feeling.

"Marcello." Her mouth is wide open as she looks in disbelief at the blood that gushes out of my shoulder, mingling with the already dried blood of my other wounds.

"I'm fine," I croak, trying to give her an assuring smile.

"Just kill me," I turn to address Nicolo. "Just kill me and let her go, please."

"Why would I do that, when your pain gives me so much joy?" He smirks, rotating the gun around his fingers. "You can't die just yet."

"Why?" I croak, still using my body as a shield between Nicolo and Lina. "I don't understand why you'd go through so much trouble to impersonate Chimera for *years* just to torment me. Why?"

It makes no sense. If he were only after my position, he would have killed me a long time ago. So why do this? Why use psychological tricks when he could have just attacked me in the open?

"That's the thing, boy. You don't even know..." His mouth curls up in anger, baring his teeth at me. His face immediately darkens, his hand still waving the gun around.

"Tell me, does your wife know you killed your own mother?" Nicolo asks smugly. Lina gasps, and she looks at me in disbelief. I shake my head.

"She killed herself. I had nothing to do with it," I declare confidently. That's one thing he can't accuse me of.

"You didn't?" He raises an eyebrow before heading to the back of the room where the burial places are. I quickly turn to Lina, trying to get her free before he comes back.

"If you see an opening, just run, okay?" I touch her face tentatively, reveling in her presence one last time.

"What about you?" she asks, her voice hoarse. I give her a small head shake.

"It doesn't matter. I'll hold him back." I know that in my current condition I won't be able to put up too much of a good fight, but maybe I can buy Lina some time to run away.

"Go to your brother. He'll know what to do," I say, barely finishing the sentence before Nicolo comes back, carrying with him an object covered by a white cloth.

With one last tug, Lina's wrists are free. I move quickly in front of her so Nicolo doesn't notice.

He spreads the cloth reverently on the floor, slowly unraveling it to reveal a human skull.

"He killed you, didn't he, dear?" He coos to the skull, a tender expression so antithetical to my uncle's usual countenance spreading on his face.

"Since *he* was born, he was nothing but a pest," he continues, his face turning malevolent as he turns to me. "You killed her, you made her sick," he spews, his words full of hate. Cradling the skull to his chest, he rises to his feet and brings up his gun again, pointing it towards Lina.

"You killed the person I loved the most, so I'll do the same to you."

"Wait!" I call out, looking for any way to delay this and get Lina an opening to escape. Nicolo clearly isn't mentally well, and that makes the whole situation tricky. "I swear I didn't do it. I watched her take her own life. I was only thirteen."

"You damned her entire existence before you were born!" he yells, the most he's raised his voice so far. "I loved her, damn it! I loved her, but Giovanni got to her before me. And because she was already pregnant, she had to marry him. She had *you*, and her life was over! You think I didn't see the bruises? The way he treated her? Worse than a goddamn whore and she was his wife! You damned her to an existence worse than death!"

Biting back a sarcastic retort, because really, I had no agency as an embryo, I keep prodding, desperate to make him talk so he can get distracted.

"So that's why you masqueraded as Chimera? To pay me back for what? For being born?" He narrows his eyes at me, and I move closer to Lina, ready to become her shield once more.

Unexpectedly, though, Nicolo laughs. He bends down, clutching his stomach. "Boy," he rasps out, struggling to breathe. "You think that was the first time I played with you?" He emits an indistinct sound, as if he's trying not to choke on the amusement I'm unwittingly providing him with. "I was Giovanni's right hand. One word here, one word there, and he made sure I didn't have to do any dirty work. For a time..."

"What do you mean?" I frown at the new information.

"Sure, your father wanted you to be a feared made man. But he didn't have to go *that* hard on you. The killings, the whores... I just had to look at you to see you were losing yourself more and more, until you became a shell of a person. You embraced our family legacy and were miserable for it. That was my joy. Liliana was suffering, but so were you. Until she died." He sneers the words, going back to the skull and caressing it affectionately. "After that, all bets were off."

He raises his eyes to give me a chilling look. "Who do you think told Giovanni about the Agosti girl? I knew the moment you started circling around her that she was different. Suddenly I had the best opportunity for revenge."

Lina's breathing becomes harsher, and I place my hand on her leg, offering whatever comfort I can.

"I'd been waiting for an opportunity like that for years. At first I thought that you'd likely OD from all the shit you were doing, but no, you had to clean up your act for her. That you talked to Agosti for her hand cemented it for me. I knew that through her I could do the most damage." He laughs, clearly proud of himself.

"What did you tell father?" I probe, willing my mind to disregard the pain in my body.

"That he should test your loyalty. The girl or the famiglia. I knew which one you'd choose." He motions at Lina with his gun, and my entire body tenses. "But I miscalculated. I didn't realize just how much you were willing to do for her. And then you both disappeared without a trace." His lips curl in annoyance. "You have no idea how long I searched for you."

"Until you found me. Two years ago," I add, the first date the fake Chimera started killing.

Nicolo grins. "After that it wasn't too hard. I've always preferred long, drawn-out wars, makes the enemy squirm. Like you did when you saw that nun."

I blink twice, suddenly realizing the connections. Adrian's forensic specialists had suggested that the female was being cared for more than the males... in a religious manner. Mother... he was doing it all for my mother.

"You were so busy feeling sorry for yourself, you didn't even realize how close I planted my people. The convent was even easier to infiltrate. Guerra, Sister Elizabeth... Mother Superior. Not too hard to give them a little push."

"You... You knew that Father Guerra was a pedophile, didn't you?" Lina whispers, speaking for the first time.

His smile is full of malice as he smirks. "Of course. That was the goal all along. She is, after all, Marcello's daughter."

"Lord..." Lina gasps, and I wish I could hug her to my chest and take all of her worries away.

Once again, everything is happening because of me.

"And then the notes," she adds, realizing the degree to which Nicolo had played both of us.

"I needed you out of the house," he shrugs. "Bonus points for despising him. Amelia told me everything about it, and it was so pleasing to hear that. Especially your suicide attempt." Nicolo turns to me and smiles, satisfaction clear in his eyes.

"Suicide attempt?" Lina turns to me, horror in her eyes.

"It wasn't like that," I shake my head.

"Of course, when you didn't *actually* die, I realized it's time to take it a step further."

"What do you mean?"

"It's rather simple. You are probably aware that even if you tackle me right now, the chances of escape are very slim. If you do what I ask you to, then your beloved might still have a chance."

"What do you want me to do?" I ask, my voice faltering from the pain in my arm. I'm already on the brink, and I know it. Whatever he may have in mind won't change that.

"I want you to finish what you started. I want you to take this knife," he takes out the rusty knife again, "and slit your own throat. Die like my Liliana did."

CATALINA

"Slit your own throat. Die like my Liliana did." Nicolo's virulent words send shivers down my spine, the implications terrifying me.

I flinch, whipping my head around to peer at Marcello. He looks awful. Blood all over his body, I can see his face twitching in pain now and then.

He took a bullet for you...

And that hadn't been the only revelation of today. If what Nicolo says is true, and at this point I know it is, for years Marcello's been living a hellish existence, tormented by this psychopath.

"You give me your word of honor that she walks out alive and unharmed in any way?" Marcello finally speaks, and my heart collapses. Surely he doesn't mean to actually kill himself.

"I give you my word of honor," Nicolo replies, a smug look on his face.

"Give me five minutes with Lina and I swear I will do it."

"You have two." Nicolo rolls his eyes and steps back, still keeping his gun trained on us.

"Lina," his voice is ravaged by so much pain and anguish that I can't help but tear up.

"Don't... please don't do this. I'm begging you." I move closer to him, lifting my hand to his face. "I don't want you to die." I don't think I've ever been as scared in my life. The thought of a world without Marcello... it leaves me cold. "I forgive you," I add immediately, knowing the words to be true the moment I utter them.

"Alas, but I don't. I can't forgive myself." He raises his uninjured hand to cup mine, bringing it to his lips for the briefest of touches. "Lina, my sweet, sweet Lina. I've failed you. Again." Tears are rolling down his cheeks. Mine too, but I need to keep my wits about me. He can't do this.

"We have a child, Marcello. Please don't do this. Don't leave your daughter without a father when she just got one." It may seem like I'm emotionally blackmailing him, but at this point I'm willing to try everything.

"That's why I'm doing this. Claudia needs her mother. She doesn't need me." He shakes his head slowly, a bitter smile on his face. "You know..." He tugs a hair strand behind my ear, his fingers lingering a little on the surface of my cheek. "I can't ever regret loving you. Not when you've been the brightest part of my life. In another life..." He lowers his head and swallows hard. "Maybe in another life, you'd still be you, and I'd be someone better. Someone you'd deserve. And maybe..." He sniffles a sob, "Maybe you'd love me a fraction of what I love you."

"I do, God, I do. So don't! Please don't do this. If you love me so much, don't leave me alone!" My fingers dig into the material of his shirt, my eyes pleading with him.

"That's just the thing, Lina. I love you too much to stay." He blinks twice, trying to clear his eyes. "I'm not afraid of dying. Not anymore." His lips make an attempt at a smile.

"Time's up," Nicolo suddenly interrupts.

Marcello winces and, leaning forward, he brushes his lips across mine.

"I'll always love you, Lina. Even with my last dying breath."

I want to reply to him, but he leans back, struggling to his feet.

He takes the blade from Nicolo and positions it at his neck.

"No. You should kneel. Die even lower than her." Marcello doesn't argue as he stoops down, his knees hitting the hard floor.

He gives me one last look, mouthing *Don't watch*. But I can't! I can't just stay still. I propel my body towards Nicolo, my only thought to stop him.

Just as I am a foot away from him, he raises his gun, aiming at me.

"No! I'll do it," Marcello yells.

"Hurry, boy, or our bargain will become invalid."

I think I hear some noise from the outside, but everything pales as I turn horrified and watch Marcello do the unthinkable.

Lifting the knife just under his jaw, he digs the blade into his skin until a small trickle of blood pours down his neck. With steady fingers, he drags it across, lengthening the wound until he reaches the other side.

Blood gushes out of his throat. Like a waterfall, the scarlet liquid bathes his skin, painting it red – redder than it was.

"Nooooo!" I yell, rushing towards him, not caring if Nicolo shoots me or not, death a small mercy at this point.

"No, no, no." I mutter hysterically as I reach for him. I put my hands on the wound, trying to stop the bleeding.

"Don't you do this to me, damn it."

His mouth moves a little, and he seems to want to say something.

"Don't speak. Please!" I take what's left of my dress and press over the wound. It immediately soaks up the blood. He can't die here. He simply can't!

"Dear God, Marcello, please don't leave me! I'm begging you." I can't even see straight for the tears leaking from my eyes. But I don't let go.

Somewhere in the distance, a succession of gunshots permeates the air. I hear it, but I register nothing but my darling Marcello, whose eyes are still wide open, staring at me in wonder.

"Please, love. Please, stay with me," I wail, my voice hoarse.

"Lina! Lina!" My brother is suddenly by my side, shaking me.

"Let go! I can't let him die..." I don't think I'm making any sense, but my tunnel vision includes only Marcello.

"An ambulance will be here shortly. Let me help." He presses his hands on top of mine, helping with the pressure.

"Fuck!" I hear another voice.

"What the fuck is wrong with him? Going by himself fully knowing Nicolo was gunning for him? Damn, Marcel, you really did it, buddy." Another man speaks, his voice full of despair.

"The ambulance should be here soon. I'll take Nicolo and Franco to the car," one of them adds.

"Fine. I'll keep you updated."

I don't know what happens next. A flurry of people are suddenly inside the crypt, and I'm being separated from Marcello.

"Miss, please, let us do our job."

"He'll make it, right? Please tell me he'll make it," I beg the paramedic. He purses his lips.

"We still have a pulse, but I can't vouch for anything. We need to hurry him to the hospital for an urgent transfusion."

"B, his blood is B," I call out, remembering that snippet of information.

"Good. We'll hook him on blood as soon as we get to the car," he assures me, and they put him on a stretcher.

Enzo is still holding me, tugging my head under his chin.

"He won't die," I say, willing myself to believe it too.

"He won't... he won't." He hugs me tighter, trying to comfort me.

———

THE RIDE to the hospital is tense. We're both aware that when we get there, he might be... dead.

"What did they do with the bodies?"

"Vlad cleaned up the scene and got rid of them."

I grunt an acknowledgement. Then I ask what's been on my mind all along.

"Why didn't you come earlier?" Enzo notices a trace of desperation in my voice, and he grimaces slightly.

"We didn't know the location," he admits. "Marcello left an automated message to be sent after a certain amount of time had passed."

I take a deep breath, things becoming a little clearer—and more alarming.

"He came here to die, didn't he?"

Enzo doesn't answer, but the tight clench of his jaw tells me he agrees with me.

"He... Nicolo was behind everything. The incident ten years ago,

Father Guerra... every single thing," I say, closing my eyes, overwhelmed at everything that had happened.

"Does it matter?" Enzo asks after a pause, his eyes focused on the road. "Does that make Marcello any less guilty? God, Lina... He raped you." He groans, emotion rolling off my brother like I'd never seen before.

"I don't think it's as black and white."

"Sure, he just raped you a little," he laughs derisively.

"Stop... please. I can't do this right now," I whisper.

"Sorry," he apologizes, and we drop the subject altogether.

We get to the hospital to find out he's been admitted into surgery. The doctor on call proceeds to tell us it was a miracle he survived this far considering his extensive injuries and blood loss. From the way he's recounting it, it seems that the wound in his throat wasn't too deep.

"There are lacerations at the level of the trachea, and it might cause some vocal impairment, but the esophagus is intact, and that's the good news. As to the other wounds, we've administered a tetanus shot, and we now have a joint team working on his throat and his shoulder."

"He'll make it, right?" I ask, a glimmer of hope blooming inside of me.

"I can't promise anything, but it looks like it. It could have been much worse."

We thank the doctor for his time and we head to the waiting room. Enzo is glued to my side all throughout, as if he's afraid I won't be able to handle this.

"I'm fine, really," I try to assure him, but he doesn't seem convinced.

"What happened there, Lina? Did Nicolo..." I quickly shake my head.

"But there's something you need to know." I take a deep breath. "Allegra was the one who took me there." His expression is tense as I tell him what happened, from the lie she'd told to get me out of the house, to the weird way she was talking.

"I'm sorry, Lina." He sighs. "I'll take care of it. I've been ignoring her for too long." He shakes his head.

"But why? What happened to her?"

"She's not well... mentally. I tried to make excuses for her because of that, but it's one thing to do crazy shit all the time, and quite another to betray the famiglia. When she took up with Nicolo, she knew what she was getting into." He mutters a curse under his breath.

"But if she's so unwell, how could you let her near Luca?"

"Trust me, I don't. She sees him briefly and under supervision. He needs to know that his mother is at least around."

"I'm sorry." I touch his arm lightly.

Marcello's friends, Adrian and Vlad, join us in the waiting room.

"Won't the police be called?" I ask suddenly, remembering the gunshot wound. Isn't it standard protocol to call them?

"I handled that," Adrian grimaces. "We wrote it off as a suicide attempt gone wrong. With his history, no one will ask questions."

"You mean the last attempt?" I probe, curious about what Nicolo had meant.

"Marcello insists it wasn't a suicide attempt, but he has a history of psychiatric problems."

"What do you mean?"

"Besides his phobia of touch, he's always had problems with insomnia," he confides, and I remember the many instances in which he'd stay up late citing work reasons, or the nightmares...

"I see." I nod, not knowing what else to add.

———

MARCELLO'S SURGERY IS A SUCCESS, and he is soon moved to a private salon. I stay with him the first night while he's out, but in the morning Enzo convinces me to go home to shower and change.

When I come back, the doctor pulls me aside to tell me that Marcello won't be able to speak for the time being, not until his vocal cords heal. Other than that, his condition is improving. Given that it's his second attempt in a month, he suggests an inpatient center. I don't want to decide anything right now, so I smile and tell him I'll think about it.

I head over to his salon and notice a nurse is coming out of his room.

"Are you Mrs. Lastra?" she asks, and I nod.

"Is something wrong?"

"Mr. Lastra is awake," she starts, and I take a deep breath, my lips stretching wide into a smile. "But he doesn't want to see you."

"What do you mean?" I frown, my face immediately falling. Why doesn't he want to see me?

"He asked me to give you this." She hands me a letter. "Your name's been removed from allowed visitors, so..." She seems apologetic, but I just nod mechanically.

I go to an empty area and numbly sit down. Unfolding the letter, I start reading.

My lovely Lina,

I'm sorry about how everything turned out. You have no idea how much I wish things were different... including what happened that night ten years ago. I can sit here and tell you countless times that I never wanted to hurt you. But the truth is, I did hurt you. Even when I tried to do what I considered best at the time, you ended up being hurt.

I stop, tears already falling down my cheeks. But I will myself to read on. He's relating everything that happened that night in great detail; how he knew he had no choice, but tried to drug me so I wouldn't be in pain; how he'd struck a deal with his brother for my safety, devoting the last decade to working to catch a criminal and betraying his best friend in the process. The descriptions are so painfully vivid, my heart aches for what he had to live with.

I simply do not deserve you. Not now. Not like this. Not when I'm a broken man afraid to face his own demons. If what you said back there is true... that you forgive me... I want to forgive myself too. I want to become someone worthy of you.

But for that, I need to help myself first. I

can't in good conscience stay in your life knowing I'm a ticking bomb that may go off at any time. I can't expose you, or Claudia to that.

I know I have no right to ask this, but... will you wait for me?

Forever yours,

Marcello

I can barely breathe as sobs wreck my body. I want to go to him and tell him that everything will be OK, that I forgive him and that I love him. If possible, knowing what I do now makes me love him even more. I can't even imagine what it's like to live with a burden like that. No, I can't even imagine how Marcello is still sane after everything he's been through.

It's hard to grasp all he's done in the past, the people he's tortured and killed... but is that really him? Or is it merely who the famiglia wanted him to be? How can he know any better when all his life he's witnessed only human cruelty? The fact that he'd so easily give his own life for me says it all. For a man who's never received kindness, he was ready to commit the ultimate sacrifice.

And that is the real Marcello. My soul recognizes his in a way that can't be explained by science or words. He's got the gentlest, most pure heart. He just had the misfortune of being born into the wrong family. No one's ever taught him kindness, and yet it comes so naturally to him.

I wipe my tears and head to the reception desk to ask for paper and a pen. Then I write my reply.

I'll wait.

MARCELLO

TWO MONTHS LATER

"Lina." I practice in front of the mirror, still not accustomed to my new voice. I clear my throat and try again. "Lina." I purse my lips. The knife had damaged my vocal cords, and while the doctors had hoped that they would heal completely, my voice now has a husky quality to it. It's not unpleasant, but it feels very foreign.

Like I'd smoked one hundred cigarettes a day for the last twenty years.

The scar healed nicely, though. Nicer than I would have expected. A reddish-pink line now mars my neck. Unfortunately, I don't think I'll be able to hide it even with a turtleneck.

After I'd received that letter from Lina, I hadn't heard from her. Well, not directly. I'd borrowed Vlad's listening device, and I've been able to listen to some of her conversations with Enzo. Both Catalina and Claudia are doing well. From the snippets I'd heard, Lina started her own business, selling some of her fashion designs and creating custom pieces for people. I couldn't be prouder about that. She's finally taking life into her own hands.

And soon, I'll be able to join her too.

I put on a blazer and head to my therapy appointment. A lot had changed since I'd walked out of the hospital, grateful to be alive. I don't think I've ever put as much price on my life as I had when Lina had begged me to live, both for her and for Claudia. But I've since learned that before I can live for them, I also need to learn how to live for myself.

In the past, all of my attempts at getting therapy had been failures. Not that I'd been too disappointed, since I've always hated talking about myself. But this time, the therapist is born in the mafia and familiar with how things are done.

After I'd been discharged from the hospital, I continued seeing my old therapist for a couple of sessions, but things weren't working out. I couldn't be entirely truthful, and how could she help me if she had no idea what the extent of my trauma was? Around that time, I'd talked again with Guerra, who'd extended his apologies for his brother, saying he had no idea what he was up to. We'd also realized that Franco had been working for some time with Nicolo, and they had planned to take over the leadership within their families. The attack wrongfully attributed to the Irish had been their doing, taking advantage of the terrible reputation the Gallaghers already had.

I'd also been trying to fix the mess within the famiglia, and Francesco had been invaluable in carrying out my orders and acting as my proxy. During one talk, he'd brought up his eldest daughter, Giulia. A clinical psychiatrist with a few years of experience, Giulia was the answer to my prayers. I hadn't been her first mob client, and certainly not the last.

At my first appointment, the conversation had flowed. She hadn't been fazed by anything I'd said – or at least she hadn't shown it. A few more sessions and she'd had a couple of diagnoses for me. From PTSD to depression, she'd tackled my self-harm tendencies and my insomnia. I don't claim to have been suddenly cured, but it feels better to know there's a scientific explanation for all of my episodes, and not a demonic possession as my mother had called it. In fact, Giulia had suggested that the bulk of my trauma comes from my mother. My father's abuse had only added to it. With her constant rejections and religious fanaticism, she'd instilled in me that I'm not worthy of anything. It had been then easy for my father to mold me into what he wanted.

The session this time focuses on *that* night, and the source of my biggest shame. I walk Giulia through everything that happened, and she listens attentively, not betraying any disgust for me — what woman wouldn't feel like that for what I did?

"I see." She pushes her glasses up her nose and makes a few notes. "What do you think would have happened if you didn't do that? Tell me your honest opinion."

"Father would have made good on his promise. He would have given Catalina to his men. Or... because he was unpredictable, he could have killed her too."

"Do you think you could have done anything else then?"

I shake my head, closing my eyes. "No," I breathe out.

"There are two things that I see, Marcello. If you hadn't done it, someone else would have. By doing it yourself, and I'm not excusing your actions, but you had control over the situation. You took care of her in a way that no one else would have. You made sure she got out alive."

"Yes, but..."

"What does she say about this?" Giulia suddenly asks, and I lower my head in shame.

"She says she forgives me, but I can't fathom how she could ever do that."

"Why? You don't trust her? Trust her word?" She leans forward, eyes trained on me, challenging me.

"I do," I whisper.

"But you can't forgive yourself." She nods, turning to her notebook and jotting down something. "You can't change the past, Marcello. No matter how much you wish it didn't happen, it did. But that doesn't mean that the man you are today is still the man you were before. Or that you can't change for the better. The past is the past. Let it go. You can still change the future."

"How can I ever feel deserving of her, knowing what I did?" I ask, my voice breaking.

"You won't. But that will make you try harder every day. Love her more every day so *she* feels that you are deserving of her. The ever-trite adage, actions speak louder than words."

"I can do that," I say confidently. "I'd do it regardless, because she deserves the world."

"Then show that to her. A wise man once said that every saint has a past, and every sinner a future. Make that future yours."

I nod numbly because I feel like I can do it. Turn my life around. Change a little day by day.

"Thank you." I stand up to leave, the clock showing that our session's ended.

"Make sure you recommend me to your other killer buddies; I give great discounts." She winks at me as I leave, and I shake my head, chuckling.

I can't believe that a mafioso's daughter would do this type of work, but I can see the usefulness of it. I still can't help but wonder how Francesco had allowed such a thing, with her being unmarried at her age. It's not at all the traditional way, and it gives me hope for the future—for my daughter and my sisters.

I'm about to head back home when I get a sudden phone call from a terrified Venezia.

"Slow down, Venezia. What happened?"

"It's Sisi... I don't know, she just started bleeding. I called an ambulance. We're at the hospital now."

Shit!

I get into my car and drive straight to the hospital. At the reception desk, I give her name and a nurse intercepts me.

"I'm her brother," I add when she seems skeptical about our connection.

"The doctor just saw her. She's sedated right now."

"What's wrong with her?"

She hesitates and instead forwards me to Sisi's attending physician.

"Mr. Lastra, I'm sorry to inform you that your sister suffered an early miscarriage."

My face falls, and I ask again to make sure I didn't mishear. He continues to reassure me it's nothing worrying. I don't think he realizes just how shocked I am to hear that Assisi was pregnant at all. With whom? She never left the house, never saw anyone...

But then I remember. Rafaelo Guerra. Damn!

"You don't have to worry. There's nothing wrong with your sister. She was about eight weeks pregnant and the placenta failed to deliver nutrients to the fetus. Sometimes this happens, but it shouldn't affect her future chances of having children. You should be supportive of her during this time. She seemed grief-stricken at the news."

"Thank you for letting me know," I say numbly. I meet Venezia right outside Sisi's room, and she's in tears.

"Did you know she was pregnant?" I ask, thinking that maybe she'd shared that with her sister.

Venezia shakes her head. "No... I heard about it for the first time too."

We wait outside until the nurse in charge lets us know Sisi is awake. I tell Venezia to let me talk to her first, and she reluctantly agrees.

When I enter the room, Sisi is sitting on her bed, head hung low, pain written all over her face.

"Sisi?" I ask, taking a step towards her.

She raises her head, and I can see that her eyes are wet.

"Marcello?" She seems surprised to see me, but then she shakes her head. "I'm sorry," she whispers.

"There's nothing to be sorry about, Sisi. Will you tell me what happened?" I take a chair and place it next to her bed.

She looks conflicted, but eventually she shakes her head.

"Who was the father, Sisi?" I ask as gently as possible. I just can't imagine who it could have been.

She's still quiet, her eyes glistening with unshed tears.

"Was it Rafaelo?" I change tactics, since he's the only man she's been in contact with outside family.

She suddenly raises her head, eyes wide, lips trembling.

"It was him," I state, more aggressively than before. "Did he force you?" I immediately question. God help me, if he did, he's dead!

"No!" She cries. "No! It wasn't like that."

"What was it like then? Do you love him?"

Sisi stares at me for a second, her eyes fearful – of what I don't know.

"I do!" She exclaims, a little too loud. "I love him, okay?"

"God! He dishonored you!" I stand up, hostility rolling off every pore in my body. I don't care about my outstanding deal with Bene-dicto. His son is going to pay for this. He took advantage of a girl barely out of the convent. What does she know about love? Sex?

"Stop, please." She utters the last word with such emotion that I do.

"We're getting married," she continues.

"Married? Says who?"

"We talked about it. He asked me, and I accepted."

"Sisi... it's too early. Please think about it. You don't have to do this just because you slept with him." I don't want her to do some-thing she will regret for the rest of her life just because she went to bed with the boy.

"No... this just makes me more sure. We're good together. We get each other. Please, Marcello." The way she's pleading with me makes it hard to say no.

"We'll talk about this. I must discuss it with Benedicto," I add, even though I know that Benedicto will more than welcome the match. It had been his intention from the very beginning. Still, knowing that makes this whole situation even more questionable. Why do I feel like there's something more? Something that Sisi isn't saying?

If I find out Rafaelo coerced her... I will not stay still.

I exit the room, trying to calm my own rising temper. Sisi is clearly distraught by her miscarriage, and I don't want that to influ-ence her decision.

Feeling like the situation is simply above my paygrade, I do the only thing I can think of.

I call Catalina.

THE MOMENT I see her sauntering over to us, I lose all sense. It's like water for a parched man. And I drink her up. She's wearing a pair of dark jeans, a first for her, paired with a tight white blouse that emphasizes her curves. Damn if I'm not gawking.

She's even more beautiful than before.

She stops in front of me and we both stare at each other awkwardly. I don't speak and neither does she. Her mouth parts slightly, her tongue wetting her lower lip. I think I might grow hard just from that sight alone.

To prevent any embarrassing incident from happening, I take the lead.

"Sisi is there. You should go." Her eyebrows knit in a frown at my words. Damn! I should have remembered that my voice is not as it used to be.

She stares at me for a second, her mouth still agape, before nodding. She reluctantly moves, going inside Sisi's room.

"What's with you two?" Venezia asks when I take a seat next to her.

"What do you mean?"

"Are you like... getting divorced?"

"No, we're not."

"Cool. That's cool." She nods, redirecting her attention to her phone.

It's around an hour later that Lina comes back, closing the door behind her.

"How was it?" I inquire, trying to keep the excitement in my voice to a minimum. This is about Assisi.

"She's doing fine," Lina replies.

"I'll just go see her now." Venezia looks between the two of us skeptically.

"Sure." I nod to her.

"Would you like to grab something to drink?" I turn to Lina once more after Venezia's gone.

"I'd like that," she replies, a slight blush staining her cheeks.

We go to the cafeteria and get a cup of coffee each, and finding an empty table, we take a seat.

"So," she starts, her gaze on the cup of coffee in her hands. "How have you been?"

"Good... I've been good." Why am I anxious? And why am I replying with the most basic things? I shake my head and tell myself to just go with the flow. There's no reason to be fretting about this, even though it takes all my willpower not to sweep her off her feet into the closest janitor's closet and fuck the life out of her.

God! I cringe internally at the direction of my thoughts. What have I become?

"Marcello?" Lina leans forward, looking at me with worry in her eyes.

"Yes?" I blink in rapid succession, trying to ground myself.

"I asked you a question."

"Sorry, I didn't hear." I grimace. I don't want her to think I'm not paying attention to her when that's all I'm doing.

"Did you know about Sisi and Rafaelo? I just can't believe that they..." She trails off.

"Had sex?"

"Yes." That blush makes another appearance, bringing her freckles into focus... making me want to kiss each one of them... one by one.... I shake myself again. Why am I like this? It's only been two months! Last time it was ten years, and I had no issues.

"I didn't realize either. But if she wants to marry him, I won't stand between them."

"That's good. She deserves to be happy." Lina adds, her fingers fidgeting. That's the one thing that tells me she's not quite at ease either.

"I missed you," I suddenly say, not being able to hold this in much longer.

"I missed you too."

"I've been working on myself, and I think I'm on the right path," I admit.

"I'm glad, Marcello. I meant it, you know. I forgive you." She stretches her arm across the table and places her hand on top of mine.

"Come with me!" My voice is urgent, and I tug her to her feet, leaving our untouched drinks on the table.

"What..."

I walk fast, remembering a small door we'd passed by. It's a long shot but... I open it, and it's a tiny storage closet. But it's enough to fit the two of us.

I drag her inside and shut the door.

"Marcello?" Lina's voice has a breathless quality to it, and it's only making me harder. Damn it! I should have more restraint than this.

"God, Lina!" I groan, backing her into the corner. "I can't believe you're here." I breathe in her scent, trying to convince myself this isn't a dream.

"We shouldn't do this... not until you're ready."

"I'm ready. So ready," I rasp, knowing full well we're not talking about the same type of readiness. I take her hand and press it on my cock, wanting her to feel how ready I am for her.

"Oh." She gasps, and for a second, I think she's going to pull back. But she doesn't. Her fingers wrestle with the zipper of my pants, and reaching inside, she takes me in her hand.

"God!" I moan breathlessly, and in a frenzy, my mouth seeks hers.

She keeps on touching me, her fingers gripping my shaft tighter.

Her tongue in my mouth is the flavor I never knew I was missing in life. We kiss like two desperate people on the brink of a precipice.

My hands go lower until I reach the opening of her jeans.

"What the fuck!" someone bellows from behind.

I barely have time to tuck myself in and zip up as a crowd gathers around.

"Shit!" I mutter, hugging Lina to my chest so she won't be seen. I lead her away from the closet. There are whispers behind us, and people laughing.

Fuck!

She's going to be mortified. What was in my head, really? I mentally berate myself for my lack of self-control. It's only when we're back in the hallway of Sisi's salon that I let go of her, expecting to see disappointment on her face. She looks at me wide-eyed before she giggles, bending forward with laughter.

"God! That was..." She starts, but can't stop laughing.

"You're not mad?" I ask tentatively.

She shakes her head, tears at the corners of her eyes from too much exertion.

"No... not at all," she says and gives me a knowing smile. I can't help but return it, and we stay like that for a bit.

It's at that moment that Venezia comes out of Sisi's salon, a look of bewilderment on her face.

"Sisi's asleep." She narrows her eyes at us, and both Lina and I can't help but grin. "What's with you guys?" She shakes her head, taking her seat and plugging her headphones in.

"We should tone it down. For Sisi," Lina says, and I nod. She's right. We need to focus on my sister right now. But that doesn't mean that I'm not taking her home tonight.

Fuck taking things slow.

CATALINA

I drape the blanket over Sisi's small body. She's curled up in bed, her eyes red from too much crying. "Are you sure you're okay? You can talk to me about anything."

I'm worried about her. She hasn't been the same since we left Sacre Coeur, and I have no idea why.

"Thank you, Lina." She gives me a tremulous smile before turning around, ending the conversation.

I sigh and turn to leave. The doctor had discharged her late in the afternoon and had suggested she'd be more comfortable at home with a support system. I just wish she would open up to me, but I know she must still be in shock. From what I gathered, she had no idea she was even pregnant.

I close the door to her room and find Marcello waiting outside, leaning on the baluster.

"Everything all right?" he asks when he sees the slight frown on my forehead. I give him a brisk nod. He holds out his hand for me, and I take it, entwining my fingers with his. We go to his office, and he pours two glasses of scotch. Handing me one, he takes a seat across from me.

"How's Claudia?" he asks.

"She's good. Mrs. Evans started teaching her at Enzo's house."

He nods, lowering his gaze to his glass.

It's almost surreal to be back here. For the past two months,

Marcello hadn't left my mind. I kept wondering how he was doing, but I didn't want to intrude or impede his progress, so I'd stayed away. I'd lost myself in my designs, and I even found a market for them. Who knew that people were so hungry for handmade stuff? It had started as a hobby, but soon I started earning money too. I think that had been the most shocking thing. As the daughter of a capo, I wasn't expected to work for money, but to leave all that to my husband. When I'd seen my first check, even though it had only been a couple hundred dollars, I'd been more than thrilled. I'd seen my first shot at independence.

But then he called. I don't think I've ever been as happy as when I'd seen his number pop up on my screen. I'd had plenty of time to think about our relationship, especially with Enzo's constant interference. His dislike of Marcello continued, and so he tried to change my mind every chance he got. But I never faltered.

I want him or no one else. I think I even convinced my brother, because when I'd rushed to the hospital, he hadn't even argued with me, offering to watch Claudia while I was away.

"And you? How have you been?" He raises his eyes just a little. Where is the confident Marcello from before? The one that was about to take me in a storage closet?

"I started my business. It's going well, I think." His mouth curls up.

"You think?"

I shrug. "People seem to like my designs."

"I'm proud of you." His knowing smile makes me think this isn't the first time he's heard of this.

"Since you called me..." I start, trying to find the courage to ask him if he's doing well enough to let me in.

"Yes," he immediately says, not letting me finish. "It means exactly that." Putting his glass on the study, he moves closer until he's in front of me. His fingers brush against my hair, tugging a stray strand behind my ear. I tilt my head back so I can look him in the eyes. "Dear God, you have no idea how much I missed you. But I had to..." He shakes his head slightly, his already husky voice sounding even harsher with the intensity of his emotions. "To give myself fully to you, I needed to find myself first."

"Did you?" I ask, almost breathless from his proximity.

He nods, his fingers tracing my lips. "It's a process, but I'm getting there. I want to show you something." Unbuttoning his shirt, he turns around, slowly pushing it down to reveal his scarred back. It looks better than the last time I saw it, but it's still an angry sight, as if someone had taken a knife and viciously ripped into a canvas. I lift my hand, and at his permission, I start tracing the ridges.

"I stopped," he notes. I raise my eyebrows in question. "I stopped hurting myself." I gasp at his words.

"You... you did this to yourself?" He nods, lowering his head in shame. "Why? Why would you do this?" My voice breaks, and I have to blink the tears away.

"It was my way of atoning for what happened to you. The only way I could feel what *you* felt." He turns and takes my hands into his own. "Your pain would be imprinted on me, and I'd never forget."

"Marcello..." I have no words. "You need to leave the past behind." I take a deep breath. "*We* need to leave the past behind."

"But how can you even stand to look at me? Knowing that I..." He swallows his words.

"Because now I know the circumstances. And I know *you*," I point my finger at his chest, "The man I fell in love with; the man who put his life on the line for me. How can I *not*?" I bring my hands to his face, cupping his cheeks and making him look me in the eye. "We're here now. Let the rest go."

"But..."

I shake my head, cutting him off.

"Even if you could change the past, I wouldn't want you to. How can I ever bring myself to regret anything that happened since it gave me Claudia? We have a beautiful daughter, Marcello." All the suffering and all the scorn I'd put up with had been well worth it. I wouldn't exchange my daughter for anything in the world.

"Lina," he groans, closing his eyes and surrendering himself to my touch. "I promise I'll do my best. You won't regret choosing me."

"I think so too," I add cheekily, moving my finger down his chest suggestively.

"What are you doing?"

"I think you started something earlier." The thought of being almost caught in the act makes me even hotter.

Marcello's eyes darken, the innuendo clear. But there's something more I need to tell him.

"Don't hold back, please. Not anymore." I don't think his guilt let him give himself to me before, with the secret still between us. Now the slate has been wiped clean.

"Are you sure?" he asks, and I nod, my cheek molding to his chest, my mouth on his nipple. "Love me like you've always wanted to," I plead, two months of pent-up desire in my voice.

He tips my chin with his thumb, laying a kiss on my nose before backing me into the study. My back hits the wooden frame, but he doesn't stop. Hands on my butt, he lifts me until I'm sitting on the desk, his torso coming between my open legs.

"I think you're wearing one too many clothes," he notes, his gaze traveling over my body and stopping at my white shirt. I'd been in such a hurry to get to the hospital I hadn't even put a bra on. My nipples are hard and straining against the material, and his eyes seem to eat up the sight.

"Take it off," he commands, his voice completely different. There's a smoky quality to it that makes me shiver. I comply, tugging the shirt off my body and throwing it on the floor.

"You have the most gorgeous tits, Lina," he rasps, staring at me reverently. He circles the nub with his fingers and I throw my head back, gasping at the sensation. His mouth is next, lips sucking, teeth nibbling. Overwhelmed, I bring him up my body, kissing him like I dreamed about these two months. My hands go to his pants, and I struggle with the zipper, impatient to feel him again.

"Easy," he chuckles, helping me slide his pants off before doing the same with my jeans. I wrap my hands around his length, stroking him slowly.

"Fuck! Just like that. God..." Eyes closed, mouth agape, Marcello is lost to the sensation. Enjoying the sight of him in the throes of passion, I take it a step further. I hop off the desk and to my knees. My face is on the same level with his arousal, and I stick out my tongue, circling the crown. His sudden intake of breath tells me I'm doing this right, so I continue to lap at him, focusing on the underside where he seems to be the most sensitive. I look up, watching his face for cues. His brows are drawn together, his hands in my hair. I wrap my lips around the shaft, sucking him in.

"Fucking hell, Lina! You're fucking killing me." His voice is harsh, and it's only spurring me on. I bob my head up and down his length, taking as much as I can. "Yes! Take me deeper. Your mouth is fucking heaven," he grits out, thrusting into my mouth and hitting the back of my throat. "Fuck, I'm coming!" He makes to move, but I wrap my hands around him, working him up and down until he empties himself down my throat.

"Shit! Are you..." I lick my lips, showing him I didn't mind any of it. In fact, it might have been the most erotic thing in my life – having him at my mercy like that.

"Damn, you're really killing me here, Lina." I lift my eyebrows in confusion, raising up to my feet and turning so I'm facing the desk. Propping myself on my elbows, I stick my butt at him, and mustering all my courage, I say the phrase I'd been too ashamed to say before.

"Fuck me, please."

He groans loudly, my words having the desired effect. But he does nothing.

"Lina... are you sure? This is..." He trails off, pain radiating from his voice.

"Yes. Please." I want this. No, I *need* this to finally close that horrible chapter of my life. I need him to take me from behind and erase all memories of that night.

He's still hesitating, and when I'm about to say something, I feel his mouth trailing kisses on my spine and down. He reaches my butt, his tongue sneaking between my cheeks.

"Oh," I squirm, the sensation new but not at all unpleasant. The flicks of his tongue make me grab onto the edge of the desk. My moans intensify as he moves lower, latching onto my nub and sucking.

"Mar..." I start, but I'm shocked silent when he inserts one finger between my cheeks, his tongue still playing with me. The movements are slow yet tantalizing as the finger moves in and out. My pleasure mounts until I'm screaming his name at the top of my lungs. Lord, I never thought I'd ever lose myself like this. But with Marcello...

Even my train of thought stops as he suddenly enters me, his length long and thick and stretching me. His hands are on each side of my hips as he pumps in and out. I gasp when he hits a spot deep within, and I tilt my butt to meet his pelvis. The thrusts start slow, but soon he's increasing the pace and driving me over the edge.

"Lina," he moans, filling me to my very soul. "I fucking love you. Adore you. Worship you," he groans. "My beautiful miracle."

The sounds excite me even further and I clench around him, feeling my orgasm nearing. I reach back, touching his hipbone and urging him to go faster.

"Fuck!" he shouts, spilling himself inside of me just as I come. He falls limply over me, hugging me from behind and kissing my shoulder.

"You're everything to me. You know that, don't you?" He speaks against my skin, the warm air making me shiver. I crane my neck, bringing his head in the crook of my shoulder so I can touch my lips to his. "I love you too," I whisper.

We stay like that for a while, him still inside of me, his body on top of my own, his arms wrapped around my waist.

EPILOGUE

TEN YEARS LATER

CHRISTMAS EVE

"The steak might not be ready in time," Lina leans in to whisper, her voice barely audible over the chatter of the other guests.

My eyes widen in horror at the news.

"You realize we have a room full of dangerous, hungry people waiting for this steak, right?"

She puckers her lips in frustration. "I can't just magically make it perfect for everyone. Enzo wants it medium rare; Adrian insists on well-done; and Bianca specifically requested a rare, bloody steak. It's impossible to please them all."

"And we definitely don't want to anger Bianca," I agree, knowing how volatile she can be.

"Plus, I need you to keep an eye on them. No talk about killing or drugs or any other illegal activities that you guys engage in." Lina jabs her finger into my arm, her expression grave.

"I'll make sure they behave," I reassure her, though I have my doubts. To distract her, I give her a quick kiss before heading back to the dining room.

Enzo and his wife are seated on one side of the long table, while Adrian and Bianca are on the opposite end. Their voices rise in a heated argument as I approach. My stomach drops at their words.

"No way! My daughter is a better shot than your son any day." Bianca stands up abruptly, slamming her palms onto the table for emphasis. "Let's have a contest and settle this once and for all."

With a flourish, she produces two pistols from behind her back and throws them down in front of Enzo with a challenging look.

"Whoa," I put my hands up. "I thought I said no weapons." Adrian shoots me a look and shakes his head.

Bianca's finger points directly at me. "You'll be the judge," she declares. "Diana against Luca for the title of best shooter. I personally trained her, there's no way his son can beat her." She wears a smug expression, clearly confident in her daughter's abilities.

"Bianca," I interject, trying to diffuse the situation. "Diana is only ten years old. She shouldn't be handling guns at such a young age."

"You're just jealous," she retorts, crossing her arms over her chest.

"And you," I turn towards Enzo. "Don't fall for her baiting."

"I'm not baiting anyone," Bianca insists, her voice dripping with pride and superiority. "I'm simply praising the exceptional skills of my daughter, far superior to those of his son." Adrian lets out an audible groan and leans in to whisper something in Bianca's ear.

"My daughter would never!" she exclaims, scandalized by whatever Adrian has told her. She turns back to Enzo with determination. "Diana would never have a crush on your son." Everyone shares a laugh at this statement, but Bianca remains the only one who seems unsettled by the idea. Personally, I wouldn't be surprised if Diana did have feelings for Luca—she's always following him around and he doesn't seem to mind it too much.

"What about you? Wouldn't you like to have Enzo as your future son-in-law?" I tease, but the look on Bianca's face tells me I should drop the subject. Especially when she reaches for one of her pistols with a fierce grip.

"Right," I take a deep breath and change the subject. "Claudia's bringing her boyfriend home for the first time. I'd like you all to behave. Especially *you*, Bianca."

She leans back, her eyebrows shooting up. "Me?"

"Yes, you." I answer drily before continuing. "Just be careful with what you say, okay? This is her first boyfriend, and she's serious about him."

"I can't believe you're even letting her date," Enzo jokes. He's mentioned his views on his daughters dating multiple times in the past, and it's always the same thing—never. Good thing his daughters are still young, one eight and the other six. He'll have time to come around.

"It's not that easy." I sigh. Claudia's almost twenty now, and there's no way I can still tell her what to do.

She had turned out to be a prodigy. She'd aced her GED at fifteen and had subsequently enrolled in college. She graduated last year summa cum laude and is now in her first year of law school. Which is also where she'd met this boyfriend.

My mood sours just thinking about it. When I'd been against her dating, she'd given me an ultimatum for the first time. That's when I realized just how much she cared about this boy she's seeing.

Of course I'd relented. I can't have Claudia be upset with me. Lina likes to joke that there's nothing I would ever deny my daughter, and much as I'd like to deny it, she's right.

From the corner of my eye, I see Lina giving me a thumbs up. I nod at her in acknowledgement before turning to the guests.

"Someone needs to round the kids up. The steak will be here soon," I say at the same time that someone knocks at the door.

Shit! They're here.

"Behave, okay?" I repeat before going to open the door.

Claudia's face beams as she sees me, and she jumps into my arms.

"Papa!" She wraps her arms around my neck, holding me tight. I close my eyes and relish the feeling. It hadn't been easy to tell her I was her father, and it had taken her quite some time to get used to calling me papa. But the first time I'd heard the word come out of her mouth, I think I wept.

Lina certainly says I did.

"Welcome home!" I say, and she steps back to introduce me to her boyfriend.

I'd said boy? Well, he was definitely *not* a boy.

"Meet Sterling, my boyfriend," she happily makes the introductions. I hold out my hand for a tight shake. I reluctantly have to admit that his grip is no joke.

Around the same height as me, Sterling is packing. And by that I mean he is either a bodybuilder or a gym fanatic. Claudia looks tiny next to him. Suddenly my fatherly instincts kick into full gear, and I have to will myself to knock it down a notch so I don't embarrass Claudia.

"Pleased to meet you," I grit my teeth.

"It's great to finally meet you, Mr. Lastra. Claudia has told me a lot about you. You are her role model." And he's polite. Now I can't quite hate him as much, and it's driving me crazy.

I smile and show them to the dining room.

Everyone is already seated, and thankfully the conversation is normal.

Claudia and Sterling make their way to the end of the table.

Just in time, Lina shows up with the last batch of steak. Placing it on the table, she takes a seat next to me. I give her a quick kiss.

"Ew!" Leo, our youngest, makes a face of disgust. His twin, Mateo, joins in and they immediately start chattering away and disrupting the atmosphere.

I shake my head, but refrain from rebuking them this time. It's Christmas, after all.

Mirabella, our eight-year-old daughter, takes charge as she tells the twins off. After they stop, she turns to me and winks. I don't know what's with Mira, but sometimes she seems too old for her age. Maybe we have another prodigy on our hands.

I quickly make the introductions, and Sterling joins the conversation effortlessly. At some point, he turns to Claudia to ask, "Where are your aunts? You always spoke highly of them." Claudia's smile trembles a little and she looks back at me.

"Sisi couldn't make it. She's currently on *a grand adventure* with her husband. I don't know what she's up to, but I'm assuming something crazy." I shake my head, a smile playing on my lips. Sisi had turned out to be such a pleasant surprise. Who knew that inside a novitiate lay such a rebel?

"What about the other one? Venezia, wasn't it?" Sterling continues, and I narrow my eyes at Claudia. Venezia is a sore subject these days. She knows it, too.

"We haven't talked to her in a while," Catalina interjects, her hand seeking mine under the table.

"But Claudia spoke very fondly of her. What happened?" Why is he so curious?

"She moved away from the family," I say, hoping he would drop the subject.

As the women head to a separate area with the children – even Bianca, to my surprise – I take the opportunity to interrogate Sterling further.

"So what do you do, Sterling?" I school my features so he doesn't realize just how close I am to snapping. I don't even want to imagine him and my daughter... Yeah, that Pandora's box is best left unopened.

"I'm a TA in the economics department." He smiles at me warmly. There's just something about him... I can't put my finger on it, but he rubs me the wrong way.

"And how old are you?"

"Twenty-seven, sir," he answers. I try to calm myself.

"You realize my daughter's only nineteen. That's quite the age difference," I comment.

"She's going to be twenty next month, sir." That smile, again. "We love each other. I'd never do anything to harm her."

"I'll be watching you, Sterling. No one messes with my girl. Just remember that." I look him straight in the eyes as I say this, the threat reflected in my gaze. I would make it so his corpse is never recovered. Not whole, that is.

He grins. "I wouldn't dare, sir."

Both Enzo and Adrian have amused expressions on their faces, and when I raise an eyebrow at them, they both shrug and tip their glasses.

Just as I'm about to continue to question him further, a gun goes off in the house.

"Fuck!" I mutter, running towards the source of the noise.

I told them to behave!

THE END

If you'd like to read Vlad's story, check out The Cute Psycho!
Join Veronica's reader group for exclusive sneak peeks at future
releases: VL's Moral Dilemma.